The Earthbreakers

The Gregg Press Western Fiction Series
Priscilla Oaks, Editor

The Earthbreakers
Ernest Haycox

with a new introduction by
Jill Marie Haycox

Gregg Press
A division of G. K. Hall & Co., Boston, 1979

With the exception of the Introduction, this is a complete
photographic reprint of a work first published in Boston by Little,
Brown & Company in 1952. The trim size of the original
hardcover edition was 5¾ by 8½ inches.

This article first appeared in slightly different form in *The
Roundup*, October 1973.

Frontmatter designed by Designworks, Inc. of Cambridge,
Massachusetts

Printed on permanent/durable acid-free paper and bound in the
United States of America.

Republished in 1979 by Gregg Press, A Division of G. K. Hall &
Co., 70 Lincoln St., Boston, Massachusetts 02111

First Printing, September 1979

Library of Congress Cataloging in Publication Data
Haycox, Ernest, 1899–1950.
   The earthbreakers.

   (The Gregg Press western fiction series)
   Reprint, with new introd., of the ed. published by Little Brown,
Boston.
   I. Title. II. Series.
PZ3.H3237Ear 1979 [PS3515.A9327] 813'.5'2 79-14924
ISBN 0-8398-2576-5

Introduction

"Fond memory brings the light
Of other days around me."
— Thomas Moore

ERNY did have a very special wish. Above all, he wanted to write an historical novel, great enough to live on after he was gone.

Seldom satisfied with his own work, only on occasion would he say: "That sentence or paragraph expresses exactly what I was trying to say."

Had Erny been granted the time, I feel the three novels outlined in his mind that were to follow *The Earthbreakers* (1952), would have made up a set of four historical novels worthy of any man's library.

He always kept office hours — nine to five. He did not believe in inspiration, saying he was never inspired to write. He often said: "I have to go to the office to sit down, put paper in my typewriter and *make* myself write." Quite often some character would come to life and stick around until Erny finally wrote a story around the character, simply to get rid of him.

Erny did not read other Western writers, admittedly afraid he might unconsciously use an idea that did not belong to him.

In the 1930s, we often took car trips to some particular place, usually a small, forsaken early-day town. A place Erny planned as the location for his next short story or novel.

How he loved to wander through the town talking to all the old-timers! In the morning he would get up around 4 a.m. for another trip—to smell the early morning air, hear the early morning sounds, see the sun rise. He could transfer himself to another period of time, live the whole story, and then go home and write it.

He particularly loved board walks, blacksmith shops, and buggy whips. And we never missed an old cemetery. Here he would wander for hours, and on returning we always had to pick off all the burrs he had accumulated before continuing on.

Once in a small dusty town a sudden rain storm came up. From then on "rain on a dusty road" became one of his favorite smells.

Erny always felt that any writer or author who becomes satisfied with himself is definitely on the way out. We saw this happen to a Western writer and personal friend. He made the *Saturday Evening Post*, perhaps long before he should have; but somehow couldn't keep it up. From then on he seemed to go downhill.

No doubt many readers know about the Ernest Haycox Memorial Library located in the Library at the University of Oregon, at Eugene. The books had been in storage for ten years and I was terribly afraid silverfish might get at them. Finally, our two children, Mary Ann Wallace, and Ernest Haycox, Jr., and I, decided to give the library to the University. I had heard Erny say more than once: "If I ever give my books away, it will be to the University of Oregon."

Erny's library is considered one of the finest of its kind in the Pacific Northwest. The books have great value; I had them appraised in New York and naturally their value increases as the years go by.

We gave the books to the University on one condition; in return, they had to give me a room, especially for this collection. We wanted the books kept together so the collection would not lose its identity. I had some trouble with the University over this later, but I held them to their promise and the Ernest Haycox Memorial Library was dedicated May 15, 1969.

From what I hear the books are certainly being used. This would please Erny so much. Special classes are sometimes held in the Library Room.

We are deeply grateful to Erny's many publishers. They responded to my requests by donating illustrations, water colors and oils of Erny's jacket covers. The most generous gift came from Transworld Publishers—Corgi Books of London, England. They gave me six beautiful illustrations. All the illustrations are framed and now hang in the Memorial Room, lending a lot of warmth and personality.

A set of Ernest Haycox novels and many, many reissues, both U.S. and foreign language, also have a place in the room.

Erny had not started a copyright renewal file before he died. I will always be grateful to Howard Cady, then with Doubleday, now with William Morrow & Co., and a good friend of Erny's. Howard helped me get the file started. He was really worried and so was I. Another friend of mine, Senator Richard L. Neuberger of Oregon, got in touch with the Library of Congress and hurried them up a bit.

Howard Cady really knew Erny quite well. He felt one of Erny's assets as a writer came from his tragic childhood. Howard said that in his experience as an editor the best writers seemed to have had great tragedy in their lives, which seemed to give them a deep understanding.

Actually, I believe Erny got started on the Western story through his great love of American history. His library proved this; his books were on every aspect of the early days. When a reader would sometimes question some detail of Erny's descriptions, Erny could always give chapter and page and prove himself right.

After Erny's death, our friend and lawyer, Paul A. Sayre, said to me: "Never sign anything that you don't keep a copy of and don't allow anyone to sign anything in your behalf." I live by this rule. I keep files on everything and know when I've been paid and when I haven't. Here I refer mainly to foreign rights. These you have to watch.

Some years ago I met Paul Gitlin, New York agent, through Saul David, then with Bantam Books. After talking with Paul, he said: "The smartest thing for you to do is get Erny's titles in your own name."

I was a number of years and involved with much correspondence accomplishing this feat. Publishers simply do not want to revert titles even if they are out of circulation. Actually, I had to go to New York, seek legal assistance and have letters written. This was the right approach. We heard from all the publishers in question. I recall ten or twelve Haycox titles out of circulation at this time. There was quite a scurry on the part of the publishers, arranging new agreements for me to sign and proposing new programs, etc.

Conrad Richter, whom I had recently met, was very worried about me, afraid the publishers would walk all over me. I was dubious myself, but had my lawyer to hide behind. I should also mention that after hearing Norman Vincent Peale one Sunday while in New York, my courage quickly returned.

In my whole life I have never wanted anything that didn't belong to me, but if someone tries to cheat me regarding Erny's material, I'll go right out after him.

I could devote an entire article to writers and even television programs that have stolen from Erny's material. Erny was even impersonated twice. No doubt this happens to other authors.

Some years ago, Neil McCarthy called me from Hollywood, telling me that a writer of Westerns had just used one of Erny's novels practically word for word. Neil, ill at the time, promised to send me the paperback, but didn't. If he had, I would have gone right after the publisher.

Neil had been head of the legal department for Paramount. Here Cecil B. DeMille had bought and adapted Erny's *Trouble Shooter* (1937) to the motion picture, *Union Pacific* (1939).

Incidentally, Erny and I met on a Union Pacific passenger train in the fall of 1924, both on our way to New York. Erny had saved $400 from his salary as a reporter for the Portland newspaper, *The Oregonian*. He wanted to meet F. E. Blackwell, who had bought his stories. I entered art school and did become a commercial artist.

We used to meet three or four times a week at Central Park. I lived nearby. Sometimes when Erny had sold a short story to *Western Story Magazine* we had a rowboat ride. If he sold a novelette we had a hansom cab ride. Mostly, we walked. Once, he walked me across the Brooklyn Bridge and back. For awhile, I didn't even like him.

Always, when I return to New York I have a hansom cab ride in the Park. Also, I visit "The Little Church around the Corner," where we were married in 1925.

Erny would simply be amazed at what I've learned about

publishers, agents, foreign rights, and copyrights—to mention a few of one's troubles.

Believe it or not—T. Y. Crowell Co., Publishers neglected to copyright the January 1, 1938 issue of *Collier's Magazine.* I found this out when I tried to renew the copyright on "A Day in Town," one of Erny's famous short stories.

I always renew in the 27th year, allowing extra time in case of trouble. Also, the Library of Congress is very slow.

After some correspondence, the Library of Congress suggested I personally renew that particular issue of *Collier's.* The people at Crowell were very apologetic and willing to loan me their file copy of that particular issue. I had to have two photostatic copies made of the whole issue for the Library of Congress. I wondered why the Crowell people didn't take care of the matter themselves; however, my main interest was to protect Erny's story so I didn't bother to ask them.

I do remember the January 1, 1938 issue of *Collier's* had some well-known names in it. I was happy to protect those names as well as the stories and articles.

Incidentally, Jimmy Stewart made his first television appearance (live) in "A Day in Town," with a title change to "The Windmill," for General Electric Theater.

Erny was about four men rolled into one. He was very public-spirited. At one time or another he held offices in clubs too numerous to mention. He was much sought after as a toastmaster and speaker.

The last office Erny held was President of the Portland Rotary Club. His year ended in June 1950. The following October 1st he was 51; he died October 13th of the same year.

During World War II, Erny had more of his novels published in the "Armed Services Edition" than any other living author. He was very pleased about this. He was also chairman of the Draft Board No. 1 in Portland. Naturally, he signed the draft cards of many young fellows going into the service. In those days the boys didn't burn or tear up their draft cards, and very few were conscientious objectors.

Often he would bring home a postcard from some soldier whose card he had signed. The boy would talk about reading one of Erny's novels in a foxhole during a lull somewhere in no man's land. Writing to say he had enjoyed the story and that home didn't seem so far away. We would all have tears in our eyes as we read those cards.

To illustrate Erny's compassion and understanding: one night as he was about to leave his office for home a very pregnant young lady burst into his room in tears. She really frightened him. Finally, she got control of herself and told her story. Her husband had been called, Erny had signed his card, and she was desperate. This was her first baby—couldn't her husband stay until after the baby was born? Erny didn't feel the delay of a week or so regarding one man would hurt the war effort—so, the young man stayed home till after his baby was born.

I must relate two items which would have pleased Erny very much. Joseph Barry, at one time story editor for the Kirk Douglas Motion Picture Company, contacted me through Little Brown & Co. He was interested in *Canyon Passage* (1945). However, this novel had already been adapted to motion pictures and was not available. Mr. Barry and I corresponded, and in one of his letters he said, "In Paris, Gertrude Stein and I shared an admiration for your husband's novels, and I inherited those she had when she died. I introduced him to her with the one on General Custer, made, alas, into a movie already."

Also, a little tribute that would have pleased Ernest Haycox appeared in the *New York Herald Tribune*'s book section a few days before his death. Ernest Hemingway, in one of a number of brief autobiographical notes contributed by noted writers, said: "I read the *Saturday Evening Post* whenever it has a serial by Ernest Haycox." This bit of praise comes from one who ranks high in anybody's list of contemporary writers.

A note of interest. Erny had very few unpublished stories in his file when he died. Later on I had time to read and go over them. Most were very early stories; however, there was one story I kept rereading and wondering why it didn't sell. I finally sent the story to *Argosy*, figuring the *Post* and *Collier's* had, for some reason, turned it down. *Argosy* bought "Court Night on the Trail" and it appeared in their June, 1958 issue, retitled "Outcast." A month later the General Electric Theater bought it for television.

Ronald Reagan played the lead; he was the wagon boss. Again there was a title change to "The Castaway." This was

Introduction

one of the last television programs the actor appeared in before
becoming Governor of California. John Hawkins, an old friend
of Erny's and mine, wrote the script.

To my way of thinking, I have done very well with my husband's material. In 1972, I had 12 reissues of Erny's titles in
this country and many more in foreign language countries.
Through the years I have made considerable money through
the renewal of copyrights; this regards Ernest Haycox titles
adapted to motion pictures. Many of Erny's titles were
adapted to both radio and television. It's hard to realize that
Erny never saw television.

I have always allowed any of his titles to be used for the physically handicapped, and am always pleased when his stories
are wanted for school books.

Perhaps I should explain that over the years I have worked
through agents; also, I have worked as my own agent, and have
personally sold novels to motion pictures, short stories to television, and placed titles with publishers.

Some years ago Bill Cox wanted to write an article about me
with regard to Erny's work. This really embarrassed me. I
didn't feel I had very much to tell and I didn't want Bill to
waste his valuable time on me; however, I did appreciate his
wanting to.

Long ago Saul David, my friend through the years and now
a producer at Metro, said: "Jill, they won't write about Erny
for perhaps 25 years." Actually, it's been 29 years since Erny
went away. Sometimes it seems a million years ago, and sometimes only yesterday.

Some day I would like to write an article on "all the dear
things about Ernest Haycox." Perhaps I shall.

Jill Marie Haycox
Laguna Hills, California

The Earthbreakers

1

A SLANTED, slashing rain saturated his wool coat while he rigged the pack animals, and coldness searched his bones. He scrubbed the wet saddle with a sleeve before he rose into it. Breakers of sand rolled from the nearby bluff to sting his face and when he lowered his head water poured from the crease of his hat into his crotch. Wind went scuffing and squealing along the earth and roared in his ears and was a cry across the world.

"*Hup-hup.*"

The pack horses moved into single file, the two cows followed and the four dun oxen came after, swinging their heads at the ground in fruitless foraging. He used both hands to jam down his hat and made his way through a camp whose hundred wagons — their canvas tops casting a pale glow against the gray flicker of sand and rain — lay on a lava beach hard pressed between bluff and river. Weather-whipped fires burned a violent yellow, darkly dotted by crouched or moving shapes, and all through camp was the constant traffic of loose stock herds moving westward into a farther wall of mist.

At the river's edge log rafts pitched in the smashing rollers, some half built, some fully freighted with lashed-down wagons and ready to go; for after two thousand miles and five months of land travel, this wagon train of four hundred people was readying itself to make the last ninety miles into western Oregon by water through the gorge of the Cascades.

Rice Burnett stopped his pack outfit before a large raft on which two wagons — Lattimore's and Collingwood's — were lashed fore and aft. Lattimore stood on the lava shore with the raft's mooring rope wrapped around him, thin body swayed back and forth by the raft's sluggish heaving. A sagged hat rim made eaves around his ears, down which water steadily ran, and on his face was the habitual fatigue of a malarial man.

"God-damn' country," he said, voice only a murmur against the shout

3

of the wind. "If I'd known it was like this I'd not come. I'm ready to go but Collingwood's off shakin' hands somewhere."

Edna came from the near wagon and came ashore to stand beside Burnett's horse. She said, "I'll walk a ways with you," and took his arm when he dismounted. A man's overcoat gave her upper body an extra heaviness; a shawl covered her head but rain blackened the exposed part of her front hair and wetted her cheeks and lodged its glittering droplets on her lashes. Her face was round and her mouth broad — an erect and rather taut upper lip lying against the lower lip's pronounced roll — and her lids partially closed on brown eyes as she watched Burnett to create an air of speculation.

Lattimore said: "Now don't rove off where I got to go find you."

"Oh," she said, "Collingwood won't be here for an hour." She moved away with Burnett. "You'll reach the portage ahead of us."

He nodded toward the river. "I expect so. You've got a rough ride ahead, on the raft."

Waves rolled high and close-following on the Columbia's wind-beaten breadth. Earlier departing rafts stood out to midstream, rising in sluggish motion to ragged crests and falling into watery valleys and vanishing behind long horizontal streamers of spray. Through the day's dullness Burnett watched the little-figured shapes of men strain at the rudder sweeps.

"I don't mind," said Edna. "Things don't bother me much. Where'll I see you next?"

"At the portage."

"We might be late — and you'll have gone on."

"Then at Oregon City. We'll all gather there."

They skirted wagons and avoided ox teams dragging logs riverward from the pine hill where the Methodist Mission lay; they watched a woman crouched and crying before a fire's dense smoke. Groups of men, heaving together with their concerted "Now — now — now," moved wagons onto the rafts and other men stood waist-deep in the November water and flinched when the breaking surf slapped them. They passed Rinearson's fire. Edna's glance went to the young men gathered there and stayed with them until Moss Rinearson saw her, and then she looked quickly to Burnett and went on with him.

At the far edge of camp he stopped. "No use for you to get any wetter."

Her voice held half a teasing note, half a sweet tone. "At Oregon City, for sure?"

4

"For sure."

"Sleep warm," she said and looked steadily at him.

"Lone man never sleeps warm."

The answer delighted her and her lids again framed a glance meant to provoke him. "It could be better, couldn't it?"

He rose to the saddle and lifted his coat collar against the slashing rain, and he looked down upon her with his smile. Wind colored him and stiffened his face until it assumed a lank length between temples and jaw point. His eyes were gray, made brisk at this moment by his humor; the edges of his hair showed a dark copper cast — rough hair, heavy hair. He had an English nose, high-bridged and prominent, and a long mouth.

"You're slow," she said.

"There'll be a time to answer that."

She shrugged her shoulders and watched him ride into the stormy morning's twilight, body bent and head bent, and when he looked back she saw his weather face — everything pulled inside. She waved and returned through camp.

Abreast the Rinearson fire she paused at the circle of young men and stood across the blaze from Moss. He was the middle brother of the three Rinearson boys and, at twenty, a year older than she. She spread her hands before the fire, slowly revolving them; she gave each man around the circle a moment of personal interest before settling her attention on Moss.

"Where's Whit?"

"Went down the trail with the stock."

She moved around the fire. "You ought to wear a heavy coat."

"Wet heavy coat's just as cold as a wet thin one."

"Ah," she said, and touched his chest with a passing hand; then she looked beyond the group and noticed Rice turned on the saddle, watching her, and she left the fire and went on through camp with her head lowered in thought. When she came to the raft she found George Collingwood ready to go. Her father's futile irritation fell upon her.

"We been waitin' twenty minutes."

George Collingwood shook his head, laughing at her. "No, I just got here." He was forty, more than twice her age, but his light blue eyes paid her a strong interest. He wore heavy buckskin gloves, a fine plaid coat, and beneath his hat the rim of curled yellow hair showed. She delayed a moment to let him have his look, then moved to the raft and entered the near wagon's half darkness, catching the voices of her brother and her mother in the far wagon where Mrs. Collingwood was. Rain drummed

5

loud on the canvas and the smell of wet wool clothes and oiled harness and bacon rose around her. She heard Collingwood say:

"You got any tobacco before we push away, Ben?"

"There's a twist in a can beside my toolbox."

She moved to the toolbox and reached for the can, but a thought drew her back and she waited while Collingwood came over the raft and crawled through the wagon's front opening. He said: "You know where his tobacco can is?"

She settled to her knees on a straw tick and lifted the can. He crouched beside her and the edge of his body came against her and stayed there while she opened the can and got the chunk of tobacco. He reached for it, hand brushing her shoulder, and his pressure grew against her; she turned her head to observe the tense line across his mouth and the bright shine of his eyes. She didn't stir, but as she watched him a speculative smile came about her mouth and her curiosity was plain. His head came tentatively forward, and withdrew; he laid a hand on her knee and pushed himself to his feet. She raised her glance to hold his attention.

Outside her father impatiently called: "For the love of God, let's start."

Collingwood murmured "Edna," in a smooth, stroking voice and turned from the wagon. She remained kneeling; she stared at the dark canvas before her, eyes half closed and her face returning to its smooth calm. The log chains began to groan, the raft increased its pitching and the wagon swayed from side to side. She drew a deep breath and smiled into the darkness.

2

THE camp and its echoes faded, the whirling rain mists closed in. Along this well-worn Indian runway loose stock bands moved ahead of Burnett toward the throat of the gorge forty miles away, but he saw nothing of them in the blind day. The river was beside him, bearing its freight of scattered rafts, and though some of these were forty feet long and sixteen wide the wind-trenched water shook them as though they were small boats. The trail, too rough for wagons, crossed an ancient field of lava and moved through a succession of sand dunes until, about two hours from camp, it rose in stairstep creases along the face of a hill.

Around noon of an already dying day he found himself following the rim of a bluff loosely covered by pine. The river was a thousand feet below him, unseen in the fog, and he was smothered by the twilight of a cloud's breaking center, and wind shook him on the saddle and the tumultuous rain came upon him in hard-breaking drops. He was thoroughly wet, his shoes were water-filled; coldness passed from a burning to an ache and finally to a lack of sensation in legs and knuckles and ears.

There was a way to handle weather and the way — lying in a man's thoughts — was to retreat from the surface misery and build a wall and when the weather broke through that wall, to retreat to a deeper layer of flesh and build another wall. There was never any danger until the last wall was breached and the weather reached that small center cell which housed the will to exist. At that point a man sat as a spectator and listened to the battle between his will and the thing which came to kill him.

Loose soil and pine stems whipped by; overhead the steady hiss of the wind kept on. The horses footed steadily forward from one rocky ridge to another, down a long slope and across the insecure ford of a swollen little river near its junction with the big river; and somewhere in the noisy day he heard a man's weak voice cry out. Fifty feet distant a horse stood on a rocky flat with its rump to the wind. A few cows stood under the shelter of a tree and a small tent, ripped from its pegs, slapped back and forth beneath a branch to which its peak had been tied. Riding in that direction he discovered Alpheus Stricklin's head stuck out from a cocoon of soaked blankets.

Burnett got down and squatted before that hollow face with its fringe of curly red whiskers. Stricklin's eyes were so deep and round that they seemed to have no pupils. A rank odor came from blankets and from man. Too sick to light a fire or to recapture the tent which had blown off its pegs, Stricklin lay in the day's full blast and could not muster energy enough to shiver.

"How long you been here?"

"Two days."

Burnett walked to a pack horse, hauled off its pack and got an ax. He chopped a set of pegs and tacked the tent cloth around Stricklin; he cut the rope which held the tent's peak to the pine bough and let the canvas lie collapsed over Stricklin. He rustled through the trees and collected a stack of wood and from the pack he got a handful of pitch kindling and crouched close to the ground to build a fire under the shelter of his coat. He stood by until the fire caught on well; and he made a frame of wood chunks around it and found his coffeepot and filled it from the river and laid it over the fire.

"When did you eat?"

"Yesterday morning," said Stricklin. "Nothing stays down."

"Any fresh blankets?"

"No."

Burnett dragged his pack near the fire. He poured half the water from the coffeepot into a small bucket, dropped a chunk of jerked beef into the bucket and a hand scoop of coffee into the pot; and put both utensils over the fire. Stricklin made a feeble scratching on the tent cloth and pulled it back until his head was in the weather. "Jesus, what a smell."

"Crawl out of there and sit up to the fire."

"Can't make it."

Burnett squatted over the man. He shoved back his hat to keep its drip from Stricklin and short, sharp critical lines of attention sprang around his eye corners. "You're a down horse and you've decided to die. Crawl out of there."

Stricklin said nothing but Burnett thought he saw the slight shining of resentment, and he reached down and ripped the protecting canvas from Stricklin's body. Stricklin brought an arm from the blankets, doubled his fist and struck at Burnett's face. Burnett laughed at him and pulled the blankets back, rolling Stricklin half over toward the fire. Stricklin kicked out with a leg. Burnett seized the man at the shoulders and dragged him to the edge of the fire.

"Sit up to it," he said and took his ax into the nearby trees to make more wood from the broken deadfall limbs. Stricklin curled himself at the fire and steam rose from his clothes and fresh rain sparkled in his whiskers. His deep-set eyeballs rolled from side to side as he kept his attention on Burnett. Burnett got a cup from the pack and filled it from the simmering bucket.

"Sit up, Alpheus."

"Can't make it."

Burnett circled the fire and took Stricklin by one shoulder and hauled him to a sitting position; he steadied the man with gentle cuffs with his palm until Stricklin made a gesture of protest. Burnett dropped his hand but stood by to be sure Stricklin didn't capsize again.

"All right," said Stricklin irritably. "All right."

Burnett handed over the cup and went into the trees to continue his wood gathering. When he came back the cup lay empty on the ground.

8

Stricklin had both hands across his belly and showed his misery. "It's started again." He lifted his glance to Burnett and dropped it. Sick as he was, he was embarrassed. "I can't get up."

Burnett lifted Stricklin by the armpits and walked ten feet from the fire; he slipped down the man's galluses and trousers and he spraddled his legs and lowered Stricklin to a squatting position. Stricklin wrapped his arms around Burnett and butted his head against the latter's stomach for support; he swayed like a half-filled sack of flour and body cramps shuddered him and the coldness of the day made fine tremors through him. "What a hell of a thing," he groaned. "Jesus, I'm ashamed."

"It's all right, Alpheus. Let 'er go."

"No use. Nothing in me."

Burnett pulled up the man's trousers and guided him back to the fire. He filled the cup from the bucket and passed the cup to Stricklin. "Keep at it." He built the woodpile until it was big enough to last a night; he fried himself a chunk of bacon and warmed himself with the coffee. Three boys crossed the little river with a band of stock and disappeared in the rain-downed twilight; wind ripped through the timber and smashed down branches and felled a tree, and rain walked across the earth wave after wave. Burnett took Stricklin's blankets from the collapsed tent and laid them flat in the rain, weighted by rocks, for washing. He pulled up the tent pegs and dragged the canvas around Stricklin. After he had restored the loose pack to its proper horse he stood a short time at the fire, attempting to read Stricklin's face.

"Keep the fire going. I'll leave the bucket with the meat in it. Just work away at it. You be all right?"

Stricklin dropped his head. He said something which was lost in the wind; he raised his voice. "Sure."

"That diarrhea lasts about three days. You've had two. Lay over tomorrow." He got in the saddle but delayed his departure; for Stricklin's eyes, fixed on him, were like the entrances to the emptiest of tunnels, and around his mouth an expression had settled. It wasn't sickness, Burnett thought, as he turned away to collect his pack outfit. He found the trail and worked his way about a rocky point and up another ridge. The image of the expression, with its unremembered familiarity, haunted him. A good mile down the trail he stopped his horses and sat still a full minute, and at last he shook his head and turned back to Stricklin's camp.

Stricklin had dropped flat before the fire and was entirely covered by the tent. He pushed the canvas back when he heard Burnett and sat up, and the stiffness dissolved from his face and left it weak; his eyes glinted in the firelight. Burnett said: "It'll be dark in half an hour so I might as well camp here." He unloaded the packs and covered them with the canvas and let the animals drift. He dragged his bedroll to the fire and crawled into it and lighted his pipe.

"What's your age, Alpheus?"

"Fifty-three." Stricklin sat up and filled his cup from the bucket; he curled both hands around the cup and sucked at the beef water. "If I'd known it was like this, I'd never come West. It's too late for men old as me. I had a good farm in Missouri."

"You'll feel different — couple nights' sleep and a few good meals."

"I'll put ten years' sweat into a new farm, but it won't please me no more than the last. It's not the constitution of a man to be happy with what he's got. . . . This stuff ain't cramping me as much. I think I'll sleep." He fell back and pulled the tent over him.

Burnett left his bedroll and squatted beside Stricklin. He straightened the folds of the tent beneath the man, and wrapped the upper part over him. He laid a hand momentarily on Stricklin's shoulder. "You were at the forks of the creek for a couple of minutes," he said, and returned to his bedroll. He was hungry, but he had a short stock of food which had to last him until he got to Oregon City or Fort Vancouver and so he lighted another pipe, stored his boots in the bedroll and fed the fire.

Stricklin said: "Been married?"

"No."

"How about that Edna girl?"

Burnett made no answer. Presently Stricklin said: "What'd you do back East?"

"A little clerkin', a little farming. I was in the Rockies trapping a couple years. Soldiered in the dragoons."

"If you'd not come back I'd been dead by morning."

"You're not that sick."

"Sick is one thing. This is another. It's like hanging to a rope forty feet off ground. Pretty soon you can't hold on and you don't give a damn anyhow."

Burnett settled into his bedroll and scrubbed hip and shoulder along the ground to make comfortable trenches for them. Night moved in full of sound; the little river roared over its stones, the racing clouds broke above camp and rain rattled like buckshot and blackness closed on him as the jaws of a vise. It was aloneness which had broken through Stricklin's last wall. Nature, hating the solitary thing — for the solitary thing has no function — had placed in man a sense of incompleteness which made him drift toward others; denied this closeness, he shrank and died. Not that she cared; for man was a vessel she created by the millions, and it didn't matter how many of these claypots were cracked along the way so long as a few survived to transmit the liquid she had poured into them; it was the liquid that mattered to her, not the pot. Man's dream of dignity was his own creation, not hers, and his suffering came of trying to make the dream real against the indifference of earth and sky to his individual fate.

3

MORNING came to him as a feeling he had slept long enough; there was no other sign of day. Wind rushed along the river's trench and burst into violent eddies; throughout the night he had heard trees, unpinned by the rain-softened soil, go down. The air had a biting chill and now and then the screen of rain thickened with the half-solid shape of snow; the little river, when he went to it, had risen two feet. He built the fire, he put on the coffeepot and fried breakfast. Alpheus Stricklin sat up with the tent around him and relished his meal.

"I'm over the hump but I'll lay by today. Tomorrow mornin' I'll be fine."

Burnett spent an hour dragging wood to the fire pile; he was another hour bringing in his strayed animals. He packed, he crouched at the fire to smoke a pipe and to soak in a store of heat against a day he knew would be bad. He rose and looked at Stricklin a moment. "Anything else?"

"No. Good luck."

The trail through the timber was a tunnel of furious sound. Wind knocked him around the saddle when he rose to the crest of a small ridge, and wet snow spatted more frequently against him. He followed a narrow strip of open land two or three miles toward a shadowy barrier, and in the first dismal daylight this barrier became a rocky point pressing hard upon a river whose half-mile surface was corrugated by spray-frosted waves closely following each other. Little by little he was crowded toward the water, the trail twisting out to the beach, climbing over the shale slopes which set up minor avalanches under the feet of his horses, threading gloomy aisles between moss-green rock pillars. Near noon he paused in the shelter of a cottonwood thicket to smoke a pipe, glad to escape the wind's beating for a short time; the farther he rode during the afternoon, the tighter was the river caught between the mountain's jaws, the more relentlessly blew the wind and harsher became the weather. From time to time he saw rafts wallowing in the water, made sluggish by the extra weight of solid ice around wheels and wagon beds.

It was growing dark at four o'clock when he came upon a meadow cramped at the base of the lava palisades and found Whitley Rinearson and the two Lockyears before a fire. With them was Watt Irish, a boy of fourteen shivering within his shabby coat; in the background the hundred Rinearson cattle stood dumb against the blast.

The boy was obviously miserable clear into his bones. He turned to Burnett with plain relief. "I got two cows mixed in with their stock and I got to get 'em out."

Whit Rinearson gave a short laugh. "You can wait till we get to the portage."

"They'll all be mixed up in the dark by then and I'll not see 'em. I got to get 'em now."

Whit Rinearson said, "Walk in and get your cows," and again let go with his brief laugh.

"I can't walk through all those horns," said Watt.

Burnett dismounted and came to the fire. He said to Whit Rinearson: "You're slow — you started three hours ahead of me."

"Cattle strayed last night and we had a hell of a time."

"It's just two cows," said Watt Irish to Burnett. "I got to get 'em out." The weather wizened his face and in the firelight he seemed to Burnett not so much a boy as a stunted man; he had his feet braced apart, he doggedly nourished his hope, but the strain of facing these three unsympathetic men had been hard with him.

It was now half snow and half rain, white flakes streaking across the firelight; wind boomed along the gorge and the river surf crashed on the rocks of this ragged shore. Burnett crouched at the flames.

"What's the harm of snaking out the boy's two cows?"

"We got trouble enough," said Whit Rinearson, shortly. "He can wait, or do what he damned pleases."

"There's your permission," said Burnett to Watt Irish. "Go get 'em."

"On foot?"

"Take my horse," said Burnett.

Watt Irish turned immediately to the horse and pulled himself to the saddle. Cal Lockyear spoke to him. "I've got some stock in that bunch. You stampede anything and I'll break your God-damned head."

"Not in this weather — they won't," said Burnett. He turned his hands at the fire; presently he lifted his chin to catch the weight of all three sets of eyes on him. '

Whit Rinearson said: "Not right for a kid to have his way against men."

"The boy's dead-beat."

"If he's goin' to play man," said Whit, "let him stand it like a man."

"You play it well as he does and you'll be doing fine," answered Burnett.

He looked beyond the group to see young Irish cut through the cattle; he brought his glance back to Cal Lockyear. The man wore buckskins, a big blanket capote around his shoulders, and a trapper's round fur hat; his neck came up as a stout column through the capote's collar to flat ears, a round heavy chin and black eyes. Chest and shoulders stretched the capote; he stood motionless against the weather and seemed not to feel it.

"If this herd belonged to me," he said in a touchy tone, "I'd not permit the kid to fool around it."

"Squirrel's pretty small game for a buffalo hunter," said Burnett.

Cal Lockyear retorted, "You can go to hell."

"Right now that would be a comfort," said Burnett.

Watt Irish came from the herd with his two cows and left the horse beside Burnett. He spread his hands at the fire, he crept closer to the heat and he watched the growing night, its anticipated misery forming around his mouth.

"It will get no better looking at it," said Burnett. "Get on before your cows stray again." He watched the small shape bend against the wind and fade with the two cows into the snow-streaked darkness; he rose to catch the fire on another quarter of his body.

Whit Rinearson had baited Watt Irish for no better reason than to cause somebody trouble. Whit was the senseless one of the Rinearson tribe, and needed to feel a lot of pain before he'd ever know anything about pity; or maybe he had been making a display of toughness for the benefit of Cal Lockyear, who was another breed of cat entirely.

Having put in his time trapping through the Rockies, Burnett understood Lockyear better than the people of the train did, for Lockyear had been in the mountains too and such a life reduced a man to the lean meat of his character. Lockyear would do as he pleased, let others take care, and that part of him Burnett respected since he had some of it himself. But there was about this muscular man a mixture of the unsure and of the threatening. He was thirty, Burnett's age, and thus old enough to have achieved some consistency of view, yet he was more frequently unpredictable than reasonable. He was by turns boastful, rudely humorous and overbearing; he could swing from a civil manner to surly silence in the space of a breath; he had spells of affable familiarity which, when not properly received, turned at once to insolence; he had great extremes in him and seemed to care nothing for the effect he made on anybody; and though he usually accorded Burnett a better manner than he gave to others — he showed little liking for the farmers and shopkeepers and mechanics composing this train — he was nevertheless offended by Burnett's defense of Watt and couldn't quite restrain his ill-humor.

"You want the kid's mother to keep you warm nights? Hell, that's not hard to do. Go ask her. Won't have to ask twice. She's lookin' around. She'd take anything that came — even a cripple like Veen."

In the background Veen stirred, gave Burnett a short glance and dropped his eyes to the fire. Whit Rinearson let go with a flat laugh. Burnett looked from one man to another, ignoring the remark; he turned again to soak in the heat.

"This ain't our country," said Lockyear. "It's Siwash country. Up in Jackson Hole we'd be fixed for winter: good cabin, plenty of meat, plenty of tobacco, no trouble."

"Plenty of cold," added Burnett.

"Dry cold. This air's too wet. What'd we come for?"

"I got to thinking like an Indian," said Burnett.

"That's all right. That's fine."

"Fine for an Indian."

"Well, by God, there's times when I like Indians better than whites. These people — I don't know. They ain't our style. Let's go back and eat buffalo hump."

"Nothing there any more, Cal. Beaver's trapped out. No market for furs. Ever meet Bill Cash?"

"On the Green once. Bigger liar than Beckworth."

"Fifty years old, looked eighty. Ate his meat raw because he was too damned lazy to cook it. Crippled up by rheumatism. Lived past his prime. Good old days gone and no good ones left. He'll drift around the mountains looking for men not there any more. Then he'll start talkin' to those fellows. Then he'll crawl off in the brush and die."

"You been sleepin' cold," said Lockyear. "What you want —"

Burnett said, "Now give that a thought before it comes out," and leveled his glance across the fire; he was cool, he was smiling. Insolence gleamed in Lockyear's eyes, the prompting of temper was there, the reckless moment was there; then he let go with a rough laugh and passed the challenge by. Burnett turned to his horse, used his sleeve to scrub snow slush from the saddle and rose into it. Riding over the clearing, he reached the rocky trail and once more followed its crooked course.

Two hours later, in the trembling blackness of a hard snowstorm, he heard the rising roar of the river rapids. Fires burned ahead of him and rafts landed from their down-river run, crowded the rocky beach. Even at this hour men worked their wagons ashore from these rafts, to remount the wheels in preparation for tomorrow's land journey to the foot of the rapids. Neither cargo nor passengers could live through that particular six miles of water; when the portage had been made, the rafts would be let go to run the cascades empty, would be retrieved in the calmer current below, and would again be loaded for the last thirty-odd miles to the mouth of the Sandy. From there on the final two days' journey into Oregon City would be by land.

He drifted forward in search of a camp spot. Traffic had churned the ground into foot-deep slush, and livestock milled about in search of forage, and wagons and fires and rough shelters lay close-crowded along a narrow strip of land between river and gorge wall. He passed and hailed the Kitchens and the Millards and he swung his horse to avoid Lorenzo Buck, who crouched close to the earth in search of some lost object. Directly beyond, Burnett came into the glow of the Gay fire. Katherine Gay saw him.

"Put up here, Rice."

A ridgepole ran between Gay's landed wagon and a nearby fir; over the ridgepole hung a large sheet of canvas beneath which several people were gathered. Six of them were Gays, Katherine, her fourteen-year-old brother Joe, her parents — John and Martha Gay — and her grandparents, Sophia and the Old Man. The Howards and the McIvers had joined the group to save the work of making their own fires. Dr. Ralph Whitcomb, who as a single man had shared one fire or another all across the plains, stood beside Harris Eby; and though the doctor was neither short nor thin, he seemed to be so against Eby, who was by far the largest man in the train, six feet six of bone and hard tissue, great feet, thick legs, maul-shaped fists, and an upper body which had a kind of treelike sweep to it; all of this topped by a blond head and a round and quiet face. On Eby's other side was Lot White, though Lot's vanity always made him step far enough back from Eby to make the comparison less pronounced; and Lot, as usual with him, was involved in rather loud and positive talk. He broke off long enough to cast a short glance at Burnett, to say "Hello, Rice," and to wait for his audience's attention to return.

Though canvas and wagon afforded some protection there was no escape from the freezing whip of the wind, or the inslanted snow, or the mud underfoot, or the reverberations of the river in its cataract. Burnett picked an empty spot not far from the fire for his pack pile and unloaded his horses with a slowness he could do nothing about; he had no feeling in feet, hands or knees, and he watched his animals drift into the night and pitied them. He stood well away from the fire to scrub some kind of sensation back into ears and nose.

Katherine brought him a cup of coffee and tested his overcoat with her hand. "Have you got anything dry?"

The heat of the cup scarcely registered in his palms though it scorched his tongue. "Buried somewhere in that pile."

She pushed him toward the fire. She looked around the circle and said to Lot White: "You've got the warmest spot. Move over."

Lot White said: "Rafts still in the river, comin'?"

"A lot of 'em," Burnett said.

"Lot," said Katherine Gay, "move over."

Lot White gave her a glance and reluctantly moved. He was a short, turkey-cock man with an upper body shaped by his blacksmithing trade; his hat, thrust back, showed a half-bald head; his eyes were a shade of blue too light for his complexion, thereby lending an unusual insistence to his glance; his mouth, though forceful, was thin enough to be without color, and his jaw was stubborn and his words came out with a kind of tumbling effect, as though sped by the pressure of other impatient words behind.

"They should have sense enough to not creep down this river by night. Out there the weather's too much to bear, and if they overshoot this place they'll be in the rapids and that's the end."

John Gay said: "We ought to keep these fires bright so they can see the way in." He looked to his son Joe. "If you're fairly warm go rummage up a few more big branches."

16

Half beyond the reach of the fire, Joe Gay was overtaken by Dr. Whitcomb's advice. "Be careful you don't get hit. The wind's knocking dead branches down like rain."

"He won't get hit," said Lot White; and said it with such certainty that Dr. Whitcomb's glance moved to him with its small amusement.

"You trying to throw a mantle of mercy over him, Lot?"

"He won't get hit."

"If he's standing in the right place at the right time, he certainly will," said the doctor.

Lot White slapped both hands briskly together and meant to carry on the talk. Katherine Gay stopped it. "Let each other alone. You're both old enough to know you can't change anything by talk."

"Lot feels he's got a call to change me," said the doctor. He settled himself at the foot of the wagon wheel, his face reddened and made cheerful by the firelight. "What reason brought you to Oregon, Lot?"

Lot White searched the doctor's face for guile. Then he said: "I couldn't abide slavery. I won't live where it is." He stared steadily at Whitcomb. "You meanin' to make fun of that?"

"No," said the doctor, "that's a good reason."

"You got a way of lookin' and just listenin' without believin'," said Lot White. "It's a way that disturbs people, for they think you're smart because you're a doctor, and if you don't believe in things, they get to wonderin' if they're right. You can't do that."

"That's right, Lot," said Ralph Whitcomb, and smiled at Lot White's renewed rise of suspicion. "So, why don't you let my beliefs alone?"

"Because you believe wrong and it's my bounden duty to make you see it."

Whitcomb was too weary to laugh outright. "You ought to be a Jesuit."

"And you ought not use education against a man that's got none," said Lot.

The doctor's smile disappeared. "You're right about that, too. Well, a Jesuit's a man who'll use any argument to gain his end."

Lot White meant to carry on with the talk but Whitcomb turned from him to John Gay. "Why'd you come here?"

Gay had been only half attentive; his thoughts were with the fire, which he pushed together with his boots. He looked back toward the raft pitching in the water, to the ropes which held it to the shore trees. He stepped to the edge of the covering canvas and shook away its load of snow, and returned to the fire. The first sloping of middle age was visible in his shoulders and the first settling had begun around his mouth, to give it an extra pinch of resolution. His arms were the long arms of the outdoor worker, wristbones heavy, fingers enlarged and slightly bowed from the year of grasping and twisting and squeezing. His face was composed rather than sensitive; without formal schooling, he was one of those natively intelligent men who move slowly from point to point in their thinking.

"Why," he said, "I suppose it was the land I wanted." He looked toward his wife. "Anyhow, that's what I told Martha." He stopped to replace a rolled-away chunk of firewood. "Most of the men of this train lie a little about their reasons. We've all got some sort of itch in our feet to try a fresh place, and that's almost the main reason in some of these fellows."

"That's what I think about," said Martha Gay, "when I remember all the nice furniture I couldn't bring and the new apple orchard just ready to bear." She looked steadily at her husband. "Sometimes I just hate the people who bought our place."

John Gay turned to the doctor. "You're such a hand to ask questions. What for yourself — what brought you?"

"My maternal grandfather was a young man in the Lewis and Clark expedition. I listened to those stories for years."

Voices roughly shouted down the trail and the Rinearson cattle broke through the fire's light toward the shelter. John Gay seized a limb chunk and waved it before them, driving them back around the wagon into the farther darkness; the steady stream of beasts moved past, and Whit Rinearson and the Lockyears appeared in the light and vanished.

"They'll knock over half the shelters in camp," said John Gay.

The doctor got up and put his hands to the fire for a last warming. "I should look at Provost's baby again."

Burnett said: "If you've got any whisky, give Mrs. Irish enough to mix Watt a toddy."

Whitcomb's departure broke the group, for the Howards and McIvers and Lot White soon left. John Gay said, "I hear somebody on the river," and moved beyond the firelight's reach as Grandmother Sophia and the Old Man, after soaking in a last warmth from the fire, entered the wagon. Katherine walked to the food box and in a moment came back with a plate of beans and molasses for Burnett. She tipped fresh coffee into his cup from the big pot on the fire and settled between Burnett and Harris Eby, the latter balanced on his heels. Wind fanned hot tobacco ashes from Eby's pipe into his face; he batted the ashes away, idly laughing. Behind

18

these three, Martha Gay looked on with a clouded interest and seemed to study her daughter as a stranger.

Through wind's blast and river's roar a man's lonely voice cried across the water from a raft; a lantern glinted on the raft and was lost as the raft sank deep into furious rollers. Shore voices called outward and the man shouted back. Somewhere behind this raft were others searching their way down-river, for far away a faint calling survived the night's rattle and rush and thunder. John Gay, lost in the snow flurry not more than twenty feet from the fire, flung out the hardest shout he could produce.

"Turn in here — be quick — turn in — bad water below!"

Katherine said: "This will be a terrible place tomorrow with all the wagons landing."

"Terrible place now," said Burnett.

"Turn around and let the other side get dry."

He reversed himself before the fire. She adjusted herself toward him, thereby placing her back to Harris Eby; and suddenly Martha Gay said, "I think I'll go to bed" — and caught her daughter's eyes and held them a long moment, and went to the wagon.

Rice said: "There'll be some weak stock dying tonight."

She said: "Be some people dying, too, if they didn't believe the trip was almost over." She took a small branch and crouched to worry the red-white coals about on their bed. The fire soothed her, her face lost its weariness and her mouth alternately loosened and grew firm as her thoughts swung. John Gay's shouted warning rode the windy night again and woke an answering halloo from somewhere on the river. The girl drew her shoulders in; a look of pity crossed her face. Upstream a short distance many men were taking a raft shoreward through the blackness, and a woman cried, and in the farther distance a gun went off as a signal.

Burnett's square pack pile slowly changed to a round lump as snow built drifts around it, and the campfire was a single bright cell of warmth in a smothered world. Wind cried shrill at the sharp wagon corners and filled the upper air with tumult as it slashed through the fir tops; a loose bucket went banging over the shore rocks, a lone horse thrust its head through the snow screen and stood with its crusted mane and its eyes shining agate green against the light. Burnett went to the pack pile to pull his blanket roll from the protecting canvas. Bitterness began one step beyond the fire's reach; he was cold again when he dragged the roll beside the fire.

"Get your feet dry first," Katherine said.

He twisted his boots between his hands and found them soaked solid to his feet. Harris Eby rose and moved over; he planted a knee against Burnett's chest, clasped his hands around one boot at a time and pulled them off with such force that Burnett fell back into the snow. He laughed, as much at himself as at Burnett. "Something had to give, boots or feet." He set the boots against the fire, smile turning his face peaceful; the shrewd blue eyes flashed in the light, fell upon Burnett and turned to Katherine. The girl's glance rose along this immense column of a man and she patted the huge hand hanging near her.

"If you ever got mad," said Burnett, "you'd do considerable damage."

Eby found pleasure in the thought. "Pull the trees down one at a time, push the cabins flat, kick holes in the earth. . . . But I never get mad. It was left out of my system."

"No, I saw you put out once," she said. "You remember the Bonesteele brothers?"

"Long time back," said Eby.

"Not so long. About ten years. It was just after my fourteenth birthday."

"Thirteenth," said Eby. "Because when you were fourteen you'd moved to the house by the creek."

"He never forgets anything," said Katherine to Burnett. "He even remembers when I was born."

"I do," said Eby. "I was three and my mother came home and told about it, and same day she got some flowers and I carried the flowers over to your mother and I saw you. They were lilacs. We had a big bush in the yard."

"What about the Bonesteeles?" said Burnett.

"I wasn't exactly mad," said Eby. "More like aggravated."

"It was about me," said Katherine. "He was jealous. The oldest one was Fred Bonesteele and he liked me. He had four brothers and I guess he thought he'd run Harris off."

"Me," said Eby gently. "Run *me* off. Fred never had any sense."

"Well," said Katherine, "Fred got his brothers and three or four other boys to help him. You tell it, Harris."

Eby said, "It wasn't a great deal. I just pushed that bunch around till the extra ones got tired and quit. Then I gathered up the Bonesteele boys." He looked to Katherine, smiling, shaking his head, and turned his attention to Burnett. "It was the backhouse. It sat on the edge of a ravine. I shoved those five boys into the backhouse and shut the door. It was

yoked and waiting. Mrs. Howard crouched before a fire with her arms thrust out as if to pull heat into her. Her husband had a hand on her shoulder, prompting her to rise, but even through the mealy blur Burnett saw the misery on her face.

Blackness was solid beyond the camp site and beyond the string of fires and there was no guide save the heaving shadow of the wagon directly ahead of Burnett. He passed the trees and crawled up a field of loose rock which ran tilted between bluff and river. At the summit of this place a man waited to warn the passing outfits. "Take the downgrade easy. You can break your wheels. Watch beyond — it's narrow." The wagon's shadow ahead of Burnett swayed and he heard the small avalanche which its wheels started among the rocks.

Daniel Rinearson's voice cried forward once again and afterwards fell still, and the column went on at its groping gait. Presently the trail moved so close upon the river that Burnett saw the exploding waters of that rough six-mile stretch which they were now detouring, the cascades leaping as white fire across the black, and the sound — like the tearing of cloth, like the rumble of smothered explosions, like the escape of live steam — trembling against him and disturbing the earth beneath his feet. He had been more than an hour on the way and had made perhaps two miles of the portage when a first daylight crept in and the scattered house-high rocks began to stand forth along the trail and the gorge wall took on substance close at hand, rising and vanishing in the upper layers of the storm. The column worked its way between narrow pillars and crossed a short lowland piece overgrown with willows. Beyond the willows, as the daylight wanly grew, Burnett had a sight of the column for perhaps three hundred feet: the straggling stock, the great wagons slowly careening, men and women trudging in the deep-churned muck with their bodies bent against the weather. Leaving the willow flats the trail entered timber, newly fallen trees indicating where the first riders had cut a way through yard-high drifts. The column halted and he sat on the saddle and felt numbness creep along his legs while the wind laid open his face with its knife slashes; later the column lurched forward and he passed Henry Provost's wagon off the trail, Provost and two other men standing beside a dead ox. A good two hours onward from this point brought Burnett to a pinched beach at the foot of the rapids where the first arrivals were already scattered through the loose trees; the cattle had begun to drift for shelter and fires showed their first feeble eyes in the grayness.

John Gay's wagon stood hard by the river, the oxen unyoked and gone,

23

the canvas shelter stretched again from wagon to tree. Gay crouched on his hands and knees — Katherine holding a blanket around him — and blew his fire into life. When Burnett crawled from the saddle thin ice rattled along his coat and his feet felt no contact with the earth and his fingers, working at the pack ropes, were iron rods which wouldn't bend. He struck them against the packs until sensation came, and struck so hard that blood began to break through the skin. From one of the packs he got a bundle of thin pitchwood and went to the fire. Katherine's face was stone-solid and in her eyes was a withdrawn expression as though, beaten until sensation had left her, she waited dumbly to be beaten again. He rubbed a finger along her cheek, he touched her ears.

"Feel that?"

"Yes."

He got down beside Gay and drew the blanket around him. The fire, scarcely larger than the size of Gay's cupped hands, burned feebly on its dry shavings. Burnett slid the pitch splinters across the flame, one by one, and Gay crowded the pile between his palms, flame licking against his skin. He strangled on the smoke and turned his head from side to side. Burnett built a wigwam of pitch and sticks and the two nursed the fire until the blanket started to scorch and the growing smoke drove them back. Gay scrubbed his crying eyes and returned to the job. Young Joe came in with a load of wood and Burnett got his ax to trim a short log nearby and to drag it to the fire for a backstop. He wanted to stay here to soak in a little heat but the weather warned him and he cruised the trees until he found a skinny fir and dropped it and began to cut the twelve-foot sections which, bound together, would make the small raft he needed to freight his pack stuff across the river. The wagon column moved steadily forward from the portage trail, wagon after wagon swinging beside the river to find camp space, and Rinearson's cattle drifted through the timber hollow-flanked, long horns tossing, turned into wild game. Burnett kept his eyes on them while he worked.

Watt Irish crawled from his wagon and ran toward the Gay fire, calling to Katherine. "Mother wants you — her feet are frozen."

Katherine still held the blanket to shield her father at the fire. She dropped it, caught a bucket and went to the river; she scooped up water and hurried on past Burnett and into the Irish wagon. Young Watt came slowly back toward Burnett. He shook, and braced his shoulders, and shook again.

"What have you got left for food?" asked Burnett.

"A piece of bacon and some onions."

"Go back to the fire and stay there," said Burnett.

Wind struck its sledgehammer blows on the camp and bent the stunted firs and ripped the snow into shredded streamers. Coldness was an acid burning holes through Burnett's body, and out of these holes his energy ran in waste. The swinging of the ax brought feeling back to feet and legs but his cracked hands continued to bleed and his motions were awkward. He dragged the raft sections to the beach and laid them together and he dropped another thin tree and trimmed out crosspieces to bind the logs. He returned to his pack for spikes, walking with his feet spread apart; coldness got at his mind as well as his muscles and he had to push himself. He spiked the crosspieces to the logs, tied a rope rowlock at each side of the raft and cut two lengths from the tree to make his oars. These he carried to the fire and went to his packs for his jerked meat and his skillet. He pushed Lot White and Daniel Rinearson aside and squatted at the fire to make his meal. The crowd had grown larger.

Mrs. Irish sat at the fire, wrapped around in a patchwork quilt. She let her head fall back against Katherine behind her; pain flickered around her mouth, put there by the revived sensation in her feet.

"I thought Oregon was gentle," said Lot White.

"We're in the neck of the funnel — it all collects here."

More people came off the trail with the telltale walk of exhaustion; it was a drunken walk, a swaying, drag-footed, loose walk; their heads bounced on their shoulders, they were mudcaked from ankle to knee and a thin sheeting of ice glittered on their clothes. Ralph Whitcomb moved among them, touching ears and noses and hands. Mrs. Howard came in and sank beside Mrs. Irish. She laid both hands over her face and softly groaned.

"Well," said Lot, "it's worse by the hour. We might get frozen in here. We had better move on fast."

John Gay said: "It's time to send a man back to cut loose the rafts and let 'em run the cascades."

"I'll be surprised," said Lorenzo Buck, "if they come through and not be torn apart."

"The risk's to be taken," said Gay.

"How'll we catch 'em when they get here?"

"Row out with my little raft," said Burnett, "and pick 'em up."

"The man that goes back can't cut 'em all loose in one batch," said Lorenzo Buck. "Let's get this timed right."

25

The men in the circle looked toward the water, visualizing the little raft going out, the pickup of the big raft, the towing of the big raft ashore, the return of the little raft.

"Half an hour," said Ben Provost.

"Ever try to tow something heavy?" asked Ryal McIver.

"Forty-five minutes," said John Gay. "That's about right."

Daniel Rinearson said, "Who goes back?" He was, at sixty, a hale man of moderate size, well-wrapped inside a buffalo coat; he had a chunk of cloth wound around his head like a turban and this, covering his ears, made him bend forward to catch what others said; the exposed part of his face — a face with frosty brows hanging above the horse-trading eyes, bold sharp nose, and a chin built forward — was whipped to a barn-red by the wind. His scanning glance stopped on young Watt Irish. "You go back and cut the rafts loose."

"No," said Rice Burnett and went on eating.

Old Daniel's arguing countenance settled on Burnett. "It's fair enough for the boy to lend us a hand."

Mrs. Irish had been listening with her eyes closed. She opened them and looked from man to man, and then to her son standing at the fire. "If it's thought he should, then he will. But I wish — "

"No," said Burnett. "He's beat-out."

"Well, then?" said Old Daniel and stood with his lower lip rolled out.

"You've got more men in your family than anybody else," said Burnett.

"Hell of a lot of free advice around here," said Old Daniel. He took his silent poll of the crowd and drew his conclusions. "All right, I'll send one of the boys."

John Gay gently said: "Which one, Daniel?"

"Does it make a difference between my sons?" said Old Daniel.

"It's a responsible thing," said John Gay. "If they're cut loose too close together we'll miss some, and then there's trouble. Don't send Whit."

Daniel Rinearson tossed his head and let go with a loud laugh, but his eyes lay resentfully on John Gay. He looked about once more, sensing the will of the crowd. "All right, I'll send Ared." Then he said, "Think he's got sense enough?"

Harper Howard said: "Send him soon. We got to get out of here. We're short of food and it's still two–three days to Oregon City. It wouldn't hurt if we had a solid meal of beef in us before we started."

Daniel lowered his eyes to the fire, rubbed his hands together, and ignored the quiet watching of the others. He said, "Well, I'll get Ared on the way," and left the circle.

"Tell him to cut 'em loose forty-five minutes apart," called John Gay. He looked to Harper Howard with a short break of humor. "He didn't rise to it."

"Rich men don't rise," said Howard. "He wouldn't miss a couple cows from that hundred. But, no, he don't give anything free."

Burnett finished his meal and shaped out the oars beside the fire. The group around him constantly changed, other settlers coming in from the trail to thaw the misery in them before they went on to make camp. The day worsened and when he carried the oars to the raft a dense snowfall blotted out the far shore. He carried a third of his packs to the beach, slid the raft into the water and loaded it. He put the oars through the rope-holes and shoved away; twenty feet from shore the current seized him and the rollers, quartering against the raft, threw it sidewise into the air; then the rollers ran away from the raft and it dropped into the troughs with a jar that snapped his head. Halfway over the river he saw a small crowd watching him from the shore but when he reached the far beach they were lost in the driving mist.

He recrossed and stood at the fire a moment, and reloaded and crossed again; on the third trip, with the last of the packs, the rollers caught him and rushed over him and only the support of the oars held him aboard; he came wet to the fire and crouched there to dissolve the iron ache in his bones.

"It's about time for the first raft," said John Gay.

Burnett got a coil of rope from his camp stuff; he cut it into two sections, making a towrope for each end of the small raft. Squatted low against the beach to scan the river, Lot White suddenly said, "Think I see it comin'," and John Gay and Ben Provost got aboard the little raft and flattened themselves on it as Burnett rowed away. He saw the big raft come through the boiling cascades, swinging end to end, sinking below the surface, rising with all the force of the current behind it to leap from the water like a clumsy fish.

Burnett maneuvered the small raft into midstream and dug the oars deep to hold it; a wave rushed under him, seized an edge of the raft and sucked it down, and buckshot pellets of spray drew a sharp shout from Ben Provost. When they rose from the trough they discovered the big raft dead ahead, slowly revolving in the current. Burnett brought the small

27

raft directly against it and waited for the collision. Provost and Gay, half risen, clung to the small raft's logs.

"Watch now," said Burnett.

The big raft came on, spray breaking over its downstream edge. Burnett checked the small raft as a roller lifted it. He back-oared. The small raft struck the big one and Provost and Gay jumped and fell flat on the logs. Provost had the towrope from the little raft; he squirmed around to make a tie on the big raft, and signaled and rose to follow John Gay toward the lashed downsweep at the far end of the big raft. Burnett swung the small raft away, taking in the towrope's slack.

It was like pulling at a stump, for the force of a ten-mile current surged on the big raft's broad surface, and against such power his two oars made poor impression. He laid his weight against them until he felt the green wood give. He used the little raft as a kind of anchor to haul the big raft around, but it was a quarter-hour before the little raft was upstream and the big raft stood below him, so slanted as to catch the shoreward push of the river. They were four hundred yards downstream when Burnett brought it to the beach. He untied the towrope and started along the water's edge with the small raft. Harris Eby came on and took the rope from him and hauled the raft upstream. Burnett turned back to give Provost and John Gay a hand with the big raft, the three of them slowly pushing it through the back eddy — John Gay using the sweep as a pike pole at the stern, Provost holding the raft's nose off the beach, and Burnett shoving from behind, hip-deep in the river.

By the time they tied the big raft to the trees near the fire, the small raft was out in the water again, Harper Howard and Lorenzo Buck lying flat beside Harris Eby at the oars; men crouched near the beach watching the little craft rise and fall in the charging current and Mrs. Howard stood at the fire with her two sons and looked into the river with her engraved anxiety. Through the almost horizontal flickering of snow, the second big raft showed itself in the cascades, ponderously bucking the water, flinging spray over its gray back. Burnett observed Eby's great shoulders swaying at the oars and he thought: "I should have warned him," for there was power enough in Eby to snap those oars.

Wind sharpened the ice-chill of Burnett's clothes; he was suddenly caught by a long, rough shuddering of muscles. He walked on to the fire. Katherine poured him coffee.

"How many rafts to come down?"

"Five or six," he said.

28

"It will be dark before then. When are you crossing your stock?"

"Tomorrow."

"How far is it to Oregon City?"

"Three days," he said.

In the semi-twilight a voice came through the trees — George Collingwood's voice — and Collingwood's wagon came from the trail, followed by Lattimore's. The wagon stopped and Collingwood called, "The women have got to get warm," and waited while his wife climbed from the seat. Edna Lattimore crawled through the other wagon's rear opening, slipped on the snow and, laughing, recovered herself.

A short cry came from the river's edge and out of Mrs. Howard's throat rose a penetrating scream. Thrown around by that wild note, Burnett saw the little raft flung half aboard the larger one, with Eby bent far back on the oars and one other man lying flat on the large raft's edge with his arm seizing vainly at the water. Mrs. Howard's scream rose again and she and her two boys rushed to the water's edge. Harris Eby backed away from the big raft and swung downstream in huge heaving shoulder motions. For one moment, on the water's surface, Burnett saw an arm rise and a face show its pale disk through the driving weather; then it disappeared and Mrs. Howard began to run downstream along the water's edge, her voice crying back through the brutal wind, "Harper — Harper — Harper, oh, my God, Harper!"

Katherine turned about to follow Mrs. Howard. In a moment she looked back to Burnett and gave him a glance, and he dropped the coffee cup and followed her.

5

THE light of half a dozen lanterns, shining through the wind-crazed snow, threw a speckled glow into the grave pit. Harris Eby came from it wet to his knees and stained yellow by the mud, and Lorenzo Buck crawled down to take his turn with the shovel, flinging the clay around the foot of the other men standing by. The shovel gritted steadily against the rocks, the scoops of dirt grew smaller. Buck called for a pick and tried it on the pit's bottom a little while and quit. "Pure rock. Four feet's the best we can do."

"Poor grave for a man," said Collingwood.

Cal Lockyear stood slightly back from the group, so indifferent that Burnett wondered why he shared this dismal chore. Lockyear said, "What difference does it make?"

Water crept through the underlying gravel and rose in the pit; it dripped from Lorenzo Buck's feet when he climbed out. John Gay moved a finger around the circle, choosing his men — Collingwood and Lattimore and Old Daniel Rinearson — "You come with me."

As they moved back through the trees toward the Howard wagon, Billy Lord stepped nearer Lot White. "Now for God's sakes, make the sermon short."

The Gay fire fifty feet away was a ragged yellow hole in the curdled black. Burnett turned to it and got a bucket from Gay's wagon and returned to bail out the grave; water spurted through the gravel as he bailed.

"Dead man entitled to be warmer than a live man?" said Lockyear.

"Might make Mrs. Howard feel easier," said Burnett. But the water continued to flow in as fast as he could take it out, and in a moment he heard people moving through the trees and he climbed from the grave and set the bucket aside. Gay and the other three men came forward, awkwardly stepping with the burden of the dead Howard between them; they skirted the grave and got on their knees to lower Howard, he covered by a faded patchwork quilt sewed fast about him. The rest of the camp walked through the trees to make a semicircle at the grave's foot. Katherine and Mrs. Irish stood to either side of Harper Howard's widow; the two Howard boys, edging forward, stared strangely at the black hole in the ground and Mrs. Howard looked at the quilt cocoon which was her husband, and put one hand across her eyes. Lot White moved to the head of the grave, waiting while the four men tried to place Howard gently into the pit. They were on their knees, each with one hand supporting themselves and one hand under Harper; they lowered him to the end of their reach and still were short of the pit's bottom. John Gay, uncertainly supported by the slick pile of clay dirt, began to slide head-forward into the pit and he let go and made a rough grab at Burnett's legs. The other three released their grasp on the quilt. Howard fell the last foot into the grave.

Lot White, removing his hat, began at once.

"God sent us to suffer, and we've done so accordin' to the plan, and God calls us back to a just reward. O you falterin' who doubt, you men that reason too much and trust too little, you people who listen to wise fools who tell you this is not so — I tell you it's so. I tell you there's a road leadin' to the gate, and the road is real as the one we traveled from Westport to Independence; and it's summer on that road, and the birds sing and there's shade for the weary and water for the thirsty, and there's a gate and a man at the gate, and inside the gate there's a stairway to the throne, and you can touch that stairway and you can feel it, and on the throne there's a body and face and a Voice — and the Voice will come upon you, and you'll hear it as plain as you hear me; and a hand will touch friend Howard and make him easy, and the Voice will come upon him with the secret of life and of death, which is one and the same secret, and he will turn to his everlastin' peace, and wait there for his wife and his children and his friends to pass through this little misery and come to him again."

Billy Lord bent and murmured to him. Lot White looked upon the roundabout people, dim-shaped in the flickering lantern light, in the relentless rush of snows.

"It makes no difference when a man dies, May or December, young or old. We die, and that's the end of it. This snow came yesterday; it'll be gone tomorrow, no trace left. We were born yesterday and tomorrow we're gone, no more trace than the snow. For the grace of man is not here; it is in heaven — and to heaven I commit this man, and I envy him the glory of his life eternal, and I yearn for the day when that glory shall be mine. O Lord, let his wife weep — for the Bible says women shall weep; and then, O Lord, let her cease to weep, for we've got work to do so long as we're here. Let her smile again, let her find a man, let her be useful till her call comes. Let her raise her children, and have more children; let her make butter and spin and weave, let her tend her garden and be a neighbor in distress, let her sing the good old songs with a full heart; and when her call comes, let her lie down with an eager heart. And we ask no questions, but only pray. Be with us, God, for there's nothin' else."

John Gay spoke a strong "Amen." Most of the women were crying but Mrs. Howard, chilled and spent, had no tears left; open-eyed throughout the sermon, she strained forward to see her husband lying awash in the shadows at the bottom of the pit and, placing her arms about her two small boys, she moved away with Katherine and Mrs. Irish. As soon as the women were gone John Gay took up the shovel to fill the grave, the first few scoops of dirt splashing in the water which now covered Harper Howard. He worked fast as though the sight displeased him, and Burnett presently spelled him, and later Ben Provost finished the job, rounding the dirt about the grave.

George Collingwood said: "This is a hell of a thing. The wolves will be down here tonight. We ought to put some rocks over it."

"Wolves or worms," said Cal Lockyear. "It makes no difference."

George Collingwood turned about and went into the shadows beyond the lantern light. He soon returned. "The rocks are too big to move, or frozen fast."

"No matter," said Lockyear. "You've satisfied your conscience and that's all you meant to do." He walked away.

The group moved toward John Gay's fire, Collingwood coming beside Burnett. "Damn the man," he murmured, "can't he be civil?" Wind crashed through the trees, dredging down the last weak boughs, and the passing lantern light touched white snow mounds drifted high against the roundabout boulders. People crowded Gay's fire. Beyond it, at the water's edge, Gay's wagon sat lashed on the raft, pitching to the shore breakers; the mooring ropes groaned quietly against the snubbing trees.

Burnett halted beside Edna Lattimore.

"Bad trip down the river?"

"No — just cold."

George Collingwood walked around the circle with his covert desire to attract attention. He had an actor's streak in him, and he made quite a ceremony of cleansing the grave's mud from his hands. He glanced at his wife, who crouched near Katherine and soaked in the fire's warmth with her fatigued disinterest; then his attention darted to Dr. Whitcomb on the other side of the circle, and fell aside. It was, to the observant Burnett, a sudden revelation.

"Now," said Collingwood, "we've got two widows, Mrs. Irish and Mrs. Howard. We've got to do something about helpin' them. They can't make it down this river alone. We're all neighbors and we'll see no neighbor suffering distress alone."

"That's taken care of, George," said John Gay. "Joe will ride on Mrs. Irish's raft, and Lorenzo's going to lash Mrs. Howard's raft to his."

The fire flushed Collingwood's face and gave to it a round, well-fed cast. "That's fine. We're all together and we'll stick together. We're neighbors. We can't let anything happen to each other."

Lucy Collingwood got up. "I want to go back to the wagon, George."

He said, "Have you got warm enough?" He buttoned his overcoat and thrust his hands into his pockets; he seemed in no hurry until Lucy Collingwood walked into the night without him. He showed a trace of fretfulness as he followed her.

Burnett turned his hands to the fire and looked about and, in one of those unexpected moments of perception which change the world so that it is never quite the same world again, he noted the abrasion of this trip on the silent people around him. It was to be seen in the bony droop of John Gay's idle hands, in the recesses of Mose Crabtree's eye sockets, in Mrs. Millard's drawn-together body; its small signs were everywhere.

The five months' crossing had taken its levy in faith and in flesh. Lucy Collingwood's baby was dead. Mrs. Irish and Mrs. Howard, married women at the trip's beginning, were widows. Summer's heat had boiled the confidence from the group, and this wintry weather had sapped their vitality so that they moved with the carefulness of the very old; and the strength with which they had started the trip — the almost insolent confidence they had in themselves as individuals — was less than it was; in this final wringing-out of their endurance, they had an intimation of what weakness was, and they sat here together with the need of closeness very real in them, and came upon fraternity.

Burnett's moving glance touched Edna and caught the signal she had for him, and he joined her and moved through the shouting night. She stumbled and seized his arm and swayed laughing against him. The harddriven snow struck like sand against his face until the repeated attack became an ache. Through the blackness other fires bloomed out their orange stains, and the beating of a maul against metal came forward from some part of the camp with clocklike strokes. A cow blocked the trail before them, its eyes shining as separate bits of opal flame. They waded through the knee-deep drifts and reached the dying coals of Lattimore's fire.

"Long day," he said. "Awful long day."

"Well, go to bed." Then Edna searched him with her lively eyes and her smile came on with its suggestions. "And sleep cold." She waited for him to lift; she laughed at his half-roused expression and she laid a hand on his arm, closing her fingers about it. But he was still slow and presently she stepped back with a display of indifference. "When I first saw you come to the wagon train this spring I thought, 'There's somebody who could be bold.'" She looked into the fire, but curiosity brought her glance back to him. "You ought to know what you see, but sometimes I don't think you do."

"At this minute a gallon of whisky couldn't make me bold."

"Ah, you're not that old, and it wouldn't take that much whisky or that much of anything." She turned to the fire. "When you came out of the mountains after a trapping season what's the first thing you did?"

"Haircut and something to eat."

"Then what?"

"Then I started to look for another job."

"But before that you hunted up a woman." The polar night rushed about, the fire flame leaped high. "What did those women talk about?"

"I couldn't say."

"Why not — why not?" Her eyes pried at him, her fleshy smile was warm. "I say things other girls think, but don't say. I trouble you, don't I?"

"No."

"Yes, I do. You're funny." She stared into the fire. "Boys don't know anything. You're older, you should know, but women still fool you." Her hands were square-shaped against the fire's light; beneath her bulky coat the separate roundnesses of her body were uneasy; she was aggressive and ready, she was uncertain. Her lips suggested their adeptness, their experience; they struck restlessly across her otherwise tranquil face. "I wish you'd talk more. I love to talk to you. Lately I don't see as much of you, and now you'll be gone in the morning and we'll not be together for three or four days."

"See you in Oregon City."

"Then what?"

"Then we'll all look for land."

"Ah," she said, "you never answer what I want you to answer." Then she said confidently, "What's wrong with you is something any girl could fix up quick. You know that, don't you?"

He smiled at her and said, "Good night," and moved away.

She crouched beside the dull coals to catch a last bit of heat before turning into the wagon, her face meanwhile settling into an expression of light-humored confidence; and her thoughts claimed her so fully that the coldness, the furious sounds and the wild motions of the night seemed to make no impressions upon her; but after a moment she rose and turned toward the wagon and discovered Cal Lockyear watching her from the shadows, scarcely fifteen feet away, and then her light expression gave way to a certain discontent.

"You been watching me all this time?"

34

"No," he said, "only a moment." He came to the fire and stood across from her. "You're cold."

"No, I'm not," she said.

"Will be if you stay out here."

"No, I won't."

There was more often than not a threatening air about this man — a combination of black brows, gray eyes and general unrest within him; at the moment, however, he seemed to wish to please her, for he made a brief gesture and permitted himself a trace of a smile. "Been a bad day. Tired?"

"Things don't bother me."

"Want me to build up that fire for you?"

"Not worth the trouble." She watched him with both wariness and curiosity, not quite at ease with him, yet not ready to quit him. All across the plains she had felt the effect of his eyes, though seldom had she caught him directly watching her; and this interest had piqued her attention so that her treatment of him was a deliberate indifference softened by an occasional smile.

"It's a mean country," he said.

"I hear it's better out in the valley."

"Wet," he said. "Sort of stuff that takes the curl out of your hair and the hell out of your disposition."

She let herself be amused. "Well, that wouldn't hurt you."

"Like a man tied to a rope, like him tame?"

She returned to her indifference. "Be what you please, it's none of my business."

He flung up his head, deviltry bright in his eyes; he laughed, he grew sober and stared at her a long interval, half respectful and half scheming; and suddenly he swung and vanished in the night. Edna turned to be sure he had gone, and settled again at the fire. Now her expression was lively, for the meeting had challenged her, and she looked a long while into the fire and at last, with reluctance, she rose and went into the wagon.

6

RETURNING from Edna's fire, Burnett thought he heard the cry of a wolf in the beaten night but could not be sure. He stopped by a group of men laboring Jubal Crowder's wagon aboard its raft and he lent his shoulder; twenty men heaved at the wagon and it should have been an easy chore, but their strength was gone as was his, and his pressure was only the dead pressure of his body, no muscle behind it, and even this exertion dragged wind from the bottom of his chest. The wagon settled on the raft and Crowder said in a reedy tone, "We ought to dismount the wheels tonight." There was no answer from the others; they leaned against the wagon, crooked shadows, silent, searching for an energy which wouldn't rise, and Crowder sensed it and said, "Well, the hell with it. Morning's soon enough." One by one men wavered through the wind and Burnett went on to Gay's fire.

The group there had diminished to Katherine, and her father and Eby, and Lot White dreaming on his haunches, and Ralph Whitcomb. Katherine rose and poured Burnett a cup of coffee and came around the fire to rest a hand on his shoulder. Harris Eby, puckering at his pipe, watched the two a moment and let his eyes fall on the flame. Katherine returned to her place beside him. She looked at Eby closely, laughed at him, and bent to rest her shoulder against him.

"Tomorrow will be bad, going down the river," said John Gay.

Burnett said, "Beyond this line of mountains it should be rain, not snow."

"Well," said Harris Eby, "we're almost there."

Whitcomb listened to the wind's beat. He shook his head. "In this gorge a lot of people will go beyond their breaking point — never quite be the same people again. Their free land's going to cost more than they think."

"We'll do what's to be done," said John Gay. "We'll do it and stand it."

"So you shall. You're a wonderful people for sticking."

"Faith," said Lot. "Faith."

"But we're all running from something," said the doctor.

"Now," said John Gay, "you're boring a deeper hole than I can see down."

"We grew up in the American notion we could start from nothing and become rich or get elected president. That's our religion, much as any we've got — that we could turn a dream into beefsteak and prosperity and happiness, leave our children more than we had, and so on. When we got older we saw that it wasn't that sure a thing. But we couldn't admit the dream was bad, for that would be saying hope is an illusion. So we saw empty land out here and we've come here to make a fresh start, hoping that what was wrong back East won't be wrong here."

Like many a man without schooling, John Gay had contempt for men

36

whose book knowledge made them foolish; but he also respected words which seemed to come from some source of wisdom denied him. "I can't say about that," he said presently. "I'd have to think on it some better time than this. You don't sound cheerful about our prospects."

"Same weeds of failure that grew back East will grow here. We bring the seeds with us. The shiftless and the ignorant will fail, same as before; the thrifty will get along. There's only one difference. Some people are going to die earlier because of the trip."

"As for that," said John Gay, "I'm not in agreement. My opinion's that our lives are in the book. The thing was set down, borning and dying, long before we began this trip. You have got a spirit, I observe, that swings mighty low sometimes."

"I don't bear misery well."

"Bear it as well as the rest of us."

"No," said Whitcomb, "it takes a particular kind of people to live this close to the mud."

Gay looked at his boots, smiling; and stamped the caked mud from them. "Well, we're damned deep in it at the moment." He gave out a sigh and turned to the wagon on the raft, his punished body seeming to be in motion only at the command of his mind. Whitcomb, hearing his name called, rose to meet Ben Provost coming in from the rush of snow and the two talked a moment and then Whitcomb, buttoning his coat, followed Provost into the night.

Lot White said, "Been hard on that Provost baby." He stared at the fire, his private thoughts making him restless, and presently he slapped his hands together and rose to follow the two. He overtook Whitcomb as the latter reached the Provost wagon. Whitcomb was on the point of climbing into the wagon. "What are you after?" he asked.

"I'll pray," said Lot.

"Pray out here then," said Whitcomb.

"No, I want to bring the Lord right in there."

"No."

"You've done your best. It's my turn to call on better help."

Whitcomb's temper slipped. He backed down from the wheel. "Lot," he said, "I won't have you dripping your wet clothes on the child, or laying your cold hands on her, or raising your voice to scare hell out of her. Pray right here. If your faith's got any power it ought to travel ten feet from you into the wagon. I don't want any more foolishness about it."

Lot White's voice rose. "Provost, it's your baby, not this man's."

"We better do what Ralph says," murmured Provost.

Lot White shouted his anger upon Whitcomb. "Your learnin' has taken true healin' from your hands, and someday you'll know it. No man can believe as little as you believe and live." Saying it, he turned away and was instantly lost in the night.

Whitcomb remained in the Provost wagon half an hour; when he came from it he started toward his own wagon, already lashed to its raft and ready for the morning trip, but within a short distance he swung aside and beat his way through the night, past McIver's wagon, past Buck's, past Mrs. Howard's. He paused there and scratched on the canvas. "It's Whitcomb. Are you all right, Mrs. Howard?"

Mrs. Irish's voice came back. "She's all right." Then he heard Mrs. Howard say, "But it's nice you came by."

He circled Billy Lord's, listening to the late scrape of Billy's fiddle, and he visualized the man sitting wrapped around by his blankets, sawing at the instrument to soothe his wife asleep beside him. They were, to the doctor, a strange and wonderful couple.

The Lattimore wagon, when he went by, was dark. Collingwood stood at the Rinearson fire with Old Daniel and the three boys. Whitcomb paused here.

"Hell of a time for you to be walkin' around," said Old Daniel.

Whitcomb spread his hands at the fire. The three boys stood across the flame, each one with his own particular character and none of the three characters in any respect alike outwardly. The oldest, Ared, was a settled close-handed man at twenty-two, a work horse with no particular imagination. Moss, the middle one, looked the least like a farmer and it had always struck Whitcomb that this boy, with an education he would never get, might have been a professional man. As for Whitley, there was no question of his parentage; he was Old Daniel thirty years younger — the same chesty build, the same push, the same self-centered interest. Neither was there any question of Whit's wildness — not only the wildness of youthful energy running in undisciplined riot, but also the other wildness which was somehow premeditated and callous. It was in Whit's large, rolling eyes; it was in the foxy brightness of his face as he looked toward Whitcomb.

"I should think," said Collingwood, "with other people's troubles and your own, you'd go to bed."

"Bed's a cold place in weather like this."

38

It was like Collingwood to be overly solicitous. He always tried to say the thing which would make him seem wise.

"Well, you're the only doctor we've got and you should keep your own health. You can't be wearing yourself out on others all the time." Then he had a thought: "Lucy's not feelin' too well. If you've got a minute to spare, go see her."

Whitcomb studied the wagons shadowed in the weaving snow and said, "That one?" He hoped that his manner was casual but felt that it was a poor try, for Daniel Rinearson watched him with a wise interest and Whit's eyes had malice in them. At Collingwood's nod, Whitcomb turned to the wagon, seeing the stain of lantern light come through the canvas. He rose to the front wheel hub and scratched on the cover.

"Who's that?"

"Whitcomb."

In a little while Lucy Collingwood called, "All right," and he pushed aside the heavy blanket draped across the front opening and crawled inside. All sorts of household equipment lay boxed or wrapped in this crowded space, piled as high as the canvas would permit; the bed was between this stuff — a feather mattress lying on the wagon boards and made up with piles of quilts. She lay deep in the mattress, the quilts drawn about her neck. Her hair had been made down into braids; her eyes were light brown, underscored by a semicircle of shadowed flesh; her mouth was pale. She hadn't smiled much since the death of her baby back at Fort Laramie, and she had lost a great deal of interest, but as he settled himself uncomfortably between bed and luggage he saw no particular symptoms of sickness. She was relaxed.

"George thought I ought to drop in."

She said: "I don't know why."

He pressed two fingers against the side of her neck to catch the beat of her heart; thus bent over her he looked straight into her eyes and had the illusion of dropping into a deep place. "Warm enough?"

"As warm as anybody else tonight."

He saw an overcoat lying over a box and he took it and added it to the pile of quilts and drew it around her neck. A small chunk of hair, escaped from one of the braids, had flattened itself to her temple; he resisted the impulse to brush it back with his finger. He said: "Do you sleep well?"

"I don't seem to need it. Listen." She moved her head toward the shouldering roughness of the wind against the wagon canvas, to the cascading rush of it through the trees, to the hundred minor sounds of things moving and groaning and rattling and snapping around camp. "It's like the earth has lost control of itself and all the wind in the world is rushing down on this spot, harder and harder, till we're blown away."

"Trip's been hard on you."

"I'm not delicate. I only look delicate."

"You don't like this kind of life."

"Did George think there was something particularly wrong with me?"

"He was being considerate. You've lost a baby and it takes a little time to come back."

"I'm over that. I couldn't grieve long for a child I never saw. It's just sad to think of that time and hope going for nothing."

"There's still time enough. How old are you?"

"Thirty-four. That's five years younger than you are, isn't it?"

"How do you know?"

"It's one of the first things women around camp would find out about an unmarried man. They wonder why you're not married. They don't like it."

"None of their business," he said. "Why should they care?"

"It's sort of a general insult. They suspect you. They'd love to catch you mixed up with some woman."

"They know better. Nobody can keep anything from anybody in a wagon train, or in a small settlement. We live naked to each other, no secrecy possible. It will be so all our lives."

"That's the thing I hate most," she said.

He drew back on his knees, taking great care not to touch her. He had removed his hat and his black, unbarbered hair rolled across his forehead. His lids were heavy, swollen by the weather, and two days' whiskers darkened his complexion. "There's nothing wrong with you," he said, "that a healthy shock of some sort wouldn't fix up. Good night."

When he got to the door blanket she called after him. "You know what I am, Ralph? I'm somebody a long way from home."

"It will be different when you get settled in a cabin."

"That's not what I meant."

He let himself through the opening and down the wheel of the wagon, and walked straight into the shadowed shape of Collingwood. Collingwood said, "I guess it's time to turn in. Is she all right?"

"Yes," said Whitcomb.

Collingwood moved around him and entered the wagon. After a mo-

40

ment's pause to orient himself in the driving weather, Whitcomb set off for his own wagon — at that moment realizing Collingwood had turned into him from the wagon's side, not from the direction of the fire. Collingwood had been posted against the wagon, listening, and as he understood this, Whitcomb's last bit of sympathy for the man ran out. Then he thought, *Am I so easy to read?*

7

HALF the morning was gone by the time Burnett got his stock across the river — towing them behind the raft — and it was noon by the time he had his pack outfit loaded. Thereafter he set forth upon a trail broken by Indians and Hudson's Bay people and by the emigrants of the two previous years. The way quartered upward into the hills, the animals had hard going; night halted him on a windy little meadow hanging to a promontory a thousand feet above the river, while to his right — northward — the mountains rolled on with their black tangle of timber.

From this high place, the following morning, he sighted the scattered rafts in the river below, and he then began a difficult passage downward through mud and rock and windfalls, the weather meanwhile changing on this western face of the mountains, the snow turning to a fat rain driven in by intermittent gusts of southwest wind. That night he camped in half-drowned lowlands beside the water, and another morning brought him to the river's narrow plain, mists rolling over him like thin cloudbanks, and the far shore receding until he judged the river was a full mile wide. Late that afternoon he sighted the log palisades of Fort Vancouver sitting hard by the water; skirting the farmed fields and the outer cabins of the place, he entered a main gate of this Hudson's Bay post — whose factor, John McLoughlin, had ruled a northwest empire for a quarter-century in the name of the company and the British.

It was a compound large enough for military drill, with the shops and houses made of milled lumber built against the inner wall of the stockade; a larger house stood not quite centered in the compound, a pole flew the British colors — the sight of the flag offending Burnett's acute sense of patriotism — and a good many men moved about the parade on various kinds of business. He was approached by a French-Canadian employee who spoke to him in bad English and moved away to the big house; within a few minutes a tall man came from the big house.

He was a physically powerful figure of about sixty now beginning to show the effects of shrinkage and infirmity; he walked with a degree of care, but with the air of authority, for there was an austere benevolence about him — in the firm mouth, in the strikingly cold blue eyes, in the direct sizing-up he gave Burnett; he wore a mane of poorly barbered gray-white hair. "Some of your people touched here yesterday," he said, "in bad circumstances. I understand the gorge has been severe and I've sent a bateau up there with supplies. What is your name?"

"Burnett."

McLoughlin gave him a hand and identified himself. "How was the trail?"

"Choked in."

"It's an early storm and won't last. You may put your animals in the pastures east of the wall and you will find quarters with the bachelors. Mr. Curry . . ." Mr. Curry came over, was introduced, and was instructed by the chief factor. "Show him where he may stay."

"I had thought," said Burnett, "to cross tonight."

"You'll save no time this late in the day," said McLoughlin. "As soon as you got across you'd find it necessary to camp in the rain. I shall have the ferry take you over in the morning. It will put you directly on the trail to Oregon City."

Burnett said: "What's the ferry charge?"

"Could you pay?" asked McLoughlin pointedly.

"I could, but I am a frugal man, and it's a fine point with me between paying and swimming."

"There's no charge. I should like you to know, Mr. Burnett, that this is a trading company and you someday may be a customer, either at this place or at our store in Oregon City, which Mr. Ermatinger runs. If you could look at our books you'd find a good many of your people carried on credit. Some of them would have gone hungry if the credit had not been extended. You will find much animosity toward the company on the part of certain of your people, rising out of nationality. It is to be regretted — but you might find that those who are most bitter toward us are also the ones who have not seen fit to repay the obligations incurred of me at a time when they were much less independent than they are now." He turned away, and turned back a moment to point toward the feet of

42

Burnett's horse. "You need a shoeing there. Tell my blacksmith that I have said for him to do it."

"I am obliged," said Burnett.

"There are only two years of migration before you; so much good land's left in the valley. Let me caution you: Take care with the bottoms — for in winter some of them are very wet. If you must settle there, make your place by the Willamette, which is the only sure road you'll have for many years. My people, when they have served their time with the company, go down there to make farms. You'll find forty or fifty families twenty miles above the fall at Champoeg. . . . If the river's not to your liking, then find a claim on the first break of the prairie near Bear Creek. The land's not quite so good, but you can build roads there."

He moved off with the abruptness of one not accustomed to terminal pleasantries. Burnett had been prepared to dislike him, for McLoughlin had been a British king out here until the American immigration of the previous two years had challenged and set aside his authority; but, watching him go, Burnett found himself impressed by a crusty courtesy which had imbedded in it a very real sense of fairness. He turned off with Curry to the bachelor quarters; he was introduced to the clerks at suppertime, and found his bed. In another gray and rainy morning the fort ferry crossed him with his outfit to the brushy south shore of the river.

The trail was clear, since it was a main thoroughfare between the fort and Oregon City, twenty-five miles to the south. Before the existence of that new town, the trail had been the well-traveled route of the company's brigades trapping as far down as the Sacramento Valley. A few miles of willow-tangled swampland ended at higher ground as he passed into the dark fir timber which covered this country wherever he looked; he saw the Willamette nearby — the river which, beginning a hundred miles or more southward, washed through the heart valley of this Oregon country and at last dumped itself into the Columbia not far from the Fort. There had been recent travel on the trail, and somewhere beyond noon of an increasingly gloomy day he discovered a figure on a horse waiting ahead of him.

He was a redhead, a lathe-shaped young man dressed in dirty buckskins, moccasins and trapper's hat. Wind and rain humped him on the saddle. Across the horn he carried a rifle, both hands resting upon it. As Burnett came up, the man gave him a searching inspection, friendliness waiting on certainty.

He said, "Oregon City?" and when Burnett nodded, the redhead fell in beside him, riding with his knees drawn up on short stirrups. "My name's Bob Hawn. Been here six years and saw the first of you people come."

"Burnett — Rice Burnett."

"I see the fringe of your buckskin coat. You been trappin'?"

"Three seasons on the Missouri headwaters."

"Know it well." He pointed to his moccasins. "Blackfoot woman made those. Who made your coat?"

"A Crow squaw."

"Your squaw?"

"No."

Hawn fell silent for as much as a hundred yards, then said, "I've got a squaw," and searched Burnett's face for a reaction. "Not a Blackfoot squaw, though. She's Calapooia — one of the tribes down the valley. I've got a claim that direction. Here to settle?"

"That's right."

"Come down and I'll show you a good place. In '43 and '44 your first people went out in the Tualatin — that's good, but the best's taken there. Some of 'em have squatted around Oregon City. Few went on farther. Not half a dozen around me. It's all open. What's news East?"

"Beaver's no good now."

"Well, she was fine while she lasted," said Hawn. "At the time — shiverin' like a dog, wet all day, cold all night, listenin' all the time for Indians — it seemed like a hell of a thing. Now it remembers good. First years out here were the same: the squaw and me and a pretty fine life. Now you people are crowdin' in and things have changed. I don't know — I don't know . . ."

They stopped at noon, Hawn making up a little fire to boil tea and fry a chunk of smoked fish which he produced from his possible sack. The timber grew thicker, giant trunks running upward in a manner to astonish Burnett, their tops making a canopy so high overhead that the wind seemed at great distance; and a kind of odd quietness lay all around. In late afternoon they reached a small river near its junction with the Willamette, crossed on a gravel ford and came upon an open piece of land at the edge of Oregon City, the new buildings of this town making two or three short rows between a high bluff and the river. Directly beyond town, a wall of black rock rose in the shape of a semicircular dam across the river, over which the current broke in steam spray and fell thunderously to its new level. The wagons of the train — such as had arrived —

were parked in the clearing, fires were burning, and people wandered idly around from town to camp and from fire to fire.

Burnett turned to a space between the Lattimore and Gay wagons and chose the shelter of a cedar tree for himself. Hawn, folding himself comfortably over on his saddle, lingered to talk and to rummage the camp with his inquisitive glances which stopped nowhere long.

He said, "Don't stay around this place. There's nothin' . . ." He ceased to talk and Burnett, looking about, saw the man's eyes pinned to Katherine Gay moving forward from her fire.

Katherine smiled at Hawn but he, making the briefest nod, said to Burnett "I'll be around town tonight if you want to talk about settlin'," and moved away.

"It's an awfully small place to be called a town," said Katherine.

"Except Fort Vancouver, it's the only town we've got," said Burnett. "Two stores here."

"We won't need them much," said Katherine. "There's not money enough in this camp to buy a whetstone." She looked through the scattered crowd and her attention rested a short time on a small, round and painfully plain girl who stood alone at a fire with a blanket wrapped about her shoulders. "Poor Roxy. The Kitchens have nothing, and I know they're out of food."

"So are a lot of others." He drove his ax deep into a fallen log and dragged it near the tree to make a backstop for his fire; he knocked down the overhanging cedar limbs and, with a few pitch shavings from his pack, made a quick blaze and dragged a pack forward to supply a seat. "Come out of the rain."

"The natives say not to think about it, for it'll rain all winter." She settled on the pack and laid her hands together and stared into the uncertain twining of the flames. She was graver than he had seen her. "How will they get along?"

"It's not your nature to worry," he said.

"You don't know much about my nature. But—land to find cabins to build, and getting something in the ground, and fences, and everything to do and so little to do it with! And waiting for harvest on an empty stomach . . . everything—just everything. How will the Kitchens make it, or Mrs. Howard, or Mrs. Irish with only poor little Watt who's half sick with working too much now?" She sat still, permitting these things to trouble her. He said nothing; he fed the fire and walked away to split a log and to bring in its sections.

45

"You're no help," she said.

"I'll save my help for those that require it. You don't need any."

She was smiling, she was a little bit wistful. "Thought I did."

"All right," he said, and crouched beside her, "we'll grieve together."

"Don't make fun of me."

"I guess," he said, "it's time for the big drunk."

"You've had a few, too."

"Had some. Missed some I ought to've had."

"Well, there's no doubt a saloon in this town."

"What would I be doing, drunk alone?"

She reached for a stick to poke at the fire's heart. "We'll be settling in all sorts of places. Where will you go?"

"Don't know. It'll take some talk and a lot of questions."

"Anyhow, here's where the train breaks up. I don't like it. I don't like things to change. Wish we'd all settle the same place."

"Four hundred people thrown together for six months is pretty close business. We're a lodge — a very particular lodge."

She said: "I don't really make out why you came."

"I'm the sort of man that always thinks there's something beyond the next mountain. I've sure crossed a lot of mountains to find out there's nothing on the far side that wasn't on the near one. In fact, I've run out of mountains. That's why I came here. I'm thirty and it's high time I settled."

"You sure?"

"Oh," he said, "I expect the wind's going to blow some mighty nice smells at me — smells of things over there, not here. Tomorrow — not today. You know — what we've not got but what we might get. Same old thing: over the next hill . . . I expect my feet will itch." He made a flat motion with his two hands against the ground. "But I'm on the blanket."

"What's that mean?" she asked.

"It's what an Indian says when he's through fighting, running around, raising hell."

She watched him. "You sure?"

"Sure."

She made half a turn and laid her hand flat over his chest, over his heart. "There's your mountain you're all the time crossing." She rose and turned her attention to Roxy at the nearby fire, and her light manner was overshadowed by thoughtfulness. "They have got to be helped," she said.

46

"You think about that. And Mrs. Irish — you think about how she can be helped."

"Why me?"

"Because," she said — "Because you should. Because I said so." She gave him a moment's austere attention; then the sudden smiling arrived. "I think I'll go look at a store — not to buy anything — just to enjoy looking." She went away.

It was then midafternoon with a light and lazy rain falling from low clouds. Burnett pulled a canvas over his packs and took his ax to walk through the scattered trees for fuel, meanwhile noting the letdown air of people standing at their fires or aimlessly traveling from one place to another. The long trip was done, yet it was not done; they were neither in motion nor settled; and indecision was plainly on them, as though they were waiting for their energy to renew itself. He heard Gay's voice call to him and he went to Gay's fire and joined a dozen men gathered there.

Some of the townspeople had come along to offer their advice. Gay turned to Burnett.

"This man" — pointing to one of the townsmen — "said it's not been settled much on the other side of the river, thirty miles down."

"What about the Tualatin Prairie?"

"Best is taken," said the townsman. "And it's low. From now till May you can row a boat from one swale to another."

"I saw a man this morning," said Burnett, "who spoke of the country off French Prairie."

"What's his name?"

"Hawn."

"Oh," said the townsman, "the squaw man. He's back of where the Howells settled, first rise off the prairie. That country rolls. Some buttes and some ridges. Timber patches and meadows between. The meadows are fine. Indians used to burn 'em every year to keep the underbrush clear for huntin'. Good game country — you're just elbow-close to the mountains. Bear Creek and a valley. Plenty of water."

"By God," said Rinearson, passing a hand through the sifting rain, "you don't have to tell us that."

"You'll get accustomed to it," said the townsman carelessly. "First year's the worst. The wetness around here is the saturatin' kind. When you get close to a stove you'll stand around in your own private cloud of steam. You won't get entirely dry until spring and you may get to feelin' like a book with the glue about ready to let go. Your cabins won't be tight and even if they were the dampness would get through. Your bedclothes will always be sort of clammy and your iron will rust, so keep your guns oiled." He was enjoying himself; he smiled at the growing and attentive audience.

"How many rivers we got to cross to get to that place?" asked Billy Lord.

The townsman shut his eyes a moment. "Molally and the Pudding — not big. And some creeks. Your first business, after cabins, is to break land enough to get your wheat in. You'll have a hell of a time turnin' over the sod. Then you got to split out rails for when your crops start comin' on. The deer will eat you lean if they ain't fenced out."

Ben Provost said: "Can't break land or seed in this weather."

"No, you wait for a spell of sun."

"Suppose it don't come?"

"Then you plow and seed anyhow," said the townsman. "You got to eat next year, don't you?" He was smiling again.

"Well," said John Gay, "to be honest about it, I'm troubled about eating *this* year."

"So say we all," murmured Lot White.

"Oh, you can borrow a little wheat from them that's been here a year or two. You can boil it, you can parch it, you can fry it. However you fix the stuff, you'll get awful tired of it. There's fish—and there's venison. The deer are meager little creatures towards spring and you'll get sick of 'em. . . . You'll make out. Don't know how, but you will. It's astonishin' how people manage to live when it don't look reasonable. Now I'll give you a tip. Look at my clothes."

He had seemed to Burnett to be a comfortably dressed man until he drew attention to himself. He let his shirt cuffs come to view, ragged as French lace; he pointed to the patching in his broadcloth suit and, turning about, he drew aside the coat skirt to display a trouser's seat of some foreign gray material sewed over the original blue cloth. He had a fine set of whiskers which came well down to his chest but when he lifted the whiskers he presented for their inspection a hole in the shirt as large as an apple. His shoes had scarcely any soles. "You see how it is. We've got food, but our clothes are worn out and there's nothing in that line to buy here yet. You've got no food but you've got a lot of clothes. The answer is, swap." Then, the cheerful smile showing again, he said: "If there's a spare shirt in this crowd of you my size, I'll give ten bushel of wheat for it."

Lorenzo Buck, standing in the foremost rank of the large circle, made a gesture to himself as though remembering something and turned away. Burnett saw him cross the camp to Mrs. Howard's wagon. Meanwhile Rinearson had another question for the townsman. "Next year, where do we sell our wheat and cattle?"

"Sell?" said the townsman, and seemed surprised. "Why bless you, brother, there's no market for anything. Hudson's Bay will buy your wheat at some sort of a price, but you'll have to wait till the country grows before you think about makin' any money. There's no money here. We don't use money. We use script, or orders on the stores, or we swap." He saw the disappointment on some of their faces and he went quickly on. "What would you make money from? Land? There's too much of it. Cattle? You can swap good stock around among yourselves, but the country's full of wild Spanish cattle brought up here years back, and roamin' now like deer. You want to watch out when you meet 'em too. No, there's no chance yet to make a fortune, but that's not what you need anyhow. What you want is to settle, make a place, fill your root cellars and your wheat bins, and get your orchards goin' and build roads and set up schools. You'll live like kings, for this is the finest country on earth, spring and summer and fall. What do you want to be rich for? Why bring that maggot out here, gentlemen, to make life wormy? Let your earth yield and let your cream pantry be full, and rest on your porch and rock in your chair. My God, men, have you got to buy and sell things to be happy?"

The audience viewed him skeptically and John Gay expressed the crowd's reaction by a pointed question. "Well, friend, wouldn't you like to be rich enough to buy a new shirt?"

"That," said the man, "is only to please the morals of my neighbors. I'd do as well with a blanket as a shirt."

Ryal McIver said bluntly: "What in hell do you do for a living?"

"My name's Sydney Moss and I run the hotel yonder — the one with its petticoats hoisted above the river."

"And do you run it for love or for money?" asked Ryal.

"I can tell you something about that," said Sydney Moss. "If every man who ate at my table had paid for his meal, I'd be rich and the country would be broke. Gentlemen, I shall not make a commercial announcement. I shall only say that if you wish to use the facilities of a hotel while in this city, you will have to use mine — for it's the only hotel we've got." With that good-humored advertisement, he tipped his hat to the crowd and sauntered toward town.

John Gay said, "Just where did the gentleman stand in the matter of money?"

"I think," said Rinearson, "he likes it but ain't makin' any."

"Same as the ten commandments," said Gay. "They're fine things when there's no sin to confuse the situation. . . . I still have got no notion where to look for land."

"The country Hawn spoke of sounds likely," said Billy Lord.

John Gay squatted and scooped his big farmer's hand across the spongy soil before him. "Rolling country," he said. "Well, that's not apt to be deep loam and what's the point of moving two thousand miles for second-grade stuff? That Tualatin Prairie interests me."

"You'll recall he said it was rowboat country in the winter," pointed out Ryal McIver. "It could be swamp-sour, and maybe wouldn't dry fit for plowin' till late in spring, and might bake during summer."

"It will bear more talking about," said Burnett, and moved toward town. He noticed Lorenzo Buck and Mrs. Howard in close conversation. Lorenzo was a short man, his head level with the woman's; he had removed his hat and the slow rain plastered his hair to his skull.

Mrs. Howard said: "I can't be leaning on you all the time. You have got your own work — and it looks to me like one man's work out here is from daylight till way after dark."

"Then what will you do?" asked Lorenzo Buck.

"I don't know. Something. I've got to do something." Her complexion was of the dark Missouri kind, her eyes gray and unlighted. There was on her face the visible remnant of what once must have been a high-strung temper and a love of gaiety; but at thirty-five these things had been quenched. Her body was thin, her mouth pressed at the corners; facing Buck she seemed on guard against an undue generosity from him and yet perhaps was hopeful of it, for she was in the cruel position of a woman who, having nothing left but pride, knew that pride was too expensive for her. "I think I can stand anything. I've told myself that more than once. But I need time to meet these things. It's not decent the world should change so fast and make me change with scarce three days to put away the things I've lived with fifteen years."

He was sympathetic, but insistent. "Maybe time, next month or next year . . . There's none now. The help that's here will be gone tomorrow. Have you got any notions?"

"No," she said, "except maybe to sell the oxen and the wagon and look for something to do around this place."

"There's nothing to do. You can't go back and you've got no relatives in the party. There some other family you can throw in with — live with for a while?"

She answered quickly, "I'd never live under another woman's shoes."

Buck swung his stocky shape to look beyond her. Rain ran down his hair and across his face. He made a gesture of dashing it away. "Well," he said, "it amounts to this, don't it? You have got two young boys and no husband, and I have got a girl and a boy, and no wife. Coming down the river it occurred to me it would be a good thing if we joined the families."

She said nothing. He continued to look beyond her, his expression fixed somewhere between kindness and embarrassment and he shifted his feet and, hearing nothing from her, gave her a direct glance. "Wouldn't it?"

"I expect it would," she said.

"It had better be done today," he said.

"All right."

"I'll speak to Lot White." Buck let his glance fall to the ground and stood in long thought, and raised his eyes to her. She made a small motion with her shoulders and he continued to watch her for a moment, and then turned away.

8

EDNA walked through the first town she had seen since leaving Missouri six months before. There were perhaps forty raw-boarded houses scattered along a street which dipped and rose to the contour of the land and had no particular order. Here and there some enterprising soul had built a fence and at intervals a section of boardwalk made walking passable; otherwise the street was two dirt footpaths bordering a lane churned to loose mud by wagons and rain. She passed a church, a hotel, a blacksmith shop and a coopering place; she paused at a store's doorway to catch the odor of goods which came from it; she saw a second store, Ermatinger's, across the way.

Other people from the wagon train cruised through this town, something like idle visitors on a holiday. She saw Moss Rinearson and looked at him until his attention came around; and she smiled at him and went on. At the farther end of town was a big warehouse and farther on some sort of mill; out in the river the falls were a great horseshoe of ragged water overhung by mist.

She paused, half an eye on the water, half an eye on the street. George Collingwood detached himself from a group of men and moved toward one of the stores; he saw her, hesitated a moment, and went into the store. Retracing her way, she noticed one of the Crabtree boys staring at her. She had no particular interest in Sam Crabtree, yet his attention was the golden coin of a man's interest and she gave him a full answering smile. Katherine and Harris Eby stood by the Ermatinger store and for a short time, drawn by the only thing that really interested her — the personal relationship between a man and a woman — she looked toward them with her warm and suspicious thoughts. Two Indian women sat on the doorstep of a house as though it were a public bench — one very old woman and one very young, the latter holding a baby across her lap. Edna stopped and her smile quickly came as she looked down at the baby's round, dark and dirty face. She laid a finger on the baby's button mouth and softly stirred it; she made small bubbling sounds with her own mouth.

Ralph Whitcomb's voice came from behind. "What's original about a baby, Edna?"

She drew back. "It's like a doll."

"Rag doll," said the doctor. The Indian mother's eyes clung to him, smileless and without motion, and the doctor suddenly said, "Do you speak English?" — and seemed relieved when she appeared not to recognize the question. "I guess she doesn't. It's just a baby, and it'll grow up half tame and half wild with no world of its own. That always happens when white people move in."

She said, "I hear Indian mothers don't have much trouble."

"No more than animals, usually."

"You shouldn't speak of her as an animal," said Edna.

"She's younger than you are, but she's already showing age. She was pretty. She isn't now. Smoke and dirt and gluttony and starvation have done it."

"We all get old soon enough," said Edna. "In ten years I'll be fat and ugly." Her broad mouth refused to be serious. "But I'm not troubled about that. The only thing that would trouble me is to think I'd never get married."

"You've got no worry there," said Whitcomb.

She lifted shoulders and head, appreciating the compliment. At such a time it seemed to Whitcomb she had been spoiled by experience. She liked men and was alert in their presence; yet there was nothing sly about her. Her actions were impulsive rather than deliberate, so far as he had noticed them, and though other and more self-contained women looked at her with reserve it occurred to Whitcomb that nature had put into her a more than sufficient capacity and that she was at its mercy. She reached out to absorb the sensations of life with a spongelike readiness. She accepted the coarseness of her surroundings and shrank ladylike from nothing. She was the exact opposite, he suddenly thought, of Lucy Collingwood.

"Your people decided where to go?" he asked.

"Dad's not said." Her eyes turned to him with speculation. "Where'll you go?"

"I'm staying here. I've found a house."

"Then we'll have no doctor."

"Yes, you will. I'll ride the circuit. I'll see you all."

"We'll miss you."

"So shall I."

"So you will." Her glance seemed to penetrate the layers he built up against the world and to come directly upon the desires he sheltered; it was an illusion of course, created by the half smile of her lips and the largeness of her eyes. "You'll miss some people more than others," she said.

"Don't you judge people too soon."

"Why, I don't judge people at all." Her smile lessened. "And I wish they'd not judge me. I don't ask them to. I don't ask anything. They like me, or they don't. If they don't like me, they can let me alone."

"It would be pretty hard to let you alone."

The compliment brought her good humor back and she walked on with her head lifted to the little sights about her. As she passed Abernethy's store she looked in to see Collingwood, and a hundred feet beyond she turned her head and found him coming behind.

She went by the straggling houses and made a turn into a side pathway which carried her by the back buildings of town and indirectly toward the wagon camp. She walked without haste and she was abreast a leanto shed half-filled with hay when Collingwood's voice reached forward to halt her.

He had been traveling rapidly and he was excited; he took her arm, cast a quick glance about, and drew her into the shed. He put both hands on her arms and he searched her face with his rising boldness.

"Why'd you come this way?"

She gave him an easy smile; she said nothing.

"You knew I was behind you," he said. "You knew I'd follow." He was sure, yet not sure enough; he tugged gently at her arms, waiting for her to come in, to give him some signal. Her body furnished him with no clue; it was neutral, responding as he pulled, stopping when he ceased. The half-smiling of her face told him nothing, but by then her closeness worked him loose from his hesitancy and he flung his arms around her, thrust himself hard against her and bore down with his mouth. She let him have his way for a moment and then, as though the moment were enough to settle her curiosity, she gave him a short push.

He was roused and his breath sawed heavily against the quietness of the shed; his nostrils were flared out, his eyes half closed. The rebuff stung him. "If you didn't want this," he said, "why'd you let me start?"

"Do what you please," she said indifferently.

"You didn't stop me," he said. "You let me go on. You want me to think you're too nice, or you want me to just run hell out of myself trying to get you?"

"Make up your own mind," she said.

He looked at her with a renewed excitement, and stepped toward her. "No," she said curtly, "that's enough."

"My God, Edna, don't you know anything? You can't encourage a man, then slap him in the face."

She shrugged her shoulders and was clearly disinterested.

"No," he said. "What was it — what'd you want?"

She shook her head and her chin moved forward, lending to her face a heavy and stubborn cast.

"I want to know," he insisted.

"Oh," she said impatiently, "I'm tired listening to you." She turned from the shed and left her order behind her. "You go the other way — don't follow me. And don't bother me any more."

"Damn cheap fun you had, wasn't it?" he said.

She kept on with the trail, passing into a light stand of timber which lay between town and camp, and as she walked she soon lost her air of resentment and began to smile at the memory of the foolish expression on Collingwood's face; and in this humor she turned a bend of the trail and found Cal Lockyear working with his ax on a thin tree which he had dropped across the trail; he was apparently hewing a plank from it. There was a complete preoccupation about him and Edna stood at the barrier created by the tree for a full minute before his eyes rose from his chore. As soon as he saw her he moved forward to chop aside the upthrust branches of the tree, and when he gave her a hand across the log his glance fell upon her with a moment of weight and afterwards he turned back to his chore.

It was curiosity which made her stand there to watch him. She was never kind to men who ran after her too hard; she was never very kind to men who ignored her, and Lockyear had mostly watched her from a distance. Sometimes she thought she saw in his eyes a certain malice or a certain belief concerning her, and that made her think he was rude. But still she knew her attractiveness and she knew he had his share of man's lustiness; therefore she was curious and observed him now with an attention which had a certain wariness in it.

"What's that you're making?"

"Plank for Daniel Rinearson's wagon," he said.

"Daniel's got three sons to do that kind of work for him."

He leaned back from his labors and showed her his rough amusement. "Daniel's got two sons out hunting cows, and one son too damned lazy to come in from the rain."

"Funny, though," she said. "You're not much of a man to do anybody favors."

"Pleases me to work, right now. Tomorrow it might please me not to. Always do what I please."

She shook her head. "Just sometimes we do what we please. Most of the time we do what's got to be done."

"No," he said, "I don't do a damned thing I don't want to do."

"Oh," she said, "don't talk nonsense to me. If you want to make men think you're a big one, go ahead. But don't tell me that. It's silly."

"You do what you want to do, I notice. With men."

She grew cool toward him, she shrugged her shoulders. "Let them mind their affairs — and I'll mind mine."

He stared at her with his bright and driving interest. "You want 'em to do that?" He sat straddled on the log, hands folded one on the other, but this attitude of rest produced no actual air of rest. The black brows made a straight strike across his face, the ash-gray eyes were intent, the long body had its innumerable suggestions of restlessness about it. As he studied her his expression shifted until some of the pointedness was gone and he seemed to find things within her which commanded his attention; when this more reasonable manner came to him, Edna let him see the more friendly side of her — let him see it for a discreet moment, and then went on through the woods to the camp. His ax remained silent and by this she knew he watched her; and she smiled to herself at the knowledge she had broken through his indifference. It was only a game he had played; and she got the notion she could beat him at it.

9

BUCK and Mrs. Howard faced Lot White; and beside them Lige Ebbett, who was thirty-five, stood with sixteen-year-old Lavina Baker; for it was to be a double wedding, both marriages fruited from poverty and necessity, from the pressure of labor which could not be borne alone, from a young girl's doll dreams, from the public insistence that in a new country women were too valuable to remain single after childhood. Ebbett had crossed the plains as a driver for another man. He owned nothing but a few personal belongings and he had no trade and no future except that which strong muscles and an illiterate mind could make for him.

All stood bareheaded in the silver-glittering slow rain, wagon people and townsmen making a half ring around the principals of the affair; none of them had changed clothes, their better clothes being no more presentable than their poorer ones, and the thinly dressed Lavinia Baker shivered as she waited and looked up to the much taller Ebbett with a sweet smile of expectation. Lot White had made a brief thing of it and now waited while the two men placed the rings. The ring which Buck used on Mrs. Howard's finger was Martha Gay's, lent for the occasion, Mrs. Gay not able to endure the thought of the woman wearing either the ring of her first husband or of Buck's first wife. While he waited, Lot White closed his eyes and tilted his face skyward and thus mustered his sermon. To him three or more people gathered together made a congregation, and a congregation was to be preached at; for the devil was real to Lot and the devil was always close by and the need to wrestle with the devil was strong in Lot's soul. The roar of the falls came as a slow drum roll through the light wash of wind in the trees, and rain mist began to crowd the earth and pack itself like cotton between the firs; campfires burned orange in the gathering twilight but the wetness of the world worked its clammy way through everybody.

Lot White opened his eyes and made a silent blessing upon the couples with his blacksmith's fist. "Rain or sun, mud or carpets, it makes no difference, for it's the Lord's will and so let it be. Maybe it's better that we should join in the mud, and in full presence of these elements. Who knows but that this ceremony is a warnin' to the disbelievers? Take warnin'. The devil's on these grounds at this moment. He walks among you in some shape or other. He's in your wagons, he's got the power to creep into your heads and he can take your tongue and make you speak words that will unsettle the people you speak to, and he can crawl into a pretty vase and make you buy it when you ought to be buyin' sugar or flour. I know it, for I can smell him when he's near — and he's near enough to me now to touch." He made a positive cut through the air with one hand and looked directly upon the newly wedded.

"Women, be obedient, for that's the way of it. Be fruitful, for how else can we populate this empty land? Dress plain, speak gentle, and be thrifty if you expect your husbands to get ahead; a careless wife can kill a man and put her children on charity. Don't gossip — it was the fault of Eve and you've got it handed down to you aplenty. There's work to do and work won't ever end till we end. Well, do it and don't complain, and don't sigh for pretty hands and a smooth face, for that will be the devil whisperin'. Men, be patient, and forbear, and let your commands be just; and bend your backs like the willin' horse six days the week; for you're sinners and you were meant to pay, and if you come to bed at night weary enough to cry, don't be sorry for it — that's the Lord's intention. God, come bless these people. God, lay your hands upon them. Amen."

The crowd moved around to congratulate the wedded ones but Mrs. Millard, listening to Lot White's final injunctions, turned to her husband in anger. "That fool with his man's advice — that conceited man — that lump of bigotry. Telling women to be obedient, like slaves, like animals. Lick your master's hand and take his blows and cringe. Oh, Millard, when's this world going to be just, to women?"

"I know — I know," he said patiently. He looked around him with his uneasy glance, for his wife's voice carried far. He saw the smile on Ralph Whitcomb's face, but that was the only smile. His neighbors found such talk unamusing and the men of the train had long since, by indirection or by blunt statement, questioned his manhood in permitting his wife to speak as she did. He was over six feet, spare and ruddy, a kind of bland good will shining below heavy eyebrows. He had a John Bull face, a great nose with its prominent bridge, lean cheeks and a forceful mouth and chin. His wife was a full foot shorter, strong-featured, positive in opinions and ordinarily kind; but when this one topic rose a sense of injustice so inflamed her that she could not be still; on such occasions Millard's expression was one of pained benevolence.

"I hate to hear him talk," she said. "Poor Mrs. Howard — every stitch she owns belongs to Buck now. The law says so. He can beat her, he can strip her of her last petticoat, but she can do nothing about it. Just because men say so."

"I know," said Millard. "Now let's think of supper."

But she was at the peak of her indignation and Lot White, coming by, was within her reach. She stepped before him and laid her forefinger as a pistol between his eyes. "You little puffed-up fool," she said, "go back and do your wife's work for a day and you'll not have so much wind left in you to lay down the law to women."

Lot White took a step backward, caught off guard yet not too surprised. He raked her with his displeased glance, but having argued with her before, he wanted no renewed argument and he said mildly, "Now, sister, it will do you no good to pester me," and escaped into the crowd.

Relieved of her indignation, Mrs. Millard said cheerfully to Lucy Collingwood, "You look better. Well, Millard, come and we'll eat." She moved away with the air of victory about her.

During the ceremony Rice Burnett had stood beside Katherine and Harris Eby, and afterwards he walked with them over the field toward his fire.

Katherine said: "If it could only have been a brighter day!" Burnett noticed tears standing in her eyes.

Eby said, comfortably, "It's funny but weddings always make women cry," and laughed at her as he moved away to his own quarter of the camp ground. She went on with Burnett, head lowered and her face half hidden from him.

"Don't be troubled about it," said Burnett. "Lorenzo's a good man. It's not a bad match for Mrs. Howard."

"It's poor little Lavinia . . . Ebbett's just twice her age."

"Not uncommon."

"He's shiftless and he won't care about her. They'll never have a thing except ten children; and he'll sit in the yard, or go hunting, and every bit of the trouble and the scraping will be on her shoulders. Such thin little shoulders. They're not strong enough for it. She'll be dead before she's thirty. I'm downright sad. It's such a long time since I've seen anybody not being punished by something — rain or dust, or heat or cold, or hunger, or something. I won't let it be that way with Lavinia. I just won't. You've got to help me make that man work."

They were on the blind side of the Gay wagon, between trees and canvas, and twilight came fast down. He moved her around to catch sight of her face. "All right," he said.

"Don't say that just to make me feel better," she said. "I mean it. I won't stand to have it so hard for Lavinia. She's been cheated out of girlhood — and that's enough. She's got a right to some good luck." She rested, silent a moment; she made a sound of discontent in her throat and said firmly, "And she shall have it. Just you remember, Rice, you promised to help."

"All right," he said.

She took hold of his arm and laughed at him. "Meek — meek. You sound like Harris when I boss him. He never minds it. You would — *you'd* mind it."

"When you marrying him?"

"Oh," she said, giving a careless answer, "I don't know. . . . Your clothes are wet. You ought — "

"Soon as he's got a cabin ready?"

"You ought to get good and dried out. . . . I don't know, Rice — I don't know. What're you so curious for?"

"Wish I knew you," he said.

"That's not hard. Just look and see."

"It's going to take a hell of a man to keep up with you."

She bent in until her head was quite near. "Where'd that start? I don't believe you meant it. What'd you say it for? You just said it to make talk?"

"All right," he said.

"Well, don't." She was silent a moment, still looking closely at him. "But why did you say it? What was in your head at that moment, Rice?"

"Don't know."

Gram Gay, moving around the wagon, came to its back end and saw them silently bent together in the shadows; and she withdrew until only her head was in view, spying on them a moment, and presently returned to the fire. Martha Gay said, "You call her for supper?"

"Not yet," said Gram.

"Why — what's she doing?"

"Nothing," said Gram, and when Martha Gay made a turn to go after the girl, Gram sharply said, "Stay here." She approached the fire, she set aside the boiling coffeepot and the Dutch oven. Her very dark face was like an apple which, evenly aging, had shrunk away without heavy wrinkling. She murmured to herself; she kept an eye on Martha Gay whose roused curiosity made her strain to hear what went on beyond the wagon; she dished meat and dumplings for John Gay, and dished for her husband — the old man who sat away from the fire and said nothing. She murmured to him, "You all right?" and got from him a small nod. Crouched, she looked beneath the wagon and saw two pairs of feet still close together on the wagon's other side.

Katherine said: "It's time to eat. Eat with us."

"I want to see Hawn again." Without warning he bent forward and kissed her on the cheek. "Tell Eby I took something of his."

"You tell him. Anyhow it was mine, not his."

"If he laid his big hands on me he'd squash me like a bug."

"Not unless I told him to squash you like a bug. He wouldn't let it trouble him otherwise."

"I'd let it trouble me."

"There's a difference," she said. She was silent, without motion; she was closely watching him through the shadows. "What for, Rice?"

"The idea came along. Fine idea. You taste good."

"What's the taste like?"

"I don't know. You mind it?"

She waited a moment before she spoke. "No," she said. "No, I guess not." Then she left him, but he got the idea that he had disturbed her.

Fires burned their yellow triangles into the fallen black and against these bright plaques shapes moved and rain sparkled. He walked to his own fire half-dead on the ground and built it, but he stood without decision over it a short time and turned toward town. When he reached the front of the hotel he thrust his hands into his pockets and felt the loose change he had and walked into the saloon. Hawn and the two Lockyears were at the bar.

Lockyear said: "You come to hear the eagle scream?"

"I'm goin' farther up the creek than that," said Burnett.

"And eat your liver raw," said Lockyear. There was enough liquor in him to draw the veil away, to let the blooded push of his arrogance come through. Now he was a trapper down from the mountains, ready for some fun.

"Have a drink," said Lockyear.

"Right with you."

"Have to hump it to keep up with me," said Lockyear.

"You won't have to look around to find me any time," said Burnett.

Lockyear's head reared back, and he laughed as he measured Burnett, and wildness was in his eyes, ready for the leap.

Hawn remembered his trapping days and was sentimental. He struck the bar a strong blow. "By God, I'd like to eat my liver raw again."

"Go out and butcher yourself a settler," said Lockyear. "They're slower than buffalo and twice as foolish. I've got no use for the entire God-damned breed; they ain't good for anything and don't even grow pelts, and if you skinned one it would be a bad hide, the grease all mixed up with it. They don't roar when they die, they make a squealin' sound. No, never mind, Hawn — they ain't game enough to make the shootin' fun. Burnett ought to know better, but he likes 'em."

"The trouble with you," said Burnett, "is you want to stay a wild man. Times are changing."

"Nothing or nobody will change me."

"Then you'll get rubbed out," said Burnett and downed his first drink. He settled himself at the bar and waited for comfortableness to begin; he swung himself toward Lockyear, and looked beyond to Lockyear's brother Veen who stood silent in the background. They were close, these two men — the able one and the cripple-footed one, the protector and the protected; they were both Lockyears in their calculated indifference to others.

"I'll tell you something about these people," said Burnett.

"Nothing to know," said Cal.

"You're wrong. They've got patience enough to fill a well, but don't let that lead you to a mistake. The first thing they'll do here is make some law to cover them. It won't be much — it'll be loose enough to let everybody be comfortable. But you better stay within it, better not make their law look foolish to them. They'll come quick when you're in trouble. They'll put up with you long after it seems reasonable. Then one day when patience is gone they'll turn more cruel than any Sioux you ever saw and kill you quick as a snake and go back to their plowin' and never give you another thought."

Lockyear said: "They don't even squirm when they die. It's like clubbin' porcupines — no struggle, not a sound."

"Sorry for you," said Burnett.

The remark struck its instant spark in Lockyear and he said, "Take care who you're sorry for," and then he laughed again. "Well, I came out here to see this scope of country. It's no good. Be full of people in another ten years and I don't want to put in my life lookin' across fences at the next man. Let's you and me light out for California. I hear there's game aplenty and a man can get a grant of land twenty miles square from the Mexicans. Women aplenty, and Indians for work."

"It's only another hill," said Burnett.

"What's that?"

"There's nothing on the other side of that hill, Cal."

"You think there's anything here?" asked Lockyear. "This miserable damned business of scratchin' a living out of a piece of land? Squatted between a lot of other people? All the time arguin'? My Christ, I got a bellyful of arguin' on this trip. Every time anybody wanted to spit they stopped the train and called a meeting. That's what you've got out here. What you intend to do?"

"Take up land and make a flour mill."

"And you the man that pulled your picket and lighted out fresh every morning. Ten thousand miles of country and you tie yourself to a yard with a flour mill in it." Lockyear gave out his heavy, jeering laugh and shook his head. "You won't make it."

"What's for you?"

"Oh," said Lockyear, "we'll winter here. Leave in the spring." He turned and hooked both elbows against the bar; and he watched the crowd in this barroom with a sparkling in his round, bold eyes; and suddenly he filled his chest and launched a wild yell into the room and watched the shocked men spring up or turn about or freeze in their chairs; and as he looked at them he gave out a ringing laugh. "Scared a year's growth from the crowd," he said to Burnett. "Poor stuff, poor stuff." He was restless and the insolence of his disposition was plainly upon him, for he looked directly from man to man and seemed to wish for trouble, and brought his hand hard upon the bar to express his discontent.

Billy Lord brought the townsman to the side of his wagon and said in a small voice, "Stay here," and climbed into the wagon. His wife was a huge mound beneath the quilts, the ruffles of her nightgown nestled about her neck; a lace cap came down over her ears, pink tie ribbon lost in the deep flesh of her chin. She was flat on her back, wide awake and waiting for him with a China-doll placidness; a small tuft of whiskers grew from a mole on her chin.

"Somebody give you a drink, Billy?"

"No."

"Pity. I wish I had a dollar. I'd let you spend it for drinkin'. What you lookin' for?" She watched him draw his fiddle and bow from its case. "What you goin' to do?"

"Man and I got to arguin' about fiddles. I got to prove somethin' to him." He returned to the man outside the wagon. He murmured, "Come a little farther," and moved on fifty feet. He tucked the fiddle beneath his chin in the drizzling darkness, he tuned it and he drew the bow over the strings. He said: "Hear that? Thing's been in my family hundred-fifty years. Came from Scotland and the man that made it learned his business from that Eyetalian that made fiddles best of all."

The townsman issued a small sound, neither agreeing nor disagreeing. He took the fiddle and played a piece of a reel; he retuned the instrument to please himself and played another snatch. He said, "It's so damned dark I can't see if she's shaken or sound."

"Give me back my fiddle," said Lord.

"I just said it, man," said the townsman. "It sounds like a good fiddle."

"It's a God-damned good fiddle," said Billy Lord.

"Well, what you want for it?"

"What you got?"

"Wheat."

"What's wheat worth out here?"

"Sixty cents the bushel. But what's that mean to you if you've got no money? This is a swap. This fiddle's worth how bad you want wheat."

"Or how bad you want the fiddle," said Billy Lord.

"I think," said the townsman shrewdly, "you need wheat worse'n I need a fiddle."

"Man don't live just on wheat," said Billy Lord, "and you know it or you'd never be a fiddler in the first place." He was silent a moment, then said: "Hundred bushels of wheat for it."

"Oh, hell," said the townsman. "I'm nowise interested."

From the wagon came Mrs. Lord's quick call. "Billy — come here."

"Hurry it," said Billy Lord, "or I can't sell at all."

"Fifty, then."

"You'd never get another fiddle like it if all the fiddles in the world came across the plains. You'll never catch me another year broke and wantin' to sell it. Don't grind a man down. You got the advantage. Don't use it so hard."

"I tell you," said the man. "Sixty."

Mrs. Lord's voice rose higher. "Billy, no — you come in here. Come here!"

"No," said Billy Lord, "I guess we can starve it out somehow."

"My last offer. Sixty."

"Billy! Don't you dare — don't you do it!"

Billy Lord said, "Give me the fiddle a minute, friend," and took it and put it beneath his chin. He drew the bow slowly across the strings. He played a measure of "Listen to the Mockingbird," and he played it over four or five times, and handed back the fiddle. "All right. Bring you the case in the morning. Tuck it under your coat."

"I'll give you a scrip for the wheat at Abernethy's," said the townsman and melted into the dark. Billy Lord returned to the wagon and made long work of hauling his three hundred pounds up the wheel and into the wagon. His wife sat bolt upright in bed.

"Oh, God, Billy, you sold it. I can't stand it. You go back — go back and get it."

"We got to get through the winter," he said. "Now don't feel bad."

Her lids crawled together and tears seeped through them and rolled down the puckered homeliness of her face. He touched her shoulder. "That won't do."

"No," she said, "you got to get it back. I got to hear you play it — you know it was the first thing."

He teetered on one foot and the other, removing his boots; he shucked his outer clothes and stood stooped and mountainous, the great folds of his belly swelling against his flannel drawers. He blew out the light and settled into bed beside her; he put an arm around her and listened to her heaving cry.

"It was the first thing, Billy. You were playin' it at a dance when I met you."

"Next year we'll get it back."

"Not that one. I'd rather sell my ring. I'd rather sell my petticoats."

"Little large for swappin'," said Billy Lord.

"What'll you do — what'll you ever do when you feel like some music?"

He was still a moment, thinking. Presently he said, "Just pucker up and whistle. Old girl, you're crying like a faucet and the damn bed's gettin' wet."

10

THERE had been no call for a meeting, but the crowd grew until there were a hundred men and women in a loose circle, dark-lumped against the wet night, reddened and roughened by the glow of John Gay's winding fire. Most of them had been in town and had found information. Privately they had weighed the next move, and in little groups they had discussed it; now they moved toward a common center to make the problem common and to come to some kind of a common decision, for though they were people of great independence they were also political animals by practice, and the push of their natures was toward the group.

A wise way of listening, and an ability to state opinions without appearing to seek for authority, had made Gay one of the leaders of the train; he was straight shirt sleeves, seeming to want nothing. Had he tried to push himself forward he would have been resented by these men who believed themselves equally capable of leadership; since he did not, they gave him the respect he hadn't asked for. He wasn't entirely without guile; he was a man of very firm notions, believing in the decency of people yet aware of the hard core of prejudice, superstition and selfishness in them; and with this knowledge he fashioned his methods of persuasion, when the need arose, to the cause he thought sound. On a larger stage he would have been a statesman tempering his cause with the practical and possible; on this rough edge of life he was the very best type of mudsill leader.

So they gathered at his fire to create a kind of tribal legislature whose deliberations gathered force by the need for order which brought them here; for they well knew they could not build roads or cabins or schools alone, and could not starve alone; argue as they often did, and violently as they might dislike each other — and there were bitter hatreds among them — necessity made the compact.

There had been much talk concerning locations and a great deal of personal opinion passed. When at last there was nothing new to add John Gay, in his mild way, more or less recapitulated the pros and cons of each location and brought the issue square-on.

"You'll go where you please, naturally, but it would be a good thing if we could get a sizable group for one place; it would make settlement a lot easier for all of us. I don't relish saying good-by to people I've lived with these six months. It seems unnatural to part, and I wish we didn't have to do it. There's no question but what the winter's goin' to be severe for us. It would be comforting if we could go through it together."

"You don't like that country off the prairie?" said McIver.

"What's the use of my coming this far to sit on six hundred and forty acres of second-best when the best is to be had? But I recognize the objections to the other land — the winter mud . . . I also know I'd rather have neighbors. So if there's a strong group inclined to that country around Bear Creek, I'll put my first preference by, and go along."

"Where's that fellow Hawn?" asked Daniel Rinearson. "He knows most about it."

Lorenzo Buck said: "He's in the saloon with the Lockyears."

"Well, where's Burnett? He talked to Hawn."

"In the saloon, too," said Buck.

"They been there an hour."

"Just well started."

Gay smiled and shook his head. Edna Lattimore, at the outer edge of the ring, turned about and walked toward town at a rapid gait.

Collingwood and his wife stood not far from the fire. Collingwood had said a great deal during the meeting. When the argument had gone strongly toward one location, he had spoken favorably; when it had veered to another location he had found good in the second place. He strained hard to be in tune with the majority. With the evening talked out, he now again sought to reflect the temper of the crowd by speaking the impatience he sensed in it.

"Well," he said, "it's time to decide, ain't it? Why don't we see where we want to go? Let's have hands on this. Who's for Bear Creek?"

Men looked upon him from the shadowed circle and refused to be moved. He waited, fire deepening the color of his naturally ruddy face, and the waiting grew to be an embarrassment to him and presently he said with a tone half between irritation and pleading, "Well, boys, we got to go somewhere, ain't we? What's your pleasure?"

He drew no response; he was the target of unsympathetic eyes, of a lurking amusement. Having committed himself, he couldn't gracefully withdraw and he faced his audience with a fixed smile. Whitcomb noted Lucy Collingwood's glance suddenly drop to the ground.

It was John Gay who quietly said, "Perhaps it's about time we did decide. If there's a group for this Bear Creek, I'll join it."

Rinearson said, "I favor it," and in a little while the circle broke into pieces, the larger part of the crowd moving toward Rinearson.

"Who's for the prairie?" called John Strang.

Somebody else spoke. "Anybody want to cross the river and go down where that fellow Moss spoke of?"

Buck and his new wife turned from the circle, moving back to her wagon. Buck said: "I'm disposed to throw in with Gay and go to Bear Creek. Have you got any notions?"

"It's yours to say."

"Don't care to take you somewhere you don't want to go."

"What would you've said to your first wife?"

"I'd have said, 'We go to Bear Creek.' "

"Then that's the way it had better be with us."

They came to the wagon and stopped. She turned and watched the shadow of his face in the rainy darkness. He said presently: "You want me to sleep in the other wagon for a few nights?"

She was silent for a long run of moments, at last placing her hand on his arm. "We can't start that way."

"It's a little quick for you."

"So it is," she said. "But you're my husband now. Come to bed."

Reaching the town's street, Edna stopped across from the saloon. When she grew tired of waiting she walked the street's full length, watched the ragged shimmer of the falls through the black, and returned to resume her station. It was a full hour before Burnett came from the place and swung toward the wagon camp. He didn't see her; he didn't seem to be drunk but he had his head down and appeared to be absorbed by his thinking. She called over, "That you, Rice?"

He crossed the mud and took her arm. He was cheerful, he had just enough liquor to make him reckless. "What are you doing around here?"

"Oh," she said, "I just wanted to walk."

"You ought to be tired."

"I never get tired. Nothing bothers me much." When they came to the entrance of the trail which led in a roundabout way toward camp — the one along which she had gone early in the day — she slackened her pace. "Let's not go right back," she said, and by a little pressure she swung him into a trail; they went past the town's houses and came to the lean-to shed. She put her head through the doorway into the darkness.

"What's here?" he asked.

"Just a shed. There's some hay I saw this afternoon. Rice — we don't get a chance to talk any more."

"All right." He followed her into the shed and heard her settle on the hay and he dropped beside her and bore her back full length and rolled her to him. Her arms came around him quick as a trap, very strong, very needy; she lifted herself and dropped over him, her mouth searching; he hung on until he grew rough and heard her wince, and then he relaxed and lay beside her, listening to the scarcely disturbed beat of her heart. The odor of her hair rose through the hay smell; her breath fluttered on his skin. "You like this?" she whispered.

"Yes. Did I hurt you?"

"Go ahead. I know you like me then."

"I could sink into you till I drowned."

"That's a good way to die." She pushed against him, sighing. "Now you're just yourself. We could have a lot of fine times. Go on, smother me."

"Fine times — misery. Like trying to drink a river dry."

"That's nice. Not true, but nice. I'm no river but I've got enough for you. Why do you keep away so much when you know you could have kissed me a long time ago?"

"No time, no place."

"People can fix things if they want to."

"Big woman — big soft woman."

"That's from sitting on a wagon doing nothing. But I'll never get fat. I don't like sloppy women. You like slim women best, like Katherine. Slim in places, anyhow. What do you think about when you look at her in that funny way-off way?"

"Don't know what."

"I know what. What it would be like to have her."

He said nothing. Her small laugh came to him. "If you kissed her you could probably have her, too. She'd be thinking about it — kissing, loving, sleeping. It goes right straight through. What do you think of me? You do think of me, don't you?"

He moved his fingers over her face, around her neck. "Not hard to think about when I'm tired, rolled up in my blankets."

"That's a good place. I think about you there too. What do you think?"

"You're like the earth."

She lay silent, pondering. Her hand patted his back steadily. "I don't know," she said. "I don't know what that's like."

"Nobody knows. Nothing to say about it. It just is. That's it. It just is."

"Ah," she said, pleased but skeptical. "There's nobody like that. You've made it up." Gently the pressure of her hands increased on his back. "If another man was lying here he wouldn't be still."

"If another man was lying here he'd catch you off guard."

"No man can catch me off guard unless I want him to." She was, from the tone of her voice, smiling in the dark. "You want to?"

"I want to — but I'm not going to," he said.

"Sometimes you're just a man, thinking the same thing they all think. Then you're not, and I don't know what bothers you. I think it's me — I mean, what I say."

"You come right out with it, that's for sure," he said.

"I'm the same as all of them only I don't bother to hide things. You'd like it if I was a little bit mysterious. That's what makes men so funny. They all would, up to a point. Just mysterious for a little while, then they don't want them to be mysterious any more." She moved in, adjusting her body to him. "You'd like to have me nights. You'd like it a lot. You'd like it right now. But you've got some other notion — I don't know, and then you don't like me so much. You ought to know me. I'm a woman. You know about women. I'll get married, I'll work, I'll have babies. It's the same for everybody. That's all it is. I can do every one of those things, and I'll do 'em fine."

"I know."

"No you don't. You think there's something else. Tell me and I'll try to be that way. If it's not foolish. If it's foolish, I can't do it, Rice. Look at everybody. I mean husbands and wives. You know how they are when they're running after each other. They make a lot out of it. Then they get married and they use each other till it's not new any more. Then they settle down — work and babies. Tell me what else there is."

"I'd like to use you up."

She was silent a moment; then she murmured, "Well, go ahead. I'd like it too."

"You want me to rape you?"

"Ah, the way you carry on, it's more like me raping you. You know what I think sometimes? I think you're afraid."

"Throwin' rocks at me now," he said.

She pushed her fingers unexpectedly into his ribs and made him jump. He rolled her away but she came back at him. He pinned her below him, wrestling for her arms and feeling laughter bubble within her and suddenly he settled himself and kissed her. Her playfulness stopped. She lay motionless, sensuously absorbing him; and in this blackness and stillness he was loosened by tender feeling and he whispered, "Edna — Edna."

Her breathing quickened, her arms pulled him; she grew dissatisfied and was all in motion beneath him, and she capsized him and was above him, rougher with him than he had been with her. He flung her around and pinned her below.

"Rice."

"No."

"Rice! Oh, damn you — please! Rice!"

She stirred and ran her fingers over his face, and whispering sounds came from her — the light, sighing groan of her pleasure; he felt ripples of laughter go through her. The pressure left; she lay content. "Well, you've done it. You happy?"

"Yes."

"I'm all rags, I'm loose feathers, I'm broken to pieces, I've got no strength. I feel like cream inside, like silk all over me. Oh, Rice." She rolled her warm, loose mouth around his face. Her breathing settled. "You're not sorry?"

"No."

"You see — what's to be sorry for? What'd we lose, what'd we do wrong? It cleaned me out, cleaned you out, just like fire burning soot out of a chimney. That's good, isn't it?"

"That's good."

"I told you I could take care of you. I watch you, I see you get nervous. You walk around, you want to fight something or break something. I know what it is. It's gone now, isn't it?"

"All gone," he said.

"Well, that's it." She lay half over him, heavy and peaceful. Her voice was sleepy. "It could be like this all the time," she said and dropped her head to his arm and seemed to rest.

She had shown him how well she could take care of him in the same unembarrassed way she might have lifted her hands to show him the strength of her fingers. She had no doubt of her ability to take the sting from him, to keep him contented; she had no doubt that this was his only need — all other needs only being the colored fancies rising from this one, like the mirages of cities and rivers rising from the violent heat of a desert. Where had she gotten that belief — from herself or from men? She waited for him, confident that her body would bring him in. For a little while he regretted having her, for he knew he'd want her again, that he'd never quit wanting her. The recklessness of the saloon's whisky had begun to wear off and, with need temporarily gone out of him, he realized he couldn't rise and walk away from her with clear conscience. For if she had been honest with him, this was not a casual act but the first act of marriage. If she meant it that way, he had to think of it that way.

She said, "You're thinking about something."

"Half asleep," he said.

"No," she said, "you're thinking. I can tell." She sat up. Her tone had changed and he knew she was disappointed in him. "I suppose there's hay all over me."

He rose. "I'll brush you."

"Oh," she said indifferently, "it's dark — it doesn't matter." She took his arm and came up and rested against him a moment, and once more he caught the waiting in her, the strong warm hope. Then she drew back. "All right," she said and left the shed with him. They followed the path through the trees into the camp clearing, passing people moving away from Gay's fire. Short of the fire she stopped. "I won't go there with all this hay on me. She'd see it."

"Who?"

"Katherine. Now you'll go there and look at her and think you see something wonderful. Just you remember she's made like me." She moved away, her manner lighter. "Think of me," she said and walked rapidly toward her father's wagon.

11

THE group at the fire had settled to the Gays, the Collingwoods, and Whitcomb and Lot White. John Gay said: "A lot of us have thrown in for Bear Creek. You decided?"

"I want a creek with a fall of water for a mill," said Burnett.

"Where'll that be?"

Burnett poured himself coffee from the pot on the fire. Katherine's face hung steady, watching him from beyond the flame. Whitcomb idly said: "Why spoil the liquor's comfort with coffee? The comfort's hard to come by."

"This was," agreed Burnett. "It set on slow and never went deep."

"Where'll you go?" insisted John Gay.

"With your outfit," said Burnett. "Hawn's going out in the morning. He can be guide for us."

John Gay turned to Whitcomb. "You going along?"

"I stay here." Whitcomb sat back on his heels; his turning glance touched Lucy Collingwood.

"I wish you were nearer," said John Gay.

"I'll ride the rounds," said Whitcomb. "I'll see you all many times." He made a gesture. "I don't like endings."

"Why, Ralph," said Mrs. Gay, "I had no notion you were sentimental."

"He ain't," said Lot White.

"You can go to hell for a foolish remark, Lot," said Whitcomb, and rose from the fire to leave the group.

Immediately afterwards Burnett finished his coffee and walked to his bedroll and soon settled inside it and lay for a short time with the flap thrown back, feeling occasional drops of rain come through the sheltering tree. His fire was black, the falls made a steady rumble in the night, wind ruffled the fir tops. Someone crossed the soft ground and made a shadow over him.

"Rice — you asleep?"

"No."

Katherine dropped beside him. "Feel better?"

"It was a waste of time."

She was silent. Presently he heard a small laugh come from her; she was appreciating some joke of her own. "Come to our wagon for breakfast. I'm glad you're going where we are. It makes me happy." Her voice went unhurriedly along. "I wish everybody'd go to the same place, stay together."

"What's up between Lucy and Whitcomb?"

"When did you notice that?"

"Tonight," he said.

"I think they're in love."

"I wonder what that is."

"What's got into you?"

"No, what is it?"

"If you've got to ask, then you've not got it."

"That's too easy. How would I know what it is?"

"You'll want a woman." She dropped nearer, catching a closer view of his face. She waited for his answer; her hand lay idle on his shoulder.

"I've wanted women without being in love," he said.

"That's different."

"Where's the difference?"

"That's being thirsty — that's just taking a drink of water wherever the water's fit to drink."

"My God," he said and sat up in the bedroll.

"You didn't think I could say a thing like that, did you? You think women just dream along. But you don't mean these funny things."

"I want to know."

She shoved him back against the bedroll. "You'd been married a long time ago if any woman would do."

"You didn't answer the question," he said.

"I said you'd know when it happened. That's enough. That's it."

"You said a hole in a doughnut is a hole in a doughnut. That's no answer. You don't know. Nobody knows."

"Crazy man." Her face hung over him, dark, serious, still. "Don't tell me about my business."

"My business, too."

"Funny man. No it's not — not so much. Never could be as much your business as mine."

"Why not?"

"Because. . . . I want you to see that Mrs. Irish gets a good piece of land. All these men will be looking out for themselves. They'll have no time for her. They might even crowd her out of something if they wanted it. First thing we get to this place — you watch out for her. You hear me?"

"All right."

She went away.

A late-arriving wagon groaned through the darkness, a tired man cursing, a baby crying; little by little the camp settled and the halloo of playing children ceased, and fires died to gleaming red eyes on the earth.

73

Ralph Whitcomb, pacing the dark, looked toward the Collingwood wagon to visualize Lucy, strongly attracted to her and believing he had seen on her face some sign of a like interest. He wasn't certain of it and his habit of viewing his acts with sometimes a spectator's irony caused him to think now that he was deluding himself; that as a lonely man he looked upon a fair woman and saw in her eyes signals which weren't there. In such a state of mind he could only believe that this was the old thing which amused him when he observed it in others. Yet he was in revolt against the reasonableness which had kept his life in low key; he was at that stage when, struggling with morals and caution, he was about to throw these things over and let himself be governed by the unreasonable, wonderful dictates of his first wants. He would make the break when he thought he saw some favor in her, and either would be humiliated by her or would be encouraged. What would come of it, he had no notion. Probably nothing good, but he was past caring; he wanted her, he had to make his try. These wagon people didn't anticipate much, they didn't drag old worries behind them. They went ahead, rough and ready and a little callous spiritually, and cried or laughed, and did what they were impelled to do and took the consequences. They were a wonderful people.

Lucy Collingwood lay awake beside her sleeping husband, and thought of Whitcomb and imagined the touch of his hands upon her, and she stirred aside from Collingwood to let nothing foreign disturb the illusion. Kneeling before a tree on the edge of camp late this night Lot White called upon the Lord to make Ralph Whitcomb see the light; crouched over a dying fire Cal Lockyear listened to Whit Rinearson speak of a Hudson's Bay messenger who rode on schedule between Fort Vancouver and this town with his gold pouch; and Cal Lockyear stared long at Whit, and murmured, "That's something interesting, ain't it?" Side by side in bed John and Martha Gay quietly discussed the long winter to come, the food they had, the money remaining, the things they might do without, the things they had to have, and Martha said: "I don't see how we can make it," and John Gay said, "We'll make it somehow. These hands can do what's to be done." But he said nothing of the one hand which of late seemed half numb. Standing alone in the night, Roxy Kitchen doubled her fists and listened for the sound of steps to come along and stop near her — a man's steps, any man's steps; and restless in bed, Edna Lattimore pressed her hands hard against her thighs and tried to think of Rice Burnett; what kept breaking through this warm reverie was the challenging

74

shape of Cal Lockyear. Billy Lord and his wife slept, both snoring. Mrs. Irish listened to the breathing of her son, remembering how worked down he was, and wondered how much more he could stand. She was both bitter and sad for the boyhood he had lost, and silently prayed: "Lord let me last till he's eighteen — then I'll not mind." Half listening to the quiet talk of her parents, Katherine Gay remembered Rice Burnett's question about love — "I wonder what it really is?" She could not believe, from that question, that he was in love with Edna. She remained long awake, thinking of him.

So the camp lay, a small world of wagons with a spurious quiet upon it; within the covering canvas all these people rested, but few were at rest and their cries, if spoken aloud, would have filled the night. Turning in his blanket roll, Rice Burnett felt the weight of Edna upon him. He loved her if love was an appetite, if it was warmth and explosion and rest, and wakening to hunger again. She was calmer than any living person he knew; and she knew him and laughed at him for his notions, and perhaps she was right. He turned again and listened into the night with an outdoor man's close perception of sound and smell, of small currents of noise twining through each other, each with a separate meaning. The rain fell in desultory fashion; the rank night odors lay heavy in the fog. All the stars were hidden beyond this low ceiling. He was lonely and not even the imagined nearness of Edna settled the loneliness. There were other things out there beyond his finger tips, beyond the next hill.

He had come to Oregon to get away from this search for things beyond sight; the search was done and it was time to settle and to accept what he saw, not what he imagined; but the yonder still haunted him; it would never let him alone.

12

THE rain had ceased, the morning mist was a silver haze upon the earth, the odors of fire and mud and fir and river thickened the air. Men caught up their stock, and wagons began a groaning march, and here and there women clasped each other, crying. Whitcomb walked through the crowd to say farewell. He shook hands with Gay, paid his respect to the other Gays on the wagon, and paused by Rice. "Best of luck. Best of everything." He came upon the Collingwood wagon and removed his hat before Lucy who sat above him on the seat. He said: "It will be a raw day — are you warm?"

"Yes."

"Pull your coat higher around your neck." He turned to Collingwood. "George, you ought to wrap a blanket about her feet. She'll be chilled in an hour."

"I'll do that," said Collingwood and grasped Whitcomb's hand with his overcordial manner rising. "We'll never forget what you did for Lucy. Come see us often. Door's always open. Whatever we've got is yours — anything, any time."

Settlers bound for the plains to the west and south of the river were already crossing on the ferry, voices calling back.

"So long. See you next spring!"

"Ride over our way!"

"Soon's we get settled!"

"Good luck!"

"Tell Josie to save that big kettle!"

Hawn rode through camp, buckskin legs loosely banging on the hide of his small horse. He said to Burnett, "We better get started." Burnett put his pack string into motion, threaded a way through the column of wagons, stock and trudging people, and fell into the town street. Somebody began to sing and in a little while the song caught hold, spreading through camp and along the column and out upon the water where the ferry was; men and women joined in, the song growing until the whole area was loud with it:

> Yes, we'll gather at the river,
> The beautiful, the beautiful river,
> Gather with the saints at the river
> That flows by the Throne of God.

A shouting rose along the column and somebody fired a gun. Hawn shook his head. "They better save that."

Beyond town a black rock bluff came forward to crowd the narrow road against the river; at the top of the bluff the column crossed a flat place and entered a long stretch of forest which ended before a natural meadow. Beyond the meadow the forest began again; and in such alternation of open and closed land they traveled twelve miles that day. On the following day the land began to open up so that they had sight of a prairie flattening into the forward haze, its plain broken by occasional groves of fir and oak which, from a distance, seemed like ships standing at anchor. Hawn took them to the edge of this prairie and swung easterly and followed a course which kept them out of the sodden bottoms. They crossed an occasional creek, a small river, and another yellow stream meandering through the country like a crooked snake. On the third day a few families fell out of the train, liking the land they saw. The hills broke into small buttes, short valleys lying between. Westward the prairie ran into a rain mist which had been with them during the whole journey, while to eastward they caught a passing sight — as the mist briefly thinned during the better part of the day — of foothills moving into mountains of great bulk and height. They went over two more creeks on the fourth morning, and at this point the train began to shrink as individual families found their favored places.

Somewhere during afternoon, the remnant of the column passed through the notch of a low hill and came into a small valley cut by a creek.

Hawn said, "My place is up that creek two miles. This is all empty. Down south you'll find rolling hills — Old Waldo's yonder — but there's only two families in the whole scope and she's a lonely place. Big prairie's out to the west, five or six families mudded in for the winter. That's all."

The wagons parked and next morning individual men rode off on their private scouting expeditions; as they returned they took their wagons away and by nightfall fifty square miles had become a settlement — this valley, the hills around it, the short prairies which adjoined it, and some of the adjacent bottom land of the big prairie. The trip was done. In twilight campfires winked at far intervals and even then the sound of axes began, and continued as darkness gathered, and rang on and on through the night. To Burnett, listening, it was something like the ticking of a new clock which, beginning with a first ragged rhythm, slowly settled for a lifetime's marking of the hours.

13

GAY was down the creek three miles from the ford, his farmer's instincts drawn to the lower, richer land. Upstream from him the

McIvers settled, and the Provosts and the Collingwoods and Lattimores. Billy Lord dropped back a short distance to claim a mile square which would include the notch through which they had traveled and the round knob of a hill on which he wanted to build his cabin. The view delighted him and he surrendered at least thirty acres of flat meadow to get it. Burnett marked off for Mrs. Irish a half-section directly above the point where an Indian trail crossed the creek's ford. "The road will probably go through here, and you'll be right on it, and you can put up people and feed 'em, and make something." The Rinearsons continued beyond the ford and beyond the shallow ridge which enclosed this valley; over there was a piece of country undulating from meadow to knoll, perfect for a stockman with its hay fields and its cool slopes in summertime; and there was enough of it to let his sons take their claims around him. Buck was up the trail from Mrs. Irish; the Millards and Walkers and McIvers and Kerns and Crabtrees and Kitchens and Purroys settled in a widening circle around the ford, so that Mrs. Irish's place was, as Burnett had forecast, a center spot. Eby dropped westward, his section entirely on the bottom lands of the big prairie, and one by one the neighbors fitted themselves in where it pleased them; for there was room enough as far as the eye might reach. The Lockyears vanished in the timber, seeking the hills, and Rice Burnett threw off his packs in a narrower part of the valley, upstream from the ford and not far from the Lattimores.

He had less tillable land and more timber than most of the rest but what he wanted was a power site for a grist mill; and he settled beside the creek at a point where it came upon a ledge of sheetrock and dropped fully two feet to create a head of water sufficient to drive a mill wheel. The surrounding meadows would do for orchard, pastures and tilled fields; the rising hill behind him had wood enough to supply him forever, and the water-level grade beside the creek made a mile road to the main road at the Irish claim an easy thing to build, or so he thought when he first looked at the land — before he had touched hands to the trees scattered along the way. What he intended to be was the miller for this part of the country.

The Lattimores were nearest him, half a mile downstream, hidden by a strip of timber which ran from hillside to water. Across the creek, opposite the Lattimores, the Millard wagon was screened by an alder clump; and so it went with most of these people: they were neighbors whose cabins would eventually be from a half mile to a mile apart yet they were shut away from each other by timber or by the roll of the land. Sometimes Burnett heard their axes ringing. At night he caught the glow of their fires. Otherwise he was alone and thrown upon his own resources.

For all these people the ordeal by work had commenced. The idea of a land of milk and honey had grown week by week on the overland journey until even their powerfully practical minds had become infected with the notion of an easy life on a beautiful, bountiful earth. This was the end of it. The rain continued to fall, not in harsh intemperance, but with a niggling persistence which, the citizens of Oregon City had warned them, might last until the following spring. The air was everlastingly damp, not bitter but clammy and penetrating; the unequal temperatures of rain and earth brought up sleazy layers of mist from the ground and these lay upon everything from afternoon through late morning of the next day, closing in until there was no distance around, no head room above.

To people accustomed to a positive climate, to strong heat and sharp cold, to full sunshine or the immediate intensity of cyclones, this damp, gray, soft drizzling indeterminate kind of weather was hard to bear. They had been born and raised in a land of dramatic and even dangerous changes and their tempers fed upon such change; this monotony of grayness and wetness and softness, good as it might be for their bodies, was hard on their souls. It didn't lift them; it flattened them until they complained of possessing no energy; they slept heavily and woke tired and looked into the rain again and found no zest in the day's work. They were moreover worried; for they had to break these tough, sodden fields and get in the wheat which would keep them alive the following year, and when they tested the soil their farming experience told them they dared not put a plow to it short of a week of dry weather — and this they feared they might not get.

Burnett's first chore was to set up a tarpaulin as a rude tent which would shelter his packs and himself. Afterwards he took time to make a survey of the falls and to dig an exploratory shovel into various parts of his meadowland. On the first day, with a baited hook on a long hank of string, he caught four trout and he looked hopefully on the creek until he remembered that other settlers, as hungry as he, would fish out this water in quick time. From the tent, actually standing inside the tent at the time, he watched a buck deer walk from the woods toward the water and he killed it at a distance of fifty feet, and he realized that within a month other settlers' guns would drive such easy game away. He dressed out his meat, took a quarter to the Lattimore's and left a quarter with Mrs. Irish.

When he had time to smoke his pipe late that night he visualized the things to be done and calculated the work which each chore required and placed the chores in their order of importance — and all this labor came at him in a lump and pressed him with its urgency; but his handworker's sense of thriftiness controlled him. Whatever he wasted in time or energy was forever lost. He was in a race with summer when the wheat came in and his grist mill would be needed; he was, when he considered it, ten years too late in the longer race of his life; for he was thirty and long ago should have settled down. So he took care to plan the proper location of the mill, to visualize his cabin in such a place that it could be, at another day, the storehouse of a frame home which sometime would rise; and he spotted his barns and sheds where they should go, and the fence lines, and the road which would run by this place. Having done this much he walked to the hillside and began to chop down proper-sized firs; he cut them into lengths, teamed them to the cabin location, and squared them; he trimmed saplings for rafters and left them in a handy pile, and found a cedar and dropped it and sawed it into bolts from which he would later rive his shakes. With this material at hand, he took his team and his tools and followed the trail to the ford, recruiting Lattimore, Collingwood, Buck and Provost along the way, these men occupied with working out their cabin stuff the same as he had been, and so reached Mrs. Irish's claim with a considerable work party.

Young Watt had brought in a few logs with the ox team and Mrs. Irish, when the party arrived, was busy with the crosscut saw; the first tier of cabin logs was already notched and fitted. Burnett took the saw from Mrs. Irish and by noon the five men had the logs ready and the cedar bolts cut. They ate trout which Mrs. Irish had caught in the creek, and corn-bread with blackstrap and coffee; during the afternoon Millard and McIver came up to join the group and at five o'clock the cabin was walled in, the doorway rough-framed, the rafters set and the fireplace hole cut.

"You needn't come tomorrow," said Mrs. Irish. "Watt and I can split and lay on the shakes — and we'll put in the fireplace."

"Dig down till you get straight clay for the fireplace," said Burnett. "Go along the meadow and cut a lot of that fallen hay to mix in. Make your first fire a small one — bake it out slow and she'll get brick hard. Who's ready next for a raisin'?"

80

It turned out that Provost had everything ready for his cabin. The gathered men agreed to meet at Provost's on the following morning and set off in the graying evening for their claims. From a distance Burnett looked back to see Watt Irish already riving shakes from the cedar bolts. Mrs. Irish was at the creek again, fishing.

"We're all going to get damned sick of fish," said Provost.

"They won't last," said Burnett. "Neither will the deer."

"Well," said Lattimore, "I've got an old pair of boots I can stew up."

Lattimore was the last to leave Burnett; passing on through a heavy stand of timber, Burnett reached his tent to find Bob Hawn squatted in its shelter waiting.

"My squaw's a fine cook," said Hawn.

"I'm your man," said Burnett and, saddling his horse, he followed Hawn upward along the creek, through one narrowing meadow after another, until the hills began to crawl down against the open flats. Hawn's cabin sat face to the water and back to the timber scarcely a stone's throw from his door. It was the sort of site that an ex-mountain man might pick, a creek close at hand to remind him of beaver, the hills for hunting and grass enough for his horses. To one side of the cabin a garden spot still contained its old cornstocks and a few rows of late vegetables; along the cabin's four outer walls deer horns hung side by side. Hawn gave a short whoop as he neared the cabin and got down with a cheerful, "Here's my lodge."

He went in first, said a few short words in some Indian tongue and stepped aside for Burnett. It was the neatest of cabins, a fireplace ablaze, a bed built against one wall, a table, two peg-legged benches to sit on and some shelves built into one of the corners; in the fourth and vacant corner a blanket had been spread on the floor and a few pouches and trinkets hung from the wall. Hawn's woman stood in this corner.

She was a pretty woman, pale brown rather than dark copper; she was, as close as Burnett could judge, somewhere between twenty and twenty-five, with obsidian-black hair, round, rich brown eyes, pleasant mouth and small nose. She wore a white woman's waist, a buckskin skirt and moccasins; and when Hawn spoke to her in her tongue, her glance went to him and remained with him until he ceased to speak; then it traveled to Burnett. As soon as she smiled her face became expressive and pointed with mischief. She said something to Hawn.

"She says you look hungry and that all my friends seem to be hungry people. Her name is Louisa."

81

"You gave it to her?" queried Burnett.

"Sure, she wanted a white woman's name. So I picked it. Then she wanted to know what girl I'd known by the name of Louisa. You can't get around a woman, Indian or any kind. The wash basin's out back."

Burnett washed and returned to take a seat before the table. Hawn sat opposite; after his woman had laid the food on the table she stood back, but Hawn hooked an arm around her waist and drew her down to the bench beside him. "I can't quite break her of that habit. Alone, she'll eat with me. With company, she goes Indian."

The woman spoke to Hawn, who said: "She's inquisitive. Wants to know what I'm saying." Then he spoke to her and she nodded, and laughed at him.

"She's not Molala," said Hawn. "She's Calapooia. That's a tribe south of this place. The smartest Indians in Oregon. I was trappin' that country three years ago and stopped in her old man's camp. Pretty soon I found myself tradin' six horses, two Hudson Bay blankets and a rifle with ten pounds of shot for her. It was a deal between the old man and me, like it always is. But these Indian women have got a way when their minds are made up and I think she worked the whole thing. If I want to make her mad all I got to do is tell her I could have bought her for two horses. I don't make her mad very much, for when an Indian gal gets mad it goes down to her bones and stays there a long time." He looked at her; he laid his arm about her waist and squeezed. She pushed his arm aside and grew solemn.

"Who are these Molallies you're talking about?" Burnett asked.

"They're up this valley, in the hills. You'll see 'em passing back and forth. They're not like Shoshones for honest, but they ain't Blackfoot for tough, either. Used to be a big tribe until smallpox reduced 'em. They ain't made trouble so far, and I get along well with 'em."

"Settlers always bring on trouble," said Burnett.

"Oh," said Hawn, "they've been grumblin'. They see what's comin'. But they ain't enough for a very big war. If a fight should come up, some white man will start it."

Burnett said, "Probably," and went on with his meal. It was a good meal, venison stewed in with potatoes and carrots and onions, Dutch oven bread baked from whole ground wheat, butter and milk and coffee, and little blue berries cooked with the stems on.

"Those things are huckleberries," said Hawn. "She picks and dries 'em

82

in cakes, Indian fashion. They look like hell till they're cooked. . . . You don't know it but she's got you sized up."

"I'm her friend. You tell her if she wants anybody killed, let me know."

Hawn laughed and spoke to Louisa, and she smiled and spoke back. "She wants to know if you've got a squaw," said Hawn.

"Tell her I've got no horses to buy a woman with." Having fed himself, Burnett lighted a pipe and settled on the corner blanket. Hawn squatted by him, and the two men smoked through a long silence while Louisa moved around the table, moccasined feet making no noise. She ignored the men and when she finished her dishes she disappeared.

"Now she'll prowl in the dark with her arms crossed, and God knows what she'll be thinking," said Hawn. "You never can get that far back into an Indian woman."

"How far up this creek the Lockyears go?" asked Burnett.

"Three miles."

"Don't leave your woman alone too much," said Burnett.

"They won't fool with her. Get killed if they do." Hawn settled to an elbow. "Louisa and me have been awful happy here. I kind of got out of the white man's way of makin' trouble. I can squat and watch a beaver workin' all day long. I can listen, I can smell, I can just soak in comfort. Don't think of money, I don't think of gettin' anywhere, don't want anything. What's to want I ain't got? Now you people come and it won't be the same. In white people's eyes I'm a squaw man and she's only a red savage and they'll make her feel it. It'll put trouble in her head, and then she'll wonder what I'm thinkin' about it."

"Wait and see," suggested Burnett.

Hawn shook his head. "I'd damned near forgotten I was white or she was red. I'd almost lost the thing that makes white people unhappy, makes 'em quarrel and scheme and grab everything in sight. I'd about got myself to where a man ought to be. Now you come, and I'm just white enough to catch the fever back from you, and there's nothin' but misery in it."

Louisa slipped into the room and settled bolt upright on the edge of the bed, watching them. Hawn beckoned to her with his hand but she shook her head and remained an observant spectator. "Look at her," murmured Hawn. "Even now she knows, she smells it coming. She's a wonderful woman." Then he made an abrupt change of subject. "What you going to do down there by the riffle?"

83

"Put up a grist mill."

"That your trade?"

"Worked in a mill for a couple years."

"You'll do business," said Hawn. "No mill nearer than Oregon City or the French Prairie right now. Where you going to get your stones?"

"I saw a couple at Fort Vancouver which can be bought. They came from England in a Hudson Bay ship as ballast."

"You people have got to learn a lot of new things out here," said Hawn and rose to face the door; the sound of horses came in and a voice struck over the yard and in a moment Cal Lockyear entered the cabin, followed by his brother. When he discovered Louisa, Cal Lockyear's glance settled on her with a round, bold interest. He stamped the mud from his feet. "That's a neat female you got there. Where you find her? Might want one myself."

"You go to hell."

Lockyear walked toward Louisa. "Had one like her once. Mandan woman. This one's cleaner, though, and she's got more of a body to her. She looks like better sleepin'." He raised his arm to touch her. Hawn spoke to him in the same idle tone.

"Keep your God-damn hands off that woman."

Lockyear wheeled about and to his face came a very close expression, a sudden peering interest in Hawn, a tenseness, an odd smiling. "Don't say that to me."

"I'm no slow buffalo for your stickin'," said Hawn, beginning to show his amusement. "I been to the forks of the creek too."

"No," insisted Lockyear, "don't say it. You don't know me, so I let you say it. But don't say it again."

"Now slap your leg and crow," said Hawn. He lifted his head, gray eyes close-fixed on Lockyear. There was a quarrel here and he was pleased with it and he threw a side glance toward Burnett and let an easy laugh drop into the room. "The man's trying to use me for a greenhorn." He shook his shoulders and laid his glance back against Lockyear. "Hell, I've heard that story too many times. You're half an alligator, half a man. You're the big wind and the trees fall down. Yellowest one started where you spit. You been havin' fun with these settlers, friend Cal, but don't try to have fun with me because I was where the fun started."

Lockyear looked toward his brother. "The son-of-a-bitch," he said. "I'll have to do it, Veen."

Veen Lockyear let his attention hang a long moment on Burnett. Then he looked back to his brother and made a signal with his chin, indicating Burnett. Cal swung to Burnett.

"What'll you do? Stay out of it or come into it?"

"I'll do what I please," said Burnett cheerfully.

Lockyear divided his interest between Hawn and Burnett. All three were coolly amused, were certain of themselves; only Veen in the background showed concern.

Lockyear said to Burnett: "You and Veen step outside and shut the door. Take the squaw with you. I don't want her at my back with a knife."

Burnett said, "It's up to Bob."

"Suits me fine," said Hawn promptly. He spoke to Louisa. She went by the men with her eyes downward and stepped into the yard. Burnett put a hand on Veen's shoulder and used a little force to swing the small brother around. "Come on."

Veen knocked Burnett's arm aside. "I'll stay here," he said. "Cut it out, Cal, and let's go home."

Burnett seized the small man at the armpits with both his hands, flung him about and pushed him toward the doorway. "You're a good rooster, Veen, but you've got no spurs."

Cal Lockyear said, "Let go him. Veen — run out and get the gun off my saddle."

"Veen," said Burnett, "if you do any runnin' I'll strangle you in the creek."

Hawn, more and more delighted by this affair, let go with a roaring laugh. "You won't get the chance. Louisa's outside the door with a knife and she'll drive it into his ribs far as the trade mark."

"All right," said Cal Lockyear. "Call off the squaw."

"Well now," said Hawn, "we ain't had our fun."

"Call her off."

Burnett turned Veen back and dropped his arms. He kept an eye on Veen, not knowing the little man's disposition; and now and then he threw a look toward Lockyear. Hawn spoke Louisa's name, summoning her into the room; she moved to the farthest corner and watched Cal Lockyear, plainly hating him, plainly wishing to kill him; she had both hands behind her. Cal Lockyear shook his head at Burnett. "You should of stayed out of this."

"I like his grub," said Burnett.

"God damn you," said Lockyear.

"And God damn you," said Burnett promptly.

"The hell with it," said Lockyear. "It was a good fight spoiled."

"Come again," said Hawn. "Any time."

"She have a knife?" asked Lockyear.

Hawn said, "Big enough to skin you."

Lockyear shrugged his shoulders, said irritably to Burnett, "Don't rub your horns on me any more, Rice," and pushed his brother through the doorway and shortly afterwards rode on through the darkness.

"Almost made his jump," observed Hawn. "It was his brother's skin that stopped him. He always protects the little fellow."

Burnett said: "Tell Louisa she's a fine cook," and rode homeward, feeling better for the visit.

14

HAWN lay in bed with his woman, watching the dying light of the fire tremble on the cabin walls. She rested, quiet, an arm under him, an arm on his hip; she said nothing, she let him alone, but she was waiting for him and would respond when the time suited him. She didn't have a white woman's ideas of partnership; she didn't argue or speak her mind. She was his woman, bought and paid for, and she was proud of it. Even when he went against her common sense or her ingrained custom, as he sometimes did, she made no fuss; on such occasions she had a short gesture she used, one finger cutting across the air before her, and then he knew he had reached a boundary. He didn't know what lay beyond the boundary; that was a country he couldn't get into, couldn't even guess at, for it was a wild land, it was Indian land, not white; and that was the one difference between them which troubled him. During most of the time he gave it no thought and the silence between them was good and he could ask for nothing better, but when he wanted to understand her and be understood by her, when he wished for that final intimacy between man and woman, he knew that no matter how long they lived they would never have it, and then loneliness would come upon him.

She spoke up. "He said something about me. I looked at your face and saw it."

"Nothing. It was a bad tongue. He wanted to fight."

"But there was no fight," she said, and he knew she wondered whether it was he or Lockyear who had backed away. It was suddenly an important thing between them, for she had the simplest standard of courage; there were no allowances in her mind, no middle ground between bravery and cowardice. What might be to him a respect for life or a sense of pity would seem a weakness to her. It made him quickly say: "The man saw it was a bad time to fight and went away."

"He's a snake, he's a Molala hiding in the brush. He'll kill you when you don't look. You better kill him first."

"That's not the way."

"Not your way, not white. It's foolish."

Nothing he might say would change her mind, but having said it, she put it aside and lay waiting. She made no motion whatever, but the restlessness called out of her and when he turned to her she came at him and then there was no boundary, there was only the man and the woman business which was the same for red or white (or brown or black or yellow). He had taught her nothing about that except one thing; he had taught her to kiss, and what at first had seemed queer to her she now liked and did well.

Afterwards, lying quiet, she asked the question she had so often asked. "As good as white women?"

"Better."

"Why don't Burnett have a woman, a white woman?"

"I don't know."

"Not enough white women?"

"Plenty of single ones he could pick out."

"Plenty for you too," she said.

So it had come to her. He sat upright and hauled her against him. "No," he said. "You—that's plenty." He wanted to tell her how he felt about her and the pleasure she had given him; he wanted to reassure her with words, but there were no words in the thin language they used. This was a lonely moment and sadness got into him for the insufficiency, and there came to him again the fear which he had felt on first seeing Katherine Gay and Edna Lattimore and the other white girls of the train. In a way he knew the ending of it already. He rocked her back and forth on the bed, speaking to her in English.

15

UP and down the creek's narrow valley, and along the trail as far as Rinearson's, the forest began to show fresh-scarred stumps as the logs fell; and crooked trails appeared where these logs were skidded down hillsides and across meadows to the various cabin sites, and crews formed and moved from claim to claim, making quick work of a chore which for the individual would have been the labor of many days. There was no such thing as a drawn plan of a cabin among them; as with everything they did, these people used the cut-and-dry method. The cabins were small, about sixteen feet long by ten or twelve wide; such smallness provided little comfort and a large family, bedded down at night, covered the floor, but the immediate need was protection from the weather and except for sleeping and for meals these families were usually out-of-doors. It was considered impractical to waste labor on a cabin which, in a few short years would be a pantry off the kitchen of the larger frame house they hoped to build.

They were thus of one shape and dimension, no man being better housed than another, the peeled logs shining pallid in the dull winter's light, ragged at the corners where the chopped butts lay upon each other in their notches. The chinking was a later labor when other chores were less pressing; the floors were plain dirt, to be afterwards covered with split and adzed logs, this again when time permitted. There was a doorway, stopped by a temporary blanket or bit of canvas; there was a window opening in each end, also closed by canvas until deerskin could be cured and oiled and used as a substitute for glass. The fireplace took a large part of one wall; the rafters were poles bound with thongs; across the rafters other poles were placed as sheeting, and on these were laid the cedar shakes. Into such a quick-built shelter were placed a few pieces of furniture carried overland; the fresh clay-and-stick fireplace was lighted — slowly to dry brick-hard; the crane was fastened in, the big pot swung over to boil, the Dutch oven laid nearby; and this was home, wind pouring through every interstice, rain trickling here and there along the inner walls, smoke belching back into the room at each strong gust of wind.

Half a day built a cabin — men specializing in chores long enough to become quick at them, some teaming in the logs, some notching and fitting, some building the fireplace, others riving and laying shakes. Lattimore's cabin went up, then Buck's and Collingwood's, and Millard's across the creek, and Walker's and Mercer's. Below the ford other crews worked, at Gay's and McIver's and Monteith's and Crabtree's. On the little hill back of the ford Billy Lord's place was a landmark to be seen two miles along the trail. When all the families were sheltered a crew came up to help Burnett on his cabin, and late of an afternoon he threw his bedroll into the finished place and watched his neighbors turn wearily homeward.

Their fatigue reminded him of his own. Ten days had passed since arrival and each day of that time, from first morning light until darkness set in, he hauled and cut logs at one claim or another, and hiked his one or two or four miles home. They had all done this; they were all dull horses plodding back and forth through the trees and over the meadows, treading out the pathways and roads which would serve them the rest of their lives. He lighted a slow fire on the fireplace and walked the meadows to test the spongy earth; and in the misty twilight he returned to the cabin and found Edna waiting with a supper she had brought from her own place.

"It's a housewarming," she said. "What have we got for dishes?"

He brought in a pack and laid out the dishes, using the bedroll as a table. She made coffee and dished the food — a chunk of venison and molasses and bread — and sat beside him on the blanket roll to eat it. "That trail through the timber's an awfully dark place," she said. "It's going to be pretty, looking out of this window to the creek."

"I'll get the floor in tomorrow and spend a day dressing it down. Don't like splinters on my feet."

"Or your woman's," she said. She waited for him to rise to it, saw that he wouldn't, and went on with her eating. Her expression was gentler than usual; she was closer to him, she was quieter in her manner.

"I'll mud the logs in, build a bunk and a table and a couple of chairs. A shelf in that corner. A door. Then, if the rain hangs off, it's time to plow."

"It'll look nice. You're handy with tools." She got more coffee and they sat silent to drink it; she collected the dishes and moved outside to find a pan for washing.

He said, "Don't bother about that," but she went on with her business and he lay back on the blanket roll, hands propped under his head, and watched her.

89

"If you've got any liquor," she said, "you ought to take a drink before you sleep."

"Haven't got any."

She did the dishes at the fire, kneeling on the ground; and the strong light and strong shadow so rounded her that when she was momentarily still she had for him the thick, indestructible quality of a statue. She sensed his watching and turned her head, and the slow smile came; and as soon as she finished her chore she sat beside him on the blankets. Her nearness kicked sensation through him. Her face was above him, loosened and heavy; her smiling ceased and she made a small sound in her throat and lowered herself and kissed him and drew back to see its effect.

"I shouldn't do that," she said. "I ought to be careful like other girls. Then you'd think I was modest."

"Can't change what you are," he said.

"Well, what am I?"

"God knows," he said and drew her down. Sometimes the thought came to him that her appetite was so powerful that it destroyed the reservations and little modesties and roundabout allures which other women maintained for the sake of men. This coming against him with her mouth was as easy and as necessary to her as the drawing of a breath.

She settled and lay whispering beside him. "I thought maybe if you were good and tired you'd just take this and let it be what it is and not make it mysterious."

"You know how it's apt to turn out?"

"Don't always be thinking about things."

"Babies."

"Nobody thinks about that when they want each other."

"Last time — Oregon City — I thought about you till morning."

"I'm glad," she said, and showed her pleasure. Then she said: "No, you make it too big. Just till you fell asleep." She knew he had stretched it; that almost clairvoyant realism was in her. Suddenly she murmured, "Oh, lover, lover," and flung herself against him, one small explosion of ferocity following another until she lighted him.

She lay beside him, looking up to the shadowed ceiling. Her hand was on his chest and now and then a flurry of affection wakened it and she patted him and grew still again. She was wide-awake, she was peaceful and talkative.

"Lot White keeps talking about this earth being pain and suffering. It

90

wouldn't be if we didn't try to make everything so important. I don't know about heaven either. Sounds like we're making something else too big. But I know this." She swung, kissed him, moved back. "I know that's good, and if it's good, why that's all there's to it, and why try to make it better by thinking things that aren't so? Look at Tansy McCormack."

"Don't know — what about her?"

"She thought Nig Blaine was the only man on earth. Then he died and she wouldn't eat for days. Six months later she married Rupe Bond, and they're happy and I don't think she feels anything about Nig any more. You see? What do you want a woman to be like?"

"Like you."

"I wish I believed it, but I don't. You like my housewarming?"

"I liked it — and I like you."

She held up a finger, and measured off a small bit of it with her other finger. "This much."

"No — it's more."

She ceased smiling, she ceased to be amused. She lifted herself to an elbow and searched him. "Is it?" she whispered. Her mouth loosened and she was during that moment almost a homely girl. She shook her head. "How much more?"

"I don't know that, Edna."

"Almost — almost. Men don't talk that way when they want a woman."

"Don't be so sure."

"No, I know. You'd get tired of me, too. You'd get to thinking again. There's no woman like you want."

"Now who's talking too much?"

"You're funny," she said. "A lot of men would run after me if I let them. An awful lot have tried — it'd surprise you if I said who. I could get married any minute I said so, to all sorts of men. You think I don't believe nice things. Well, if you'd seen what I've seen on men's faces, and the lies they've tried to fool me with . . . I hate people that try to fool people. I won't say things I don't believe. If I could, you'd think better of me but I just can't do it."

He sat up and bent over her. He ran his hand over her forehead, he traced the edges of her hair; he was close to it, the feeling rising, the belief growing, the words almost there. She saw it and waited dead-still. But the impulse stopped somewhere; it couldn't come freely and he said nothing. As soon as she sensed it she put his arm aside and got up. "Time to go home." There was nothing in her words.

"I'll walk through the trees with you."

"No. I'm not afraid. Things don't bother me."

He went with her as far as the timber's edge, but she turned him back there and went on alone through the blackness.

It was a quarter-mile through this timber, from Burnett's to Lattimore's, the trail winding around huge trees which, twelve feet in diameter, had been growing there through the hundreds of years. The water was beside her, dashing over its shallow rock bed; a small wind ruffled the boughs far above her, and in this close damp air the odors of the forest lay heavy. There was no variation to the dense shadows; all Edna had for a guide was the trail's yard-wide track in the soft humus, beaten out by Indian feet generation upon generation. Neither blackness nor animals bothered her, and the fear of the unknown wasn't in her system, but she had grown up on the usual Indian tales told by her people — of murder, surprise, captivity and torture — and these made some effect on her placid imagination; therefore when she heard the sharp break of a branch directly before her she stopped with strong fear.

"That you, Edna?"

It was Cal Lockyear's voice, pitched low to reassure her. His feet lifted slick and sucking sounds from the mud. "You, Edna?" he asked, closer by.

"Yes."

"I'll walk through with you."

She said, "How'd you happen to be here?"

"Oh," he said, "I'm a lean hound, always on the run."

"How'd you know it was me?"

"By your footsteps," he said and gave out a short laugh.

"The ground's so soft I made almost no sound," she said skeptically.

He had a dry answer. "If you'd spent your time sleepin' in Indian country, you'd sharpened your ears to hear grass rustlin' two miles off."

She went along the trail before him. Like all women in whom the sex power is heavily packed, she had a keen sense of the constant intrigue between men and women, the surreptitious game of chase and seduction they played. Thus she believed Lockyear to be lying. He had come here, she decided, because she had at last attracted him out of his indifference so that he was now running after her. She had never doubted her ability to bring him around, and suddenly she was a little scornful of him.

"Go on," she said. "I don't need any protection."

His brief laugh came again. "I said I'd walk through with you, and so I shall. I can't be handled as easy as Burnett or Moss."

She quickened her pace and said nothing more until the trail fell into her father's clearing, across which the cabin lamp thrust a golden bar of light. She turned to him. "You're just talking," she said. "You don't know anything about Burnett or Moss."

"Indian country's where I learned to keep my eyes open, too."

"You're funny," she said.

"You don't like me much."

"Well," she said, "you're a hard one. You hurt things."

"Oh," he said, "there's hell enough in me." Then he showed a bit of his underlying truculence. "Who's been telling you stories about me — making me out some sort of a damned animal?"

Now that she had him openly interested she grew a little cruel with him, partly to punish him for his previous indifference and partly to defend herself against his willfulness. "Oh," she said, with a touch of mockery, "you're not that wild."

"I'm a damned long way from being as tame as the men you been running with."

"You don't know what I do, and it's none of your business."

"Know more than you reckon I do," he said. "Like to get a man stirred up, then knock him down — that's what you like."

"Don't you get stirred up," she retorted, "and then you'll not be knocked down."

"I'd not be so easy to stop as the others."

"There'll be no starting, so there's no stopping."

"Then what have you been looking at me for?" he said sharply. She said nothing but when he leaned forward to catch some sort of a view of her face he saw that she was smiling to herself. "You don't know me," he said. "You don't know me at all."

"I know you well enough," she answered promptly. "You like to make trouble. I mean, you're not kind to other men."

"Ah," he said impatiently, "these dishwater men."

"You're not better than they are," she said promptly.

"Let them try to follow me on hunt, let them stand up to me in a fight — we'll see who's the better."

"Fight — fight," she said. "That's what you think about."

"Well, by God," he said, "I have stayed alive because I kept my mind on fighting; your gentlemen, in my shoes, would have been dead for their easy manners." He was silent and he was dissatisfied, and stirred and stepped slightly forward to keep his view of her face in the shadows. "Certainly I'm proud of myself. I have got good reason to be, for I followed a livin' which kills poor men quick." Again he was silent, and still not pleased with the way things stood. "As for being easy with your people — have they been easy with me? What family invited me to share its fire or meals on this trip? Not any. I ain't one of you — you make that plain. Lockyear's the greasy trapper; let him alone, let him shift for himself, keep away from that man."

"More your fault than anybody's," she said. "You've not been agreeable."

"It's not required that a man should beg his way," he said. "You people think me no better than a savage, no manners, no talk worth listening to, no feelings. It amuses me to let you think it. Do you know why I have no use for your men? Because they are barn-fed creatures and they've lost the gift to smell, or see, or hear. For sleeping under a roof they've forgot what the sky looks like or what comes when you think on it; and for living safe the spirit's died out of them. No, you don't know me." He stopped speaking, he drew a long breath, and peered into her quiet face and gave her his intolerant advice. "Go back to the men you can do what you please with. You don't know me — you never would."

She remained still for a while, seeming to reflect on what he said and afterwards, unexpectedly, she put her hand forward in a kind of impulsive gesture and touched his arm; and then she laughed at him. "What's there to know that's so mysterious?" she said, the mocking manner returned.

He reacted at once; he clapped his hands around her arms and gave her a rough pull against him, and threw his arms about her waist with an intemperate squeezing; when he kissed her the pin-sharp whiskers of his face stung her face and she drew aside but he lifted a hand and pushed her face back to him in a kind of cuffing motion and thrust himself against her and increased his pressure around her until her breath began to draw fast and short; a short sound in her throat warned him; he released her and gave her a small shove. "I'm more than the men you've been tinkerin' with," he said. His tone was guttural with excitement. "If there was a full-out man in the lot, you'd stay with him, but there's not and you fool with one and the other. I could teach you what it's like. Whatever you think it is, I'd teach you it was more." He sucked in an enormous breath and let it go. "I don't know," he added, coolly, "I don't know if you've got

94

enough to give back," and he turned and entered the trail, immediately vanishing.

She was angry because he had left her before she had sent him away, and also because this scene, which she had been so certain of controlling as she wished, had gotten away from her. He had responded as other men responded, up to a point; beyond that the surly independence in him had asserted itself and he had defied her and walked away. She went on to the cabin more and more dissatisfied with him, yet restless with herself and made increasingly curious by his final taunt.

Burnett stacked a pile of wood inside the cabin and dragged his blanket roll near the hearth so that he might keep a slow, even flame burning against the damp mud of the new fireplace. He brought up a bucket of fresh water from the creek; it took a great deal of water to kill the odd cravings which long hours and a limited and monotonous diet created. He covered the pile of packs with a tarpaulin and stood in the darkness, listening to the distance-gentled clank of the bell on the white mare. All the stock would be feeding close around her. There were cougar aplenty in this country; he had seen those big cat tracks printed frequently in the loose mud at the creek's edge, and he thought about the risk to his animals, and meanwhile let his senses test the night for rain. The sky was closed out and dim banks of mist hung over the meadows, but the vagrant wind was from the northwest, directly opposite the prevailing storm winds. He turned into the cabin, undressed, laid his rifle handy and rolled the blankets around him on the hard floor.

She came to him now as she had so many nights before; she settled warm-flanked beside him, laughing a little, whispering. This was the imperative reverie of a lone man, flesh's need tangled through the soul's need so that as he used her he endowed her with grace. Without grace it was brutal; without flesh it was bloodless. Lot White would have said that one was evil and the other perfection, but Lot was wrong, they were not two separate things, they were parts of one thing and so long as he was alive these alternate thrusts would have their way; the conflict had been built into him and he could no more change it than he could chop himself in halves and live. So she drew him on by the shape of her body, by the shock of her vitality, by the smiling temptation of her face.

He heard the scrape of a boot on his threshold and turned his head to find Lockyear in the doorway's dark square, the firelight rubbing its rouge stain into the man's cheeks and starting up a glass bright flashing of his

eyes. He was a cat animal prowling, and the sign of his predatory discontent was all about him. Burnett rose to an elbow, irritated by the
soundlessness of Lockyear's arrival.

"Next time you come here at night, sing out. Don't play Sioux with
me."

"Sioux was good enough for you once," said Lockyear indifferently
and stepped forward to settle on his heels before the fire. "Now you're a
fat settler snorin' on your back. You're a fool to leave that door open."

"This is a settlement of white people."

"White or any color, I'd not trust anybody standing yonder in the dark."

"If you did a day's work," observed Burnett, "you'd get over this spooking around. Walk off that rock patch you've got up the creek and find
yourself a claim you can farm."

Lockyear spread his hands to the fire and stared steadily at them. "You
think you're going to like scratching holes in the ground the rest of your
life?"

"What's better business?" countered Burnett.

"We're squatted between these ridges like frogs at the bottom of a well.
I've not had a decent breath since I got here — my lungs are full of fog. I
can't see anything for the timber and there's no light. It's a damned dull
world, it's a country for gophers. Think a minute of what it looks like
on Wind River right now. Sun's shining and you can see for a hundred
miles." He turned shoulders and head toward Burnett and he said ear-
nestly, "This is no way for a man to live," and made a sweeping motion
with one hand which seemed to include cabin, settlement and valley.

"What's a better one?" asked Burnett.

"This place will break you before you get it broke," warned Lockyear.
"You'll be a damned old man in five years. You need a woman to cook,
but she'll drive a hard bargain with you. She'll tie you with a wedding
ring and load you with ten kids and you'll not be free to pick up your
gun and roam a hundred miles for the fun of it." He struck a hand across
his thigh with an odd impatience and murmured, "God damn these white
women, they'll have their way. They wring a man dry and trap him with
work; then what's left of him? Squaws are better — they let a man stay
a man. There's your white settlement, kids to raise and cows to milk and
fences to keep up, and cabin-broke men, and women that have got things
their own way."

"Go find your squaw then," said Burnett.

Lockyear said in the gentlest tone, "God damn these settlers and all their kind." Changeable humors played over his face and he rose and looked down on Burnett with his half interest and his half intolerance. "Think you'll stick it out?"

"I'll tell you next spring," said Burnett.

"That business of you siding with Hawn — I didn't take that well. Next time, don't do it."

"Next time," said Burnett, "I'll do as I please. You know that, Cal."

Lockyear turned to the doorway and passed through it and swung back. He stared a steady moment at Burnett, dry and tense and preoccupied, and he had something to say; but finally he stepped aside and vanished in the dark with no further comment.

Burnett turned on his blankets, listening for Lockyear's steps but hearing no sound of them; and he knew enough about Lockyear to realize that the man would tramp the trail with an increasing unrest, at the mercy of one of those storms of discontent which swept through him at regular intervals — the same kind of discontent which, in mild or furious form, was the common misery of everybody.

16

GAY had built a pit outside the cabin, in which a deep bed of coals, three days' burning, had accumulated; and over the pit he had erected a scaffolding of poles from which hung the butchered chunks of half a dozen deer. Over the fire too hung Martha Gay's largest iron kettle — her soapmaking kettle — filled to the brim with potatoes boiling with their jackets on. On a three-day trip to the French settlement along the Willamette, Harris Eby had picked up the potatoes, several sacks of onions and half a wagonload of squashes. Wanting a community meeting to discuss roads, among many other problems, Gay had sent out word of the feed, knowing there would be no absentees.

It was late afternoon. Gram had a basting pan and a jug of meat sauce — onions and flour and salt and pepper and water — and as she turned the meat she ladled the sauce on each chunk and caught the drippings in the pan. Now and then she tore a sliver from one chunk or another to test the doneness.

Martha Gay came from the cabin. "Pity we've not got flour enough for bread, or butter, or pickles, or that damson jelly I made so much of and left in the old cellar for the new owner's woman." The memory of it deepened the fretful lines of her face. "Have we got enough? It's such a lot of people. I wonder if he sent word to the Lockyears? I hate those men; but Gay — his heart's like a barn door, always open. . . . I hope that meat gets done. I won't have Nellie Lattimore making remarks."

Accustomed to these moments of irritation, Gram sometimes scarcely heard Martha Gay's words and said nothing now. Gram was small, weighing little more than a hundred pounds, but she was one of those people whose vitality would go on and on, outlasting the personal satisfactions of living or hope of reward or fear of death, until one day she would turn her mind about and actually kill herself by ceasing to wish to live. In the tireless way of an old person, she rose early, found work to keep her moving and at dark lay abed to think of the past, her memory an attic trunk crowded with the miscellany of seventy years' living; names, incidents, the ring of certain voices, the sight of the first dead face she had seen, the odor of lilac in a room whose identity she had forgotten, phrases spoken, a boy's hand creeping over her and the excitement and guilt printed on his face, her third son's body lying smashed after the horse had killed him, the velvet sensation of summer's deep dust on her bare feet, the scream of a girl in Turner's woods, the sound of Sunday's church bells, the flash of Simon Burke's eyes across the dance hall to her after she was married — a confusion of such things lay in the trays of her mind; mostly the sentiment was gone from them, but once in a while she touched something still powerful enough to stir her and then she worked through her day in absent-minded silence. She was close to only two people.

For the Old Man she had an ancient wife's mixture of affection and irritability. They were two old horses teamed, sometimes scarcely able to abide each other, yet so long accustomed to the pairing that they were lost when alone. More than once he had failed her, the original heartache of that failure severe but now of no importance, and long ago she had discovered that her original faith in him was only girlhood dreaming, for as the years rolled on he had settled into his obscure place of no great force, actually insignificant. What held them together was their sharing of things which meant nothing to anybody else; when one died the other would be lost in a foreign world.

She paused from her work to look out upon the plowed field beyond the cabin. In the gray light of late afternoon four figures moved over the field at spaced intervals casting wheat seed — John Gay, young Joe, the

98

Old Man and Katherine. The field was rough and wet, but neither John Gay nor the other settlers dared to wait longer on the seeding; and the four, trying to keep steady pace for an even cast of grain, hauled their mud-clogged feet along like iron boots. The Old Man was tired; Gram watched his shoulders and watched the way he flung his arms, and sent a silent message to him: *You come back.*

Four people filed from the timber beyond the meadow, the first to respond to John Gay's call, and at sight of them Katherine swung from her work and moved toward the cabin. She was good as a man at almost any sort of rough chore, but she was woman enough not to want people to see her dirty. Such real affection as was left in the old woman was reserved for this girl. The strong salts of Gram's disposition had been inherited by Katherine. Martha was mild, she was worried over small things, she believed everything other people believed — she was one of the soft ones; but Katherine belonged to the other kind, to the rough ones. There were only two kinds of people, in Gram's judgment: those who did what they wanted to do and made no bones about it, and those who were afraid to act and afraid of the consequences after they acted.

Katherine wore an old dress spattered with mud, a heavy sweater and a pair of her father's shoes round as cannon balls with the clinging loam. Work and damp air reddened her cheeks, her eyes had bright blue shining, her light hair was tumbled on her head and at the moment she reminded Gram of one of those bulky, fair-featured German immigrant girls who had come into Iowa in earlier years. There was a difference; most of those girls were placid, whereas there was nothing placid in Katherine. She lifted the seed sack from her shoulders and stood by the fire.

Gram said: "Who's that comin'? I can't see from here."

"Lattimores."

"Edna, too?"

"Yes."

"I'm surprised she didn't wait to tag along with Burnett. You need to wash — fix up your hair. You look like a hired man."

The Lattimores came on, and elsewhere, out of the timber and over the roundabout meadows, other people began to appear. The Gay men made their last round of the wheat field and returned, and the Gay yard took on something of the cheerful spirit of the trail. Moving about her chores, Gram watched these people grow warm as they touched each other again. They were tired with the steady labor of two weeks, they had their worries, and the climate had not been kind; it was worse on the women than

99

on the men; the women showed the grinding-down caused by their in-cessant chores and by the monotony and loneliness. It was in the pinched expression around their mouths, in their higher tone of voice, in their nervous, restless motions. But the meeting calmed them. For the women it was the chance to talk — and their talk ran around the yard in swirling little gusts of sound, exclamatory, incomplete and running on and on as if some dam in their minds had burst. For the men, it was talk too, a slower talk; but it was also the smell of food and, for the younger men, it was the presence of the girls.

Gay had doweled long split logs on trestles, thus making a table; and the visiting women brought what they could spare from their small stores, a bit of relish, a jar of preserves, a pan of bread. Mrs. Rinearson, having swapped a string of cheap beads for dried huckleberries from a passing squaw, came to the meeting with ten huckleberry pies; the rough table began to have a picnic appearance. Gay and Eby carved the venison, lay-ing up mounds of meat in various pans; the potatoes were drained and the huge kettle laid at one end of the table; the coffeepot stood at the other. Gay lifted his voice:

"Now here it is! Come and get it or I'll throw it away."

Men moved to the table at once, using dishes their own women had brought; the women were slower to come, having more pride in the mat-ter of showing their hunger before other women. Gram Gay collected the little dibs and dabs of coffee brought by the families, and threw them into another pot of boiling water, meanwhile observing the crowd with her greedy interest. Katherine, changed into a clean dress and shoes, moved among the women, just talking her way along to find out what had hap-pened to them and how they'd been; and when she came upon Edna Lattimore, Gram's following glance saw at once the contrast between the two girls. The trip over the plains had pulled Katherine down; she wasn't thin, yet against Edna she seemed thin. Gram, a rock-bottom realist, had no doubt that it would be Edna men looked upon first; she was the feather bed in which they wanted to lie. It took a little longer to see what Katherine had.

She found more joy in watching the scene than meat could have given her. Ralph Whitcomb rode in with the first shadows and went around shaking hands; he flattered Gram with his attention. "You'll live to be a hundred and ten. They don't make people like you any more." After-wards, as he walked about, Gram noticed him search the crowd — for Lucy, Gram understood.

It was full dark and the men had gathered in a wide circle around the fire to discuss roads when Burnett arrived. She had never seen the man look so tired; he walked to the stripped table and stood by it a moment, as though his mind were somewhere else; and then Katherine came from the group of women and paused beside him; she said something to him and gave him her smile, and Gram saw him look upon Katherine with an extended thoughtfulness. Presently he answered her, returning her smile. Katherine turned and got a plate and began to hunt him a meal. She was reserved — not like Edna; she didn't show Burnett a thing.

Gram turned her wandering attention now to John Gay. His shoulders were round with their weariness and the angles of his face bones were sharp across his face. Even in the firelight there was a shadow, like the shadow of a cross on him — and Gram closed her eyes and felt a chill go through her; there was death on him, there was death in his voice. Powerfully it came to her, powerfully she conjured the feeling into prophecy. She opened her eyes to see what real thing might have cast the shadow, and found the shadow gone. She thought, "It'll come three times." She crossed the yard and circled the cabin until she was in the darkness, and she stood there and let the superstitions of her nature have their way, the haunted currents coming out of nowhere and everywhere, the witchery moving, the evil conjunction of stars and moon and earth. *That wheat won't grow. Everybody'll quarrel tonight.* She thought of thirteens and sevens and threes. Six deer on the spit — *two sets of threes. It might be that. Wheat field and wrong moon* — it might be that. Somebody could have walked around the cabin too many times? A bird had flown inside the cabin two days ago. She had stepped on a snail last night. She stirred and felt a small rock underneath her shoe, and she picked it up and turned into the cabin and laid it on the bed in which John Gay slept. Rock could soak up evil, if it were the right kind of rock. But it was too late, the sign had appeared; it was too late — he would die.

John Gay said: "Well, folks, it's good to get together again. I been a little lonely to sit around with everybody again and hear some good lies."

"Where'd you get them spuds?" asked Lattimore.

"French people over by the river."

"Hell of a long distance to go for spuds."

Jackson Monteith said: "We'll go farther for grub before the winter's done."

Gay let the talk go aimlessly on for a while. Men lay close to the fire; they knelt or stood in the background. Somebody said, "Where's your fiddle, Billy?" Billy Lord shook his head. Ben Provost said, "I hear there's some wild cattle around here, strayed from Ewing Young's place a long time back. Anybody seen any?"

"No, by God, but I hope I do."

Moses Crabtree said, "I came here to get rid of fever and ague, but I still got it. Anybody else got it?"

"The old stuff's still in your system," said Whitcomb. "It'll burn out next summer. Or it may be your belly. How've you been eating?"

"Damned poorly," said Moses Crabtree, and set the crowd into laughter. John Gay sensed the ease around him and brought the meeting to its business.

"We ought to talk about a few things. Some things ain't timely and will wait, but we ought to be thinking about them anyhow. There's a marshal for all this country, but he's at Oregon City, and we ought to think about making a county and electing a sheriff. We have got to think about a school. None of these kids have been in one since last spring. We ought to talk about roads. Not the little ones leading into our places — the main one to go through the settlement."

Ben Lattimore shook his head and came right in with his objection. "Now, wait, John. You're hell-for-leather to put a load on us. What's a sheriff for, when nobody's goin' to shoot anybody? The schools — let them that have kids build the school. I have got no kids for school. As for roads, let's just keep the plan of wild animals. They just walk back and forth the easiest way and pretty soon they've got a road."

"That's fine, Ben, but if we all decide on the place for a road, we'll waste no labor. Don't know about you, but I'm an old horse and I can't be spending wind on false starts. I ain't got that much wind."

"No," said Lattimore, "it just sounds like settin' up some more gover'- ment, some more expenses. It's the start of taxes again, damn it, and I didn't come two thousand miles to saddle myself with taxes. I came to get away from 'em."

"As for me," countered Gay, "I didn't come here to run away from taxes or sheriffs or schools, or anything people ought to have. I was born inside a government and I expect to die inside one. You can't throw things away, Ben. We're not Indians."

"Well, by God, they ain't got sheriffs and taxes."

"And they ain't got anything else, either," said Gay. "It's a poor argument. You don't intend to squat in the mud and itch fleas like they do."

"I'll build my own floor and I'll take my own bath. Don't expect anybody to do it for me, don't expect to do it for anybody else."

Daniel Rinearson, listening in, suddenly pounced on Lattimore. "The hell you'll build your own floor. You had help on it, like the rest."

"I could of done it alone," said Lattimore stubbornly.

"Now," said Rinearson, "don't argue yourself into a corner you're too stubborn to get out of. We're all wheat dumped in one sack. We got to keep the sack sewed tight or we spill out."

"What's schools got to do with that?" countered Lattimore.

"Let's just talk about roads," said Gay, in his reasonable tone. "If we all go to cuttin' trees and diggin' stumps in the wrong places, we'll get nowhere. Better to think where we want the main road to be and all work on it as the occasions come. Where should it be?"

Cal Lockyear stood at the outer edge of the circle, present but scarcely a part of the crowd; his brother, shadowlike as ever, stood near him. Lockyear had come late, hadn't eaten with the crowd, and seemed to hold himself aside from it. His voice went roughly at Gay. "You're askin' where should the road be when we've not decided we need one. What do we want a road for? We got here on a piece of a road. A piece of a road goes stragglin' through the settlement. What more do you need?"

Ben Lattimore nodded. "That's what I said." Then he looked around to Lockyear and his expression turned and he seemed unhappy with Lockyear's company in the matter. He caught Ryal McIver's eye and shook his head.

"A piece of road it is," said Gay. "And a damned poor piece. It took four days to come here on it. That's too much. We ought to bridge the creeks. We ought to do a little grubbing on the hillsides. We should knock down some trees."

"What's your hurry?" said Lockyear. "Where we going?"

"Straight down to hell in the mud if we don't do something about it. When the wheat's in and the cabins are floored and chinked we'll have time on our hands. It's better to start these things or they never get done."

He stooped at the fire to light his pipe. Having expressed his own view, he was wise enough not to press it for a little while, for he had gone through this business times enough to know how opinions were formed when men got together. The core of any crowd was common sense, self-interest and a tendency to do the right thing — these elements, loosely blended. He was old enough to know that men talked somewhat better than they performed; they had a Sunday suit of good intentions which they liked to wear in public, but when the chores got burdensome they frequently put on the shabbier jeans of indifference. What had to be watched for was the unintentional offense which might put some perfectly good men on the wrong side of the fence, out of injured pride; what also had to be watched for was too great shock to that selfishness which all men had and which could waver them from the standard of public necessity. In each crowd there were some men who stood fast to reason, some who sought some personal gain, some who objected to any program because of an ingrained principle of resistance in them, and a great many who would listen and at last go along with what seemed to be the prevailing sentiment. It was a matter of steering a course through the divergent personalities before him, and it required some skill. Gay had enormous faith in the rock-bottom decency of his neighbors; he believed devoutly in the shirt-sleeve system and, as a product of that system, he could neither understand nor like any other system. As his neighbors did, he depreciated the need for leaders and he subscribed to the notion that though men might vary greatly in capacity, they took on a sort of God-endowed equality in the matter of making public decisions; then, the foolish, the illiterate, the selfish and the able stood on equal ground, all equally endowed with wisdom for the voting moment. Had the proposition been put to him, Gay would unhesitatingly have preferred government by a thousand fools to government by one wise man; for at least the thousand fools would be speaking the common wish, whereas the wise man would be speaking only for himself. He would have explained it by saying that if the thousand wanted to go to hell in their own style, that was their privilege; but that it was certainly not the privilege of one man to lead them to heaven against their desires. Yet though he subscribed devoutly to this theory, his practical streak would not permit him to stand by while the foolish had their way. By instinct rather than by reason he felt that a shirt-sleeve order carried the two streams of redemption and destruction side by side and that it was the duty of good men to reason with the foolish and temper the prejudice of the ignorant and the selfish; thus in a society which disliked authority and distrusted leaders, he was one of those unwitting minor leaders which such a society thrusts up to protect itself against the farthest limits of its own theory.

He renewed his argument. "If we get a main road through here before somebody starts it somewhere else, we'll see a little town grow at the ford. It's better for us to have it there than ride twenty miles to somebody else's town. It'll give value to our claims." Then in mild manner he asked his question again. "Where ought the road to go?"

Collingwood discovered Whitcomb across the circle. He moved past the fire, shook hands with a quick turning-on of his cordiality. "Lucy's not well. I wonder could you drop in and see her a minute?"

"Come along," said Whitcomb.

"I'd like to stay here and talk this out with the boys," said Collingwood. "It's directly up the creek, first cabin this side of the ford."

Whitcomb looked into the man's rather handsome face, and thought to himself, *You're a damned fool.* But he said aloud, "I'll go see her," and moved toward his horse. Riding into the darkness he hoped his eagerness hadn't shown; the wish to see her was so powerful that he had a guilty man's fear that even his thoughts were visible.

17

WHEN he saw the light of her cabin shining a hundred yards distant along the creek he began to feel the mixture of embarrassment and eagerness he hadn't experienced since boyhood. At that time this surge and urgence had been shot through with reveries of the ideal, and passion transmuted into the beauty of one constant lifelong love. It was, he thought, perhaps the high-water mark of a man's imagination — that capacity of making the perfect blend of body and spirit. Now that he was older, the terrible skepticism of experience came in to unsteady the things he thought about Lucy. He was hungry for a woman. He was poaching after another man's wife. Strip it down and what else was it? A jury of twelve men he most respected would have shaken their heads at him; or perhaps, being men, they would have laughed at him and told him to go hunt his peach in a less dangerous orchard. It was against his wishes and against his training but it was happening to him and there seemed no sort of reasoning or moral judgment he could use to stop it. He had passed the point of wanting to stop it.

He left the horse and knocked at the door and heard her say, "Who's that?"

"Whitcomb. Your husband said you were sick." Then he added, "He asked me to come."

There was a moment's delay, and then she said, "Come in."

She stood with her back to the fire in a gray rough dress against which a gold locket made a small point of light. Her hair was loose, coming to a tie at the back of her neck, pulled together carelessly as a girl might have done it. She had her hands behind her and she looked across to him with her chin lifted, manner grave. He thought she seemed less ill than disinterested.

"You always manage to find me," she said, "when I'm a poor sight." Then a smile destroyed whatever dullness or hint of poor health she might have had. "It's so good to see you, but I wish George would quit making me out an invalid."

"Maybe he's concerned."

"Let him wait till there's cause for it. I do my work." She took the coffeepot from a corner table, spilled hot water into it from the crane kettle and added coffee and set the pot into the fire.

"You'd better hoard that stuff," he said. "Long time till spring."

"So long as it lasts I'll have it for visiting doctors." She had her back to him at the moment and he sensed some sort of waiting in her. The silence pulled at him to finish what was unfinished.

"Then there's apt to be a doctor around here pretty often," he said.

She turned about and again put her hands behind her back. Her chin rose; he made out the working of excitement within her, the moment's tenseness of her body. Her voice was pleasant to hear, level but slightly hurried. "I think that will be nice."

He motioned for her hand and took it and settled his fingers on her pulse; and meanwhile he found satisfaction in watching her eyes. They were a heavier blue than Katherine Gay's, almost a gray-black. Her pulse was faster than it should have been. "Lie on the bed a few minutes," he said.

Her smile came back. "Oh, I've been turning and stooping."

"Nevertheless . . ." he said, and waited while she settled on the bed. "Feel stronger than a week ago?"

"I suppose so. How strong am I supposed to feel? I don't know."

"Sleep all right?"

"When I get to sleep."

"What keeps you awake?"

"Oh," she said half in laughter, "what a question! You've got no medicine for people who watch ceilings. Anyhow, I'm healthy. It's a good thing to lie awake at night. It's about the only time when anybody's alone. I've got a solitary streak in me. I like to go away off by myself now and then

106

where nobody can find me. You know about that? Sometimes, people, people — people . . . they get to be too much. Maybe I'm queer."

She was relaxed, she was grave. "We've all lived too crowded on this trip, so close together that at night times it seems to me we were all lying in one big bed, snoring together, sweating together, doing the most intimate things together. It's not good when you see somebody look at you and you know he knows everything about you; and you know everything about him. There were times on the trail when I could hear so much from the next wagon that I cringed. I even know the words Ben Provost uses on his wife when he loves her."

"You tell George this?"

She shook her head. She said, "George never gets enough of people. I could have gone to the meeting tonight, but the thought of staying home alone seemed awfully good."

"Maybe," he said, "I ought to get out and leave you to your solitude."

Her fingers curled back on his hand and remained with a moment of pressure; a softening expression moved over her face. "You stay right here." Then she shook her head. "That's not exactly what a female patient should do to a doctor." She rose, murmuring, "The coffee's ready," and set a pair of cups on the table and poured coffee, and found sugar and spoons. She had her back to him. "Other women have tried that with you, haven't they?"

"That coffee smells good."

"But they have," she said.

He sat down to the table. She took a place opposite, crowding her body into a rounded comfortable position. She laid her arms on the table. "I guess they've poured everything out to you, one time or another."

"I guess they have."

"Petty things, terrible things, things real, things imagined. Are the stories all different?"

"Variations of the same few things."

"That makes me seem more like others." She sipped at her coffee; her velvet glance came over the cup's rim. "What things?"

He made a tumbling gesture with both hands. He had a large chest and shoulders, with a first showing of extra flesh of the middle age he was coming upon, and his hair had some gray at the base of the sideburns. His profession had given him its particular manner of listening, half personal, half detached. To Lucy, who had a romantic imagination, it often seemed that he must have had an unfortunate love affair, for behind his settled kindness she sensed an ardent disposition, a love of the colored and fanciful; and on his face, particularly about his mouth, she noted a taste for the good things of living. Experience had made him kind; only occasionally did she see anything disturb the kindness, this a quick flashing-out from his eyes of an accumulated unrest with himself and other people. So then he had moods in which he was sharp, perhaps even cruel, in his judgment.

He looked up from the table. "I believe we were meant to give, and to receive. When there's not enough given out and not enough taken in, we're cheated. I think there's no complete happiness unless we're altogether absorbed by somebody else and we've absorbed them."

"It doesn't happen much."

"Which is why I make a living by tapping sick bellies."

"I think you've put on weight."

"I'm living in better style. I've got a house and a woman to cook. I'm not rushed with work. This is good coffee."

"I'm a good cook."

He put down the empty cup; he looked into it. "And a good wife."

She rose from the table, turning from him toward the fire for the coffeepot; but she became still, arms wrapped across her breasts. There was strain in her, for he saw the pressure of her fingers against her sleeves and the same strain got hold of him. The critical fragment in his head told him that this was an opening maneuver in an old game, but it didn't matter. He had the feeling of being young again — the same heated images returning, the same formless wishes, the beautiful pictures, the desire to possess, to hurt, to pour out. It was all back.

She said quietly: "I didn't say that. I'm not sure George would say it."

Now he thought he saw half an opening, but he was awkward and lacked the courage to take the step; much as he wanted her, he couldn't manage it and for an instant he despised the luggage of propriety and self-analysis which stopped him from performing this simplest and most direct act of a man. So he stood silent.

She swung, her returning smile quickened by an awareness of the thing moving between them. It took the indifference from her; it made her feel good. If he judged her rightly, it had been a long time since her husband had troubled himself to go through the extended niceties of love-making with her; and no doubt she had earlier learned what the wagon train people had discovered about his character, so that affection was pretty much dead between them. Her eyes, with so much aliveness in them, were beautiful; her face was expressive. She was amused, she shook her head. "Oh, Ralph —"

"What?"

"Nothing. It's funny."

"No," he said, "it's not a damned bit funny."

She moved around the table and laid a hand on his arm. "I didn't mean it that way. Have I hurt your feelings?"

He thought to himself, *I'm thirty-nine and acting like a fool boy.* He found humor in it, and the rankling instant vanished. "No," he said, smiling.

"You know I'd hate it if I did. Things are so mixed up."

He turned from the cabin and got his saddlebags and came back, and found her staring at him with a changed expression, solemn. He opened the saddlebags on the table, found a bottle and shook out a dozen pills. "I want you to take one of these each night when you go to bed."

She said: "You left the room so abruptly. I thought you were going away without saying a word."

"I guess I had my mind on the pills."

"You were a little bit angry."

"No."

"You can't hide things. It was there. Please be gentle — please be."

He left the pills on the table and put the bottle back and buckled the saddlebag. It came again. His heart beat quicker and he thought, *Now — right now.* In her eyes was that peculiar obscurity which so often came to women at the end of their emotional tether. He stepped forward, meaning to take her. What stopped him, more surely than a club across his head, was the slightest expression of dread which seemed to stain the expectancy, as though she had drifted beyond her restraint and was at his mercy. She could have done nothing more effective.

"I'll make a try at it," he said. "I think I'd better get out of here."

Her manner grew impersonal and a coolness came from her and he became uneasy with the feeling he had failed to do what she had expected. She said: "One pill each night." She counted the pills. "That's twelve nights. Then what?"

"I'll be back," he said. He took up the saddlebags and moved to the door.

"Ralph."

He turned to find her smiling. He had somehow gotten adrift in the crosscurrents of feeling but she understood them and was sure of herself.

She said: "What kind of a cook have you got?"

"A good cook," he said. He looked closely at her. "She's fifty-five," he said — and suddenly they were both laughing and the air was clear again. "You know," he said, "I'm a clumsy man."

"Ralph, think well of me. Please — always do."

"Sometime I've got to tell you what I think."

She looked down, she moved one hand idly across the other; in a moment she lifted her head. "All right," she murmured, and he felt she had made up her mind. "Sometime," she added, and sent him from the cabin with that deferred promise.

He rode toward Gay's in a strange mood. He was angry at himself for not seizing the opportunity he thought he had seen; the cautions in his nature had got the best of him, as they so often did. Then this sober reflection was chased away by the exultation which came of knowing that she had responded. It was a young man's intoxication all over again, the great well-being, the fancies shooting off in all directions, the senses wide open to the goodness of the night and its flavors, the desire to sing, to shout, to spill out. His realism whispered that this too was the old reaction to chase and conquest, but he would not believe it and he rode on alternately rising and falling to the mood. He was in love with her.

18

DANIEL RINEARSON said: "Take the trail the Indians made. Widen it, and you've got a good road with the least amount of work. It should come past Billy Lord's, same as now. All you need on that slope is some zigzag grading. It ought to cross the creek at Mrs. Irish's. That makes it right in the middle of everybody in this part of the settlement. We ought to put a bridge there. Then it should go right through the notch valley, pass my place —"

"There's the coon in the brush," said Elam Walker. "You're damned big-hearted where this road ought to go till it gets down your way. Then you want it right past your place. That leaves me a mile off the road, and you right on it."

"I'm only figuring the work we'd have to do on a new road," said Old Daniel with his best show of reasonableness.

"And throw a mile of road building on my shoulders," said Elam.

"All right," said Old Daniel, "let's all pitch in to help you build your side road. It would still be less work than swinging the main road."

"That ain't what you're thinkin' about," pointed out Walker. "A claim on the main road has got value. My claim, a mile off the main road, won't have much value. That's what you want. Well, I don't see it."

"I'm thinking of the others," protested Rinearson.

"Let's just do that," said Walker. "There's Kitchen. He'd be closer to a new road than to the old one. Ain't that so, Kitchen?"

Kitchen, not a firm man, found it an embarrassing matter to be caught between two personalities. "Well," he said, "it might be. I never stepped it off. Depends on where the new road goes, don't it?"

"Fifty-fifty," said Rinearson. "You won't gain or lose, one way or the other."

"Probably so," said Kitchen.

"All right," said Elam Walker, "there's Purroy. What you think?"

"Swing it up the creek a quarter-mile, and I'll be pleased," said Purroy.

"Oh, hell," said Rinearson, "you can't wrestle a way by that hill. Be a damned mudslide in wintertime."

"You got an answer for everything," said Elam Walker.

"Now, men," said Rinearson, "let us raise our sights above what might be best for any one man and think what would be best for all."

That caught the crowd's humor and a quiet laughter went around. Rinearson spread his feet and shoved his head forward — a stubborn little man, penny-grasping as everybody knew, foxy in the maneuvering of things toward himself. His face was like nothing so much as a piece of baked wood split by countless small crisscross seams. His eyes were very small, quick in their roundabout searching; he was good-natured, infinitely sly, profane, a hard trader; he was a dirt-common man grown wealthy because he schemed where other men grew tired of it; but though he schemed and took delight in skinning a man, he also made it a point to keep his word and could laugh at his bad luck if a smarter man skinned him. If others sometimes resented his wealth, it was also a fact that they admired his shrewdness more; in a society of hardshells he was harder than the rest.

"Well," he said, "it's true."

Elam Walker would not be sidetracked. "I'll tell you something else true. Be damned if I work on a road for your benefit. Either it's for the rest of us or you build your own road."

III

Collingwood had done somewhat less talking than usual, for the issue was not one on which all were agreed, and his instincts shied away from unpopular argument; it occurred to him now that there was a shift away from Rinearson and he thought he saw an opportunity to show his common-sense quality and his ability as a diplomat. "Well, there's two sides to everything. Daniel wants it favorable to him, and that's nothing against him, and Elam's got a point too. Why wouldn't it be a good idea to split the difference — put the road through that little pass, then swing it halfway between Daniel's and Elam's places?"

Walker stared at him. "What the hell good's a road that goes nowhere and passes nobody?"

Old Daniel said: "We'd *both* have to build side roads to it, and so would everybody else!"

"Well," said Gay, "let's have a vote on this — just among the men living beyond the ford. Those for the old road. . . ."

There were fourteen in that district. Rinearson had his three sons and Ebbett with him in the vote; the rest of the neighbors were against him. Kitchen, sensing the majority, joined it as a matter of comfort.

"I suppose," said Elam Walker to Rinearson, "you won't go along with us, not gettin' your way."

Rinearson shook his head. "You're dead wrong on the road. You'll have something stragglin' like a snake with the bellyache all over the hillslope, the damnedest roundabout thing you ever saw, full of bad grades, mudholes and stumps. You fellows think I was scratchin' my back and so I was, but so were you. But we got to have a road and if the majority's for this one, I'm for it because I'm no fence jumper, which is more than I can say for you, Elam, and to hell with you."

"All right," said Walker, feeling generous with his victory. "It's all right."

Ben Provost said: "Should be another road straight up and down the creek."

"That's the easier thing," said Gay. "It's mostly level and if every man will brush it out across his own claim and scrape it a little, the thing's done."

Cal Lockyear, long silent, spoke up. "I'm three miles beyond anybody. Don't I get any help, or is this lodge closed?"

"It's your corn if you settled to hell and gone back in the hills," said Lorenzo Buck.

Lockyear shouldered men aside and came into the circle; he approached

Buck. "Who you proposin' to dress down with that tongue of yours? God damn you, don't talk that way to me."

Buck said in surprise, "What riles you?"

"Don't give me your advice. Don't ever do it."

Buck, growing on toward middle age, was the mildest of men. He had made his remark casually, using the common talk of his neighbors. All the argument had been in the same vein, heated and sometimes rough but not vindictive. This was something else again, this growling man ready to make a personal quarrel of it. Buck couldn't match Lockyear in a fight, yet he couldn't pass over the way Lockyear went at him. He held his voice on its diplomatic level. "You've got no reason to be riled, Cal. Your temper's too touchy."

"It's mine, not yours, and watch out for it," said Lockyear. He swung to face the crowd with his air of unruly intolerance. "You'll help anybody, but not me. Well, to hell with you."

"There was no offense intended," said John Gay.

Lockyear gave Gay the raking edge of his eyes; he laughed at Gay. He threw back his head, silently challenging the men around him, and had no takers. A good rough and tumble fight they didn't mind; but Lockyear's vindictiveness, with all its consequences, was another thing.

John Gay, however, felt impelled to give an older man's advice. "Cal," he said, "you've got some notions of the rest of us. It's your business if you want to think that way but it's not your business to let that temper run wild around here."

"Let somebody take it up," said Lockyear promptly.

"That's not it. We have got to live together and there can't be bad blood. I'll be damned if I make out why you figure your pride's such a tender thing. You're no better than the rest of us. It sounds to me like this Southern honor business, and I had a bellyful of that in Missouri. By God, Cal, you can't go rummaging around the settlement like a wild bull, hooking your horns into us at your pleasure. Think it over."

"Let someone stop me," said Cal, and laughed. "There's your rub: nobody wants to." He nodded toward his brother and the two wandered toward the table and stopped to feed there on the scraps.

Rice Burnett had earlier moved to the table for coffee; propped against it, he watched shapes move around the yard. The fire threw a red half-light over the people; the sound of women's voices and the sound of men's voices moved through the night in two layers — rumbling undertone and quick, nervous overtone. Edna Lattimore's smile came across the yard to him and passed to Moss Rinearson, who walked toward her. For Moss or for him, the smile was the same, and a ragged irritation moved through him and unexpectedly he realized he was angry at her. He watched her teasing way with Moss; he watched Moss respond to it.

The Lockyears came toward him and Cal said: "You know anybody that wants to educate me?"

"It would be a chore," said Burnett.

"A damned long one," said Lockyear.

"Short one," said Burnett. "You and I take education about the same way. A quick hole through the head."

Lockyear let go with a rough laugh and helped himself to coffee. He wanted trouble. Mildness kept most men within bounds; Lockyear's extra energy tossed him farther out to extremes. "Who'll pull the trigger? Not any of these country lads. You heard me offer a fight. Nobody took it."

"Nobody's mad enough tonight."

Lockyear stared at him. "What's it take to make you mad enough?"

Burnett grinned at him. "I'll let you know."

Lockyear said, "Come on, Veen. There ain't a fight in the crowd." He crossed the yard to the horses beyond.

Men broke from the fire, business done, and drifted idly around. Burnett watched George Collingwood pass through the crowd and pause to speak, to shake hands, to move on; he went about it with a single-minded gravity as though he had to cover everybody. Ralph Whitcomb remained at the fire, listening closely as people came to him, occasionally asking a question, nodding his head. Katherine came to the table with Gram Gay. The two gathered bits and pieces of the meat and potatoes into a set of bowls.

"I want one for the Kitchens," said Katherine. "And one for the Lords." She moved away with the filled bowls, discreetly searching out Mrs. Kitchen and Mrs. Lord. She came back to the table.

Gram murmured: "Mrs. Buck?"

"No," said Katherine. "Buck will rustle. But one for Lavinia Ebbett."

Women moved against the table to recapture what was left of the things they had brought, and their talk went on in bits and inconclusive fragments, some compulsion making it necessary for them to exhaust themselves completely of words. Mrs. Irish came forward with Watt and studied the table and got a deer shank with its few shreds of meat. She handed it to Watt, murmuring: "You didn't get enough."

He said, "I'm not hungry."

There were women near her. She lowered her voice until its meaning was lost to Burnett. Watt chewed reluctantly at the bone while Mrs. Irish looked on as though she were trying to will some of her strength into him. She murmured, "Don't waste it — put it in your pocket — it'll make a soup bone." She turned her back to Watt and fell into talk with Provost's wife.

Somebody said: "Well, great Lord, here's the squaw man and he's brought his woman!"

Hawn rode into the firelight, the Calapooia girl following. When she stopped she pulled up her horse behind him, not coming abreast; her head remained steady, her round black eyes darted their quick glances about her. Burnett moved forward to speak to Hawn.

"Get down," he said. "There's something left to eat. You're late."

"We had supper," said Hawn and saw the women standing in their groups, watching his woman; they didn't come up. He added, "We were just traveling through."

"Well," insisted Burnett, "get down."

"It's late," said Hawn.

Katherine stepped forward. "Tell your wife we're glad to see her."

Hawn spoke to his squaw without turning on the saddle. When he heard what she had to say to him, Hawn looked again beyond Burnett and Katherine to the white women so silently gathered, unfavorably watching, and he said in a shortened voice: "No — just stopped in to say hello." And he turned about and moved back into the darkness, with the squaw following.

Mrs. Millard's voice was clear enough to be heard around the yard. "Look how she tags after him. Lord of creation, he is, and she ignorant enough to let him be."

"Well," said Ryal McIver, "he's got his bad furrow. A squaw man's a hard lot."

"He ought to marry her," said Lot White. "I'll talk to him about it."

"An Indian woman?" said Mrs. McIver. "What makes you talk like that? He ought to send her back to her people."

"His wife, ain't she?" countered McIver.

"She's nothing — she's a savage."

"Kind should stay with kind," put in Mrs. Crabtree. "What'd he bring her here for?"

"Maybe he wanted to get acquainted with his neighbors," suggested Burnett.

"Would you take them into your cabin?" asked Mrs. Rinearson.

"Certainly. They took me into theirs."

"Rice," said Mrs. Rinearson, "you're a nice man, but a fool. It won't do."

The resistance which these white women had thrown across the yard at the Hawns surprised Burnett. Nothing had led up to it or had prepared for it; it had come at once, out of the deepest of prejudice, out of some wrongness. He shrugged his shoulders at Whitcomb, and Whitcomb pretended to enlighten Burnett with his amused and lightly stinging words.

"The woman's not married to Hawn, and these ladies regard that as a threat. They don't like the precedent. And she's a different color. Any color which is not our color, Rice, is a bad thing. If you ask me why, I can only say it's because it's not our color."

Mrs. Rinearson refused to be shamed or baited. "That's what any *man* would think. You're all alike, and really you'd none of you mind being in Hawn's place. It suits your instincts fine. Just you remember, Ralph, it's the children who suffer. Their blood's mixed."

"You know the blood of your people a thousand years back?" asked Whitcomb.

"Oh, that's far-fetched and you know it," said Mrs. Rinearson. "Then's then. Now's now. What did Hawn bring her here for? To get us to make her one of us? Why doesn't he go sit in the tent of her people? No, he wants to be with us because he don't want savage company. Well, he can't have both things, a savage woman and white friends. She's not welcome in my cabin." She looked around for her husband. "Rinearson, don't you ever bring either of them around, not even if it's mealtime."

"Had no intention of doing it," said Old Daniel testily.

"Well, don't."

"All right, all right. God damn it, don't shout at me for things I ain't doin'."

Burnett shook his head at Mrs. Rinearson. "Hawn guided us here. I'm surprised you'd be willing to let a squaw man do you that favor."

"Now there you go," said Mrs. Rinearson, "trying to string one thing to another. All you men do it and call it being reasonable. You're the most impractical people on earth, trying to make things add right, or sit in a straight line. And don't you be gallant about it, either, Rice Burnett. It's not gallant, it's just wishy-washy. She's a female thing with doe-eyes and pretty enough to turn your head, or Rinearson's. But five years from now she'll sit on the floor with fat loppin' all over her and dirt on her face.

That man Hawn knows it, too, and he's regretting his bargain. That's why he came here, because he's lonely and he can't talk with her." She nodded her head with vigor and said, "I get so aggravated listening to you men, sometimes."

Daniel Rinearson rolled his eyes at Burnett. "I get to thinkin' that maybe women use their feet to think with."

The crowd broke up in a sudden yell of laughter. People began to call back and forth over the yard as they moved homeward. Edna Lattimore paused at the fire, waiting to catch Rice Burnett's eye — and from the background Katherine Gay watched her beckon to Rice with her smile; then, as though the mood had passed or as though she had seen slowness in Burnett, she turned to Moss Rinearson, spoke to him and moved away with him into the darkness. Katherine observed Burnett's glance follow them and she tried to read him but found nothing to read. She turned to the crowd, saying good-by to the last stragglers, and discovered the massive block of Harris Eby's body before her. Somebody, she thought, had given him a drink, for he took her arm and gave it his notion of a gentle lift; she had to catch hold of his sleeve to keep her balance. He laughed at her and steered her across the yard and around the cabin into the thicker shadows.

"Katherine," he said, "I want to say . . ."

"Who's got whisky around here?"

"You a temperance woman?"

"No, I was only curious."

"Well," he said, "I wouldn't mind a temperance woman. Liquor don't mean enough to me to be an effort to give up. Tobacco's a different thing. Your father don't smoke. That your mother's idea?"

"She persuaded him."

"No," he said, "I have got to smoke. It's a comfort and I'm damned if I see what's unholy about comfort. You ain't that set against tobacco, are you?"

"I never said a thing about it."

"That's fine. Now, Katherine, I want to — "

"That your horse pitching around the other horses?"

He turned and he bent his head and searched the shadowy line of tethered animals across the yard at the meadow fence. "No," he said. "Think it's Ared's — that fiddlin' sorrel that dumped him in the Snake." He straightened himself, he looked down upon her from his height and collected his thoughts to say again what he had twice started to say.

She made a short and restless swing with her body. "There's a bite to the air all of a sudden."

"Like to see a little snow," he said. "Would remind me of home."

"Home's here now, Harris."

"All right," he said. "So I go back to my cabin and think it's home. Well, it's not quite home yet. What I been squarin' off to talk about is right along that line —"

"Somebody's calling me," she said.

He reached out and took her arms and held her still. "Be quiet a minute — don't head me off again."

"Whisky — whisky."

"No, by God, it's not whisky. It's me, and I want you to come to a stand and answer my question."

"Not tonight."

"Well, when?"

"Oh, sometime. Sometime when we're more settled."

"Never be more settled," he said. The exuberance brought on by the liquor seemed to leave him and his moment of impatience was over. "Well," he said, "I can see it's nothing you want to take up now. But I want you to think on it. I want to settle and start a family."

"I know," she said.

"Think about it." He took her arm and moved back to the yard; he looked down, half smiling, and said "Good night," and moved from the yard, an enormous shadow which took a long time to fade.

Katherine drifted to the table, coming beside Gram. Her father and Ralph Whitcomb and the Old Man and Burnett were at the fire; the other neighbors had gone. She was restless, at odds with herself. She watched the men at the fire until irritation swung her to the table and set her to work with the scattered dishes. Gram's voice came at her with a mysterious whispering.

"Pride — pride. When you eat with it, it's a stone in your stomach, and when you sleep with it your bed's death-cold. Pride's got no lips to kiss you, no flesh to cover you and keep the lonesomes away. It will give you no delight and make you no babies."

Martha Gay crossed from the cabin to the fire and began to talk to the men in a tired, half-fretful way and Gram looked on a moment and presently walked over, leaving Katherine alone at the table.

"It was a good meeting," said Gay.

"Talk, talk," said Martha Gay. "Men can't do anything without arguin'."

"Takes time," said Gay. "But we got the idea of the road started. I expected more trouble, but when Lockyear bucked it, a lot of others changed their minds to favor it." He smiled. "I hoped he'd do that."

Ralph Whitcomb said: "You're a sly man with a pious face."

"I know how to use mine enemies," said Gay. He drew a breath and passed a hand across his chest in a massaging motion. Martha Gay watched him, the pessimism of her nature taking fresh concern.

"You been doin' that lately," said Martha. "What's wrong?"

"Just a kink," said Gay. "Well, it was a good get-together. There's not really such an all-fired hurry to do road work, but if it hadn't been brought up, Old Daniel might have laid out the road where it pleased him; then there'd been a scrap, the whole settlement full of bad temper. Now he knows what we think, and he'll abide the vote. That's one thing he respects — the vote."

"They ate us clean," said Martha. "I don't begrudge it, except maybe the Provosts, who'd eat anything free if it bust them."

Whitcomb said: "Any Indians been around?"

"They've been to Rinearsons, begging, and one buck popped his head into the Kitchens' cabin and scared hell out of Miz' Kitchen. They're a poor lot. Goin' back tomorrow?"

"After I make the rounds, though there's not much sickness here. You're a healthy lot."

"We better be," said Gay with a touch of grimness. "It's a long winter yet."

The Old Man, silent on his haunches, rose and moved to the cabin without a word. Burnett swung to warm his back and noticed Katherine alone at the table; he walked toward her, "Coffee left?"

"Yes, cold," she said, and continued her work with the dishes. He got himself a cup and filled it. He filled a second cup and watched her circle the table. When she came along his side of the table he put the second cup before her. She said, "I don't want it," but he reached for her hand and laid the cup into it. She said "What do you want?" Then she laughed at him and murmured, "You — you're only trouble." She tasted the coffee and took his cup from him and threw the coffee into the pot. "Put it on the fire."

He carried the pot to the fire. Katherine followed him, settling on a log beside the flame; she propped her elbows on her knees and laid her chin in her hands, and almost at once the tawny core of the fire drew her attention and carried her a long way off. Gram and Martha Gay disappeared into the cabin. Presently John Gay went away.

Whitcomb stood a moment longer at the blaze. "When women speak of love, they mean possession and security, and these women were outraged that Hawn's squaw didn't bargain for it with Hawn."

"Is it a bargaining business?" asked Rice.

"Certainly. You heard Mrs. Millard say that men's instincts were loose. They all feel it. So they want it signed and sealed."

Katherine looked up to Whitcomb. "You're talking crazy, Ralph."

He looked at her with his smiling easiness; he glanced at Burnett and moved to his horse. He stripped it and let it go for browsing; he carried his outfit past them to the shed.

Burnett settled on the log beside Katherine. She said: "Does he do it just to tease us?"

"No."

"He saw Lucy tonight. Maybe that's it."

He moved around to the coffeepot, filled the cups and came back to the log. She nested her cup between both hands. "It was a good meeting," she said. "Except for the Lockyears. I don't like Cal. All the women are afraid of him — and a lot of the men."

"That's his fun."

"It's not right."

"Let them stop him."

She said: "No, it's not fair. Lorenzo Buck couldn't fight him."

"Lorenzo could use a bullet on him, but Lorenzo won't. That's the way Lockyear judges men — whether they'd kill or not. That's the threat he hangs over them. And they back up from it."

"No man's got the right to do that to anybody."

"Let them stop him. People that want their pride respected have got to risk their necks for it."

"You sound like Lockyear."

"We both went it alone a long time. He's still going it alone, but I'm changing — I'm a tame Tom now."

She turned to him. "You don't like it, either." As she grew interested her attitude lightened. She rested a hand on his arm, looking back to the fire with a soothed expression. Her nearness affected him and drove its momentary aggressive flash through him and he found himself remembering the many expressions her face had shown him; the practical air, the mysterious manner when she stared into the firelight, the stubborn resistance to misery, her helpless resentment toward Lavinia White's marriage, the bright side-strike of her eyes when curiosity got the better of her. Her moods were varied and lively.

"What was it like — the way you used to live?"

"Too cold or too hot. Plenty of food or none at all. Looking for a better creek to trap over the next hill. Some fighting, some drinking. Camp here tonight, camp there tomorrow. Trouble never out of your head — that was the main thing — trouble never entirely out of your head. Never was a time you didn't listen for it or look for it. It kept your bristles lifted so much that they finally got the habit and wouldn't lie down."

"That's like Lockyear," she said.

He lifted his head to listen into the night. Beyond this bowl of light lay the heavy-accented darkness and night fog hung close down and all odors were strong around them. There was no wind, no motion. He said: "Never feel safe close to a fire at night. That's part of the old business in my bones."

"But you're calmer now than when I first saw you in the wagon train. You were more like a stranger — not like a settler."

She laid her arms across her knees and bent forward to the fire. Her lips were round and idle, her whole face at peace. Light danced in her eyes and cast its red stain against her hair. "Tonight I feel at home. It was seeing the neighbors all together that did it." She turned her attention to him. "You wear a beard in the mountains?"

"Clear down to my chest. Curly."

"Couldn't be curly. Your hair's not curly."

"Was though."

She narrowed her glance to visualize his appearance with a beard. "No, I'd not like it. Don't wear one." Her next remark ran into the rest of her words, without a lift of voice and without a change of breath. "I hear most trappers had squaws."

"Common thing."

She bent for a small stick and used it to draw tracks along the ground. Once she looked back to him, the question formed and almost spoken; then she resumed her aimless pattern making with the stick.

"No," he said.

"I didn't ask."

"The hell you didn't."

"I guess I did. What if you'd had a squaw? Would you've told me?"

"No."

"That's best. These Indian women — do they love their men?"

"Tell me what that is."

She dropped the stick and let her laugh spring out. She laid her palm on his hand and closed it. "Rice — Rice." She gave his hand a rough shake. Sensation ran through him again.

"But," she said, "it can't be any different, one kind of people or another. It must be the same thing all over."

"Part of it's the same thing all over."

She dug the tip of the stick deeper into the ground. "Part — part," she said, and shook her head. Her face lost serenity. "Oh, no. There are no parts — it's just one big round thing."

He rose and kicked a log into the bright coals and watched the brilliant ash flakes stream upward; he circled the fire and studied Katherine over the tip of its flame. Her eyes were a different blue, the smile was gone. She drew herself straight on the log, shoulders squared, and she became entirely still as her thinking seemed to close in on a thought. In a moment the thought went away and she raised her eyes and smiled. He circled the fire, coming before her and standing over her.

"Why are you so restless?" she murmured. "Always restless."

"Time to go home."

"So soon? I hate to leave a fire — hate to go to bed."

He turned over the yard to his horse. She rose and followed him and stood beside the horse after he had mounted; and she cocked her head, listening into the night, to a cowbell's steady clanking in the meadow, to the undulating rumors of the creek. "Will you get tired of this, Rice? Will you pull stakes and go back to the mountains?"

"Nothing there to go back to," he said, and rode away.

She returned to the fire and clasped her hands behind her and took in long, deep draughts of the night air; a thousand odors rose from the earth in shimmering waves, and rolled in from the timber and from the hills, and the damp atmosphere blended all these into a pungent, impalpable liquor. Somebody stirred in the cabin; her mother, a coat covering her nightgown, came out to the fire and made a spurious gesture of chilliness with her hands. She had her hair braided down for the night and she tried to appear sleepy but her mind was in one of its lively worrying spells.

"What was Harris talking to you about?"

"Same thing," said Katherine.

"What'd you tell him?"

122

"To wait awhile."

Her mother's voice took on a lightly nagging concern. "Why? He's got his cabin up. He's got supplies enough to keep himself and a wife. He's ready, and I should think you'd be too. I just don't make out why you stand off on Harris like you do. When I was fifteen I prayed for a husband and a cabin of my own. I couldn't wait. I was miserable under my mother's feet. I can't understand why you're not that way. You mean to have him, don't you?"

"Yes," said Katherine.

"Well, then . . ."

"Oh, I don't know," said Katherine, interrupting the inevitable question. "There's no harm in waiting till spring — it's a better time."

Mrs. Gay shook her head. "You're not wise to make him wait if he wants to get married now. Suppose the Snyder girl got it in her head to make eyes at him? Suppose she went down to his cabin and fooled around?"

"Well, then?" said Katherine.

"It's happened before," said Martha Gay. "Men can't defend themselves very well — and if Debby Snyder trapped him away from you I'd never hold up my head again. I've been hurt already by the talk about you bein' nineteen and still single. I just don't understand why you stand off." She looked curiously at her daughter. "You've not got strange notions, have you? You don't want things perfect, I hope — moonshine and nonsense? It's well enough to talk of love. That's for people in parlors, with money and time, that's for those who can send their daughters to fashionable places, for those who don't have to make their way, scrub their own clothes and cook and raise their own children. Don't you get such notions, Katherine — they're not for you. You have got to get married and make your way. You have got to take one of the young men that's here. Harris will turn out a well-to-do man someday, and he'll not be a willful man, he'll not break your heart or your back — he'll not be hard for you to manage."

Katherine stared into the fire, saying nothing; and Mrs. Gay, knowing the futility of argument with her daughter, gave a small sound of distress and turned away. An afterthought swung her about. "Maybe Harris is good-natured, but if you keep so friendly with Rice, and people get to talkin', maybe Harris won't stay good-natured." Then she went on to the cabin. Katherine settled on her heels and began to poke at the fire, dreaming into the yellow flame.

19

COLLINGWOOD returned to his cabin late, he having stopped in at the Monteiths' for further talk. The fire was down to its last ruby coals and Lucy lay curled wide-awake on the bed. He settled on a bench, he pulled off his boots; he lighted his pipe and settled for a spell of that secretive dreaming whose signs she knew so well. He lived a great deal in his fancy; and in his fancy he was quite a man.

He said: "What did Whitcomb say?"

"Nothing, of course. Why did you send him?"

"I thought he ought to look at you again. You don't always seem well."

"Stop talking to him about me. I'm as well as anybody. I keep up my work."

Turning on the bench, he crouched to smoke his pipe and to stare into the ruddy coals. She knew, by the short shifts of expression on his face, that he was reviewing the meeting; he was remembering what he had said and the little victories of personal attention he had won. It was vanity, for he was an actor; but it was more than vanity — it was a consuming hunger to be thought well of. Sometimes it seemed to her that he fought a terrible battle with himself, for in many ways he was a small person, and perhaps he had moments when he knew it and hated himself and tried, by standing before his fellow men, to gather into him the character which he lacked. He was as transparent as glass in most things, yet in some respects he had an obscure roundabout method which made him complex to her.

"Well," she said, "I do keep up my part, don't I? Or have I failed you?"

"No, you've done well. You've had a hard time. I don't blame you for a thing."

"Where have I failed you?"

"I didn't say you had," he said; and she knew that though she might pry at him all night she could never break through the secrecy of his nature if he chose to be still.

"Stop telling anybody that I'm not well," she asked.

"I only thought I was being honest about it."

"No you didn't. You only say it so that others will say, 'What a thoughtful man and affectionate husband.'"

He gave her a short, sidewise look and stared back to the fire; his mouth settled and she thought he meant to relapse into one of his extended moody silences. But he surprised her; he became talkative. "I saw everybody tonight. We got the road business straightened out. Some of the boys bucked, but Gay and Rinearson and I more or less settled it. By the way, I asked Rinearson for a cow. Not as a gift, but as a loan till we're able to buy one."

"What did he say?"

"He would have done it, except for one thing." He gave her a fuller look, making a smile of it. "He said if you didn't dress so well when everybody else was so poor he wouldn't mind, but damned if he would otherwise."

"What did you tell him?"

"I let it go. You can't argue with Rinearson."

"You didn't tell him I make these clothes out of scrap stuff? If I like to sew, that's my affair. If I like to look well, it's none of his. Tell him that — or I shall."

"Don't do that, Lucy. It only makes hard feelings."

"Then let *him* not make hard feelings."

He shrugged his shoulders. "He means nothing by it."

She turned on the bed to look toward the ceiling; she lay still, hands folded, eyes half shut. "You always have some reason but I never get it out of you. You've got a reason for asking Whitcomb to come, too."

"Well, you could be pleasant to him."

"Why?"

"He travels a lot, he sees everybody, knows everybody. He could put in a word for me wherever he goes."

"What for?"

He surprised her again. He rose, and he tried — she actually saw him go about it — to be impressive to her. "There'll be an election next spring for the legislature of the provisional government. There'll be a man from this district. Nobody much wants it. But I want it. That's why I'd like to be on friendly terms with people."

"What good will it do you? How will you work the claim?"

"Oh, somehow."

"But what's the good of going to the legislature?"

He started to tell her something, changed his mind, and only said: "It's something to start with."

"For what?"

125

He shook his head and returned to the fireplace. For a moment she thought she had the bottom layer of George Collingwood brought to light, but it slipped back suddenly into the obscure parts of him. Then she thought: "But he's willing for me to be nice to Ralph. I'm part of his horse trade." She turned on her side, away from him. Some of his trouble began with her; very soon after marriage she had come upon that pliable and elusive streak, the shrinking-away from the harshness of even small decisions, the extreme vanity interlaced with extreme sensitiveness, the ambition coupled to a courage so frail it wouldn't endure the lightest shocks; and from then onward, their marriage had turned into the monotony of acceptance, endurance and personal isolation. She knew he felt his failure with her and perhaps this was why he wanted to be in the legislature, to show her and to show his neighbors that he was better than they believed him to be. It was sad; for her feeling for him was dead and no dramatic triumph he might achieve could substitute for the solidness he lacked. It was more than sad: it was the tragedy of a man who with bottom and forthrightness might have been great, but who was otherwise only shabby and laughable in the eyes of his neighbors. She recognized the tragedy but couldn't feel it; all she could feel was pity, and even this was gradually crowded out, as time went on, by the desperation accumulating within her. She was alone, she was unused; the wealth of spirit and passion which should have passed so freely out of her into him lay painfully clogged within her, the pressures casting a most lurid light across her fancies. She was his wife and came to him when he made his demand, but when they were through she lay with the urge to love still unquenched; gradually the fear came upon her that this urge, too long repressed, would clot into the impotent bitterness of a woman no longer able to give or to receive. Lying silent, she thought of Ralph Whitcomb and the wish to have him passed beyond restraint.

20

THE cabin was up, the rear meadow plowed, and the wheat in. Those were the first things. Afterwards Burnett sat down to arrange the endless chores in the order they ought to go; for when the peaceful mood was upon him he was the most methodical of men who wanted a recognized pattern in his work. It was December, four months until planting time, seven until wheat harvest. He needed to run fence lines, to fell cedar trees and buck out bolts from which to make posts and rails; he had to slash brush, to lay a footbridge over the creek, to hunt a spring on the hill, to build a barn and a smokehouse; he had to cut a road as far as Lattimore's through the dense stand of timber which lay between; he had to lay out his mill, build a raceway, square his timbers and begin the long drudgery of sawing lumber; and somewhere during the winter, he had to make a trip to Oregon City for supplies and to Fort Vancouver for a pair of millstones and enough strap iron to bind his wooden construction.

He built a saw pit, and one evening walked down to Mrs. Irish's cabin. "I'll need Watt for a week or two. I'll give him a dollar a day and pay you in supplies when I get stocked up at Oregon City."

Watt stood in the saw pit, under the log laid over the framework, and got the wood dust and splintered bark in his face as he guided the saw at the bottom of its cut; straddled above the log, Burnett hauled the saw up and down, traveling lengthwise with the log. A deep slab cut from four sides of the log created a square timber; from this timber he took his inch-thick boards and stacked them out to season. At the end of a week he had a hundred boards cut and, observing Watt Irish climb from the pit like a half-drowned swimmer climbing ashore, he knew he had a dead-beat boy on his hands. "We'll let that do for a while," he said, and watched Watt move homeward through the graying twilight, small and sharp-pointed body as loose as a sack of meal.

He knew what the feeling was, for he had some of it in himself and would have paid a stiff price for a drink to take the accumulated ache from his bones. He cooked supper; he milked; he built the fire till its brightness filled the room and took up the chore of planing out cedar boards for shelving and furniture. At midnight of one more of the many eighteen-hour days behind him he fried a meal to take the place of lost rest and walked along the creek to catch the sound of his stock; all the animals had drifted to the upper end of his place, liking some kind of feed they found there.

Darkness was a packed-down thing between the ridges, layer upon layer of it squeezed together by the million miles of weight above, and the thick mist rubbed his face with its cobweb tickling. In such a night the various odors of the land rose from their separate places like the bubbling water of small springs, a bit of mint smell here, the aroma of an occasional cedar, the vague pollen scent of bracken fern; and these rivulets of odor joined and became invisible creeks coursing the night, to meet other creeks of more pronounced size, the resin flavor of the firs, the acrid cast of skunk musk, the reek of smoke from his cabin fire, the effervescence of mud-rotted grasses through the meadows; and all creeks fell into one broad river of odor flowing sluggish and strong and rank and wild through the night. He turned back to the cabin, rolled into his blankets and was at once asleep.

He rose in morning's dark, and he rose stiff and cranky and drank half a pot of coffee before his mind would move or his muscles would respond. The cattle rattled across the creek and stood soft-breathing in the yard, waiting for him. He milked and went back to the saw pit; morning's damp cold shocked him and pulled his shoulders together; his footsteps were ragged prints in the crystal-beaded grass. It was Sunday and at noon he carried two big buckets of milk down the trail for Mrs. Irish and returned as far as the Lattimores' for dinner; afterwards he returned to his saw pits until dusk unrolled its gauze through the hills. When he had finished his chores he stepped into the house to make supper. He had the frying pan on the fire when suddenly the four walls of the room closed in on him and he couldn't bear the thought of his own company. He pulled the pan aside, took his gun and saddled his horse and rode to Hawn's.

Hawn heard the horse coming and was at the door, not in the frame of light but outside the cabin and shadowed against the wall. "Wondered how long it'd take you to get cabin fever. Come in. We got salt pork and beans."

"The salt's fine. I'm sweated flat."

Inside, Louisa smiled at him. She listened to Hawn talk, and the smile grew broader. She made a motion with her hand and spoke to Hawn. "She says it's a shame your bed's cold."

"That gets right down to facts."

"Women always do," said Hawn. "When a man bays at the moon and thinks it's poetry in his soul, his squaw figures different. She loads his gun and sends him out to fight or she turns down the blankets and takes him to bed. Far as she's concerned, it's one thing or the other he needs."

"Might be right."

"Might be," said Hawn. But he was quiet as he said it and there was a change in his old, free manner. They ate and settled to smoking, comfortably silent until Hawn unexpectedly said: "You think so?"

"I was only making talk, Bob. Damned if I know."

"I knew a trapper once," said Hawn. "Tab Boyer. We were up on the

128

Yellowstone and the Blackfoot jumped us and Tab got an arrow through the liver. It took him two hours to die. He wasn't afraid of dyin' — he'd lost too much blood to give a damn but kept sayin', 'I'm twenty-seven and I ain't done nothin', and now I'm dyin' and I'll never get it done.' And I said to Tab, 'What you ain't done?' and Tab put up a hand and closed his fingers around the air and he said, 'It's a pity — it's a God-damned pity. I had fifty years comin' to me and I ain't goin' to get it. I ain't goin' to do what I'm for.' And I said, 'What's that, Tab?' And he said 'I don't know but I'd sure found out, because what's eyes and ears and a brain put in a man for? Not for nothin'.' Tab was goin' out and I was curious, so I said: 'You see anything, Tab?' And he said, 'Where?' And I said, 'Across the river, where you're goin'.' He said, 'Not a God-damn' thing over there. But I see somethin' here and I wish I could live. Because livin' ain't no accident. Does a man crawl out of a woman just to die at twenty-seven with an arrow through his liver? That's no sense — not when grass grows for a reason and dies for a reason, and comes again for a reason. Grass is for buffalo and buffalo is for man, and man for somethin' else, but man's such a God-damn' fool he won't keep his part of it like the grass and buffalo do. If a man believes a thing, it's so, and he can go out and make it so, but he won't. He's got to get drunk or he's got to die before he sees it, and now I'm dyin' and what I see is no good to me, and it's a God-damned pity.'"

Hawn tapped out his pipe; he filled it again. He looked at Burnett. "You believe that?"

"I'm like Tab," said Burnett. "It comes when I'm drunk. Maybe once in a while when I'm not drunk."

"What got me," said Hawn, "was the grass and buffalo business, for that's dead true. It reasons out nice. It sort of stretches a man's thinkin', he sees these little things tie up. Like the pattern in one of Grandmaw's comforter quilts. You can't see the whole quilt — it stretches to hell and gone out there, way out. But you can see the pieces of the pattern and you can see the stitches, so you know there must be a quilt, or what's the pattern for? Like Tab said, it's not for nothin'."

"Now you're lookin' into the hole that's got no bottom," said Burnett.

"I never knew a hole without a bottom," said Hawn. "It's not in nature."

"There's no such thing as a hole without a bottom," said Burnett.

"Then," said Hawn, "this hole that's got no bottom, has got a bottom."

"There you are."

"Sure enough," said Hawn.

"All you've got to do," said Burnett, "is find the difference that makes the two things the same. Then we'll know what we're doing here."

Hawn chuckled and adjusted himself more comfortably on the floor blanket. "We got to look a little farther down that hole."

"The man that looks too far down," said Burnett, "falls in. Then he can't come back to tell us what he saw."

Bob Hawn's glance followed Louisa as she walked through the doorway into the night. "Those damned Lockyears are makin' whisky. They packed a lot of wheat from Oregon City last week. It was covered up on the pack animals but some of the kernels dropped along the trail."

"Whisky and trouble," said Burnett. He lifted himself and stood at the fire. "Didn't see much of you at Gay's."

Hawn rose and crossed to the doorway and swung his head from side to side as he made his search for Louisa. "God damn those white women, they made a ring around her and stood back and looked at her like she was an animal."

"They don't know her yet. It takes a little time."

"There ain't any more time for that. She's got their faces memorized. She'll spend a little time every day keepin' those faces alive in her mind and every day she'll make a ceremony of hating 'em." Hawn turned and moved around the room, speaking out his regret. "I wish none of you had come to this country. We were doin' fine. I had damned near gotten over being a white man, but it's all back. I'm lonely for my people, and she knows it, and things ain't the same with us any more."

"Maybe you'd better pull stakes and get away from us."

"I did that once. I came out here. You caught up. If I moved again, you'd catch up again. There's no runnin' away from nothin'."

Burnett said, "Tell Louisa thanks for supper," and left the cabin. When he was a ways down the trail he heard Hawn calling for Louisa.

The timber closed in upon the trail and Burnett rode thoughtfully on through this intense blackness, hearing the nearby rush of the creek. He crossed a small meadow whose wet grasses cast off the palest light, and entered timber again. His horse grew restive beneath him, head flung up, body tense, and at this warning Burnett lifted the rifle from the saddle and cradled it in his arms. At the upper meadow he heard his pack horses scudding around the soft earth, sent into aimless flight by something. The cattle were motionless, the cowbell had ceased to clank. He reined in, hearing nothing above the clatter of the creek and though he waited half

130

an hour he saw nothing in the night. It was not until he was in his blankets that he understood the nervousness of the animals; from the ridge came the undulating cry of a wolf.

Hawn waited for Louisa to return; and watched her come silently into the cabin and settle on the corner blanket. She looked away from him. He said, "Why are you angry?"

"I make you sad," she said. "You want your people. You want a white girl."

"No," he said.

"Yes," she said. "I saw it."

He rose up from the bench and pushed the fire into a small pile; he went to the yard and circled the house and came back to latch the door. She was in bed and when he got in beside her he put his arms about her and said, "Now I'm happy. Women are foolish. They think wrong things."

But even then her body didn't respond and he knew that she had sensed the wavering in him, the growing wish to be one of the settlers. This was why he had taken Louisa to the meeting and this was why the failure was so painful. He had tried to conceal it but the girl looked through him as though he were a window. He saw the end; even now he saw it coming forward and knew there was nothing he could do to stop it.

She made a small sound and sat up in bed. He said, "What is it?" She turned and laid herself across his chest, not crying, not speaking, not moving; she was back from her unreachable place but she was sadder than he was and this was her way of trying to tell him how it was with her. He knew they would never be closer than they were now; he knew they would never again be this close.

On Monday morning Burnett returned to the saw pit and all that week made lumber without help. When Sunday came he oiled the crosscut and hung it in the cabin. He had the one-by-twelve planks in one stack, the two-by-fours in another, with each layer of boards held from the next layer by cross boards so that air would flow through the piles and dry the boards evenly.

It was a comfort, after the long roaming years, to stand on his own land and to see these possessions, for it brought to him a revelation of the only way a man could capture the fleeting hours of his life. The footprints of the roamer faded from the dust at the first wind's puff and his breath fell into the air and was lost; but in the ax marks along the cabin logs each swing of his shoulder lay frozen, translated from nothing to something. This was what wealth meant, this trading of the impermanent days of life into the permanent things before him. He could touch one layer of boards on the pile and say, "This was what I was yesterday," and touch another and say, "this was what I was the day before." There stood his day, boards and cabin and fence rails and plowed fields; these were his hours captured and brought forward into the future for so long as he lived, and at the end of a lifetime he might look down from the ridge and see that life lying before him, each day and week and month of it visible in familiar form.

In the afternoon of that Sunday he borrowed Lattimore's wagon and oxen and set out for Fort Vancouver to get his mill wheels. Having scratched one chore from the list, the next one pressed in on him; and each particular piece of work, as its turn came, rode him as hard as the rest.

21

WHIT RINEARSON said: "That stuff scrapes goin' down." He flinched as the liquor hit his stomach; his mouth stretched tight along his teeth. He poured the last drop from cup to palm and rubbed it with a finger. It spread like oil, it had an odor which sickened him.

"You liked it last night," said Cal Lockyear. "For a pup you drink steady."

"Two cups."

"Two cups, hell," said Lockyear. "Veen died on three and you fell down on four. You were reachin' for a gun to shoot me. You get ambitious when you're drunk."

"Don't remember it," said Whit. He shuddered in the damp morning air and plunged his hands into his pocket for warmth. His pale blond hair lay coarse-matted around his skull; his eyes were flushed and the soft skin around them was darkly puffed. Lockyear laughed at him and moved to the creek with four half-filled jugs and added water enough to cut the whisky fifty-fifty. He put the jugs in the pack rig of a horse standing by. "Well, let's go."

Veen said: "I'm not goin' up there, and you're a fool if you do."

"It's all right," said Lockyear.

"Drunk Indian's a drunk Indian," said Veen.

"We'll have a little fun," said Cal. He looked at Whit Rinearson. "Comin'?"

"Sure," said Whit and got on his horse.

Morning mist rose from the narrow clearing between trees and water, and smoke lifted from the chimney in blue curls, and along the water at this hour gnats hovered in cloudy clusters. On all sides of this pocket the mountains roughly rose and the trail into which Lockyear and Whit turned was immediately smothered by the massive roundabout timber. From time to time as they ascended the hills a small meadow broke the firs and at intervals they skirted the creek at some rocky narrow place through which the choked water thundered in whiteness. Fog rolled sluggishly about them and when they struck low branches the lodged moisture fell upon them in heavy sheets.

The trail was a broad trace beaten deep into the forest mold. Lockyear's head never ceased turning as he searched the way ahead and the dark coverts to either side of him. They passed another meadow in which beaten-down sections of ground and blackened fire circles were testimony of a recent camp.

"We're bein' watched now," Lockyear said and threw his rifle across his arm. "I been at this too long not to know when an Indian's lookin' at me."

"How many up here?"

"Twenty–thirty. Don't know. They shift around."

He halted, he tilted the rifle downward on his arm. Twenty paces forward on the trail stood an Indian who seemed at first to be scarcely more than a fat boy; a second look showed him to be a full-grown man, five feet tall, fat, round-faced and dirty. His ragged hair fell somewhat below his ears; he wore moccasins, white man's pants and a short blanket shirt. He carried a carbine which he took care to point away from the two white men. He said something in his tongue.

"What's that?" asked Whit.

"Don't know. Molally, I guess." Lockyear pointed to the Indian's gun and to his own gun and shook his head. He patted his chest over his heart, he pointed to the pack horse and made a drinking motion. The Indian stood still. Lockyear said, "These people ain't smart. It wouldn't take a Crow or a Sioux long to catch on." But he waited until the Indian, waggling finger across air, turned about and took the trail at a half trot.

133

The Molala village, when they came upon it, lay in a brushy meadow beside a very small creek; it was less a village than a temporary camp of eight lodges, constructed partly of brush and partly of dressed skins, pitched helter-skelter among the alder saplings. A band of children wheeled and fled away; the little guide called forward and men and women came through the alders and out of the tents until there was a group of perhaps fifty standing in wary semicircle. The little guide made a speech, frequently slapping his chest. Lockyear said dryly: "Makin' medicine for himself."

"Scabby-lookin' lot," said Whit.

The men, on average, were taller than the chubby guide but scarcely up to the stature of either Lockyear or Rinearson. Few looked particularly muscular and most were scarred by smallpox. They were dressed in nondescript fashion, some in straight Indian style, some half Indian and half white; the women were, with few exceptions, homely, heavy and sullen. The largest man of the group detached himself from the crowd and spoke first to the chubby guide and then to Lockyear.

Lockyear dismounted and walked to the pack horse and got out a jug. He put the jug on the ground. He removed his beaver hat and ran his hand around the fur; he laid the hat beside the jug. Almost immediately the Indian spokesman began to shake his head and to talk in a louder voice; other voices rose up from the crowd to quarrel with the chief.

"Chief's been bitten by that stuff before," said Whit. "He don't want it."

"He'll bite again," said Lockyear. "Watch his eyes roll around. He's talkin' against himself. They'll all be drunker than hell in ten minutes and we'll have our pick of what's good around here."

"I don't see anything good except a couple of those young squaws."

Lockyear grinned. "You want one?"

"Not to take back."

"Didn't say to take back. Here we go."

Men broke from the crowd and moved into the lodges and came out with pint-sized Hudson's Bay tin cups; suddenly a few women ran for the lodges, returning with similar cups. They came nearer Lockyear, watching him, watching the jug. Lockyear pointed to the beaver cap. The chief said a short phrase sharply and the chubby little man turned to Lockyear and made a pushing gesture with his hands. He pointed north, made the sign of a man on a horse; pointed to Lockyear's pack animal and pointed north again.

Lockyear shook his head. The chubby man laid a hand across his

134

mouth, thinking. He turned into a tent and came out with a blue, heavy-woven blanket. He pointed to it, to the beaver hat, and once more pointed north.

"Hudson's Bay blanket," said Lockyear. "I make out they've traded their furs to the company. Well, we ain't got much to get here this time. But maybe a little drink will wean 'em from the company." He picked up the jug and held it under his arm. The gesture was misunderstood, for a young Indian gave a short shout, rushed from the circle and pulled the jug from Lockyear; he held it over his head like a scalp for the crowd to see and was immediately surrounded by men and women with their cups.

"I see a couple guns in the crowd," said Whit.

Lockyear stepped back to his horse and laid an idle arm on his rifle. "Might be a little trouble here, but when they sober up they'll come to me and sell anything they've got for another drink."

The young Indian took his drink straight from the jug and surrendered the jug. It went around, cup to cup, mouth to mouth; the chubby little man said something and pointed to the pack horse, whereupon the crowd moved around Lockyear and Rinearson; the other three jugs were taken and passed about.

"Don't get separated from me," said Lockyear. "I've seen this business before."

He moved through the group with slow care, for suddenly it was touch-and-go. These people had no resistance whatever to liquor; the moment it struck their stomachs it broke such restraints as they had and inflamed them to an unnatural pitch of anger. The first people to drink were drunk before the last people had managed to catch hold of the jugs; within five minutes the liquor was gone and every man and woman in the camp milled about in a smaller, more excited cluster. Half a dozen women rushed a man holding an empty jug. He swung the jug around him, caught one woman on the head with it and dropped her senseless to the ground; the rest of the women seized his arms and began to claw at him, tearing his clothes into shreds and entirely stripping him. They slashed him with their fingers until, shouting his misery, he broke through and rushed into the timber. The jug, rolling free on the ground, drew the crowd's attention and squaws and bucks rushed at it, fell on it and fought with silent venom for its possession. Lockyear and Rinearson got to a tent and put their backs to it.

Lockyear held his rifle steady, and seemed to find satisfaction in this

135

swift changing of people into beasts. "I said I'd show you something. Always the same. In about ten–fifteen minutes they'll start fallin'. Then it's over, but we might get rushed first. Don't shoot. Use the barrel over their heads."

"Indian skull hard?"

"No harder than a white's."

"I never hit a white man over the head."

"Try out on one of these — then you'll know."

"Brain him?"

"Hell, yes."

Part of the crowd moved toward the pack horse, searching for more liquor; the horse reared up in sudden fright at the confusion and a Molala, whipping out a knife, slit its throat in a single motion. "Now, then," said Lockyear, "that's blood and more's to follow. Watch sharp." Women wavered slow and sullen along the grass toward the tents. A pair of bucks fell into a fight over an empty jug and a knife appeared in one man's fist and left its bright red track, yard long, diagonally over the other man's body. Up the street another buck lifted a gun and fired at the crowd and somebody let out a short cry and dropped and next moment the crowd, hunting fresh trouble, came about and advanced toward Lockyear and Rinearson.

Two Molalas came crouched, came running. "Yours," murmured Lockyear. He stepped aside; he gave Rinearson a clear field and the younger man, raising the barrel of his rifle, brought it smashing down into the first Molala's head. The Indian pitched forward, making no sound; his legs squirmed a moment in reflex and were still. The second Indian gave a cry and crouched lower to rush in but as he came on his courage ran out and he wheeled away and afterwards the crowd gathered caution and its aimless interest settled on a man-and-woman fight near the creek. The woman struck steadily at the man, screaming; the man had a piece of short wood in his hand. He knocked her back, he slashed the wood downward and broke her arm and as she fell he came upon her and straddled her and beat her until she made no further motion.

A Molala man settled and crawled a short distance on hands and knees, and slowly capsized; and now the energy of these people went away and they moved in slow motion to and fro, past each other; they stepped into the creek and went down, they staggered toward their tents and one by one they disappeared or collapsed in the grass. Lockyear let his rifle sag and walked to an adjoining tent and he put his head through the flap and withdrew it, motioning Rinearson forward. He was sharp, he was laughing; he pointed into the tent. Staring through, Rinearson saw two young squaws, half upright on blankets, stare outward with an owl-round interest. Rinearson straightened; he nodded at Lockyear. "They got knives?"

Lockyear said, "Never handled a woman with a knife before?" He gave his rifle to Rinearson. "Keep watch," he said, and went into the tent and closed the flap. Whit made a walking stick of the rifle and rested his arms on it, counting the drunk-still shapes on the ground. He got as far as twenty-four and ceased to be interested. The buck he had clubbed was dead. The woman beaten by her man was dead, and there was another dead one near the creek. A very old man walked along the grass, peering into the faces below him; he raised his eyes to Rinearson, he looked away, and went on with his search.

Lockyear came from the tent in a little while. He said, "No knives." He let go with a long laugh and pushed Rinearson into the tent and for a moment he observed the old Molala and he idly lifted a gun and took a trial sight on the Indian, but presently the notion left him and he let the gun drop. A squaw, more ancient than the old man, crept from the timber and went on to the dead pack horse. She studied the horse and turned about, going from one liquor-dead man to another until she found a knife, and returned to the horse and began to cut a chunk of meat from its ribs.

Lockyear got the two saddle horses from the brush, collected the empty whisky jugs and tied them to the saddle thongs, and stopped by the dead horse to strip it of its gear. The old squaw was in his road. He laid his foot against her shoulder and pushed her backward, flat into the grass, and went on with his chore. Presently Rinearson came from the tent and the two, with jugs and pack gear loaded around them, started down the trail. Looking back, Lockyear saw the old buck staring at him; the squaw had returned to her butchering.

When they got home Veen looked at the empty jugs. He said, "Where's the other horse?"

"Indian cut its throat," said Cal.

Veen narrowly sized up the good humor he saw in both men, the flicker of deviltry, the sly joke between them. "You're a couple of God-damned fools," he said.

"I'm hungry enough to eat a gut," said Cal.

Rinearson tossed down the pack rig and said, "See you later."

"Showed you something, didn't I?" said Cal. "Want to go again?"

"Sure," said Whit, "Oregon City next."

Cal Lockyear said, "You're all right, kid," and watched Whit ride down the trail. Veen, unfavorably listening, waited until the boy got beyond hearing and suddenly was jealously angry. "Played hell up there, you two. Feelin' fine, ain't you? The kid's a jackass and he'll get you in trouble. By God, Cal, you don't learn much. You got to bust things up whenever you feel like it. You got to bust things up just for nothing. Someday it'll sure come home."

"I'm hog hungry," said Cal and went into the cabin to find himself a meal. A good humor kept with him during the afternoon. He pulled the charge from his rifle and cleaned the gun thoroughly. He sharpened his hunting knife, he cut off a chunk of bar lead and melted it and molded a pouch of shot, he tinkered with the nipple spring of his powder flask and, soon hungry again, he butchered out a chunk of jerked venison and crouched against the cabin wall to warm himself in the pale moments of sunlight, hound's body settled into a rare interval of rest, energies for a short time soothed by the morning's adventure; even his face — that lank copper-cast face with its prominent bones and slate-gray eyes — achieved a state of composure. He watched a hawk sailing its steady circle around the tip of a fir tree across the creek; he swung his head to consider the dark mouth of the trail gaping at him from the timber and his glance ran slowly along the base of the trees, pausing to explore the shadows within the trees and to witness occasional flurries of motion rippling up from the ground through the brush tops. He dredged the day for its news.

Veen came to the yard. "We better knock down a couple deer while they're fat."

"Do it tomorrow," said Lockyear.

Veen moved an old maple at the rear of the cabin and renewed his job of bucking it into small sections of wood for the smokehouse. In every partnership of men there was a wife and a husband, and Veen was the wife of this partnership, the smaller, steadier man who did the cooking, the washing, the petty chores which Cal refused to recognize. It was not only Veen's size which cast him in the role; the difference lay in that thoughtfulness which a crippled man develops and it lay to an ever greater extent in the push of Cal Lockyear's maleness. Had the two men been equally matched in vitality the partnership would long since have dissolved in a quarrel, for this kind of union — common along the frontier — depended on complementary qualities; and though two men might begin

138

such a partnership on equal terms, the inevitable struggle between personalities soon or late brought either a dissolution of the partnership or an adjustment in division of duties and authority much like that of marriage.

Somewhere short of twilight Lockyear rose to make a patrol through the timber which surrounded the house and returned for supper and stood by the fire to warm himself. By now the ease was fading from him and he was once more at the mercy of that energy which rapidly renewed itself and created its tensions throughout his body; and his mood darkened and he began to stir restlessly around the cabin floor. There was in him no cushioning layer of reflection to absorb the shock of his impulses; there was only the terrible immediacy of force felt and act performed, and when he could no longer bear the cabin's confinement he seized his gun and ranged the hills, half bent over, half trotting, pausing to crouch and to listen, prowling. He came to the edge of the Indian camp and lay flat, listening to Molala voices inside the tents, and when this had satisfied him he returned home and fell asleep. In first daylight he was in the hills again. He shot two buck deer and dressed them and packed them to the yard; he helped Veen butcher and slice them for curing in the smokehouse. He was preoccupied and scarcely heard Veen speak.

"You workin' up to somethin' again?" Veen asked.

Cal went into the cabin, put a chunk of jerky into his pocket, took his gun and started for the lower trail.

Veen called: "Where you goin'?"

He didn't answer; the flood rush of energy was again in control of him, carrying him forward to its certain explosion. He walked with a nervous and loose-gaited stride, head pitched down but completely aware of his surroundings. He passed Hawn's, ignoring the redheaded man, who sat in the doorway and watched him without comment; he moved on through the timber toward Burnett's and as he came near the latter's place a notion arrested him at the clearing's margin and for a short time he listened to the ringing of Burnett's ax somewhere near the cabin. Then he backtracked on the trail — and moved forward again, deliberately setting his weight into the trail's soft soil to produce a clear print; thereafter he turned to his right and then went quietly up through the timber of the hillside, climbing the slope until he had cut another trail, running from Burnett's meadow into the higher ridge; he then descended this trail, once more leaving deep-cut moccasin prints in the dirt as far as the meadow's edge. Stepping into the brush beside this new trail, he settled to observe Burnett splitting rails in the yard.

Burnett's habits, Lockyear knew, were still a mountain man's habits; he would watch for signs and as soon as he saw these tracks he would trace them out and try to read the story. Lockyear found the idea amusing and meanwhile kept his eyes on Burnett.

The latter drove his wedges into a cedar log, split it, quartered it and reduced the quarters to rails. He laid the rails in the growing pile and straightened for a moment's rest, his glance going idly around the meadow; that was the mountain man's suspicion still working in Burnett, never trusting silence, never trusting calm. He let his ax fall and walked beyond the cabin and toward the creek, passing from sight. *Drink of water,* Lockyear thought, and waited. Burnett came into view at the edge of the creek, and dropped to his belly. Lockyear squirmed his heels into the ground and made himself comfortable. He calculated the distance from this spot to the house; he reached forward to snap a huckleberry bush for better view, and saw Burnett move back to the yard. Burnett got his sledge, tapped a wedge into a new cedar log — the metal ringing like a sharp-struck bell — and straightened to begin his steady swinging. Lockyear raised his rifle and took a long aim on Burnett's upper body, below the shoulders and above the small of the back; he steadied the gun, not following Burnett's motions but waiting for Burnett's body to come into his sights. His face assumed a dry and preoccupied hunter's cast; he checked his breathing, and in his mind he made the shot to his satisfaction and lowered the gun; then he rose, retreated into the timber and completed his circle. Reaching the Indian trail, he passed through the timber between Burnett's and Lattimore's.

He went as far as the Lattimore clearing. Flattened behind a tree, he observed Lattimore chinking the outer cabin wall with mud. It was cold work on a raw day and Lattimore, never a forceful man, plainly went at the job with half a heart, frequently pausing to slap his long arms around the thin shirt he wore. Mrs. Lattimore washed clothes at the back of the cabin and Edna was inside, now and then passing across the cabin's doorway. Considerably down the trail, from the direction of the ford, Lockyear made out a solitary rider coming on, a short man riding a thin horse. The short man presently turned out to be Lot White and he, dismounting before the cabin, spoke to Lattimore and to Mrs. Lattimore and went inside.

From his position, Lockyear had a poor view of the inside of the doorway. He moved along the edge of timber until the opening was better squared before him and through it he managed to make out the blocky shape of Lot White and the figure of the girl. Lot had removed his hat. Lot's arms rose and spread themselves and fell as he talked.

Damn fool's deliverin' a sermon, thought Lockyear.

He continued to observe this scene until both White and Edna, shifting position, got into a corner of the cabin beyond his view. Making a gesture of discontent, Lockyear retreated a quarter-mile along the trail, toward Burnett's. Here he turned into the heavy brush and threshed around it; he began to beat it down with his feet, snatching and breaking the brush with his hands; he tramped back and forth across an area as long and as wide as his body and he removed his blanket coat and spread it over the beaten spot as a mattress; and then he stepped to the edge of the trail and, placing his glance westward through the dark aisle toward Lattimore's he drew a rough breath and settled to a waiting. His body continued restless and tense and occasionally, as though the waiting were almost unbearable, he struck his fist against the coarse-ribbed bark of the fir beside which he had posted himself.

22

"DAUGHTER," said Lot White, "I have come to speak o you."

Edna turned from her breadmaking chore at the table to give him her moment of smiling attention. Her hands were dusted with flour, her face had small patches of it, placed there when she pushed back the wayward bits of hair falling over her forehead. She wore a loose dress, the sleeves cut off between shoulder and elbow, and the neck low enough to show the upper half-moon of her breasts. She noticed the brief conflict of man against preacher within Lot and was amused by it, and let Lot see her amusement.

He said, "Why don't you wear more clothes?"

"Because I'm working and it's warm."

"You ought not stir men," he said. "They're easy stirred."

"Then let them not trouble me."

"You know the ways of men," he said. "No woman around here knows 'em better."

"Men enough have tried to teach me."

"You brought 'em on to it," he said.

"They needn't come my way if they don't want to."

He removed his hat and laid it on a chair and he faced her with a single-minded certainty as to his duty. He was powerfully built but short and when he stood before her she seemed slightly taller, and this bothered his vanity enough to make him rise a little on the toes of his boots. So poised, with his stubborn nature showing itself in the bulldog chin and in the zealot blue of his eyes, he was to Edna a somewhat ridiculous figure. He was a man, not the least trace of saintliness about him. He had eyes enough to see her charm and to be bothered by it; lacking any sort of education to set him apart from his neighbors, as Ralph Whitcomb was set apart, he had no mystery in him to impress her.

"They come your way, daughter, because they're men. They can't help it."

"Then it's none of my business."

"God made you to haul the water and hew the wood. He made your flesh to close about man, he made you to be the tabernacle of man's faith. But the snake crept in and now the devil finds his best hidin' place right there in the creases of your body."

Edna ceased to smile. She was not offended, but her intense practical-ness rose against Lot White's rush words. "That's foolish talk."

"Well, they come awhorin' after you, don't they? They do, don't they?"

"Don't come tryin' to drive any snakes out of me. Go drive your snakes out of men."

"It won't do. Man's frail that way. Woman has got to stand above him. Woman's got the curse of wantin', same as a man, but woman's got the glory of turnin' the want into somethin' else. That's what you got to do, daughter."

"I don't see any curse on it," said Edna. "How'd you get your wife if you didn't want her? Was that a curse?"

Lot White settled on his heels. "Never you mind about me and my wife."

"Then don't you mind about me," said Edna. "I saw you looking at me and I know what you were thinking."

"Cover yourself up," shouted Lot White, "so men ain't tempted. Don't swing your hips every time a man comes along. Stand still and let 'em pass by. You got Eve all over you. The devil's in your eyes now amockin' me."

"That's smoke stinging my eyes."

142

"You got too many men around here thinkin' things. Get yourself married, and do it soon. What you need to take the hell out of you is ten babies nine months apart."

"When I get married," said Edna, "it won't be to a man wastin' his time in other people's business." She bent forward, tolerating Lot White, even sympathetic toward him. "Why," she said, "you must be old — you must be forty-five; and still you go rammin' around like a young man bad off for something."

Lot White's color thickened. His pale eyes flickered, his lips grew thin between pushing jaw and heavy nose. He pointed directly at Edna Lattimore's face and lifted his voice. "Devil — devil, I see you in there and I'm agoin' to get you out!" He seized the girl around the waist, he kicked her smartly across the legs with his foot and made her cry out and stumble against him; he sank to his knees and brought her down with him. She slapped at him, leaving flour prints around his coat. She said, "You old fool, let me go! Poppa — Ma — come in here!"

Lot drowned her cry with his roaring words. "God, come down here — come down here this minute! Here's the devil. I got my two hands around him, and I smell him all through this room — I smell the brimstone, I smell the burnin'."

"That's wind blowing ashes out of the fire," said Edna. "Let go me."

He held her when she tried to rise; and since she was a strong girl he was lifted half from his knees by her force and shifted around on the floor. He grew crimson; perspiration formed on his upper lips. He flung his words about the room. "O Lord, I have got him — come now, come quick! Rid this girl! I got my arms around him. Use my arms, Lord. Send down your lightnin' bolt. Send it right through me. Paralyze my arms, Lord, I don't mind, but get the devil out of this woman." Edna walloped him on the face. She got hold of his hair and twisted a hank of it until he squirmed. "Damn it, girl, don't do that! Lord, he's usin' her fingers to get at me! I will stand it. I'm your servant, but how long I got to stand it? Hit him hard so I'll know. Make her cry out when he leaves her body. Then I'll know!"

Mrs. Lattimore ran through the cabin's back doorway, alarmed by the outcry. She stopped, she called: "What you adoin' there, White?"

"I'm tryin' to get the devil out of your daughter!"

"Oh, God," screamed Mrs. Lattimore, "how'd he get there?" She flung her apron over her head and began to cry. Lattimore, slower moving, stepped through the front door.

143

"What the hell's goin' on here?" he said.

"The devil's got her," said Mrs. Lattimore. "Lend Lot a hand."

"It looks to me like Lot's got her," said Lattimore. "You got anything in you, Edna, you ain't supposed to have?"

"The devil!" shouted Lot.

"Don't see a thing," said Lattimore and broke into a long laugh. "If this ain't the damn'dest sight I ever saw. Hang tight, Lot, you're agoin' to get bucked off."

"Lord," shouted Lot, "show me a sign!" That was the end of his calling — for Edna, gathering outrage, began to fight him. She loosened him with a pair of hard slaps to the face; she put her arms around him, twisted him and threw him to the floor and lay crosswise over his squirming body. She drove her sharp elbow points on his chest and pressed down with her weight. He tried to roll her body around and get it beneath him but she was too much weight for him. They were both silent, both stubborn, both breathing hard; her hair came down across her face and she squirmed herself tighter to him when he tried to roll her away and at last she got part of her body over his face and used it as a pillow to shut off his breathing. He began to kick his legs at her. Mrs. Lattimore dropped her apron from her eyes and seized a broom and struck at Lot while Lattimore, sagged against the doorframe, laughed until he had to support himself. Lot released his grip and Edna got to her feet.

"You plain fool," she said. "You old, ignorant, interfering fool! Wait till I tell this story around."

Lot rose. He looked at his coat, he ran a hand around his face, he drew a great breath to calm himself. "Daughter," he said, "I'm tempted to use my fists and beat the devil out of you."

"Now, then," said Lattimore, "you've had fun enough and that's all."

Lot White got his hat. He held it between his hands and looked long at it, the stubborn quality fading slowly from his face. "It was too strong for me. I wrestled, but it was too strong."

"You didn't get any help from the Lord, either," said Edna.

"It wasn't time. When time's right, he'll come. And I will call till he does."

"Well, just do your calling somewhere else," said Edna.

Lot stared at her, slowly shaking his head. "Devil's found the best place of all, right in you. He'll make use of you, too. Someday when you're clear of him, you'll know it, if he ain't ruined you by then."

He left the house, got on his horse and for a moment sat undecided. He

144

had meant to go on to the Hawn's, but he had failed here and his energy was spent and finally he turned back on the trail. As he rode he remembered that, looking on this girl, he had felt a carnal impulse and for the first time a hole opened in his armor of self-certainty. He recalled he had shouted for the Lord's assistance in the loudest voice he owned and had got no response. "It wasn't time," he said. "I got no right to ask questions about it." But the robustness of his faith was shaken and he found himself wondering. "I been a good servant, ain't I, Lord? Ain't I worthy? You goin' to pass me by for some other servant? What ain't I done that I ought to have done? Let me know — let me know. Don't go away from me, don't go 'way, Lord."

23

NOTHING disturbed Edna for long. By the time she had combed her hair and washed her hands she had ceased to be angry with Lot White and she returned to her breadmaking and found herself laughing. "If he wasn't a silly sight!"

"You sure can wrestle," said Lattimore and went back to the yard.

Mrs. Lattimore gave her daughter a strange look. "You sure get men stirred up in funny ways, but I never before saw one stirred up that way."

"He's a fool," said Edna. She separated the dough and fashioned the loaves; her face was sweetened by humor. She was pleased.

"All men are fools," said Mrs. Lattimore. "But they make fools out of us, too. What you been doin' to Lot?"

"I guess he's just interested in my soul," said Edna and looked at her mother and laughed again.

"Old boar," said Mrs. Lattimore. She tilted her head to consider her daughter in a worried, admiring manner. "You can just look at a man and do it. I was like you. I had 'em crazy, too. No girl had a better time, right up to the last." Her voice acquired a light melancholy. "But don't you wait too long. Popular girls always do. You know what, baby? When you're young you don't like to let go the fun."

"Work and trouble comes soon enough," said Edna.

"That's what I thought — that's what we all think. And when you get married that's the end of it for sure. Nothin' but work, nothin' but babies, and the old man snorin' in bed, not the same man he was when he sparked you any more. It sure ends fast. You want to hang onto the fun and I don't blame you. But you pass good men by, and they marry somebody else, and pretty soon you get older and you get scared, and you take somebody half as good as the ones you could of had."

Edna was thoughtful, her lips were pursed; her fingers made spatting sounds on the bread dough. Her mother murmured: "Who you want most?"

Edna shrugged her shoulders, "Oh, I don't know."

"Yes you do. It's Rice. You better watch out for that Katherine."

"I don't care," said Edna.

"Yes you do."

"No, I don't care. It could be Moss, too."

"Those Rinearson's are thrifty. They'll all do well, except Whit."

"I don't care about that either," said Edna.

"You better care. You want to live like Lattimore and I have lived? Nothin' — nothin' — never nothin'? You think I ain't been ashamed in front of other women most of my life? The poor never get so dumb they can't feel bein' poor, and no woman ever gets over havin' a shiftless man."

"It's not been that bad," said Edna.

"I could have borne it better," said Mrs. Lattimore, "if I hadn't known that every neighbor we ever had laughed at us behind our backs. Don't you make that mistake. God, I wish women could know when they're young what a man's goin' to be like later. Pig in a poke. The fancy ones say nice things and they fool you, and they turn out poorly. The plain ones you don't want but they wind up well off and their kids have fine things and their wives look down on you. Don't you do it. You got it in your power now to pick what you want. You ain't goin' to have it long, but you got it now. You think of yourself and you pick right."

"All right," said Edna.

"They'll take what they can for nothin'. They're all like that. If they can't get it for nothin' then they'll do it the way a woman wants, but not till she makes 'em do it. You got to be awful hard, Edna, because it's so easy to be soft, and men know it, and they try."

"All right," said Edna, smiling.

"Well, don't forget it," said her mother, sharply. Then she said, "I wasn't born yesterday," and returned to her washing in the back yard.

Edna molded the last loaf into its pan and laid a damp cloth over the pan. She washed her hands and stood in the room's center, thinking of other things to be done; but she had lost interest and stepped to the front

146

doorway and stood there with restlessness working at her. She hadn't seen Burnett for two days; except for Lot White and her father, she had seen no man for two days and this made her lonely. She had too much liking for people to be happy when left by herself and moreover her own situation increasingly troubled her. She didn't need her mother's reminder of time passing and chances lost; these things were frequently in her mind. Neither did she need coaching from her mother, since her own experience was ample; but no matter how much she knew and no matter how skeptical she might sometimes be, the pressures within her were greater than any wisdom she might acquire, and these forced her to a decision. If her realism rejected the notion that love was registered in heaven, binding one man and one woman to a full and happy life, and if she sometimes rebelled at the narrowness and monotony and drudge-labor and blind chance of marriage, still the insistence of her tissues drove her to it. There was no rose-glow within Edna to soften the forty years she saw coming; she viewed the marriages about her, the injustices, the stolid acceptance, the accumulated resentments, the poor matchings, the rare pleasures, the things illy hidden; and these she transferred to herself and saw her days in much the same pattern. She could smile about it, she could be sad about it, but rarely could she permit herself to dream of anything better.

It was early afternoon. Her mother's knuckles drummed a steady rhythm on the washboard and her father had curled himself in the shed and was asleep. She looked at the sky to judge the weather and left the cabin, calling back: "I'm going to Rice's."

She traveled rapidly along the timbered Indian trail, paying no attention to her surroundings. Her curiosity was all for people and in people she found a fascinating variety; nature — trees or animals or the changing colors of the earth — interested her very little and roused neither poetry nor speculation within her. She had Burnett on her mind; she was thinking of the things she might say to him, of all sorts of small stratagems to soften the gentleman's streak he frequently raised against her. Most men, but not all men, had some of that gallant streak. So far as she could make out it was an illusion they created to make their dream the more desirable, to clothe the raw act of possession with some sort of golden gauze. She didn't believe in it and frequently laughed at it, yet she had much earlier learned that it was a weapon to be used against men when they grew ardently unmanageable; they could be restrained by a word or a look which threw them back on their honor. She admired the quality in Burnett and was flattered to hear it in his voice when he spoke to her, but as time went on she grew impatient and now, walking along, she tried to understand him better so that she could bring him on. Honor was well enough, but it had nothing to do with living or eating or making babies.

The trail took her around a bend and, raising her glance from the ground, she saw Lockyear ahead, one shoulder against a tree, gun half lifted at some object in the timber. On this he appeared to have his attention when she reached him and stopped. "What's there?" she asked.

"Was a bobcat. Gone now."

"They harmless?"

He nodded. "Nothing around here to trouble you this early in the winter. Later, take care walking through the place — there'll be wolves and cougar around, hungry enough to jump." He lowered his gun and his rough gray glance struck her and she saw how tense he was behind his seeming idleness. She guessed at once that he had been waiting for her and her sureness came back and she watched him with her covert smiling. Recognizing the amusement, he turned his attention to the timber with a curtness that offended her. She moved on.

Yet she could not quit him this way, no matter what her better judgment told her. Her curiosity was too much stirred and her need to have better command of him too urgent. She swung and caught his eyes on her; that revived her amusement. "Oh, no. It was no bobcat that brought you here."

"No," he admitted coolly, "it was no bobcat." He stared at her gravely, observing the willful certainty upon her and the old, old knowledge harbored in her eyes. "I've been here a couple hours, waiting for you."

"How'd you know I'd come?"

"Sooner or later you'd come."

"Might have been days."

"I can wait days if my mind's made up," he said. He set his gun against the nearby tree and faced her. "I shouldn't have kissed you."

"It didn't do you any harm," she said tartly. "But don't blame me for it."

"You don't know me," he said.

"Ah," she said skeptically, "you're no different than the rest. I know what's in your head right now."

He looked beyond her, his powder-colored eyes catching the low light seeping into the woods. He was for that short time unusually thoughtful.

148

He brought his attention back to her. "This is what I came here to tell you. If you've got no interest in me — pay no more attention to me at all. None of your looks or your smiles, nothing of that kind to give me notions. If it's only fooling, as you do with other men, I want none of it. I don't fetch and carry like these settler boys. I don't dance in and dance back like a trained bear. Men have found me dangerous when they crossed me. You'll find me the same way if you're just havin' your fun. I say it again to you, let me alone if you mean nothing."

She tossed up her head, prepared to be high with him, for her pride was offended by his blunt speech; but as she studied the combination of intensity and stubbornness he displayed she changed her manner. Curiosity bested her again — curiosity and that heavy appetite which a man's interest always set into motion. She said, half irritated and half kind, "Don't put yourself in my way and you'll not be troubled."

"A woman's got a thousand tricks," he said; "a man's got damned few. Use none on me or you'll regret it."

She gave him a narrowed glance, and her sense of intrigue was strong within her; and suddenly — to challenge him or perplex him or keep him further in excitement — she said, "I'll do whatever comes to my mind," and laughed at him.

He seized her arm, whirled her and caught her at the waist, dragging her back to the tree and past it into the brush and to the beaten-down place where the blanket lay. She fought with him, not speaking or crying out; she fought with her hands and with her feet, she tried to drive her elbows into him and to butt her shoulders against him. He got her to the blanket and released her. "Stop it," he warned, "or I'll knock you down."

As soon as she noticed the blanket coat on the ground she went at him again, compelled not only by anger but by the outrage of a woman who, however generous she was, had always been in command of herself. What Lockyear violated was her deep-rooted sense of mastery over men. She arched her fingers and clawed his face, she kicked him on the legs, she seized his reaching arm and bit into it. Then he got her around the waist and threw her roughly to the blanket and pinned her arms and laid a knee lightly against her stomach. "Stop it," he said. He bent down to kiss her; she threw her head into his nose and lips, drawing blood. He slapped her twice full-force across the jaw.

That was the end of her fight. She said, "Oh, no," and closed her eyes and rolled her head aside.

He got her beneath the shoulders and shook her and he said in a rising voice, "I don't trust you. You've got every trick there is. Open your eyes — don't play possum." She said nothing and his voice came at her, still rising, growing rougher. "Stop playin' with me. You're not hurt."

When he slid his hands to either side of her face she opened her eyes. He was quite close to her, so close that she noticed for the first time the smallness of his lips against the rest of his face, the suggestion of the sensuous and the savage in them. There was no peace anywhere on his features, no light, no sympathy, no relief from the combination of self-centered anger and melancholy. He stared at her. He murmured, "Do what I tell you. Always do it." He was gentle at this moment. He lowered his face and kissed her with a lightness that puzzled her; but she saw the anger move cloudy over him again. "Give me something back." That was the end of his gentleness. He dropped his mouth on her and bore down, rolling it back and forth over her, shaking her with his arms, giving out queer half-grunted sounds, and when he failed to move her from her passive silence he raised himself on his arms and cursed her.

"Have I got to beat it out of you? Have I got to strangle you?" Then that gust of anger passed and he put his cheek against her head, whispering, "If I were a dumb ox I'd never look at you, but I've got to have you. There's no man ever looks at you that don't wish he had you, and I'm the same. No, I'm different. The rest of 'em have not got the nerve to do more than wish. Come up to me now."

She met his self-centered stare and remained silent beneath him. He dug his fingers into her shoulders and wrapped his arms about her and drew her to him; he let her drop back and the bilked desperation went through him with its particular agony. He groaned and smashed his fist into the earth beside her; he fell silent, his breath hard-laboring against her; he grew quiet and talkative. "You could pick me up in the hollow of your hand and carry me to hell and gone," he said. "What's my life now? It's walkin' through these hills. It's eatin' and sleepin' and growin' older. It's a damned trap and I'm a animal inside a fence, goin' round and round till my feet hit the trap, and then I'm done. I have got more in me than ten men but it won't come out. There's nothin' to bring it out. They think I'm a wild man. Sure I'm a wild man. If I was happy to see nothin', think nothin', do nothin' — I wouldn't be wild. I have got to have you."

He bent down to kill her again and his talk came muttering from him. "You want a better man than Moss. Or Burnett. I'd wear out that body

—that's what you want. I prowl these hills same as a wolf. I can walk softer than a wolf. You come with me and there'll be no prowlin'. Listen to the way I talk. You can hear the creek in me, can't you? You can hear the wind and the rain. Lightnin's in there, too, and all the damned Sioux in the hills hellin'. You can even hear murder if you listen for it but don't listen for it and it won't be there. Come up to me now. Turn into me. Give me somethin' when I kiss you. Then you'll know what I am." He settled on her, waiting; but when he realized the waiting wouldn't bring anything from her, he flung himself back and rose cursing. He seized her by the arm and hauled her to her feet; he gave her a shove that unbalanced her. She caught herself and walked out to the road and stood still, looking back at him.

She was no longer afraid of him but neither was she indifferent toward him. She was a little bit dazed by a handling far more intense than any other man had displayed; and though she resented his domineering manner, her appetite, much more powerful than her reason, responded to Lockyear. She said softly: "Why didn't you do what you meant to?"

"I don't want anything. You've not got it. You're nothing to me. It's all on your face. It don't go any deeper. You're a board wall painted pretty, but there's nothing behind the wall."

She watched him steadily; "You don't know," she said.

"I know."

"No you don't," she said. "You're like all the rest."

"I'm not like any man you ever ran into," he said. "By God, I'd get tired of that smilin' that don't mean anything. I'd probably trade you for a squaw."

She started to speak — and checked herself, and went down the trail toward her house. Twenty feet away she heard him call her; she turned.

"Next time do better by me."

"What next time?"

"I mean to have you," he said. "You're trying to fool with me now, same as you do with everybody else. It's too late. I won't be fooled with. I am going to teach you how it is."

She went on. At the trail's bend she looked over her shoulder to find him still following her with his glance; then she moved out of his sight, straightening and brushing her clothes; she touched her cheek and felt the tenderness where he had struck her and her eyes narrowed at the memory. She crossed the meadow to the cabin.

Her mother said: "Quick trip." Then she gave her daughter a closer inspection. "What bruised your face? It's all red."

"Walked into a branch," said Edna.

She went on with her work, silent and preoccupied. In late afternoon she left the cabin, arms crossed before her, and traveled the trail idly toward the Irish ford, walking simply to be walking. It was dusk when she got back. Her mother said: "Where you been?" She shook her head and was silent through supper; she did the dishes and, still saying nothing, she slipped on a heavy coat and stepped into the night. Her mother came to the doorway, calling after her. "Where you goin' now?"

"Rice's."

The earth breathed its fog around her, its silky sensations tickling her face. In such still, thick air the creek seemed farther away and the hoarse rustling music of the frogs came muted about her. Distant in the timber she heard a lumbering bear move carelessly through the brush but she had no concern. Beyond the bend she caught the blurred winkling of Burnett's cabin light and soon came to his door and knocked on it. At the sound of his voice she opened the door and found him lying dressed on his bunk, so turned that the firelight fell on a book he had been reading. "You're comfortable," she said, and smiled at him. "And you oughtn't be. What's that you've got?"

"*The Miller's Practical Guide.* I'm figuring how to put this thing together."

"Just let the stones grind against each other. Is it hard?"

"You want flour or you want cracked chicken feed?"

"It's not those things I want. You're practical tonight. You always practical?"

"No."

"When?"

"Now," he said.

She watched him a moment. "You're fooling me." She looked to the floor. "You've got the floor in. It's nice and smooth."

"Sawed blanks instead of split logs. Then I used the plane. No splinters."

She settled on the edge of the bunk and reached down to unlace her shoes; she moved her feet back and forth on the floor. "That's good — that's good," she said, and closed her eyes. "I'd never wear shoes in here." She had her back to him; he hooked his arm around her waist and she swung her head and looked down. She was serious, she was

152

alert. He tightened the pressure of his arm. She said, "You're different."

He drew his arm away. She laughed at him and seized his arm and replaced it where it had been. "You're slow." He pulled at her, drawing her back against him. She resisted him gently, she mocked him, murmuring: "I let you have something and now you're brave."

"Edna . . ."

"Yes — don't talk — yes." She turned about, very easy in her motions, rolled herself on the bunk and settled comfortably against him.

"Cold?"

"No. Things don't bother me. You want to talk now?"

"No." He felt the tremor of amusement in her body. "What's that?"

"It's a sure cure for talk. All those funny things in your head go right away. You're just happy. That ought to show you something, Rice."

"What?"

"You make too much out of things. It's just this. There's nothing else."

He didn't answer and presently she said: "Don't you think so?"

"Must be a few other things. People can't stay in bed fifty years."

"Oh, working and raising a family, and a dance now and then, and worrying about money, and fighting sometimes. Sure. But you know what I mean. I mean hunting for something that's not there. I used to take a needle and pick away the center of a daisy just to see where it began. When I got it picked away there wasn't any beginning. It was all gone. That's what I mean." She settled closer to him. "I could go to sleep."

"Go ahead and sleep."

"Then I wouldn't wake up till morning."

"Think so?" Then they were both laughing and in a rough gust of affection she drew her arms around him.

"Proud of yourself," she said. She was warm and heavy; her heart beat steady against his chest, her mouth settled into the side of his neck; she patted him much as a mother would soothe a baby. She was sleepy, she was restless. "Talk to me."

"You don't like talk."

"Not before. It just drives me crazy, waiting while you talk. Now I like it — afterwards."

"You're good."

"I know it." Then she said, "Oh, you mean the other kind of good, nice good, afraid good, lady good? No. I'm just what I am and you can't make me out anything else. Talk to me."

"Beautiful Edna."

"Ah, that's dreaming. You're only seeing what you want to see. Men say that to girls before they're married. They don't say it to their wives. I'm not ugly but I'm not beautiful."

He said: "Who'd wear out first?"

"That's years off. There's lots of time to do this."

"Time's not a steady thing. You can't depend on it. One time on the Sonora Desert my outfit marched all day in the sun. Five men died. I remember that. I remember a few other things that happened to me. I'll remember this. This hour. That's all we've got — a dozen or two dozen things that stick. Add those things together and maybe they covered a month of our lives. All the important things lumped into a month. The rest of our lives — maybe forty years — we don't do much worth remembering."

"Don't. Don't think like that. Don't think. How many other times, like this, with other girls, stick in your mind?"

"I don't know."

"Everybody lies about that."

"Same reason everybody wears clothes."

"You believe in Adam and Eve?"

"I think that's one way of saying there was nothing bad until people made sin in their heads."

"Old people. It's always old people that say things are bad. This isn't bad. I don't feel it that way. You don't either, do you?"

"No."

She was silent a moment. Her hand, so steadily tapping his shoulder, fell still and he sensed a change move through her; he sensed it in her motionlessness, in the currents flowing out of her; it was as though a damper came down to shut off the warmth. She said: "You've changed. I mean, now you're sure you can have me. Like a wife."

"No," he said.

"Now it's easy, no trouble at all."

"No," he said, "that's not it."

She lifted herself to an elbow and put her hand against the side of his face and turned it into the light; she was solemn, she was critical. She gripped his hair and lifted his head and dropped it, murmuring, "Just

154

easy, no trouble. Damn, damn you. Oh, Rice." She settled against him. "I ought never have let you have it."

He held her in. "That's not it," he said.

"I guess it's just me," she said. "But I can't help being what I am. If I thought I was wrong maybe I'd change. Maybe not — I don't know. I think about old people. People that don't do this any more. You see any of them make love, or look at each other, or rub together, or anything? No. It goes away when they're old. Those words they said about love being forever — I wonder what they think about those words now? It don't last that long. It goes when this goes. Then they just live together and the things they said are silly."

As he held her he realized he had lost some of her and he remembered what Hawn had said about Louisa going across the boundary, beyond reach. It was the same here. *They're all Louisas,* he thought. He got the notion that she had removed herself from him, had turned to look back at him in a new light; that suddenly she had discovered something in him she hadn't noticed before. There was a sense of waiting in her strong enough to pull at him, and as time went on, she motionless in his arms, the feeling grew into a strain.

She broke it at last by a short motion back from him, by an impatient rising to her elbow. She looked at him in a way that was absent-minded, distant from him. She said, "You're funny — you'll always be," and when she left the bed and moved across the room he felt he had failed her.

"Come back," he said.

"I'm going home."

"Come back."

"Talk, talk. No."

She was preoccupied and she had a different expression on her face — settled, tired, determined. She said, more to herself than to him, "No use wasting time on what won't happen. There's not that much time to waste."

He got up. "I'll take you home."

"You don't need to."

He said nothing. He freshened the fire while she put on her shoes; he left the cabin and went across the meadow with her, and trailed her through the timber as far as Lattimore's clearing. When he put his arms around her he received from her the impression that she was impatient with him. The warmth and willingness weren't there. He had meant to kiss her but he drew back embarrassed and even her quick smile didn't help, and the kindness of her words made him feel too young. "People don't change. A lot of misery comes from thinking they do."

"What's that mean?"

"Nothing. Did you like me tonight?"

"My God, Edna, what a hell of a word for it. I wish . . ."

"I know."

"I wish you did."

"Ah," she said, "you're just trying to make something plain into something complicated. I'm glad you liked me, though. You should have. You had your way. Remember — you had your way. That's what you wanted and you got it — but you don't know what you want. Don't forget — you had your way. Good night."

She went on before he had time to answer. Going back through the timber, he felt the barb of her last remark work itself into him and he realized then he would never shake it free. The remark was unfair. She had been willing — it was her way as much as his way. It was even on both sides. *No*, he thought, *it never is. Makes no difference whether a man's in love with a woman, half in love with her, or not at all in love with her. Once he gets that thing from her, there's no giving it back. The thing's done and he's mixed up with her. From that time on, he's accountable.* Lying with him on the bunk, she had waited for him to understand it. He had failed her.

Her father was asleep; her mother waited up. She gave Edna a searching study. "What was it?"

"Nothing," said Edna.

"Oh, God, baby, I told you not to — I told you not to. You went to him too much."

"I won't be what I'm not," said Edna.

"If he hurt you, baby, I'll go slap his face raw. You're as good as any girl around here."

"That's not it," said Edna. "I'd just get weary of being something I couldn't be, and he'd get tired of me as soon as he found he'd fooled himself and he'd think I'd fooled him and I couldn't stand that."

Mrs. Lattimore came over and put her arms around her daughter. She was sentimental, she was half in tears. "My poor baby — my poor baby. I'd like to cut his damned heart out." Edna said nothing and in a short while Mrs. Lattimore drew back and gave her daughter a curious glance. "Why don't you just let it go and have a cry?"

"What for?" asked Edna and turned away.

"Sometimes," said Mrs. Lattimore, "I think you got no feelin'."

"I've got feeling all right," said Edna in a rare moment of candor. "I've got so much feeling that I like men too much. I'm just sloppy with feeling. I know what I am. I don't hold back like Katherine does. What's she? No different than me, but Rice thinks she is, because she holds back. If I held back he'd think I was different too. But what's the good of that? It wouldn't last. Afterwards he'd still have his funny ideas. She's just as much a slut as any."

"Baby — baby," said Mrs. Lattimore, "don't say it."

"Well," said Edna sullenly, "there's that in all of us and I won't pretend, like she does. If it's there, it's there. I didn't put it there and I won't cry about it. I won't be ashamed of it either. I'll get married to a man that's satisfied with me just like I am. I'll be good enough for him — I know how to do that, I know how to do it better than girls that pretend. I'm going down to stay with Irene Shafer. Might stay two days."

She left after breakfast, walking the four miles across the ford and through the end of the notch to the Shafer place. She went over for a while at Daniel Rinearson's, to leave her mother's good wishes with Mrs. Rinearson. That night Moss Rinearson dropped in at the Shafers and the two went for a walk. By the time they returned to Shafers, she had kissed Moss and she had given him courage enough to ask the proper question and she had taken him.

24

BURNETT reached Lattimore's in the graying afternoon and joined the neighbors standing in semicircle before the cabin. Everybody was here, even Hawn, even the Lockyears. Billy Lord drifted toward him, murmuring, "Hell, Rice, I thought she was your woman," and stared at him with his eager curiosity and walked on. A fire burned in the yard and a coffeepot hung over it; and he heard Katherine, close by, say, "She's pretty." Edna came from the cabin and joined Moss, and the two came before Lot White.

Lot said: "Neighbors, we're here to make a marriage," and began the ceremony at once.

Burnett lowered his head and felt a rough inner wind blow him empty.

Maybe he had been mistaken. What else could he have wanted? She was the warm room into which, tired and lonely, he could have gone, closing the door behind. He heard Lot White finish the words of marriage; he watched Moss, embarrassed by the crowd, kiss his wife.

"Now then, you two," said Lot White, "put away the fancies of bein' single and lay by your notions you can go on doin' what you've done before. It's a young man's nature to hunt and girl's way to run ahead of the hunter. That's the wine, and the wine's good so long as it lasts. But it don't last long. The Lord gave you your runnin', and this is the end of it, so make your hearts firm and your minds steady, for life is aketchin' up and you have got to do what you're supposed to do. What's these older women cryin' for now—what's these gray-haired men lookin' solemn for? Because they know what young was, what no care was, but that was a long time ago. They had it one time. They ain't got it now. You had it till this minute. You ain't goin' to have it any more. You shall be useful, and sweat and pain's comin' with it. You shall struggle and your hearts are agoin' to break, and mend, and break some more. It may be you'll have peace and plenty, and only small trouble, but don't count on it, for Beulah Land is on the other shore, it ain't here. There's only one thing in this world, and you've got to learn it. You have got to endure — you have got to endure."

Edna, with her pleasant half-smile, seemed to pay full attention, but Burnett knew most of her thoughts would be elsewhere. She was her own world, no other world half so interesting to her. The smile held on, meaning anything, everything, nothing; it was the same smile which, looking down upon him with its affection in the cabin, had at the same time concealed her decision to leave him. He looked away from her, not wanting to see her again in that particular attitude, softened by that particular light.

"O Lord," said Lot White, "come down here on these people. Open the doors of darkness just a crack and let them see light. Not too much light, O Lord, or you'll blind 'em, for they're mortal and they can't stand the full light. Just a little."

Turning his glance about, Burnett noticed how tired his neighbors appeared to be; they stood faded within their clothes and upon them was the silence of worry rather than of peace. He knew them all, their names, habits and values; they were strongly themselves, like sharp separate pickets sticking up from the earth, of unequal length and thickness, no picket being like another. Yet as he continued to watch they became something else to him, their separateness blurring into oneness, the bent heads and stilled bodies joining into a yeasty lump which clung to the earth and spread shapeless over the earth.

Lot White said, "Amen," and voices rose around Burnett. He heard the sudden disturbing laugh of Cal Lockyear, an insolent laugh meant to draw attention. He noticed Lucy Collingwood's expression of fixed and heavy unhappiness.

Lucy was more than unhappy. She was lost within herself and could find no way out. She thought of Moss and Edna: "He'll cause her no trouble. She'll manage him and he'll never know what's in her head, but he'll never be very curious. But why wasn't it Rice?" Lucy tried a short side-glance toward Rice and saw nothing on his face, but her active imagination supplied him with a broken heart and pity rose to touch off her own loneliness. "We're all standing here wanting things we can't have." Invisible strings crossed this yard, dozens of them, leading from one person to another. Back and forth the strings ran until they wove a web in which everybody was caught; respectability made them lie quietly in the web but hope cried at them to tear free. Looking at Katherine, she thought: "She ought to be glad it's turned out this way."

Katherine heard little of Lot White's sermon. She watched Roxy Kitchen move forward step by step until she stood directly behind Moss and Edna, the girl's interest in the scene for a little while making her unaware of herself. Ragged, homely, simpleminded and disregarded, she fed her greedy soul on what she saw. Katherine thought: "Poor thing — poor, poor little thing." It was only a short break in her main thought. What did Moss mean to Edna? Nothing. Nothing but a man to marry. Why wasn't it Rice? Edna had wanted Rice. She had done everything to get Rice. Everything. She turned slightly to catch another quick sight of Burnett, and turned back. It was hard to tell what he thought. "I'll wonder about it till I die," she said to herself. She was sorry for Moss, poor Moss with his young man's belief that he had won Edna by his own effort, or that he had won her at all. In his bed she would be a stranger, though he'd never know it.

Old Gram stirred beside her, thinking: "She'll shrivel him up and suck him dry and spit him out like a seed. She's had a dozen men and she'll have a dozen more." Mrs. Buck thought: "A baby every ten months until she can't drag herself around, and they'll run wild, no care from her — shiftless and dirty and no-account." George Collingwood, dreaming of the touch of her mouth, condemned himself for his poor effort and believed he could have had her. Mrs. Irish said a kind prayer and from her own experience she saw the misery coming to Edna, and then the worry settled down again and she wondered how she and her son would survive the winter. Mrs. Millard whispered to her husband, "Now, she'll learn what it's like to be a slave." Martha Gay thought: "Well, she's married," and the feeling of satisfaction which came to her was the same feeling shared by all the older people around her. As a girl ready for marriage and needing marriage, Edna had troubled them by her conduct, for their realism made them see much and guess more. She violated their concept of usefulness; she was a girl who ought to be at the business of making her family. There was a form to be observed and since all others had fitted themselves to it she could not be the exception without bringing against her the quiet pressures of the group. It was this pressure which, as much as her own need, brought about this marriage, and now that she was inside the stockade of their general customs much would be forgiven her and much allowed.

Women immediately surrounded the newly married, their silence erupting into voluble talk. The men delayed their congratulations a little while, forming their own group.

Old Daniel Rinearson said: "I'd give a lot for a keg of whisky."

"There's coffee yonder," said Lattimore.

"Coffee's for warm, and I ain't cold. Whisky's for fun."

Lockyear came up, his brother Veen trailing him. Cal said: "You want whisky?"

"I said *whisky*," answered Old Daniel. "When I want half blue vitriol and half gun oil I'll make my own."

Lockyear said: "That gut of yours could stand anything."

"It's my gut, and you keep your stuff for the Molallies. Don't you know that's makin' trouble without need?"

"I'll make what I want to make," said Lockyear. "Keep your damned mouth shut to me."

Old Daniel straightened his turkey-cock shape. His jaw moved forward, his scarlet color quickened, and he set the anger of his eyes on Lockyear. Lockyear stared back. "Old man," he said, "that's a bluff. You ain't got the mustard."

"The hell I ain't," said Old Daniel. But it was, for him, a quiet answer, an answer not in keeping with his known character, and the feeling of witnessing something improper came again to Burnett as it had when Lockyear had treated Lorenzo Buck the same way at Gay's meeting. Old

Daniel looked around to see his oldest son, Ared, move beside him. He gave Ared a short nod. "That's a comfort." Then he turned his attention to Whit who was a little behind Lockyear. "Come over here."

Whit avoided his father's eyes. The lightly flushed face took on balkiness. He shrugged his shoulders and he tried a smile which faded as he became aware of the hard-watching and the hard-listening of the crowd. Cal Lockyear laughed at him. "Well, boy, your pa's callin'." Whit's stubborn embarrassment increased. He flung up his head and gave Old Daniel a resenting glance; he said something nobody understood and whirled about and walked away.

Burnett thought: "The yellow son-of-a-bitch." Old Daniel had been punched through by this blow and he showed the hurt. The stillness in the circle got worse. Nobody moved and nobody said anything until Cal Lockyear's voice grated them with its malice.

"You want a drink, Rice?"

"I'll say when," said Burnett.

Lockyear laughed. He pointed to Edna among the women. "Why wasn't you standin' in Moss's shoes?"

"I'll tell you when the time comes," said Burnett.

"I guess you forgot to say when," said Lockyear, and laughed again. But the carelessness spread only as far as his eyes. He moved gently on his feet, keeping nimble. He had some liquor in him and knew it, and he guarded himself. "You ever say when?" He walked toward Lattimore's lean-to barn at the edge of the meadow. Veen limped after him.

Ryal McIver spoke to Burnett in a mild, careful voice: "Wasn't he sayin' something to you, Rice?"

The soft question brought men's glances to him and he knew what they were thinking. "That's right," he said.

"I didn't quite make out what he was sayin'," said Ryal, gently.

"You heard it," said Burnett.

Old Daniel hauled himself from his heavy thoughts. "Well," he said to Gay, "we ought to get some crews together one of these days and start road work."

Burnett left the circle, moving toward the creek. Behind him Old Daniel said, "Now, take care," and he turned to see Ared Rinearson walking toward Whit. Ared came before his brother and he said something which brought up Whit's head and drew an angry answer. Ared took half a step back, raised his fist and slammed it into Whit's face; the younger man lost his balance and fell on his buttocks. He came up like an angry cat, he made half a rush at Ared and checked himself and he stood a long moment before his brother, saying nothing, and at last wheeled and walked deeper into the meadow. The circle broke and men moved around the yard, toward the coffee, toward the horses, toward the new bride and groom.

Burnett flattened himself at the creek. He wanted a lot of water but he took a short drink and rose and turned back. Katherine was at the corner of the cabin. She looked at him; she looked away from him. "Go kiss the bride," she said idly.

He pointed to her hand. "What's that cut?"

"A dull knife. You want some coffee?"

"No." He took her hand and ran a finger along the scar; he reversed it and saw the small calluses in her palm. "Been swinging an ax?"

"Dad doesn't feel good." She grew restless; she pulled the hand away.

Lockyear was still standing near the lean-to with his brother. Burnett watched him a little while, thinking: *He'll fight alligator-style, hands and feet and thumbs. His gun's hanging on the horse, but he's got a knife and he might use it. Hit him in the belly first. If I go down he'll try to kick my brains out. Watch him when he walks toward his horse. He might use the gun. He pushed twice — now he thinks it's easy. He'll try it. He's figuring how to start it.*

Katherine said: "What's in the air? What's wrong with Lockyear?"

"Feeling mean," said Rice.

"You're feeling mean, too. I know that snaky look. You two quarreled?"

"No," said Rice. "He just needs a fight."

"You need a fight?" she said.

"Have to take one if it's offered."

Old Daniel pushed himself through the crowd to Edna and led her beyond earshot.

"Daughter," he said, "I want you to know I'm glad you're in my family. Moss ain't a fool. He's reliable. He'll take care of you. Treat him well."

"I'll do it," said Edna.

Old Daniel's wrinkles of smartness sank deeper into his face. "You got a baby started?"

Her pleasant expression broadened; she laughed at him.

"Well," he said, "once I was young and did my chasin' and I know how these things are. It could be you got a baby started. It could be it ain't

Moss that started it, too. You're a big girl all over and when the urge comes, it sure comes. I want you to know that if you're foolin' me I halfways know it and I don't care. Moss ought to take care of you. If he does, you stick with him and give him no trouble. If he don't do it enough to make you happy, I wouldn't blame you much for findin' an extra man." He shook his head and sighed out his regret. "By God, I wish I was young enough to make you a run."

She bent forward and gave him a kiss and stood back, smiling at the brisk scurry of interest about his face as he turned away. She remained where she was, noting that Katherine had left Rice. She looked at Rice and waited for his glance to come to her; and she grew tired of waiting and went over to him.

"I thought you'd come to wish me well," she said.

"I wish you well."

"You knew I'd do it, didn't you? You knew it when I left your place the other night."

"No."

"If you're sad, I'm awful sorry. But I don't think you're as sad as you think you are." The shortsighted and wondering glance came to her eyes. At such times, not so certain of herself, she had a soft, faithful expression which made him believe he had missed much that was in her; and these were the times when he drew nearer to her and regret moved through him with its suggestion of love. She shrugged her shoulders and gave him a small laugh. "Well, it's just more talk. It'll do no good. We never get anywhere with it. It had to be done."

He looked at her in a sharper way. "If it had to be done, I should have been told about it."

"I don't mean that. I mean it was time for me to marry."

He shook his head. "I guess I've got nothing to say."

She sobered; she took on a dignity before him. "It's my problem, it's not yours. Why do you care? You didn't before — not much. You had your way. If there's been a mistake made, it's your mistake. Remember that. It was your mistake."

"Maybe it was," he said. "Clear back to Oregon City, maybe it was."

She looked about her and saw Moss moving in. She said hurriedly: "Oh God, Rice, why do we just look at each other and make mistakes? You like me a little don't you?"

"If there's anything you ever want from me, tell me."

"I'll see you," she said, "I'll see you soon." Then Moss walked over and said, "We better start home pretty soon." He didn't look directly at Burnett. He took the girl's arm and moved toward the cabin.

Ben Provost came through the crowd to Burnett. "Powell Baily said he heard Lockyear say he was going to tree a coon."

"Where's the coon?"

"Cal was lookin' in your direction when he mentioned it."

Lockyear, at the moment, walked in from the lean-to, his knees stiff when he struck ground with his boots. *He's got a pint of that stuff burning a hole in his belly,* Burnett thought. He crossed the yard and joined John Gay and the half-dozen men around Gay. Lockyear walked toward Edna who stood by the doorway. She noticed his approach and turned into the cabin, and Moss shifted around and blocked the doorway, trying to make the act casual. Veen overtook his brother and spoke to him and Cal swung and came on to Burnett.

"You want a drink now?"

"I'll say when."

"Man," said Lockyear, "the word's not in your head." He seemed for a moment to forget Burnett; he stared at Moss Rinearson at the doorway. "Now there's a man who said when."

"Let it alone, Cal," said Burnett.

"She said when, too," Lockyear went on. "She'll say when any time . . ."

Burnett stepped on, struck him in the stomach; and as the man broke backward, half bent over, Burnett advanced to hook a leg behind Lockyear and drop him. Lockyear struck, squirmed like a cat, and flung himself to his feet. He let go with a crowing cry, he shouted, "Here's my coon," and poised himself for a rush.

Men rushed forward with their released eagerness to make a circle, closing Cal and Burnett within it, closing Veen Lockyear out of it. Veen yelled, "Let me in there — watch out, Cal — let me in!" He rammed into Powell Baily. Powell wrapped Veen in his arms, revolved three times and flung the little man into the meadow.

"Here's my coon," said Cal and laughed and made a forward run. Burnett stooped low, body clipping Lockyear across the waist. He gripped Lockyear by the legs, came up with him and threw him sidewise; he whirled to fall on Lockyear and pin him to the dirt, but checked himself at the sight of Lockyear's out-striking boots and waited for Lockyear to rise; he struck, missed his blow and felt his mouth ripped by the wallop of Lockyear's fist. The force set him back and dropped him and a red curtain fell over his eyes. As soon as he fell he curled himself to shelter his stomach; he pulled in his head, he heard a warning shout and took Lockyear's hard kick into his kidneys. He rolled against Lockyear's legs and brought Lockyear down and rolled free and rose and plunged into the half-upright Lockyear, driving him back to the ground. He fell on Lockyear and thrust his knee into the man's belly; he got his forearm over Lockyear's windpipe and let his weight fall. Lockyear's fingers made their window cuts across Burnett's face and the steady surging of the other's body began to unseat him. Reaching aside, Burnett scooped a handful of dirt into Lockyear's eyes and sprang away.

As he rose, Lockyear sought to squeeze the dirt from his eyes and in such a half-turned and unprotected position, Burnett found him, mauled him on the head, in the belly, on the temple. Burnett closed on him, wrapped his arms around the other's waist and drove him straight against the circle. Men jumped aside and tripped against each other in their hurry to clear away. He brought his knee into Lockyear's crotch, he drove that resisting body on, he rammed his head against Lockyear's chin, he steered the man straight at the nearby fire. Lockyear stiffened his legs, sensing what was behind him, and tried to veer; but he was too close and his legs caught on the burning fire log and he went haunch-flat into the flame, dislodging the big coffeepot hanging there. He rolled wild-crying across the fire's bed, kicked the supports from the fire crane and crawled away. Burnett seized the coffeepot and flung it at the man, and missed. Lockyear got on his hands and knees and began a patient, bearlike crawl toward the meadow. His trouser seat, in one full contact with the fire coals, had been burned away and the raw black cheeks of his buttocks undulated as he moved.

The broken circle of men re-formed itself beyond the fire, hemming in both Lockyear and Burnett. When he saw he couldn't get through the circle, Lockyear shoved himself to his feet. His arms were down, he was absent-minded with pain, both hands were burned, the sleeves of his coat smoked. He slapped himself, he watched Burnett with a close attention. He waited for the beating to go on and he slipped a hand underneath his coat and held it there.

"That's a knife," said Billy Lord.

"Take it and stick it into him," said Lattimore.

John Gay's grave rebuke followed quickly. "That won't do."

Burnett said, "Here's your coon, Cal."

Lockyear cocked his head crookedly and caught sight of Burnett through his dirt-clogged eyes. He bit his mouth together until it was no mouth and endured the rising misery of his hurts. He shook his head. Burnett waggled his hand at the circle. "Let him out of here."

Men stood in their places, reluctant to move. Lockyear waited with his dead-centered patience; his head slowly revolved to cover one man and another until this individual searching out began to trouble them; they were still afraid of him and as his eyes pried away at the ring some of these settlers grew uneasy and in a short time the circle lost its tightness as men drifted from it. Lockyear walked toward his horse and toward Veen waiting by the horse.

Lattimore grumbled: "He'll be back, worse than before."

Burnett said: "Lend me your gun." He watched Lockyear pause and lay both hands on the rump of his horse. Veen stood close to Cal, talking to him. Lattimore came from his cabin and handed over his rifle and Burnett stepped to the edge of the crowd, holding the gun ready. His beaten nerves began to cry and his legs quivered. His mouth was bleeding, his ear had been cut by Lockyear's fingernails; the broken skin across both rows of knuckles lay pleated back from the red underflesh. Cal Lockyear circled his horse, made two tries and finally got into the saddle, bending forward to take the weight from his scorched buttocks; and he rode very slowly over the meadow and disappeared in the trees, Veen behind. Directly before he passed from sight, Veen turned and shook his fist at the crowd.

"Little fellow's brave today," said Old Daniel.

Gay said, "He won't be sweetened by a lickin'. You feel bad, Rice?"

Burnett pressed his shoulder against Elam Walker and moved by. He was still groggy, not so much from Lockyear's handling as from the pure poison dumped into his blood by the fight, and gusty tag ends of violence caught him off guard and made his motions jerky. He left the rifle against the cabin wall, went to the creek and flattened for a long drink; when he got up he found Katherine waiting.

"Have you got anything for that?" she asked, and pointed to his mouth. "No."

"Heat a stone. Wrap something around it. Lay it against your mouth." Her glance went back and forth across his face; he saw the tightening of her expression, the faint constrictions of hardness come and go. "You wanted to fight. You wanted it." She lifted a hand to lightly touch his scarred ear. "You'd look fine with one ear, you'd look well with your teeth knocked out. I've got some salve Ralph Whitcomb left."

"You mad, Katherine?"

"I guess so." She looked at him; she was critical, she was hurt by his hurts. "My poor man," she said, "why has it got to be so hard with you?" and left him.

He returned to the yard and found his hat near the fire. Moss was at the cabin's doorway, waiting for Edna. He met Rice's glance, held it only a moment and looked aside. Rice went on to his horse and rode soon into the trees; now the ebb was on him and he was dull-minded and paid no attention to his surroundings.

Katherine said little as she walked the narrow trail ahead of Eby. He had seen a big timber wolf during the week and took time to tell her his experience with it; and this occupied him all the way to Mrs. Irish's cabin at the ford. When he finished the story she said, "I wouldn't want to be alone and see one," and fell back into her silence. Past Kern's, past Provost's and Collingwood's they walked; it was between twilight and full nighttime when they came through the last short patch of firs and arrived home. Eby said cautiously, "Feeling bad about something?"

"The fight bothered me."

"One of 'em could have got killed easy. They were both tryin' for it. I wasn't surprised Lockyear should try, but I didn't think Rice would get that crazy."

"How can you fight gentle? Fighting's fighting." She stepped inside to light a lantern and hang it on a rafter. Eby made himself useful for a little while, lugging in wood for the fireplace. "We arguin' about something?" he asked mildly.

"No," she said and returned to the yard.

He followed her. "It didn't settle anything," he said. "Now he's got to watch himself when Lockyear's around. He ought to've known that when he started the fight."

"Did he start it any more than Lockyear?"

"Now we're arguin' again."

"I'm picky tonight."

He reached forward to turn her so that the lamplight fell against her face. "You think I ought to've fought Lockyear instead of Rice?"

"You had no reason to do it. But he did. Lockyear was picking a fight with him. All the men saw it. They expected Rice to fight him." Then she got to thinking about the scene and saw something new in it. "They made Rice fight Lockyear — they pushed him into it."

"Something to that all right," he agreed. "He couldn't back down before his neighbors."

No, she thought, that wasn't it. They forced Rice into the fight, not by words so much as by a kind of soft pressure. They expected him to stand for them. She checked the impulse to tell this to Harris, knowing it would trouble his pride; for if strength to speak for them was what they wanted, this huge and amiable man was the better choice, his enormous fist capable of destroying Lockyear at one blow. But they had turned to Rice in this matter as they had, along the trail, occasionally turned to him in other matters. She hadn't thought much about those qualities in men which drew the trust of other men, but it was plain to her now that Burnett had grown in the train's estimation since he had joined it in the spring. It was a strange and powerful and quiet thing — this crowd judgment which cast some men aside and brought others forward, and put all men in their places regardless of their own seeking. How hard Collingwood tried, yet was rejected; how worthy Harris was, and still would never be more than a voice in the background. Whatever it was that commanded the respect of men, her father had it and Burnett had it, and because of it there would be demands made of them they couldn't escape. Burnett had spoken for them and as time went on they would require more of him. He couldn't escape that service if he stayed in the settlement. *If he stayed,* she repeated to herself, and again wondered about his intentions.

Harris Eby had been watching her during this long silence, and drew her interest back to him. "You got no patience with me tonight."

"I'm just out of sorts," she said. "Don't know why."

"What I ought to do," he said, "is get boilin' mad and raise hell with you."

"Go ahead. It's what you ought to do."

"I've not got that kind of a temper."

"Oh, Harris," she said, and took his arm, her smile reassuring him. "You know me well enough to put up with my spells. You'd better — you've got a whole life to endure them."

"Then you've made up your mind to endure *me?*" he said, quick to take the opening he saw.

Her reply was not quite an answer. "You'll not make a hard husband."

"Well," he said, "what you require you can have, so long as you don't expect more than I can do. There's not half a dozen things I stick fast on. On those I shall want my way. The rest of it can be what you want." He laid his hand on her shoulder, of a notion to force the decision; but he couldn't bring himself to be aggressive and stood rather awkwardly before her. She reached up and brought his hand down, and held it; and she changed the subject.

"Did you get the well finished?"

"Water came in at thirty feet. I am going to put a coolhouse around it, with shelves for the milk and butter."

"You remember what Mrs. Dancey's coolhouse looked like in Poplar Grove?"

"Big square box, like a small room, built into the top of the well."

"Build it that way," she said.

"You had better come down and look around," he suggested, "before I get things put together the way you don't want."

"All right," she said. "Now you go home — it's a long walk."

She knew him well, but on occasion he had an insight into things which surprised her; he surprised her now. He stepped back and made a balancing motion with his hand. "It's yes and no with you, ain't it? You lean, but you're afraid to fall."

"I don't know," she said. "Maybe it's that way. Maybe I get scared when I think of it — a lot of girls are like that just before the wedding."

"Buck fever," he said. "Lot of men that way, too."

"You feel it, Harris?"

"No," he said, "my mind's made up and I'm in a hurry to do it."

She gave his hand a quick tap and dropped it. "Well, good night," she said, and watched him go. He followed the trail with no seeming haste but his great stride soon took him to the trees; he was a matter-of-fact man, she thought, his sentiment well contained, for it never occurred to him to turn to wave at her as he passed into the trees. Turning to the cabin, she found herself relieved, as though his presence had pressed her too close to a decision and she said to herself, *There's not that much hurry. After Christmas is time enough. Or early spring. March. For then I can do summer's work before a baby puts me indoors.* She set on the coffee and started supper and her mind went in another direction and she remembered how Rice had watched Edna at the wedding. Why hadn't it been Rice instead of Moss — and did it really change anything between those two? Moss — poor Moss, he was nothing. The family came home and she listened to the supper talk without interest, and afterwards the three women did their chores. The moment the men left the cabin Gram began to talk, as though the silence had been hard on her.

"That Edna — she had to do it."

"I don't doubt," said Martha Gay. "Wonder what Miz' Rinearson thinks? I'd not be happy were I she."

"Moss don't mean anything," said Gram. "He's just a boy that got fooled into it. That girl's been an excitement to men so long it's in her blood. She likes it too well to quit. She'll keep right on. Pull the wool over Moss's eyes half the time, honey him out of being mad the other half."

"I don't understand it," said Martha Gay. "It was Rice she was running after."

"He had her, too," said Gram Gay. "More than once."

"Well, then, why didn't she marry him?"

"Something about the girl boggled him. Girl like Edna thinks it's easy to let a man come on — then get him that way. Sometimes it is. Lot of husbands in this settlement were got that way. But sometimes it boggles them."

"I don't know," reflected Martha Gay. "Maybe she did the best. That Rice has done a lot of wandering. It's in his blood; he'll wander some more. Moss will settle down. She's got something certain to count on."

"*Certain — certain,*" said Gram. "Don't talk *certain* to me. That's for scared people. Get a man you're certain of and you'll die a thousand times listenin' to *certain* all your life, watchin' *certain* all your life." She touched the silent Katherine with her glance. "Nothing more certain than a rock, but what's in that kind of marriage to please a woman?"

Two days later Lockyear walked into the Kitchen house, spoke to the Kitchens for no more than fifteen minutes and walked out with Roxy. They found Lot White, were married and at once turned into the hills, Lockyear walking so fast that Roxy now and then broke into a trot to keep up with him. All her possessions, the few ragged clothes and the fewer pitiful trinkets, were wrapped in a cotton towel under her arm. The news spread around the hills, from mouth to mouth, and was known by everybody that same day. A special messenger could have carried it no faster.

25

AS with nearly all other things in this land, the weather made its change in quiet fashion; the wind swung to the east, the fat gray clouds dissolved, the sun shone down with its reddened year's-end mildness, the nights were crisp. Near Christmas it was bright and clear, and people's spirits lifted as a sense of elbowroom and distance returned. Eastward the massive Cascade chain showed a white dusting of snow along peak and alpine timber masses. To the west the valley — whenever the settlers caught sight of it through the intervening timber — rolled toward the prairie and then far-off mountains of the coast. Vine maple had earlier flashed its light scarlet against the green background of fir, but now those leaves were gone, and the alder leaves had dropped — leaving behind the memory of their last amber-yellow glow. Beneath russet oaks acorns lay scattered; the ferns were wilting back to form another layer of mulch for the earth, the berry bushes — interlaced with weedy growth — were ragged and old-purple; an occasional wild rose bush still held its last red seed pods; the willows stood bare along the creek. In every new-plowed field winter wheat made its pale green cast against the black soil.

It was strange weather to people who at this time in the East would have been knee-deep in snow and whipped by bitter winds. They liked this blandness, they marveled at it, but they couldn't quite trust it and waited for blizzard time to come. Meanwhile they used the opportunity to burn the slash piles accumulated from their land clearing, and everywhere around the settlement ash-blue clouds of smoke rose and the wild-flavored residue of burning wood permeated the air; at night the dragon-eyes of fire gleamed through thickets and across meadows.

Burnett made fence while he tended his fires, and as soon as he had his home lot closed in he brought the stock down from the upper meadow each night; for both cougar and wolves were moving in from the higher mountains, the wolves sounding in the dark, the cougar printing their presence in the soft earth beside the creek. Colder weather shrank the creek until it fell over its rock barrier as a thin sheet of curved glass, and at this low stage he had his best chance to survey the millrace which would cut the creek above the falls; the actual digging could wait, for he had begun the fencing and, as with any chore he did, he liked to complete one thing at a time. He crossed the creek to run his fences along the farther upper fields.

The self-discipline of the settlers loosened as the year straggled to its end. The holiday season came on with its increased sentiment, with its memories of the far-off East softening and saddening them, and in this mood they wanted company and began to set out on their nightly visits. Hawn came down from his place with a big red hen and fifteen eggs.

"She's been settin' for a week. There's your start of fowls." Then he grinned. "Now you got a female around the place."

"That your idea or Louisa's?"

"Louisa's," said Hawn, and was reminded of some news. "Some Klamaths have crossed the mountains to join the Molalas for the winter. Thirty or forty families. They're tougher people. Seen any bucks around here?"

"No."

"Probably will. They'll get hungry and go to beggin'." He lighted a pipe and stood lazy in the sunlight. He knew he had stopped Burnett's work and ought to go; but he had no work of his own to occupy his time. He was outside; he was a squaw man on the edge of the settlement, not in it. "The hen's name is Crazy Girl. Louisa named her." He made up his mind to go. "I wish," he said, "I could tell Louisa about Christmas, but damned if I can get it across." He went away, habit causing him to walk in long fast strides though he had no reason to hurry.

After supper that evening Burnett heard Millard's voice calling over the darkness and when he had banked his cabin fire he took up his gun, crossed the creek and made his way through the thicket to the Millard cabin. The Provosts had dropped in, and the Collingwoods and Mrs. Irish and Watt, and John and Martha Gay; and Katherine. Lot White hailed the cabin a little later.

"We got some tea," said Millard. "What you packin' a rifle for, Rice?"

"To balance my weight crossing the creek." He said "Hello" around and settled on his heels in a corner. Katherine sat on the bed beside him. His pipe, and Millard's and Provost's, presently fogged the little room. Katherine reached down, took the pipe from his mouth and tried a few draws on it.

Mrs. Millard said: "Women get bad habits enough from men without learning that one, Katherine." She laid out cups for the tea; exhausting

172

the cups she used mush bowls. "I better give you one of the bowls, Lot. Your mouth's pretty wide for a cup."

"Sister," said Lot, "is it agoin' to be war or peace tonight?"

Mrs. Millard passed around the tea. She moved to her cupboard and found a piece of bread and spread it with jam from a crock. "I don't guess we'll ever see those wonderful wild Iowa plums again. They don't grow here." She gave the bread and jam to Watt Irish. "You're the hardest-working man in the crowd and *you* don't waste time talking or roving."

John Gay, seated next to his wife, laid his head back against the wall and smiled at Mrs. Millard. "Nancy, don't strain your mercy so thin."

"She was bit by somethin' when she was ten years old," said Lot.

Mrs. Millard laid the edge of her glance against him but held her tongue. This crowd was easy, tolerant. Gently, gently it lay here. Burnett thought — the thing that bound them. It hovered over them, it moved softly through them.

"Any Indians?" asked Gay.

"Saw one across the creek late yesterday afternoon," said Provost.

Burnett said: "Hawn tells me there's some Klamaths living with the Molallies."

Martha Gay's face darkened; here was something new to worry about. But it was John Gay's odd motion Rice Burnett noticed then — the way he reached over with his left hand to turn his right arm half around; and he observed again, as he had at Edna's wedding, the falling-away of the man's flesh from its bones. He was older by ten years than in the spring of this year at the trip's beginning; and straight across his lips was the precise streak of pain. Katherine dropped her hand to Burnett's shoulder. "Tell an Indian story like the one you told on the Snake."

"Oh, Katherine," said Martha, "they give me the miserables."

"Tell it," said Katherine.

"Murphy and Jo Gantt and Ben Kimmel — this was in the Yellowstone country, four years ago. Big party came up the Missouri and made camp. We worked out from the main camp, up the creeks, three and four men together, trapping beaver. One night, week or two from camp, these three fellows cooked supper and settled for sleep. That's Sioux country and you don't sleep close to the fire. You get away from it and sleep light. Beyond midnight the horses made a racket and Murphy and Gantt got up and went over to what was left of the fire. Kimmel was a different man — always expected trouble; so he stayed back and he was half out of his blankets, in the brush, when he saw Murphy fall down. Arrow went through

Murphy's chest and came out his back — point on one side, feathers on the other. Gantt started to run, and ran right into a big buck. The buck raised his gun barrel first and crushed Gantt's skull. Maybe you don't know the sound of that — it's somethin' like what you'd hear when you break open a good hard squash with an ax handle. Well, Kimmel was still in the brush and he thought he wasn't seen, so he crawled away, and he'd got maybe twenty yards when something hit him on the ribs and a gun went off right in his face; he felt the powder burn his skin when he faded out."

He bent forward to catch a splinter from the wood pile, to light it in the fire. He wavered the flame back and forth over his pipe bowl. Katherine's fingers dug into his shoulders. "So what'd Kimmel do?"

"Maybe he was dead."

"Then that'd be the end of the story. Go on — you always stop to light your pipe."

"When he got conscious the fire had gone out entirely and he was cold — it gets awful cold in the mountains that time of year. His face was sticky, full of blood, so he figured he'd been wounded by the explosion of the gun in his face, and he felt around to see where'd he'd been hit. When he passed his hand over his hair, he didn't have any hair. He'd been scalped. Well, he had some hair — sort of a rim around the scalped place. The Indian's bullet had missed him, though his face was powder burned, and when he wrapped a bandanna around his head the blood caked and quit running. It was pretty close to daylight, the horses were gone and Murphy and Gantt were dead. All he could do was start back for the main camp, about thirty miles away.

"When daylight came he went back into the timber, and pretty soon he topped a small ridge and found out he was being followed, so he crossed the ridge and got to a lake and broke a big bullrush and sank under the water, using the bullrush to breathe through. He couldn't see or hear anything under water, and he didn't want to risk looking, so he stayed under most of that day; then he crawled out, much dead as alive, and began to walk for camp. By that time it was dark again and he missed his way and started up the side of a ridge. Next thing he got into an old rock slide and fell into a sort of a pit about fifteen feet deep and maybe twenty feet wide. Couldn't see a thing but he began to smell something — the sort of a smell you only have to smell once to remember; and he began to hear some funny noises and then he knew he was in a rattlesnake den — snakes all around him. Somehow he'd landed on his feet without stepping on any of 'em but he knew if he shifted around he might. It was a pretty cold night and he suffered some, but the coldness helped him some, too, for it made the snakes sluggish. Anyhow, he never moved — not so much as an inch all night long. Eight hours is a long time to stand still.

"When daylight came again he looked around and saw thousands of snakes, all twined together in masses big as barrels at the bottom of the pit, and when he looked at the broken sides of the pit he noticed snakes curled back in the ledges sort of like Navajo cliff dwellers. It was a pretty ticklish business climbing out of the place, because he had to put his hands and feet on these ledges and once when he was pulling himself up the side of the pit his face came dead level with a rattler, he staring at the snake and the snake staring at him, not a foot between them. If it hadn't been so cold, and the snake so slow, Kimmel would have been bitten right between the eyes.

"Finally he got out of there and crossed the ridge and found a river. He didn't know exactly where he was but he stopped at the river and had a good drink and worked his way downstream. About noon he got a little careless and next thing he knew he was jumped by a dozen Sioux. Only thing he could do then was run for it, so he struck out, Indians a quarter mile behind him. He took to the timber but they were fresh and he wasn't and pretty soon they closed in and he thought he was done for, ducking in and out of the trees and climbing a small hill. They all took shots at him and missed him. By the time he got to the top of the hill he was ready to quit. Then he looked down the other side of the hill, and there lay the big camp — tents and horses and trappers. He just let out a hell of a shout and ran down the hill into the camp.

"The Indians stayed on top of the hill and started shooting. Pretty soon some more Indians came up and the trappers had a hot time for three or four hours fighting off the band. They lost some horses and a couple men got scratched. Otherwise it wasn't much and by nighttime the Indians pulled away. Kimmel didn't pay much attention. He was too weak to stand up so he dragged himself into a tent and let the rest of the crowd do the fighting. He'd done his. Well, when it was all over the booshway — the leader of the party — came into the tent and gave Kimmel hell. He said 'You damn fool, when you come into camp, come in alone. I ought to brain you for bringing all those Indians with you.'

"That's all the story. Kimmel put a lot of bear grease on the scalped spot and went back to trapping in a week. It never bothered him much except when it got hot — but he's always been mighty sensitive to flies

175

walking on the top of his head ever since. He once told me that without hair and hide up there a fly's foot weighed ten pounds."

Katherine reached down and pulled his head about to catch a straight sight of his face. "*Thousands* of snakes?"

"Maybe that was a little large," he said.

"It was a wonderful story," she said.

Martha Gay shook her head. "I don't see how you can bear to hear such things." She spoke to Mrs. Millard. "Nancy, have you got any big buttons?"

"Lord," said Mrs. Millard, "when did I see one last? I been using cut-down nails for buttons on Millard's trousers."

"There's so little to do with," said Martha Gay.

"I've got some," said Mrs. Irish. "How many you need?"

"Three," said Martha Gay. "And that reminds me I've got a stout piece of cloth at the bottom of my old round trunk. It will make Watt a shirt."

Billy Lord's sudden laugh came out of him in short scratches of sound, like a broom sweeping back and forth. "My God, I ain't thought of Hugh Paddow for most a year! . . . The shirt reminded me. . . . Hughie went huntin' in the Ozarks and got trail of a bear. Trail got pretty warm and Hughie got careless. He following the tracks through a thicket. Pushed through the thicket and there was the bear on a log, lookin' at Hughie. It was kind of sudden. Hughie was sure surprised, and so was the bear. Hughie tried to get his gun raised, the bear made a run. Bear wasn't after Hughie — bear just wanted to get the hell out of there, but it was kind of close quarters, so the bear knocked Hughie down and walked right over him. I guess it would of been all right but Hughie rolled to get out of the way, and got on his hands and knees. That was sure unfortunate because he had his back end to the bear and the bear took one swipe at it and kept right on going. It didn't hurt Hughie much but he didn't have no back end to his pants — none at all. So he walked home. When he got to the village he sort of traveled sidewise along the street with his back end against the picket fence, and this looked kind of peculiar to Hughie's wife who was out on the porch with some other women and saw him comin'. After he got to the gate he didn't know what to do — there was the women in front of him, and somebody was comin' along the street behind him. Hughie just sat down and pushed himself feet forward across the yard toward the porch, like a man rowin' himself home. Hughie's wife got right up and ran into the house and pretty soon she came out with a broom and laid it around Hughie till she broke the thing, and she said

'You old creature, you're drunk again.' That's what hurt him most. Usually he was, but this time he wasn't."

"Want more tea?" said Mrs. Millard. Nobody did. Mrs. Millard said: "It just offends me not to give company something better. How I yearn for somethin' green — it's been such a long time — it'll be such a lot longer."

"I got some onion sets planted behind the cabin," said Mrs. Provost. "I go out day after day to see if they've sprouted any more."

Mrs. Lord sighed deeply, and Lord said, "You got an ache?"

"No, I was thinking of such good things to eat."

"Hell, girl, you and me can hibernate all winter and still come out plump."

"That Cartwell girl," said Mrs. Provost, "she sixteen or fifteen?"

"Sixteen," said Martha Gay.

"Her mother keeps sayin' fifteen."

"That's just to make it seem she's too young to know what she's doing," said Martha Gay.

"What's she doin'?" asked John Gay.

"Now, you know."

Burnett closed his eyes, listening to the softened talk, to the back and forth play of easy words. It was here — softly it touched them. The room was a small bright cell set in the downbearing blackness, in the empty blackness, in the windy, endless blackness; inside the cell fourteen people crouched together, like common passengers in a crowded coach. He opened his eyes and saw Lucy Collingwood's face tipped toward the ceiling, darkened and soft. Billy Lord said:

Moses, Rufus, Jackson, Joe,
Think of Egypt — there you'll go.
Think of hell and hell's for you.
What you think is what you'll do.

"That's pretty, Billy," said Mrs. Lord, "but thinkin' won't bring a big cake a sugar to me."

"It's the spirit we got to nourish, girl."

"Then what'd you sell the fiddle for? Wheat — wheat — that's not spirit."

"Now you're contradictin'," said Billy.

The green skirt slipped and the green skirt fell,
And I kissed her in the loft by the big church bell.

177

The gray skirt whirled and the gray skirt rose,
And I kissed her in the meadow where the lilac grows.
And I loved them both, but I went away.
Oh, where is the green? Oh, where is the gray?

"That's what I mean," said Mrs. Millard. "Men do it and run away, and they make songs to brag about it. I wish I could make up a song for what women feel."

Billy Lord said: "Man or woman, it's no difference. The song's to soak up the cryin'. We all got to cry, but we got to sing to quit cryin'."

"Ah," said Mrs. Millard, "a man might cry till he filled a river but it'd be thin water. A woman's tears are mighty few and strong as poison. Ever break your heart, Lord?"

"Every Saturday night till I met Fanny."

"Then you never did."

Collingwood bent forward. "There's no doubt. Women have it hard out here. I have thought about it a lot, it's a sad thing, everything they've got to do. Morning till night, no let up, no end to it. It would break a man's back to follow their steps all day long. Mothers and helpmeets. They keep the fires lighted and the cabin warm and say nothing about their sorrows or their aches. Well, there's a special place in heaven for women. Closer to the throne than men will get, I'm entirely certain."

His wife cast a short glance toward him and dropped her eyes. Mrs. Millard studied him with a puzzled, skeptical glance and for once had no immediate answer. The room was quiet. Collingwood looked about from face to face and settled back.

"Well, now," said Gay in his comfortable manner, "let's not make out this world such a terrible thing. I don't pity myself for the work I've got. What would we do if there was no work — walk all day down the road pickin' buttercups?"

Burnett's cramped legs fell asleep and a thousand needles pricked them. He rose, he stamped his feet, he walked into the night. Millard's brush fires were a cherry red on the meadow, the guttural song of the frogs was a carpet of sound along the earth. He walked to the nearest fire and squatted before it, and he heard steps come lightly behind him, and Katherine's voice.

"Any snakes in Oregon?" She settled near him and took up a half-burned stick and began to poke at the flame. "What's that wood?"

"Alder."

178

"It's crying."

"Sap in the alder."

"The devil crying. For once he got himself in the wrong place. Lot would be pleased." She turned the stick steadily in the flames. "I feel good — I feel sad."

"Devil ever get in you?"

"Sure, I've got a place for him, I invite him in once in a while." She stirred uncomfortably in her crouched position. He peeled off his coat and laid it beside him and steadied her while she settled on it. She turned to prop her back against his shoulder. He moved his shoulder and she straightened away from him and looked around while he adjusted himself; then she dropped against him again. He braced himself to her weight and circled his arm around her waist. She folded her hands over his arm and her head tilted on his chest until she faced the yeasty foaming of the stars.

"Never changes," she said. "Up there — always the same."

"Everything changes."

"No," she said. "Everything's old. Every time I look in a fire I feel something move around me. I've done this before, way, way back. What's new? How long have people been kissing?"

"Pretty old habit," he said.

"That's what I mean — old."

"Damned good habit, too."

Talk went on in the cabin; the creek clucked over its stones and the coyotes prowled the close-by timber, sounding off with their half bark and half howl. A lifting thread of wind blew the fire brighter.

"Heavy on you?" she asked.

"No."

"Christmas — Christmas."

"Feel it coming?"

"Two days ago. I looked at Joe and I thought, 'What shall I get him?' Made me sad to think there'll be nothing to get this year. Then I thought, 'We're a long way from home.' Rivers, mountains, deserts — a long way off. We'll not see our people again, we'll not go back. It's like stepping off Noah's Ark. I don't like to lose track of my people. I like things close around me, place I was born, everything I knew, old sights, old things. I feel like a moved tree that's not taken hold. Any old wind could blow me down."

"No it couldn't."

"The air's good, the wood smells good. Night's peaceful."

He lowered his head to catch the scent of her hair and possessiveness went through him as a quick puff of flame through dry leaves, and he rose to drag over the burnt-out heart of the fire, bringing on a brighter blaze. She sat upright, curiosity alive. "How much weight have you lost?"

"Don't know. Should weigh a hundred seventy-five."

"It shows here," she said, and pushed in her cheeks with her fingers. She turned her attention to the fire and he waited for the faraway expression to come to her again; but she was in another mood, her thoughts bringing on little shifts of comfort, of luxurious reaction around her mouth, and her eyes were bluer than the nap of old velvet and sweetness rose from her as pitch might rise from a summer-heated tree. She raised her glance, found him observing her, and erased the expression with a smile. She motioned, pulled him toward her, and caught his hand to rise from her place. He got his coat and went into the cabin for his gun; when he came out she had drifted farther along the meadow.

He caught up with her and they moved on to the creek's shallow riffles above the Lattimore place. Wet earth's odor and bland air and creek's coldness met here and became light whirlpools of turbulence around them. The glow of brush fires wavered against the alders; voices came from the cabin, echoes bobbing in darkness like corks on choppy water.

"How deep's the water?"

He put his back to her and she got her arms around his neck and rode over the creek. "Last time I did that was when Harris and I went to school at Poplar Bluff — that was a muddy little creek. I wouldn't put my foot in it because he scared me with stories about cotton-mouth snakes."

They crossed Lattimore's clearing. Rice said, "Where we going?"

"I don't know. Where we going?"

He turned to the left, then along the trail, toward Irish's. She passed a hand back and forth in front of her. "Air's thick. Smell what's in it — trees, fern, brush smoke, mountains, mud. Like syrup. I feel good. You taking me home? I don't want to go home. I want to go up there."

"Where?"

"In the mountains. Way up there, where nobody's ever been. What's a cougar look like?"

"Big, tawny, short-cropped cat. Beautiful head, clipped ears, round green eyes."

They passed into the trees, all light vanishing. She moved nearer to him and took his hand. "Cougars in here?"

"Might be."

"How old you think the Lords are? It's hard to tell about fat people."

"I'd guess forty."

"Wonder what they were like? I think she must have been one of those big pretty girls that never ran out of energy and danced all night and loved everything. It's still in her eyes."

"Forty don't mean anything to them. They're still young."

"Once in a while I see a look on them," she said. "Sad look. They hate to get old."

"I can't fight or drink the way I did at twenty," he said. "I hate to get old, too."

"I wish I'd known you then," she said, and immediately changed the subject. "I like the way my father is. I know he wishes he'd done other things, but he's never sorry about the past." Her mind moved from thing to thing; he felt the bubble of her spirit, the light and active swinging of her thoughts. "I like trees. They stand right here and don't change."

"Trees don't need much."

"If we could only know what the lives of people were like. Grandmother, now. Why do some people stay like that, and others fade till they're nothing? When she was a girl she had a fine time. I can imagine her then. But I can't imagine Grandfather then. He's been old since I first knew him." Her mind was arrested by that notion; she went silently on through the trees and into the Irish clearing. She made a small sound. "It must have been hard for her."

"Why?"

"She so lively and Grandfather so quiet."

They passed into the woods beyond the Irish cabin, hearing the hallooing of voices across the creek at Millard's. From the ridge beyond Lord's hill came a coyote's cry, short yipping notes breaking into a sustained howl. Timber's blackness fell upon them again. "I like that sound," she murmured. "I like the darkness in here."

"Tonight," he said, "you like everything."

"I do. I wish there was a dance. I wish there was an excursion boat going down the Mississippi. I wish I could get on a horse and travel all the way to California. If I were a man, I'd go. Then I'd come back. Why are you so silent?"

"Like your grandfather."

"Not the same. You're thinking something. But not sad — I don't feel it's sad. What is it? I wish you'd tell me."

"Now you're your grandmother. You want somebody to say something to you."

"I'm my grandmother all over," she said. "Lock, stock and barrel. I want to be like her, do all she's done and do it as well — that would make me feel good. She even shot at an Indian. No, I don't want to do that. An outlaw came to her house once, made her cook a meal, left her a gold piece, and kissed her. She's got children, grandchildren, great-grand-children. She's plowed land, killed and butchered meat. She's lived in all kinds of country and weather, she's had every sort of experience. I wish I knew the things she's done she's not talked about. Things have been hard with her, but look at her now. I watch her hands and admire what they've accomplished. It makes me angry sometimes when I hear Lot White saying what miserable and helpless creatures we are and how much forgiveness we've got to pray for. Grandmother's never been helpless. I never saw her cry. Never knew her when she wasn't busy. I'd like him to tell me what the Lord ought to forgive *her* for. She's done her share here."

The trail took them out of the trees into the Collingwood meadow and past the dark Collingwood cabin. Katherine fell silent, engaged in an interesting set of thoughts which held her all the way to the Gay cabin. When they came to the yard she turned on him. "Coffee?"

"No, I'll reach out for home."

"Next time we walk, you do the talking." She stepped nearer, laid a hand on his arm, and looked up to him with her curiosity. "Next time you do the talking."

The short, dry flame once more licked through him. He remembered Edna's words: "She's no different than I am — we're all the same." Maybe, but even so it wasn't the same with Katherine; not the same thing at all.

Gram's shape darkened the cabin doorway's yellow rectangle. "That you, Katherine?"

"Yes," said Katherine. She dropped her hand from his arm, the lightness and laughter within her seeming to increase. She was new to him tonight, she was like a piece of glass which, under the changing sunlight, threw off varied colors. "Come to supper when you're lonesome."

"All right," he said and turned away.

As soon as he took the trail her manner changed; the confusion of emotions subsided and a kind of flat quiet came upon her, the strong sense of well-being growing less, and she listened until his ranging pace died on the trail, and turned to the cabin.

Gram said: "It a good visit?"

"Yes," said Katherine. She moved around the room, too restless to be either idle or useful.

After their departure the other families began to move away into the night, over the meadows, into the charcoal blackness of the timber, through brushy thickets — voices calling across the night and fading tone on tone until the Millards, listening from their yard, heard no more.

"Do hope the Lords don't fall, crossing the creek," said Mrs. Millard and turned into the cabin.

"Not a foot deep at the ford right now."

"It was good to have everybody," she said. "Lately I've had the lonesomes. Seems like everybody's got the lonesomes. I guess it's Christmas so near that makes me feel bad. Do I see John not looking well?"

"Somethin' wrong there," said Millard. "But he'd be the last man to say what."

"I wonder," said Mrs. Millard, "how long it'll be?"

"What'll be?"

"Katherine and Rice."

"He only got through with this Edna business. You think men got to be runnin' every minute of the time?"

"Just hounds with their tongues lappin' out a foot."

"Look here, girl," said Millard. "Any time a woman won't want a man runnin' after her she can stop it in twenty seconds."

"No we can't, not after a man starts it. There's where you men have got us, Millard. Touch the match to the tow and we burn till we're destroyed."

"Ah," said Millard in disbelief.

"I wish," said Mrs. Millard, "they lived closer together so they'd see more of each other. Then it wouldn't take so long."

"I thought you thought he was a hound dog."

"She's got to get married soon or late and he's the best she'll be able to do."

"Well, by God," said Millard, "he's a damned good best for her."

"He's a man, like any other and when the newness wears off, he'll bully her — try to crush her spirit." She turned on Millard. "You certainly took your good time watching Lucy Collingwood."

Millard said cautiously, "Don't seem to remember that."

183

"Well, you did. In a man old as you it looks silly. But I'm sorry for her. Her spirit's dyin'. I could cry."

"Collingwood ain't much, and that's a fact," said Millard.

"That came against the grain, didn't it, Millard? Men hate not to stick up for men. He's such a vain creature I could strike him. Those meechin', nice-nice, polite ways of his — all a big lie. I just see those shadows around her eyes get deeper and deeper."

"They ain't so deep but what they wouldn't disappear in about five minutes with Whitcomb."

"Oh, the egotism of man. You give and you take away, and women ought to be proud to do your slavework and stroke your heads and give you pleasure, and crawl away humble when you don't want them. God, Millard, you make me so mad!"

"There you go," said Millard. "You think of something some man did to some woman, and you take it out on me."

She moved around the cabin, silent, her motions made brisk by irritation. She finished her work and turned on Millard with a changed manner. "I've caused you a lot of trouble, haven't I?"

"Times, you have," he said noncommittally.

"I know I have." She came over to stand before him and to lay a hand on his arm. He watched her with an air of puzzled resignation — and this was his defense, for it pleased her to think he didn't understand the complexity and depth of her nature. It was true that he had no knowledge of what made her as she was; when he reflected on it he was sometimes inclined to think that an extra pinch of sulphur had been carelessly measured out in her making; at other times he searched the past in order to understand her, seeking for the things she wanted and hadn't gotten, considering his own treatment of her. Wondering if there had been some other man she had preferred. To that extent she was mysterious to him, but otherwise he had a most accurate knowledge of the things which set her into revolt; he knew the pattern by heart, the oncoming storm, the course it ran, the fury it generated, the period of calm — almost of happiness — which followed. He was, himself, a man whose days made a kind of steady flat line forward; but his wife's soul demanded a different rhythm, rising to peaks of fury, falling into valleys of calm. For her there had to be bursts of thunder to dissolve the tensions built up.

"Why do you put up with me when I'm like that? Why don't you just up and strike me?"

"That's just talk," he said. "If I did, you'd rile up again."

"No, you ought to do it. I swear, I must be hard to live with. You're such an easy man. If you knew me better you'd exert yourself more and stop it."

"Kind of late for that."

She looked closely into his face. "Millard, are you saying you wanted to strike me a long time ago? You been unhappy with me all these years?"

"Said nothing like that."

"It sounded so. If you're not pleased, speak it, don't hide it."

He shook his head, smiling. She said, briefly, "It'd be better if you didn't always close up like an oyster. When I get mad, why don't you get mad? Then we'd get over it."

She turned from him, the quickness of her motion notifying him of her renewed displeasure. The scene was done. He stepped into the yard to make the round of his slash fires, piling on great mounds of wet brush. It was a wonderful way she had of touching a match to her discontent and blowing it to hell and gone into the sky; it gave her the feeling of something accomplished. Now she would hum to herself and forget about it and expect him to forget about it. He stood in the meadow, catching the sense of the night. There was no feeling of rain. Tomorrow would be another fair day.

The Lords crossed the creek with the Gays and the Provosts and thereafter went on alone, westward up the hill to their place. Mrs. Lord said: "Where's the trail, Billy?"

"God-damned if I know. Black as the gut of a cat. Come over here. You tired?"

"Visitin' makes me fresh. I just love it. But I wish you had your fiddle. Ain't ever goin' to get over bein' sorry. Oh, God, Billy, I could of snatched that bread and jam from Watt Irish. Sugar — sugar, I'm so starved for it. I'd just like to get my greedy hands on a barrel of honey. I'd eat till I was sick. I'd smear it on me. I'd drown in it." She went on up the hill, making little mournful sounds as her imagination tortured her.

Billy Lord reached deeper and deeper for his wind as he climbed. "I have got to lose weight," he grumbled. "It's killin' me."

"Now don't talk of that. What'd I do out here alone?"

"Marry a man that'd buy you sugar."

Her huge bulk moved over, bumped into him. Her voice was girl-like. "Oh, Billy, I never said it. I never meant it. You know I was just talkin'."

"Sure," he said. "But I wish you had it. Wish I could find a bee tree. Ought to be bee trees out here."

26

WHEN Lockyear brought Roxy home, straight from Lot White's reluctant blessing, he did an odd thing: he paused at the edge of the clearing and looked at her with nothing kind on his face.

"Go on ahead, I'll be there in a minute."

So she walked into the cabin. Veen was at the fire, back to the door; he turned and he rose in surprise. "What you doin' here?"

She was out of breath from the long hike; she said nothing. Her clothes were muddy; her hair, shaken loose by her exertions and caught in overhanging branches, lay half down her neck and half down her forehead. Never a pretty girl, never noticed, accustomed to nothing but the strays and scraps of attention, she stood mute before Veen with her heavy lips and irregular features fixed in anxiety.

He said: "Where's Cal?"

She motioned toward the door.

Veen said, "Jesus Christ, is this one more of his crazy notions?"

She moved her hands, she tried a strange laugh which came to an abrupt ending and wheeled when she heard Cal come into the place. He was grinning. "Meet my wife, Veen."

Veen looked long at his brother, and let his glance fall on the girl; he turned to face the fire, he turned back and spoke quietly. "You son-of-a-bitch."

"Stop that," said Cal. "Don't tell me . . ."

Veen said, "Shut up," and took Roxy's arm and went through the doorway with her. He pointed to the creek. "You go over there and stay till I call you." She didn't understand him and he had to give her a small push to start her away.

At the creek she turned to find him watching her. He motioned for her to go farther on and she walked another twenty feet and squatted beside the water, hearing the voices of the two men rise — Veen's voice running on with almost a shrillness in it, Cal's words breaking in. She made nothing of the talk, but the brawling quarrel was plain enough; then presently it died to a lower pitch. She dropped one stone after another into the water, becoming so absorbed in the chore that Veen, later appearing, had to shout twice at her.

She returned to the cabin. Cal lay on one of the two bunks, hands over his chest, eyes on the ceiling. He said nothing to her. Veen stood at the fireplace.

"Well, girl," he said, "you're the cook — you keep house."

She looked around anxiously; she saw a broom and went to it. "Floor's swept already," said Veen. She laid the broom back and stood in the corner with a straining-to-understand expression on her face. He spoke to Cal. "I'll make my bed in the shed."

"Don't do it if you don't want," said Cal indifferently. "What difference does it make?"

"You son-of-a-bitch," said Veen.

"Take your turn with her, too, if you want," said Cal.

"You want to know what I wish right now, Cal? I wish there was a God and I wish he could catch you and slice you lengthwise one inch at a time till your screamin' filled the world."

Cal Lockyear swung his head and stared over to his brother with his pressed grin. Roxy suddenly came from her corner and took Veen by the arms. She said: "I won't be in your way. You'll like me. I like you a lot." She kissed him and peered into his face with her hopeful eyes; her unpracticed laugh made its brief sound in the room. Veen patted her shoulder and said, "That's all right, Roxy," and moved to the door. He paused there a moment. "Oh God, how I wish it," and went into the yard.

She settled into the cabin without authority or place and without encouragement. Her power of self-expression had never been developed; ignored by Lockyear, she had no chance to develop it here. She was a poor cook and Cal swore at her and sometimes Veen stepped in to give her help. Whenever she was puzzled or in trouble it was to Veen she turned. Time went on. Rarely did she speak to Cal unless he spoke first; when he set off on his frequent trips she stood in the doorway to watch him go with the half-lighted expression on her countenance and afterwards resumed her one solitary amusement of walking by the creek, head down, toes kicking at the rocks. At night she sat at the corner of the fireplace, looking at nothing in particular, listening to nothing in particular, for it was a silent cabin with little said between the brothers. Occasionally a quarrel born of some silent conflict between them which she neither saw nor understood would rise and she would watch both men and be terrified and crawl deeper into her isolation. Gradually the little dream of being a wife with the possession and the assurance of other wives faded. It had never been a clear dream; it had been only a shapeless thing moving across the dim light of her world. She learned she could expect from Cal nothing better than rough usage during the moment he wanted her, and nothing but indifference afterwards. During his peaceful periods he scarcely looked at her; when his mood of silent fury came upon him, he frightened her. Since Veen was always kind to her it came naturally about that she turned to him, and this was presently noticeable to Cal. She was inept with her hands and one afternoon she badly burned herself on the big kettle hanging over the fire; she was usually stoic enough to endure injury without comment but on this occasion the long accumulating fears and repressions caught up with her in her pain and she burst into a wild crying, and paced the cabin floor, and grew more incoherent until she had worked herself into hysteria.

Summoned by the sound, Veen came in and caught her shoulders; and she flung her arms around him and locked her body against him, and in this attitude Cal found her when he walked through the front doorway.

"Foolin' around my henhouse, ain't you, Veen?"

Veen pushed the girl into the yard and closed the door; and the sound of quarreling rose inside again, higher and higher, and presently she heard things slam against the walls, and Cal's steady cursing, and the whacking of fists against flesh, and the crashing of a body on the floor. She ran in from the creek and flung open the door. Veen lay in the corner, mouth and nose bleeding; he had taken his gun from its peg and now held it cocked against his brother. Softly he said one thing over and over, "You son-of-a-bitch, someday you'll scream. Oh, you son-of-a-bitch someday you'll scream." Cal turned from the cabin.

He was soon back, his whole manner changed; he was excited about something and seemed to have no more interest in the quarrel. He seized his gun and went rapidly from the cabin. Veen said, "What's up?" and followed him. Roxy, moving as far as the doorway, watched the scene. Cal was laughing; he pointed diagonally across the yard and across the creek to a small break in the trees. The break became a ragged corridor extending perhaps a mile southeastward; something along that corridor drew Cal's attention.

"See there," he said. "Way down. Looks like the back end of a deer."
Veen squatted and set himself for a long look. "Indian," he said.

"Been there, same position, for half an hour."

"Indian watchin' somethin'," said Veen.

Cal lifted the gun and clapped it snugly to shoulder and cheek. "How far you say it is?"

"Half-mile or better. Don't do that. It'll just cause trouble."

Cal settled into a long silence as he took aim; the muzzle of the gun steadied itself, then crept fractionally upward. The explosion was dry and flat, bouncing over the clearing, bounding through the timber. The object on which Cal had aimed made a slight turn and fell and became an indistinct blur on the ground. Both men watched it a long time.

Veen said: "Just for nothin' you do things like that. He's squirmin'. Gut shot. Don't leave him like that."

"Hell with him. One shot's enough."

"You finish it, or I will."

Cal rammed a new charge into the rifle, shook powder on the pan, made another long aim and fired. Veen, watching from his crouched position, said, "He jumped." Then, a long time later, he added quietly, "That's all," and rose and went around the cabin.

It was then middle afternoon. Cal disappeared into the timber with his rifle and was gone until suppertime. The savage mood was on him — the swollen energy, the taut nerves — and he ate without a word and lay on his bunk to stare upward through the gray spiral of his pipe smoke, his very motionlessness sending strain into the room; and suddenly he sprang from the bunk as though he had passed his endurance and took his rifle and again disappeared.

When he returned an hour later his gray eyes had a cat's green shining in them. From his place beside the fire, Veen narrowly watched the signs of deviltry on his brother's face. Cal laid out the tin cups and hauled the whisky jug from beneath his bunk, he filled the cups, he took his own, he signaled at the others. Then he said to the wondering Roxy: "Go on — might do you some good." He watched her sip at the liquor, and press her mouth together, and sip again.

"Go slow, Roxy," said Veen. "You don't know that stuff." He stared at his brother. "What you up to now?"

Cal sat on the edge of his bunk and made short, urging motions at Roxy. "Drink for the bottom."

She was soon drunk. There was no more tolerance for liquor in her than in an Indian. She stood spraddle-legged, she let the cup and its remaining whisky drop. Dumbness came upon her. Her lips thickened, her jaws moved stubbornly forward, her eyes turned on Cal, round and roused. She moved toward the bunk with difficulty and sank beside him. She got her arms around him, and buried her head in his chest, and began to undulate her body against him.

He brought his half-closed hand against her chin, knocking back her head; he laid his forearm against her chest and broke her grip and shoved her away. She slid from bunk to floor. She got on her hands and knees and crawled a few feet and settled and rolled on her back. She closed her eyes; she opened them and looked directly at the ceiling.

"She likes you best," said Cal.

"Let her alone," said Veen.

"Ugliest God-damned creature I ever saw," said Cal, "but just right for a lame bastard like you."

"What'd you bring her here for?"

"I wanted a white woman for a change. This is all I could get. That ought to make you laugh. This is all I could get. The country's full of women and they're marryin' men I could break in two with my hands, slow cattle that won't fight, that stink when they sweat, that huddle in herds like sheep. And all I can get is a woman even those cattle won't have."

He rose from the bunk and stepped over Roxy, a foot on either side of her. Her glance wavered from the ceiling to his face; she rolled her head slowly on the floor. Lockyear reached out, caught her dress at the neck line and ripped it apart in one long motion, and he gripped her petticoat and tore it straight down. She made no protest; she watched him steadily.

"You son-of-a-bitch," said Veen.

"That's all I could get," said Cal. "I hate the whole God-damned race of women. They've got us, they can make us crazy, they can laugh at us and go away. She'd do it too if she could. If there was one other man in this world who'd have her, she'd run away from me. That's why I've got her, because nobody else wants her. I don't know whether to use her or put my foot in her belly and kick her to pieces."

Veen reached over his head in a quick motion and brought his gun down. "You fetched her here. I didn't want it — but you fetched her and now, by God, you take care of her."

Cal stepped away from her and settled on his bunk. "You sleep with her tonight. She might as well be useful."

Veen rose, watching Roxy, watching his brother. "When you're crazy, God knows what you'll do." He put his gun aside and went over to Roxy. He lifted her with some difficulty and carried her to the shed and laid her on his blankets, and returned to the cabin for his gun and for the blankets on the other bunk. He said nothing to Cal, who sat crouched, eyes fixed to the floor, big shoulder muscles hardened, lost in his discontent. When he got to the shed, Veen settled beside her and felt the occasional tremor of her body before she fell asleep.

27

THE deer were well away from the settlement and Burnett cruised the ridges a full morning before he saw a buck working at the brushy browse in a ravine below him. The better part of the afternoon was gone when he got it home and butchered it. Half of it he hung in the shed for himself; the other half he divided again and set off down the trail, leaving some of the meat at Lattimore's and taking the rest on to Mrs. Irish.

"Well," she said, "you sit right here and I'll make supper."

She had been doing man's work as well as woman's work; she was thin and her hands were rough and the smile she gave him came out with the crackling suddenness of unaccustomed muscles responding. She was about four years older than he was. He remembered her at the beginning of the wagon trip as an attractive, slightly careless married woman whose high-tempered husband had more than once staged a quarrel with her inside their wagon; but that liveliness was pretty much extinguished. Going into the yard to chop wood while he waited for supper, he began to think of his other neighbors, to estimate the changes made within them by the trip, and he was on this line of thought when Watt Irish came in from the hills with his gun, empty-handed and discouraged. He said, "Hello," to Burnett and went to the cabin. Burnett heard Mrs. Irish speak to Watt and heard the boy's short answer; then Watt, obviously instructed to keep Burnett company, emerged from the cabin and sat on the woodpile.

"No luck?"

"No sign," said Watt. "Where'd you get yours?"

"About three miles south and east of Lord's."

"I'll try there," said Watt. There had been no change in him since the gorge. He had gained no weight, and perhaps had lost a little, for his shoulders were sharp points beneath the cotton shirt and his arms and hands were bony. He talked as a man would talk and on his face was a dry weariness.

When Mrs. Irish called them in for supper Burnett noticed she had taken time to do over her hair and change her dress. Watt gave her a curious stare as he sat down to the table, and thereafter concerned himself with his food. She had cut three good steaks from the venison rump and had ground enough wheat in her coffee mill to make gravy; from this same whole dark flour she had made biscuits. This, with coffee, was the meal.

When they were through Mrs. Irish rose to clear the table. "Watt," she said, "we've got Gay's big file and he'll be needing it. You put on a coat and take it back."

Watt left the cabin with some reluctance and Mrs. Irish followed him into the gathering twilight and walked on a few yards with him; when she came back she was livelier than Burnett had seen her for many weeks.

He said: "I'd better be moving on."

"Oh," she said, "sit awhile and light your pipe. I've not had the smell of a man's tobacco smoke for so long."

Winter's darkness rolled over the meadow and familiar landmarks vanished. From the doorway Burnett watched Billy Lord's hill turn into a conelike shadow; the roundabout tree spires scratched a ragged silhouette across a star-speckled sky, the far lights of Collingwood's cabin set forth their wavering wink. He got a big root chunk from the woodpile and laid it on the fire; he filled his pipe and found a towel for the dishes.

"You don't have to do that," said Mrs. Irish. She stopped her work a moment and bent her head into the smoke of his pipe. "That's so good. I used to hate it. I was spoiled."

The firelight and her own mood erased the lines of her face. He had never thought of her except as Watt's mother or as a widow, but it occurred to him that she was younger than his notion of her. She had round arms and her mouth was pleasing; her hair was black and heavy, her body looked comfortable to him.

She said: "I had an easy life as a girl and when I got married to Irish and started house with a very poor man I sometimes was sorry for myself. I wish I could tell girls how foolish it is to be proud. They're young, they're good-looking, they make men dance at their heels — and they've got everything their way. It's nothing they've earned, it's just being young. One day they'll wake to find the tide turned, and they've got to beg for the smiles they used to take for granted. I think it's the most cruel day in life." She looked thoughtfully into the dishpan, and corrected herself. "No, the second most cruel day."

"What's the other?"

"When you look at your child and know he's missed too much, and it's too late."

"Watt's going to be all right," he said.

She raised her head and shook it slightly and he saw how brutal the thought was with her for a moment; then she went on with her washing. "You've been nice to us. I don't know why you should. You're nice to a lot of people."

"Common thing."

"Not so common. People have to be hurt before they understand much. Healthy people and happy people — they don't know."

"I'll be damned," he said mildly. She threw him a side-glance, and presently they both laughed. When the dishes were done he hung up the towel to dry; he hunted for the broom and swept the floor and shook the fire together and stood by it with his pipe. "How much wheat have you got left?" he asked.

"About three sacks," she said. "Watt's awful sick of it. Boys hate plain food. I've got a little corn but I hate to touch it."

"Don't do it. That's your seed. The first good day of spring I'll come around to break your garden lot. Any salt meat left?"

"Barrel's empty. We've a little molasses and some tea. It marvels me to see how little people can live on. I don't know how we're doing it and I lie awake so scared sometimes I shake. When I think of how much we wasted from the table in the old days, it just seems sinful. I'll never again throw a scrap of food away, so long as I live."

"We may get hungry before summer, but nobody's going to let anybody else starve."

He watched her move about the small room to finish her chores. Her glance came to him and she smiled and went on with her work, but the smile faded and she seemed to grow hurried or disinterested in what she was doing, and she removed her apron and came to the fire. "It's nice to know we've got somebody to lean on. I wish I had some liquor to give you a drink. I wish I could help somehow. Have you got any clothes you need mended?"

"What I've got's too ragged to patch."

"You take good care of yourself." He caught a remarkably direct glance from her and noticed the growing color on her face. She seemed uneasy with herself, she made another aimless circle of the room and returned to the fire. "People think crazy things sometimes, don't they?"

"That's living alone."

"It's not good." She turned to the doorway and watched the night; he felt tightness close around and sensation rippled through him and he was alert. Her voice roughened. "My neighbors are good to me — in every way except their advice to accept my lot and be cheerful. They don't know — they have got their comfort. I swear, I sometimes think if a one-legged heathen of a man should come through here I'd make eyes at him." She caught herself. "I shouldn't say that."

He knocked the ashes of his pipe into the fire and crossed the room. She had her back to him, blocking the door. "Cabin fever," he said.

"It's a good thing when we're young that we don't know what waits us. Lot White says we deserve what happens to us because we're sinners. What sin did Watt commit to grow up like he's growing? It'll take more preachers than the world's got to make me believe that. When Lot gets to talking about how wonderful a place heaven is, I think of how Irish used to say what a wonderful place Oregon would be. It's the same thing. We keep fooling ourselves."

"Look here," he said. "Watt's going to wind up with six hundred forty acres of land and you'll both look back and laugh at the troubles you've had. He's not going to starve, and neither are you."

"Oh, food, food," she said. She continued to look into the darkness. Her stillness seemed to grow and to become a waiting. He noticed the preoccupied expression she wore, the rigidness of her body. She drew a long breath, murmuring, "I suppose it'll be at least an hour before Watt gets back," and she swung and let her eyes touch him. She held the glance long enough to embarrass him and when she observed it she gave out a small laugh and stepped aside.

He moved into the yard, conscious of the air's coolness on his face; he had grown very warm. "Thanks for the meal," he said.

"Come again, Rice."

"All right," he said. The stirred-up expression had left her; her eyes were rather sad, rather puzzled. She murmured, "Good night," and turned into the cabin.

194

28

HOMEWARD bound, he found neighbors gathered at Lattimore's and Lattimore shouted, "Come in — come in." He spoke to the Bucks and the McIvers and the Kerns and the Millards. Moss Rinearson and Edna were there. He hadn't seen her since her marriage, but there was no change; she came around Lorenzo Buck and put a hand on Rice's arm and kissed him.

Lattimore said, "Look out, girl, you got a husband here."

"Ah," said Edna, "Moss knows I like Rice."

"And whut else does he know?" said Lattimore cheerfully. "Never mind, Moss. First month of marriage is always the hardest."

"Why," said Moss, "I figure the first month was mighty good," and ducked his head at the crowd's laughter.

McIver turned to Burnett. "Been a couple of Molallies sneakin' around today. See anything along the trail?"

"No."

Lattimore said, "Long hike to Gay's, ain't it, Rice?" and winked at the room.

Mrs. Lattimore said, "Everybody don't think what you're always athinkin'."

"Well, that's too bad," said Lattimore. "Makes damned good thinkin'."

Edna stepped to the back of the small room and watched Rice between narrow-shuttered lids. She ignored Moss, she ignored the others; she watched Rice and her lips were warm pillows waiting.

"They were over at Crabtree's," said McIver, still talking about the two Indians. "Crabtree was gone and they scared hell out of the women. Bullied 'em around and got some food and went away."

"Hungry season," said Burnett.

"I don't like it," said McIver.

Mrs. Buck drew her shoulders together. "It reminds me of Grandma Hedges when she was captured."

Buck looked at her. "I don't believe I've heard that story."

"We've not been married so long I've told you all my stories," said Mrs. Buck. "It's wise to keep a few for something fresh."

"Men don't think so," said Mrs. Millard. "They tell 'em, and tell 'em, and tell 'em, and each time the story gets bigger and the man's more of a hero."

Buck said, "Tell that story, Sophie."

"My grandmother lived in Kentucky, back on the edge — way back where the Scotch-Irish went to get away from people. I don't know why those men always hated to live in towns or near anybody. Grandmother says there weren't any neighbors around her closer than twenty miles. She was fourteen and had ten brothers and sisters and her mother at the time was only thirty-six. They had a big cabin and a barn and maybe twenty acres of clear land, everything else was hills and trees. Her father was a great hunter, and when he wasn't hunting he'd be scouting for the soldiers that went through, or he'd be trading horses a long way off. Grandmother's mother raised that family. Well, it was a time when the Indians were bad and Grandmother's father was gone. One afternoon, a little before dark, the Indians came. Grandmother's mother got the children inside the house and barred the door. There's one thing Grandmother's father had done — he'd built a tunnel from beneath the floor of the cabin to the barn, and the barn was close by the trees. So when she got the door barred Grandmother's mother kissed Grandmother and the girls and the youngest boys and sent them through the tunnel. The oldest boys stayed to help fight.

"Grandmother got to the barn and sneaked through the back way into the trees with the other children. By then the clearing was full of Indians and the top of the cabin was burning. A lot of Indians were roaming around the barn and Grandmother figured they'd find the tracks of the children pretty soon, so she led them to a creek and told them to wade along the creek as far as they could; then she went back to the edge of the clearing thinking that maybe her mother and the other boys would come through the tunnel. But while she was there the Indians broke into the cabin and in a little while they brought her mother out — the boys must have been killed in the cabin, because she never saw them again. She said her mother's hair was very long, almost to her knees; she'd measured it once when she brushed it. The Indians unpinned the hair and one Indian, very tall and powerful, gripped her mother by the hair and brained her with a club; and then he scalped her and went around the meadow, waving that long hank of yellow hair.

"Grandmother went back to the children and told them to keep wading in the creek for another hour — it was growing dark then — and then she told them to strike straight north toward Fort Mims and she showed them the star to go by. After that she began to walk in the other direction. She was about ten miles from home when daylight came; and about an hour later some Indians came right through the brush and caught her. She saw more scalps in the party. She recognized every one of the little brothers' and sisters' scalps. So she was alone. Well, she was fourteen and a large girl and they didn't kill her. They marched her all that day and all next day and finally brought her to a village where some Indian women took her and beat her awhile and set the Indian children against her. But an Indian man liked her and made her his squaw and she lived in that village for about three years. She had two babies by the Indian but each time she smothered the babies. She said that when she was a captive she'd sometimes get awful blue and then she'd go to the lodge of the big Indian who'd killed her mother. He had all his scalps hanging in the lodge. And she'd go touch the hair of her mother's scalp — she said the color of the hair hardly changed at all — and it would make her feel better. I remember one time asking her if it wasn't a bad feeling to see it hanging there. 'No,' she said, 'life's life and death's death and that's all of it, and there's no use borrowin' from one side what belongs to the other.' When she was almost seventeen a band of white men came onto the camp — they had heard there was a white woman captive in it — and killed almost every Indian, even the women and the older children, and took Grandmother back to the settlements. There was a young man in that party and he took her to the home of his people, and about a month later they were married."

Mrs. Lattimore said: "She ever see her father again?"

"She was about thirty when a man came through the country and stopped to ask some directions and he looked at her a long time and he said 'Ain't you Maria?' — and it was her father. She said she cried a little, not so much for her father, but because it brought back the memory of her mother and her brothers and sisters. Her father stayed over one night with them. Next morning he said good-by and went on. She never heard of him again."

Silence hung heavy over them. Mrs. Buck looked into the fire with a kind, dark expression; she was thinking far back. Mrs. Lattimore stirred uneasily. All the men were thoughtful.

"Things were hard on people in those days," said Mrs. Buck.

"I don't like the notion of those Molallies creepin' around here," said Mrs. Lattimore. "Who knows they don't mean to come down here some night and kill us all?"

"If they get to botherin' us much more," said Ryal McIver, "we better go up there."

Burnett said: "Not worth worrying about. They're just a few miserable people living in half a dozen hardscrabble lodges."

"You'd regret saying that if they came down and did it," said Elam Walker.

Burnett held his peace. A winter in a Crow lodge had shown him the inside of a people as vain, as gentle, as easily hurt, as lovelorn, as practical, as faithful as these here in Lattimore's cabin, but nothing was gained by saying it; for cruelty and infidelity between red and white had put the thing past saving. Beyond the cabin somewhere a sound began to grow. He turned through the doorway, listening. In a moment Ryal McIver came out. "What is it?"

"Hear that?"

McIver listened. He said, "No." Then he said, "Yes, I do," and called quietly into the cabin. The rest of the men stepped into the yard and women stirred around the room with their growing nervousness. The sound grew stronger on the trail eastward and became the ragged running of somebody. Ryal returned to the cabin to get his gun, followed by the others, and Mrs. Lattimore said sharply, "Oh, God, Lattimore, we goin' to be scalped?" With the steady rushing of the unknown person's feet came presently the harsh in-and-out sawing of breath. Stooped down, Burnett saw the wavering outline of the fugitive in the meadow. He spoke to Lattimore, who seemed inclined to shoot.

"Don't — just one out there."

The runner rushed over the yard and entered the fan of cabin light. It was Roxy, hair down from her running, mud splashed over her clothes. She brushed by Burnett and the other men and went into the cabin; she slammed the door against the men in the yard.

"Well, what the God-damn' hell," grumbled Lattimore. He lifted the latch and gave the door a kick with his foot to show his displeasure. Over the shoulders of the other men who followed Lattimore in, Burnett saw Roxy backed against the fireplace. She used her fingers to throw her loose hair behind her. "I ain't goin' back," she said.

Mrs. Millard said: "He hurt you, girl? He mean to you? Beat you?"

Roxy watched Mrs. Millard with uneasy suspicion. "I ain't goin' back," she said sullenly, "but I won't tell you why."

Burnett retreated from the doorway, turned the cabin's corner and waited in the shadows; for he had caught another sound on the trail, this time the rapid beating of a horse's feet; then he corrected himself — no, two horses. The horses left the trees and ran on over the meadow into the cabin light. Cal Lockyear was on one horse and led the other. He said, "Roxy," and got down and faced Lattimore at the doorway; he laid an arm on Lattimore's chest and shoved the man aside and stepped into the room. His voice went roughly at the girl. "If you want to leave me, do it in the daytime. Tell me you want to leave and I'll furnish a horse and take you to your people, but, by God, don't play this running-away stuff with me and make folks think I'm bad to you. You come out here and get on this horse."

Burnett turned the corner of the house and passed through the doorway, thus coming directly behind Lockyear. Roxy faced Lockyear, chin and mouth stubborn, eyes flat, the anxious and peering look upon her. She shook her head. "Don't make me do that again."

"Do what?" said Mrs. Millard.

Lockyear said to Mrs. Millard, "It's none of your business."

Mrs. Millard's rage rose and she dumped its acid into Lockyear's face. "You dog, you! You jackass — you overgrown baby goin' around making faces at people. Tell me what to do? Why, I'll tell you what I'll do. I'll take this gun and do what these men have not got the spunk to do. I'll brain you with it or I'll shoot you with it as somebody ought to have done it long ago."

Mrs. Millard lifted the gun and glanced at its pan; she made a wicked sound of annoyance when she discovered no powder in the pan and she started forward in the little room with the gun poked forward like a sword. Millard reached out and seized it from her. "That will do," he said.

"Millard!"

"No," he said, "that will do."

Lockyear stared at her. "Your husband ought to break your damned neck."

"That will do, too," said Millard.

"Don't talk to me that way," Lockyear warned him.

"I'm about out of patience in both directions," said Millard. "Now you mind your business or I'll grab you by the neck and take you to the creek and drown you like a cat."

Lockyear said, "Don't talk to me that way."

"Do your business here and get on."

Lockyear turned to Roxy. "Come out of here."

199

"You don't have to do it," said Mrs. Millard.

Millard shook his head at his wife. "It is not your affair. He's the husband and she's the wife and what goes between them ain't for us."

"Come out of there," repeated Lockyear.

"Roxy," said Burnett, "do what you please."

Lockyear pulled his shoulders around, saw Burnett and swore at him. "Where were *you*?"

Burnett laughed at him. "Roxy," he repeated, "do what you want."

The girl had no mind for all the voices going at her. She laid her peering glance upon Lockyear. "You won't do that to me any more?"

"Come out of here," said Lockyear.

Satisfaction quickened Roxy's expression. Rarely in her life had she received notice and this scene comforted her, for she was the center of it, she was looked upon, talked to, made important. She lifted her chin and was proud of herself. "Well," she said, "I guess I'm your wife," and went over the room. Burnett stepped back through the doorway to let Lockyear and Roxy come out; he watched them rise to their saddles and he watched Lockyear's glance reach for him.

"Played Sioux with me," Lockyear said to him. "You want to play Sioux, I'll play Sioux, and we'll see how that comes out."

Burnett laughed at him. "Always get yourself in a crossfire, Cal."

The two moved across the meadow. Going to his own horse, Burnett heard Mrs. Millard's voice intemperately rising.

"You heard what she said. She said: 'Don't do that to me again.' Oh, God, it's horrible to think about! He'll kill her. You men, have you got no feelings?"

Drifting over the meadow Burnett caught Millard's dry rejoinder. "Man and wife is man and wife — foolish to interfere." When he reached the edge of the timber Burnett turned to discover Edna in the doorway, the light framing her unmistakable figure. She had wanted to talk to him. She was experienced enough to see into him and to understand there were parts of her scattered all through him as coals waiting a breath of air to flame again; she was certain she could carry on where she had left off, if it pleased her.

Half through the woods he stopped the horse to listen into the curdled shadows. There had been no definite sound — only the impression of a sound, only the feeling that somewhere a motion had occurred; it was the kind of thing to which he was particularly responsive and always had been from his earliest outdoor training; and so he sat quiet a long while, moving his head in compass-needle fashion to catch the next warning; there was none, and he went on to the clearing, put away the horse and entered the cabin.

The fire was only a splinter of red on the hearth. He stood before it a moment, catching the steady wash of the creek over the rock ledge; then he turned to the doorway and squatted down, scanning the yard before him, and in another moment he retreated to the cabin's back side, pulled away the canvas which served as a temporary break against the window aperture, and crawled through. He stood against the outer wall, searching the night; he lifted his gun and drifted toward the lean-to barn, and circled it and paused to watch his front door from the distance of fifty feet. Beyond the cabin a streak of shadow floated against the greater backdrop of black, and when he noticed it Burnett went to the ground and crept forward belly-flat.

The shadow strengthened before him; the shadow swung, advancing upon the cabin's door with short stop-and-go motions. Twenty feet from the door the shadow rose higher and went the last twenty feet to the cabin in a silent rush and lodged motionless against the log wall. Burnett crawled on until the intruder's shape took form against the logs — bent over and now beginning to creep toward the nearby doorway. Burnett changed his direction, angling for the cabin's corner; when the shape reached the doorway and hung close upon its edge, Burnett ran his hand along the earth until he found a creek's stone the size of a musket ball, gathered his knees beneath him and threw the stone across the yard.

The small report of its landing flung the prowler around and sent him away from it, straight upon Burnett. Half risen, Burnett wrapped his arms around the man as the latter plunged into him. The smell told him enough; it was an Indian he had trapped. He threw the Indian to the ground, struck him hard in the belly with his knee and weathered through the explosion of the Indian's energy. He had learned from Hawn the skeleton words of the Chinook jargon and, both arms anchoring the Indian's hands against the possible use of a knife, he tried out his learning. *"Tillicum — kopet, kopet."*

The Indian surged against Burnett and brought his stony knees into Burnett's flank. Burnett said, "Well, the hell with you, stop it, *kopet*," and let go his grip long enough to bring the jarring heel of his palm full force against the Indian's head. That stilled the Indian. He grumbled something between the in-and-out saw of wind. Burnett slapped his hand around the Indian's waist and found the knife he expected, and hauled it from its sheath and threw it across the yard. Then he got up.

"*Sikh tillicum*," he said.

The Indian remained still on the earth — too still. Burnett stepped farther back and waited. The Indian rolled and rose in one motion and flung himself into the night, the padding of his feet dying at last below the sound of the creek. Burnett got his rifle from the ground, found the knife and went into his cabin to build a fire.

It was three days until Christmas and somehow the encounter with the Indian took him back to the rougher years, reminding him that during his adult life most of these holidays had been spent in the camps of men a long way from home. Going backward in his mind, he tallied them: Winter camp in Jackson's Hole; the Crow village on the Green; on the side of a bare mountain in Sonora with fourteen men, nine of whom he knew were dead; in a freight camp halfway between St. Louis and Santa Fe. They were a little difficult to pick up as he moved farther into the past. One of them stood out bright against the rest, this one shared with a woman in New Orleans. Down in the Old Quarter he ran into Steve Rich, who had made the march with him across the Sonora desert, and they got to talking about it, and two women came along and Steve knew them and they went to supper. All Steve ever said about her was, "This is Rose," and then he went off with the other woman.

At this moment, reaching with his memory to bring her before him, he recalled only a face — now anonymous — against black loose hair on a pillow. She had believed too much in other men to believe him, and he was careless and had no honor to think about; and it went well with them, nothing asked, nothing expected. In the beginning he had expected it to be a meeting, a parting, and no change for either; at the end of it he knew that nobody walked away intact from such a thing. For on the last day he had felt loss; and her voice, murmuring to him, was no longer hard. Nothing was free, nothing without consequence. When he thought of her now it wasn't the physical pleasure which came back; he had not wanted to walk the streets of New Orleans alone and she had not wanted to be alone; and they had joined to escape the loneliness. That's what he had learned from her — that loneliness was something nobody could live with too long. When he got to thinking about it he realized that so much of what he believed true came of these chance meetings with other human beings. He touched them and something of their quality rubbed off on him. As with old Frank Mount who had said: "Old Ben's out here and

202

I got to help old Ben," and had walked from the safe shelter of a winter cabin into the blind wall of a Rocky Mountain blizzard. Whenever he thought of courage, his own or another man's, it was Frank Mount who set the standard. Pierre Lazarus had set another standard for him. Pierre showed up in camp one night as the sole survivor of a trapping party jumped by the Blackfeet. He had been twenty days lost, he was skin and bones and his bare feet appeared as two chunks of decayed meat. But all of that ordeal he boiled into a few words. "Ran three days, walked ten, swam one, and crawled six." Then he had laughed at the sight of his feet. "Sure as hell got rid of my corns."

Good people, good people, walking from God knows where to God knows where, with nothing but bad water, poor luck and not much relief along the way. Tick Petty had said that. Then he had said, "But there must be a big village at the end of this trail, or why's everybody walkin' on it?"

That was the year they worked the Yellowstone and Joe Torpenning was in the party; and Joe said to Tick Petty: "What you want to do in that big village, Tick?"

"Well, I want a bath and I want a shave, and I want a meal. That'll take me a couple hours. How long we goin' to spend in this place, Joe?"

"Eternity," said Joe.

"Then I want a big drunk. That will take a couple days. Then I want a bed I can sink two feet deep in, and I want none of your damned wool blankets or your lumped-up quilts for cover. I want my blankets to be six beautiful women. And that's eternity for me."

Joe Torpenning said: "There's the trouble with heaven. It's too good, it's everything we ain't got here. It's no mud, no fleas, no rheumatism, no work; it's perfect. You ever find a place like that?"

Burnett turned to his bunk and drew out his money belt to count his wealth. A sound rose over the creek's clatter. He pushed the belt back into the blankets and got his gun and left the cabin, finding shelter at the edge of the lean-to. The beat of two horses came on, from the direction of Hawn's; he saw the shadows rise against the black, he heard the rattle of bridle chains and the windy heave of the pressed animals. Cal Lockyear's voice was distinct. "Ease off, Whit."

The horses dropped to a fast walk. Lockyear and Whit Rinearson came abreast Burnett and went by. He heard Whit say:

"Take a shot through the logs?"

"Keep on now. We got a long way to go." Horses and men presently faded into the trees westward.

He returned to the cabin and sat by the fire, thinking of the money; thinking of what he meant to do. The idea had come to him suddenly.

He was rigging the horses of his pack outfit, when Edna walked into the yard the following morning. She said: "Where you going?"

"Prospecting around," he said. "See what the country's like."

"You're not going to move away?"

"No."

She stepped into the cabin and paused at the fire. He kept on with his chore and didn't follow her until he was finished with it. She had a smile waiting for him but she was displeased. "You're so busy you can't talk to me? It wasn't that way once."

"Where's Moss?"

"He went home. I'm staying a couple days with the folks."

"Trouble?"

The question amused her. "Don't you think I know how to be a wife?"

"Damned well."

She laughed, and her head lifted with its gesture of self-confidence. "You ought to know," she said. But as she continued to watch him her attitude changed. She was dissatisfied with him. "You're different."

"I'm different, you're married, we're both different."

"Ah," she said, "don't talk silly. People don't change because Lot White waves his hand at them and says they're married. Am I supposed to quit talking to everybody else because I'm married? I'll not do it."

"Moss has got something to say about it."

"I took him as he was, and he can do the same with me. I won't shirk anything. But I won't change." She grew restless. "What do I bother talking about it for? I shouldn't have come. It's for me to worry about Moss, not for you, but if it bothers you, I won't come again."

"That's better."

"You said if there was ever anything you could do for me, I was to tell you. You didn't mean it. You were just trying to make me think you were grieving because I married Moss."

"What do you want me to do?"

"Nothing. I only wanted to say hello."

"You want me to say how much I miss you. You want me to look bad and feel sad, to be all busted up."

She said: "You never meant anything you said to me. It was just playing, so you could have your way. You had your way and you were glad when I married Moss, so you wouldn't have to worry about me any more."

"You're angry because I don't cry. You want to scratch me."

"Well," she said sullenly, "is it so easy for you to forget everything? It must be. You're running after Katherine now. You turned right from me to her. It didn't cause you any trouble at all."

"You're the one that got married. I didn't."

She said: "That had to be. But does it change anything about you and me? Can you be close to me and not think of — of that?"

As soon as he came to her she had her arms ready for him and her kiss was the same lively thing. She made a groaning sound in her throat, she put her mouth aside, murmuring: "All week long I've thought and thought. You didn't want me enough. There was always something, always something. It just got longer and longer and I knew Moss wanted me and I couldn't wait any more."

He brought her head back to him and felt the laughter inside her body. "You've not changed." She looked to the bunk for a moment and then caught his glance. The hint was there. "I know I hurt you when I got married. I saw it. I almost cried. I hate to think of you lonely, Rice. I just don't want you lonely." She made half a gesture with her hand, she whispered, "It wouldn't be the same with any other man. But we know each other, don't we? Would it be so wrong?"

"How about Moss?"

She said, "Oh, never mind him."

"I don't," he said. "I don't give a damn about him."

"I knew you didn't. Men don't think about that. So don't talk about him."

"I think about you, though."

Her manner shortened. "I can think about myself. You had your way. What's to be sorry for now?"

He had never been able to speak to her as he wished. Looking upon her, the fancies in him went wild; but when he came to say the words, they wouldn't match his feeling — they were like the squeaks of a slate pencil against thunder; and her smiling way of listening to him did the rest — for he knew the intense practicalness of her nature would make the words seem foolish to her and, in turn, to him.

"You know what I'd do for you," he said. "You know you can come here, any time, and start the whole thing over. I'd break my damned neck, I'd cheat Moss or kill Lockyear. I don't know what we had between us, but so long as you're around I can't keep my hands off you. Maybe there was more than that — I don't know — but it's a little late now to find out. What do you want to do, come around here once a month, keep the thing burning? I don't want it. Whatever it is, I want it dead."

She listened to him, head tilted, a trace of laughter in the engrossed interest of her face. She should have been offended at his bluntness but instead it pleased her to hear him, it was one more meal for her self-confidence. She murmured, "All right, Rice, go ahead and kill it," and she moved to him and put her arms around him. "Lover — lover." She kissed him and passed through the doorway. She was happy. When he followed her to the yard she teased him with her returned smile. "I won't like it if you go around other women, having your way. I know too much about you. I know just what you'll say, just what you'll try to do." Her imagination made a picture of it and she ceased to be pleased. "And, damn you, you'll probably get your way."

"You've got a man, Edna. What's this for — what for?"

The smile dimmed, her face settled and became heavy. She shook her head. "Well," she said, "someday — maybe — someday . . ." She shrugged her shoulders and started down the trail.

"Wait," he said. He saddled his horse, banked the fire and closed the door. Then a thought took him into the cabin again and he came out with the Indian's knife and stuck it into the outer cabin wall. Walking the trail with her he explained the fight with the Indian. "If he comes back he'll see the knife."

"He tried to rob you, maybe kill you. Why fool with him?"

"I want him to understand I put the knife there for him to take. All his life he's been trained to be afraid of anybody strange. White people have got the same thing in them. So, somebody makes a quick move and somebody gets killed — and there it goes again."

"Don't you trust an Indian. You'll get killed trying to be kind."

"If you lived in one of their lodges," he said, "you'd hear them say the same thing about us. People get afraid and build walls. Tribes build walls. Settlements build walls. The world is full of walls. That's a hell of a way to live."

"That Indian won't thank you. He'll think you're easy and try to rob you again. Indian or white people, don't you take on anybody's troubles. Don't be like Mrs. Millard, always fretting about things that are wrong. Nobody likes her for it. She ought to mind her own business. We all

206

ought to." Her smile took on its meaningful form. "You and I. That's our business."

They came to the Lattimore clearing. He got into his saddle and looked down and for a moment he regretted not taking possession of her in the cabin. The shadowed mockery was in her eyes as she witnessed his disturbance and she was inwardly laughing at him. It was a queer thing that they should know each other so well in this one thing, and fit so well, yet be strangers otherwise.

"We'll see each other soon," she said.

"I expect so."

"Next time don't be so slow."

He said: "There's an end to this, Edna."

"Ah," she said, "don't always be troubled about how things ought to be, or end, or start, or anything. Let things take care of themselves." She smiled at him as he moved away.

He passed Buck's and Monteith's and stopped at Mrs. Irish's for a moment. "You hear anybody go by here last night?"

"They went over the meadow and through Lord's notch. I think I heard two."

He followed the creek past one donation claim and another; he paused at Gay's and in another hour he reached the break of the bench and let himself into the prairie. Winter's soft, blue-cast atmosphere dulled the scene before him, the board-flat miles running on toward a distant penciling of hills, the occasional groves standing at anchor on this calm sea of space, the curl of smoke rising from an isolated cabin, the ragged course of brush-bordered creeks. Yonder, somewhere short of the hills, lay the Willamette and the settlement of the French-Canadians.

29

ON Christmas morning Martha Gay watched wave upon wave of fine-spun mist move over the earth, dissolving timber and rolling hills into unidentifiable shadows. There had been rain the night before but this was not rain; this was water whipped finer than she could have whipped egg-whites, layers of it settling lower and lower, chunks of it adrift and curling visibly around the corners of the lean-to barn. When it touched her face she felt it change into a cool sweat; and every object in the yard was crystal-beaded with it. Katherine and Gram stood by a big fire burning in the yard, scarcely fifty feet from the cabin, yet so wrapped about by the fog that they were indistinct to Martha in the cabin's doorway. John Gay and Joe were in search of a strayed cow. The Old Man sat by the fireplace, hands idle, mind idle. Martha stared at the fog, at the crawling moisture which lay upon everything, at the churned mud, and turned into the room without a word. When Katherine and Gram came to the cabin they found her seated opposite the Old Man, hands folded and expression despondent.

"Back home now, there'd be two feet of snow between house and barn."

"Blessing it's not that way here," said Gram. "I ain't sentimental about misery."

"But everybody'd be coming in. Even Alice, and she lived two hundred miles off. It was always the one time of the year when I could stand her husband. The house would just be wonderful crowded."

"Work — work — work," said Gram. "I remember it well."

"This miserable place," said Martha. "It ought to be full of cookin' smells. It ought to be just suffocating strong with things roasting and frying and bubbling. Well, it won't ever be the same for us again. Last year this time I looked on a table with twenty-five people, and we had twelve kinds of jam, and suet pudding, and those two suckling pigs and eight ducks — "

"Ten," said Gram. "I picked the dratted things."

"We left a whole crock of mincemeat and right this minute I suppose that new woman's making pies with it, and saying it's *her* mincemeat. She didn't look like much of a cook to me. I don't know why Gay wouldn't let me bring the rambler roses. I don't know why we had to leave most everything that's been ours since we been a family in America. I don't know why we came at all. We had all we wanted and we didn't have to lower our heads to anybody. Why have we got to start all over again? What's the good of it?" She was silent a moment, working herself into a more rebellious mood. "I wonder if Tade's alive. I wonder what kind of a baby Mary Lane got. I wonder — I just sit and wonder and I can't get anything out of my mind."

"Well," said Gram, "we lived in that one place eighteen years and I hated every minute of it."

Katherine said, "I didn't know that, Gram."

"I did. It wasn't my country to start with. I hated the heat and the mosquitoes and the bareness. I never got accustomed to the people. They had no fun in 'em like the people of my old home. I saw one of my boys grow up and get drowned there. I watched another get killed by a horse. That didn't make the country any dearer to me."

"We shouldn't have moved," said Martha. "We had all we wanted."

"Look at him," said Gram, and nodded toward the Old Man, who seemed beyond hearing the things they said. "He worked too hard there."

"*We're* working too hard here," said Martha.

"First year — first few years. But you won't have to fight the land and the climate like you did there."

"I don't know why we came."

"Because your husband brought you," said Gram tartly. "How long's this spell going to last?"

"You remember that jolly man in Oregon City? He said there wasn't any mail service. If you want to send a letter you give it to somebody who's going East, and maybe it's the long way around the Horn. It's a year before the letter gets home, if it ever does. It's a year waiting for an answer." Martha lifted her darker and darker countenance to Gram and Katherine. "We'll never see them again. We're dead and buried out here. We'll never see them till we're in heaven." She turned her face away and sat stiff on the chair and cried without a sound.

The Old Man lifted his glance from the floor, looked at her incuriously and turned his eyes away. Katherine crossed the room to stand behind her mother. She dropped her hands to her mother's shoulders. "Wait till the sun comes out. You'll feel better."

"No," said Martha Gay, "I never will."

Gram Gay said: "It won't do for you to go around like that."

"I know," said Martha.

"Won't make it any better for John."

"There's something wrong with him, and he won't say what. What would I do — what would I ever do if I lost him?" Martha murmured.

Over Gram's face moved the fleeting shadow of her superstitious other self. She reached down to lift and throw a clod of mud into the fire. The expression passed. She said, "Don't bring things on before their time. Now, if we're goin' to have Christmas supper in this house it's high time the bread goes in the oven, and where's that piece of meat?"

Martha said, "Don't ever tell him I said he looked sick. I don't want him to know I know it."

Katherine returned to the bonfire in the yard and covered it with wood. Over the fire hung the largest of iron kettles and in the kettle lay the slow-melting chunks of fat from the half-dozen bears John had shot during the previous month or two. After she got the fire burning properly beneath the kettle Katherine moved to the leach barrel which her father had built on a platform behind the barn. Into the barrel went ashes from the cabin's hearth and from the yard fire. Rain and an occasional dousing of bucket water trickled through the ashes, came from a spigot hole low on the barrel, and fell into a waiting keg. It was this filled keg of lye water which Katherine carried to the fire, adding it to the melted grease in the kettle; the two elements of soap now being combined, she settled herself to a tedious waiting and skimming and stirring while the mixture boiled itself to the proper consistency.

It was one of those jobs in which hands went one direction and mind went another.

Heavy shoes and heavy coat gave her the false immigrant-girl air Gram had noted; on her light hair the fog particles lodged and built a kind of crystal lacework; fire and weather tinted her complexion, and her general feeling of health laid its optimism across her face and added to the blue eyes an alertness and an expectancy. Far off in the fog she heard her father's voice calling the strayed cow. The brindle cow — that was another cow — was not more than two hundred yards beyond the barn, but the fog had gradually thickened until the cow was a shadow that had to be looked for. The oxen had not strayed far from the barn; one of them, Dan, stood a few yards from Katherine with its dew-frosted muzzle and watched the fire steadily. She could almost see thought moving behind the animal's eyes. She stepped to the big beast and rubbed the stony spot between the horns.

The timber at the meadow's edge had become a tall shadow, the fences were gone, the wheat field lay foreshortened; and with the fog had come too a soft, thick stillness and a world-slowed-down feeling; in such quietness the talk of Gram and her mother in the cabin sounded more than life-size.

It was a wonderful land. In the East at this season everything would be odorless, growthless, life withdrawn to some deep-protected cell for survival; and the ground would be ungiving. But here the earth still contained a mucky ferment and there was warmth enough in it to keep the meadow grasses emerald green. She gave the kettle a good stirring and crossed the meadow to the brush fire which her brother Joe had been tending until the strayed cow drew him away. She piled on layers of new wet slash. Fresh flame licked up and gray ashes rose, and the strong smell of green limbs burning rolled against her. Beyond the meadow, somewhere along the fog-hidden trail, she heard women's voices briskly break the stillness. Visitors coming.

She returned to the kettle, gave it another stir, and went to the cabin. "We should send Joe to the Kitchens with some butter."

"I used to be sorry for them," said her mother, "but I despise them now for letting poor Roxy go with that terrible man."

"I think Roxy decided that."

"She's not got mind enough to decide anything. It just makes me shudder."

"I don't know . . ." said Katherine. "Maybe it pleases her to have a husband when she never thought she'd get one."

"Well, she ran away from him."

"But she went back. I don't think it's for us to answer. How would I feel if I knew I never was to have a husband, and then I saw the chance?"

Martha Gay stopped her work long enough to place a well-known glance upon her daughter. "Might be a good thing if you'd just give that a thought — for yourself. I never expected to see the day Roxy Kitchen got married before you did. And you could have been married long ago. And I just can't understand why you make Harris wait. I never will understand it."

Katherine smiled. "We should send the Kitchens the butter."

"Well, all right, but my heart's not with it. We ought to give Mrs. Irish some, too."

"Not butter," said Katherine. "Rice gives them part of the milk from his cows."

"And why's he so good to her?" challenged Martha Gay. "A widow and a single man . . . I don't say anything's wrong. I just say pitch and fire oughtn't be too close together. He's thirty. Why wasn't he married before? How many women's he been mixed up in?"

"How do you know there's been any?" asked Katherine.

"At thirty? Well, if he's not been there's something wrong with him. You know all about Harris. You grew up near him. You know just what he is. You know he's good. He's thrifty. He works. He'll never cause you trouble."

Gram turned from the fireplace. "And that's why she don't want him."

"Don't make light of it," said Martha Gay. "When I think about it I just can't sleep nights. What do you think the neighbors are wondering about Katherine?"

"She's not getting married for the neighbors," said Gram.

Katherine said: "I've not seen that little brooch Uncle Ben sent me from New Orleans."

"It's in the bottom of the green chest. Between the comforters. Why?"

"I want to give it to Lucy Collingwood. It would look so well on her. Ivory and gold, and delicate. It just matches her."

"Delicate — delicate. Not so delicate when Whitcomb's around."

"How do you know that?"

"Pitch and fire — pitch and fire. And I will tell you something else, too, since you think Rice Burnett's such a man. Edna went up to his cabin. Helen Provost told me. It was the same day he came by here with the pack outfit."

Gram said: "You're a nice woman for talk."

"Well, she did."

The Old Man turned his head. "Where'd the boys go?"

The three women halted their private conversation to look at him. Katherine stepped behind him and laid a hand on the brown bare top of his head. "To hunt for the cow that strayed."

"Why didn't they say so? I better go help."

"You stay there, Old Man," said Gram.

"Well, why didn't they tell me?"

Katherine returned to the kettle and began a steadier stirring as the brew thickened. She had heard of Edna's visit to Rice's — there were too many ready eyes and tongues in the settlement for a thing like that to remain unnoticed. She put her mind to it as she stirred, puzzled a little but not too much, growing angry at Edna. Gram came from the cabin.

"Knew about Edna bein' there, didn't you?" commented Gram.

"Moss doesn't mean much to her, it's clear, or she wouldn't have done it."

"No man means much to her, so long's it's a man."

"That's wrong. She wanted Rice. So it must have been Rice that broke off."

"She's a miser for men. What she gets she won't let go. She's chased all her life and she don't want to quit."

"But he's the one that broke it."

"It ain't broke. She'll hang on. She knows what she can do. She knows she can shame him, too. She's got that string to pull. You know why she's got it."

Katherine turned the stirring stick around and around into the kettle;

her face was thoughtful. "It would be hard for him to stay back from her. Damn her, I'd like to drive her clear out of his life, out of his mind. She's not made him happy."

"There's ways of doing it," said Gram. "But just thinkin' about it ain't one of 'em."

30

JOHN GAY walked with his son through the dark aisles of timber, calling for the cow. The drifting fog tangled itself in the matted fir branches as ragged hanks of strange moss and the forest, condensing this thin dew, manufactured its own private rain. Young Joe's voice broke against the trees and seemed to become separate voices sounding down one corridor and another. "Co' boss — co' boss." They left the grove and crossed a meadow and circled another grove, John Gay traveling slower and slower; they came to the lower meadow of the Gay claim.

"I think," John Gay said, "we'll stop a moment," and settled on a windfall. Young Joe waited, not quite understanding his father's delay.

"Not feeling good?" he asked.

"It's maybe a cold," said John Gay. He breathed harder than he liked, he was conscious of the unaccustomed tightness of his face. He turned himself to let his right hand fall into his lap and he began to massage it and got almost no sensation from it. Higher up, somewhere around his shoulder, the steady ache had grown worse; no matter how he carried his shoulders, the bound feeling remained across his chest. He thought to himself: *Six weeks of it's not accidental. It must be I've had a stroke without knowing it.* Young Joe ranged the meadow, calling, and came back. "Don't see any tracks here. She didn't get this far."

"She's sly," said Gay. "Probably not a hundred yards from the house, playin' possum in a thicket. Cows take notions. Well, dark will bring her home."

"You want to go back now?"

"We'll wait a moment," said John Gay. "Like this country, Joe?"

"It's all right."

"If it were just me, I'd not come West. But this is a better place for you. There's more chance. We only had a middling-fair farm back East and land was getting too high for me to go buy a better one for you. All that country's growing but it won't profit the farmer so much as the speculator, the fellow starting towns, the lawyer and the storekeeper. It's the speculator who pushed up land prices and if I'd bought good farming land I'd had to go in debt for it, and you'd spent half your life paying it off. If a bad year came along you might have lost the farm. So we came here. The land's cheap, there's plenty of it and there'll be no debt on it. You have got to remember that in your lifetime you may see a dozen years when hogs and cows and hay will sell at a good price. The rest of the time prices will be low and you'll do well to break even. So you can't farm on land that costs too much; and debt will kill you. Don't ever buy anything you've not got money to pay for. Don't mortgage this land. Don't buy any more land unless you see a clear way to use it. Never buy land to speculate on and sell. No man can be two things at the same time, and you can't be a farmer and a speculator any more than you can be both black and white. God made the land to use. He didn't mean for it to be passed back and forth like a dollar piece from one fool to another."

His son nodded and looked beyond John Gay into the deepening mist; his mind was half elsewhere, and Gay lowered his head a little while and let the silence go on.

"You want to go back now?" asked young Joe.

"We'll do that in a moment. I'd like to tell you something to keep fast. You hear talk about this free land. But it's nowise free. Nothing's free. A lot of men, coming on this trip, lost something out of their lives by the trip, and that's a costly thing. We've got to do everything here, build everything, fence in, plow, fire stumps, clear brush. We have got to travel forty miles for everything that goes on this place — and that's time out of your life. We have got to build roads and schools. We have got to wait, we have got to do without till better times come. Someday when you're plowin' I want you to stop and think that the plow you're using came two thousand miles in a wagon and it took six months of your life and mine to get it here. There's nothing free and the fools that talk free are the men that don't know and won't thrive and will end up busted." He had looked across the meadow while he talked, but turned to catch his son's glance. He said, "Remember it."

"All right . . ." said young Joe. "Maybe the cow went up the trail toward Collingwood's."

"We'll go home now," said John Gay and rose from the log. He laid a hand momentarily on his son's shoulder, let it drop and walked across the meadow with his very slow, very careful pace.

214

Katherine used a paddle to transfer butter-soft soap into a keg. She washed the kettle and laid it away, and cleaned her hands and went into the wagon to change her clothes. She found the brooch in the green box, intending to walk to Lucy Collingwood's with it; but she returned to the cabin to spend a little time listening to the talk which Mrs. Provost and Mrs. Buck brought down the trail with them. Her mother had made tea and sat temporarily happy. The Old Man was gone.

Her mother said: "I'd not be that outspoken if I were Nancy Millard. It makes Millard no more pleased."

Mrs. Provost said: "Men ain't ever pleased to hear the truth about themselves. They take great stock in their pride."

"Well," said Mrs. Walker, "I do admire Nancy's spunk for spittin' out her mind. More than once, I've wished I could."

"I don't know," said Martha Gay. "Seems to me men do *try* to be reasonable."

"Oh, yes," said Maude Provost. "They make such a great to-do about reasoning things out, one side against the other, so much for this, so much for that, the good of it, the bad of it. Lord, sometimes I could just scream to hear Provost, for I know all the time which way he'll decide. He'll decide it the way he wants. But he's got to go all through the rigamarole. They love to be reasonable all right but it always turns out their way."

"I don't know," murmured Martha. "Gay usually asks me what I want to do."

"Well, he asks you but does he do it your way?"

"If it's best, he does."

"There you are," said Mrs. Provost. "If you side in with him, you get your way. But if you don't there's a long argument why your way ain't wise, and on and on through the whole rigamarole again till you just get weary and tell him of course he knows best. How many times have I said that! Sometimes I'm so mad I could cry. Sometimes it's so funny it's all I can do not to laugh. You'd think men would catch on to that but they don't."

"They're thick-hided, that's for sure," said Mrs. Buck.

"I wonder if they're so thick?" said Mrs. Provost. "Sometimes when Provost looks at me so innocent, I think, 'You rascal, you being sly with me?' They can be awful sly."

"Ever tell him that?" asked Mrs. Buck.

"Oh, no. Then he might be slyer still. I'd rather know what he was doing, and not tell him, than not know what he was doing."

The remark delighted Mrs. Buck. "That's it. We just play a game but the men, they don't know it. It's bad to laugh at a man. I did it once and Harper like to never got over it. How can they be so thick and still so sensitive? They're funny."

Martha Gay shook her head. "Pride means a lot to them."

"Means a lot to me, too," said Mrs. Provost, "but I've swallowed it plenty of times. Whenever did that start, I wonder — that it's woman that's got to bend and let a man keep his pride?"

"Men started it, where else?" said Mrs. Buck cheerfully.

"It was the men that got us out here," said Mrs. Provost. "Who would have come if women had had any choice in the matter?"

"I don't know," said Martha Gay. "I'd despise a man who let me run him. There's such a thing as bein' so considerate that the wife don't respect him. It's almost that way with Millard. Poor man gets trouble from her, and trouble from all the other men because he don't make her mind."

"They do hate her," said Mrs. Provost. "Because they're afraid she'll show us how to be independent, and that would be the end of their lord-and-master business."

"Lord-and-master," said Mrs. Buck and dropped both palms on her lap and bent forward to laugh. "Until they get sick. Then they act like roosters swashed around a rain barrel. Such moaning and groaning and complaining! You'd think they were about to die."

"Sick or well," said Mrs. Provost, "they always got to be the center of things, they always got to be important."

"Not all men," said Martha Gay. She thought of Gay, and grew still.

"Never saw one different," said Mrs. Provost. Then she looked toward Katherine and brought on a brisk smile. "You must think marriage is a poor thing, listening to us."

"I wonder if men talk about their wives this way?" said Katherine.

Mrs. Provost said: "If I ever heard of Provost doing it I'd kill him."

"You'd never know if he did," said Mrs. Buck. "Men don't tell things about other men."

"And I wonder," said Katherine, "if it's such a trial, why married women always try to marry off single girls."

The other women were silent a little while. Mrs. Buck, who had contributed her share of this talk in good humor, made a smiling gesture of resignation; but Mrs. Provost found humility hard to come by. "What else could you do? God made us the way we are — "

"And he was a man," said Mrs. Buck.

"There you are," said Mrs. Provost. "It's a trap that's got no way out. If only men didn't think they were such superior creatures! That's always the thing. You wait and see, Katherine."

Voices came through the fog and the brisk tingle of a harness bell announced a pack outfit. Turning through the doorway — the other women with her — Katherine found her father and young Joe walking into view with Rice Burnett. Behind them plodded Rice's pack animals, each one broad-loaded; even Rice's horse had half-filled sacks swinging from its saddle thongs.

"Merry Christmas," said Rice, and halted his string in the yard.

"What on earth have you got there?" demanded Mrs. Gay. "Do I hear geese? Where've you been?"

"The French-Canadian settlements," said Rice. "It'd do you good to look into their barns. Damned near made me cry — poor man looking at plenty."

Everybody went along the line of horses, Mrs. Provost patting the crates and sacks and bundles as though they were animals, Mrs. Gay issuing small sounds of pleasure for the things she saw. One pack animal carried three slatted crates tight-packed with geese; another had crates of chickens. There were big willow baskets from which wheat dripped, and sacks of onions, and squash and pumpkin and potatoes, and other baskets of shelled corn. Katherine placed her nose against a sack and caught the odor of apples. From every peg and rope-end of the pack outfit something hung, a few strings of peppers, a cheese in a calico bag, small hams, smoked fish wrapped about by a coarse cloth. Mrs. Gay never got farther than the geese; she put her fingers between the slats, murmuring, "Beasties, beasties, you wonderful beasties!"

Gay said: "All you need is some tinware and calico to have a travelin' store."

Burnett for a moment watched Martha Gay's complete preoccupation with the geese, then he walked over to her and ripped open a slat from one of the crates. "It's like Noah's Ark. Here's your start of geese — two geese, one gander. Same of chickens — one speckled rooster, three hens. Ought to get a setting of eggs out of that many hens in four or five days."

"Gay — Joe!" said Mrs. Gay. "Come here, help. Put 'em in the cabin and shut the door till we get something provided." She took the big goose in her hands and hugged it, and she went toward the cabin, murmuring, "You beautiful, beautiful beastie."

"Bring some buckets and pans," said Burnett. He went along the line of packs, loosening ropes; he took off half a sack of potatoes, he measured out some of the corn, some of the vegetables.

Katherine said: "What will you do?"

"Spread it around the neighbors."

"Then that's enough for us."

He left one of the hams and he had Martha Gay lift her apron and he put into it an apple apiece for each of the family, and he found another sack and added a few hands of nuts they knew nothing about. "Hazelnuts — wild." From still another sack he took a small covered crock from which honey oozed. Then he went down the line of horses, tightening the pack ropes. He said to Mrs. Provost and Mrs. Buck: "I'll stop by your cabins and leave a little of this. It spreads sort of thin but it'll make a taste."

"Wait a minute," said Katherine. She went into the house, got her coat and came out. "I'm going along. I've got to see this."

"Rice," said Martha Gay and called him about as he started away. She came to him and looked up at his face a moment, and she turned to her husband and said, "Now don't you mind," and swung back to kiss Burnett. She started away but Burnett, smiling, reached out to seize her around the waist.

"Been a long time waiting," he said and returned the kiss. When he let her go she said, half embarrassed, "You needn't be so rough with an old woman," and she stared at her husband and seemed to be displeased by his sudden let-go of laughter.

The pack outfit went on. They stopped at the Collingwoods', and Kerns'. Katherine noticed that Rice then left more with Mrs. Irish than at the previous places; that he left nothing but a token at the Rinearsons' — a small cheese; that he was almost as generous with the Kitchens as with Mrs. Irish. He detoured by the Purroys', Walkers', Crabtrees' and by McIver's, he stopped at the Mercers' and moved up to the Millards'; he returned across the ford to climb the notch to the Lords' — leaving a jug of honey there; he went roundabout to the Monteiths' and made his final stop at the Lattimores'. By the time they reached his cabin the cargo had shrunk to a ham, a few potatoes and onions, and a little cheese; he had saved a rooster and two chickens; and when they entered the cabin he laid a bottle of wine on the table.

"Your people drink at all?" he asked Katherine.

"Mother made Father take the pledge when they were married. Come back to our place for supper?"

It was five o'clock and half dark. He made a short fire to take the chill from the room and went out to unsaddle his pack string. His two cows had come down the meadow and waited with their noses at the fence. Katherine let them into the yard and got a pail and did the milking. She strained the milk and poured some of it into the skim pans in the lean-to; she mixed milk and wheat for the setting hen and went into the cabin while Rice put together a shelter for the chickens.

As she waited she took in the bachelor's arrangement of the room, and she looked at the bunk and she thought: *She's been in it with him;* and she thought of that affair very closely. What had it been like, and what had he gotten from Edna, and who had ended it, and what did he think about her now? Something must be left. How could anything like that end with nothing?

He washed himself, making a big noise of it, and came in to stand by the fire. He was in the best of spirits, he was lighthearted, he seemed to be thinking of something along the route which pleased him, or touched his humor.

"None of that was free," she said.

"Those French-Canadians have got stuff to burn."

"But it cost you something."

"It's Christmas. We've had a hard year. We're pretty sober. I don't know why we have to be so sober."

"When did you think of the idea?"

"At Millard's the other night."

"At every cabin it was a little different," she reflected. "Billy Lord's place was the nicest of all. You almost made Billy cry. . . . Open the wine."

He looked at her with his approval. "That's a fine idea." He used his pocketknife to dig out the bottle's cork; he half-filled a pair of tin cups, he touched his cup to her cup. "To what?"

"To everybody in the settlement."

"Down she goes," he said.

"No, sip a little at a time."

"I don't much like to nibble at things. I like the whole thing at one wallop."

"Then what's left?"

219

He took his sip; he watched her taste the drink and like it. "We can fill the cup again."

"When the bottle's gone — what?"

"Another bottle."

Her mouth moved along the cup's rim; her glance came over the rim. "This is good. I can see why people get the habit." She let the cup drop a little; the next question was soft. "What do you do with your empty bottles?"

He said carefully, "I never throw away the kind of a bottle you're talking about. I never emptied that kind of a bottle. That kind of a bottle can't be emptied. The more you drink of it, the fuller it gets. If it begins to empty on you, then it's not the drink you thought it was. Am I talking straight?"

"I'll think about it," she said; and then they were laughing at each other.

"Want some more in that cup?"

"Don't know what I'd do if I had another drink."

"Want to find out?"

She looked at him, still smiling. "Is this how it goes? I mean, a man and a woman — is this one of the ways?"

"I'll ask somebody that knows and tell you what he says."

She fell into serious thought. "I wonder if that was why my mother had Father take the pledge — if she saw something in him she was afraid of? It's hard to think of him as having been young and wild. Young people never know their parents. Once I tried to imagine my father kissing another woman. It shocked me. The younger we are, the more we think that excitement is all in *us*. They know we think it, and they know we'd be displeased to see it in them. My father and mother rarely kiss each other in front of me or Joe. But they're not so old. Where does it go, Rice? Does it really go — for all of us?"

She put her tin cup on the table and turned to spread her hands at the fire; and the fire captured her attention, as it always did, and the shadow and shift of her thoughts got stronger. "No, I don't believe it."

"There wasn't a hell of a lot of smiling going on today at any cabin we went to."

"Everybody is tired."

"Why don't they see it a little clearer — like Billy Lord sees it? When we grow old enough to know anything we know the game's got an end and the end's rigged against us. So we get solemn, we get into arguments, we fix up a lot of rules to make the game worse."

"Well, what do you want — how do you want it?"

"Tune up the guitar, and play it away."

"You're just talking. No more to drink for us. Remember we've got to go home for supper."

"I thought I had the answer — roving around the country for ten years or better. But it wasn't. Being a shadow's no good. Now I'm piling up some logs and some stones in this spot so I won't be a shadow but they'll fall down someday and I'll still be a shadow."

"Your sons will be here."

He looked through the door and saw the solid blackness move in. He stepped to the table and got the bottle and put it under his bunk. "I trust people, but not this far. Ready?"

She held her glance on him; her expression quickened when he came to her and turned her. She made no protest.

"This is my mistake," she said. "I ought to have Mrs. Provost or Mrs. Walker around. That's what they were doing when you came by — telling me about men."

He dropped his hand from her shoulder and got her coat and held it for her. Laughter was sharp-creased around her eyes. She said: "I didn't think you'd be scared away."

"You can scare me awful easy," he said. "Because I don't want to be wrong with you."

"Would you like it now?"

"Yes."

She smiled and shook her head as she put her arms around him. "I never thought it would be this way." She closed her eyes and the smile stopped.

Her mouth came to him, confident as Edna's but reserved as Edna's had never been. Half of her came through, half of her held off — and he checked himself and put no force on her. She stayed with him longer than he expected and when she drew away she was, in some fashion, still with him. She was smiling again. He tightened his arms on her and she touched the top of her head against his chest, whispering, "That was nice," and stepped into the yard. She was cooler than he was, for the kiss went knocking through him and made him absent-minded for a moment.

He closed the door and looked at the shadowed outside wall where he

221

had stuck the Indian's knife, and saw that it was gone. He got a bucket of milk from the lean-to and came back to give Katherine a hand up to his saddle; she sat sidewise on it, following him through the dense ground shadows and into the trees.

"I expected it to be different," she said. "What held you back?"

"I don't know."

"You're not sure about it."

"About what?"

"Talk — just talk," she said and avoided an answer. He left half the milk at the Lattimores' and the rest with Mrs. Irish. When they moved into the timber again Katherine said, "Give me a hand — it's too lonesome back here," and got off the horse and walked arm in arm with him the rest of the way.

Supper was ready. Martha Gay, whose anxiety was sometimes stronger than her fortitude, said, "I'd begun to worry — you're late. Sit on the milk stool, Rice." Gram went around the table to see that everything was on, and then stepped to the yard. In the shadows she looked back through the doorway at Katherine and Rice.

31

THE neighbors had come again. They sat close-crowded along the walls of the cabin, on the bunks, on the floor. Firelight stained them with its dull red, the leaping of the flame was bright in their eyes. The Old Man crouched in his corner, nodding at what he heard but only half understood.

Burnett watched Katherine's hands stir on her lap, come together and grow still. Her head rolled back against the cabin wall; she watched the ceiling and lightness made a visible wave over her face, eyes changing, lips changing. He had his back against the logs and thought he felt vibration. Turning his head, he flattened his ear to the log and picked up the thready rumor of a traveler in the night.

Gay watched him. "Something out there?"

"Horse."

There was a rider in the yard, hailing, "Hello there!"

The barrel-round voice created the image of a big man; and it turned out to be a big man when he stepped into the doorway — a spectacular man in greasy, blackened buckskins so shrunk by wetting and drying that they fitted like tights at buttocks and calves. He wore moccasins and a round trapper's hat, and a beard covered most of his face and fell over his collar button in iron-gray magnificence. His mouth was largely lost behind the whiskers but his nose stood out in Roman style and his eyes were lively and black and cheerful. He was around fifty, Burnett decided, and he seemed familiar though Burnett couldn't place him.

Nobody in the crowd knew him but the stranger attended to that immediately.

"Meek, Joe Meek, neighbors. I'm your U. S. Marshal, and I thought it time to come out and mend my fences. Think I met some of you when you passed through Oregon City. This man I know" — nodding at Gay. He edged and squeezed and sidled himself through the crowded room, identifying people, shaking hands. He stopped before the fireplace and turned his back to it and lifted the skirts of his hunting shirt to warm the bottom of his breeches. "Snug as a bear's den — and that's snug, for I've slept in some."

"I'll make coffee," said Martha Gay, rising.

"No — had some back a few miles."

Gay said: "If you've got a family why ought you travel on a day like this?"

"This country's got more corners to it than an old maid," said Meek. "She goes from there to there, and she goes off there, and crosses the river and goes off there." With each "there" his lifted hand made a poking gesture in a different direction. "Keeps me humping to cover it."

"Well," said Gay, "I don't think I'd travel on Christmas Day to shake the hands of the President, Pope or presiding elder."

"Depends on the requirements of your soul, I do suppose," said Meek. . . . "Looks fine down here. You people have dug in quick. You ain't quite got the Oregon mildewed look yet. Another winter and you'll have moss on the north side, and then you belong, and you won't talk about going back. Who's beyond the creek?"

Collingwood began to tell him, anxious to strike up a conversation. Meanwhile Gay let his attention quietly move to Burnett, and something like doubt came out of him.

Meek's Christmas Day traveling seemed to stick in Gay's throat. Burnett closed his eyes a moment, listening to the rumble of the marshal's voice; he opened his eyes and watched the marshal's glance make its short darts about the room as he listened to Collingwood. Gay was right; the marshal wanted something.

"Who'd you say?" asked the marshal.

"Beyond this valley? Daniel Rinearson."

"Didn't I meet him in Oregon City? Had sons?"

"Three sons."

"Sure—sure . . ." said the marshal. "Well, you certain got good country to settle in. . . ." He thrust his hands into his pockets and rocked a little on his heels; the heat sent him slightly farther from the fire, and his upper cheeks grew redder. Casually he drew one hand from the pocket, bringing with it a round stamped silver medallion with a pair of buckskin thongs extending from it—a saddle ornament fallen from somebody's outfit.

"Anybody lose this? I found it on the trail."

"Where on the trail?" asked Gay in a voice which had grown dryer.

"Few miles back."

Provost caught it then, for his chin lifted slightly and he set his eyes on the marshal. John Gay raised his good hand, passing it back and forth across his chin. His face took on a speculative, horse-trading expression.

Meanwhile Collingwood bent forward to have a clearer look at the ornament. "Not many of us have got fancied-up saddles. I only recall—"

Burnett cut him off with a question for the marshal. "If you were a few miles back on the trail, wouldn't it have been dark?"

That was when it came to McIver. So far not much interested in the talk, he now straightened his shoulders and seemed to see the marshal as a new man. He passed a glance to Mercer. Mrs. Buck bent toward Buck, whispering, and Buck turned a little on his chair and placed both broad palms on his knees to stare at the floor. Lucy Collingwood's hand dropped on her husband's hand; he looked about with a small rise of interest. He was the last one in the room to sense it.

"Well," said the marshal, "it was just getting dark. Thing had a shine to it or I wouldn't of seen it." His quick eyes went from person to person; he caught the quality of the silence, he caught the withdrawing; his question went light and quick at Collingwood. "You say you know who this belongs to?"

Collingwood said, "I couldn't be sure."

"It's no matter," said the marshal carelessly, and thrust the ornament into his pocket.

Gay straightened and laid his lame arm in a more comfortable position. "Any news from anywhere?"

"She rocks along — she just rocks along."

Gay said: "That won't do. I am thoroughly able to see through a picket fence."

The marshal let go with his strong laugh, and slyness sprang over the visible part of his face. "So you can, neighbor, so you can. Well, the messenger between Oregon City and Fort Vancouver was robbed and killed last night."

"That's where you got the ornament — and you want the man who owns it."

Burnett rose and edged the marshal away from the fire. He used his boot to roll the logs together. "This thing needs some help," he said and went to the door. He looked at young Joe wedged in the corner. "Where's the woodpile?" he asked, and set his eyes on the boy before he stepped into the darkness. Young Joe followed him.

Burnett drew him deeper into the night. "Take my horse — walk it easy out of the yard — get on — go to Rinearson's and say the marshal's here with one of Whit's saddle fooforaws in his pocket." He watched young Joe fade; he circled the cabin and got a chunk of fir and carried it into the cabin.

"Two men?" Gay was saying.

"Two men," said the marshal. "We don't know nothing about one of 'em. We know something about the other, though."

There was half a suspicion in the marshal's head and he looked to the doorway and was about to say something when John Gay diverted his attention. "They make any money of it?"

"I expect there was five hundred dollars, and that's a hell of a lot of money for Oregon. Any of you men get that much money together the next two–three years in Oregon, and you can say it's an accident. When I came here wheat was money and furs was money — and a day's work got you credit at old John McLoughlin's fort, but no cash. Ain't so bad now but she's tight, boys, she's tight." He looked again at the doorway and his question came in at the tail end of his other talk, without a break. "Where's that boy?"

"Sleeps in the wagon," said John Gay. "Might be there."

The marshal drew a breath, unlaced his hands from behind his back and gave his buttocks a sharp slap. He wasn't angry. He moved his glance around and laid a civil, wicked set of eyes on Burnett. "Did me, didn't you? Halfway to Rinearson's, ain't he?"

"Set your trap on the wrong slide."

"I thought you wasn't altogether a farmer," said the marshal. His short, strong laugh came out again and for an instant white teeth and red tongue showed in the aperture of his whiskers. "But if I get there, and he's run, then I'll know I'm on the tail of the right man, won't I?"

"You want to find him, or you want him out of the road so it won't be bothersome to you?"

There was at once a rough deviltry in the marshal's side-rolled glance. He laughed again, but it was the laugh of an unamused man. "Next time you go to Oregon City ask if Meek's for fun or fightin'." He looked at Gay. "No hard feelin's, neighbor, but it's got to be done."

"Then do it and ask nothing from us," said Gay.

"Why," said the marshal, "I tree my coons alone and always expect to."

But he wasn't quite through with Burnett and at the door he turned and left his last pleasure with Burnett. "It's my authority to deputize help; and if I got to chase this man to hell and gone, I might swear you in and wear your legs right down to the knee joints chasin' him with me."

"Were I you I don't believe I'd do it, though," said Burnett.

The marshal said most gently, "You tell *me* what I oughtn't do?" The deviltry grew brighter and paler in his restless eyes.

"How many coons you want to hunt at one time?"

The marshal studied him and his teeth showed again and small half-explosions of laughter rumbled around his chest and throat. He was interested, he was tempted; that bull boldness was about him. Then he changed his mind and said, "Good night, neighbors," and passed into the night.

Martha Gay could no longer keep her anxious question back. "Who?"

"Whit's saddle ornament, of course," said Gay, and added: "The wild, ignorant damn-fool kid!" He looked at Burnett. "You sent Joe up there?"

"Yes."

"Well, that's good. Whit'll probably slide into the hills."

"That's where the marshal wants him," said Burnett. "Easier to track a man in the brush than to walk up to a front door for him."

"Lockyear's the other one," said Provost.

"Certainly," said Gay. "But he was too smart to be caught. It was Whit who had to get himself caught. The fool kid, traveling around with a bad man so he can make out he's a bad man himself." He shook his head, he

226

was both bitter and sad. "There's grief for the Rinearsons. Those three boys are Old Daniel's life. Whit might as well have shoved a butcher knife right through Daniel." It seemed to come closer and closer to him. "I can't abide murder, but as to that, who knows whether it was Whit or Lockyear that killed the fellow? Well, it makes no difference, there's that murder — and there's one more evil against Cal Lockyear. My God, the man ruins anything he touches, his hands are bloody red to the shoulders, his mind's squirmin' with the maggots of destruction, the inside of him is black — black. Tell me what good he is on earth? If there's a place for him, then I have got to doubt creation." He was pale and beyond his own strength. Tissue and features lay tighter against the bones of his face, the eye sockets seemed rounder, the lips were shrunk, the outline of the skull itself grew prominent before Burnett. Disease, so long working its secret way in this man, made its first visible break-through. The Gay women watched him, Gram with her crone's attention, Martha Gay close to crying; and to Katherine came the familiar closing down of expression, the discipline, the bracing against disaster.

"Well," said Buck, "I expect the Lord will take care of him; but if we got to wait too long for that, maybe patience will run out and we'll do it ourselves."

McIver said: "That marshal get paid?"

"Certainly," said Gay.

"One more man at the public tit," said McIver, "growin' fat doin' nothin'. I've got no use for government. Nothin' comes from it but the excuse of them that work for it for more government."

"We got to have some government," said Gay.

"Better none than too much. It is a corrupter, a seducer; it panders to the weak and selfish. It feeds us sugar till we like sugar too much, and then it has got us, because we need the sugar more than we need self-respect."

"That's a strong view," said Gay.

"I fear government more than I fear hell, starvation, anarchy or the devil. I fear it because I fear the instinct in all men to want things for nothing. I never heard of a government that stayed small. They all get big and suck the sap out of the people they serve, and finally kill people, and kill themselves."

From the trees, from the southward darkness, came a long-ringing shout with a note of emergency which tumbled these men at once into the yard. A pair of feet pounded the earth at a labored gait, a shadow

227

grew, Harris Eby stumbled into the yellow arc of the cabin light. Branches and briars had skinned him, his hands were bleeding, he sucked the insufficient air into his deep lungs with an effort painful to hear; he had extended himself almost too far. Burnett caught him by the arm but the big man's momentum carried him to the cabin wall and he laid head and shoulder against it and braced his feet to keep himself erect. Martha Gay cried, "Harris — Harris — is it Indians?" His head rolled from side to side. Nobody else said anything. Burnett stepped to the bucket and got a dipper of water; he poured the water on Eby's head. He filled the dipper again; he pulled back the collar of Eby's coat and dashed the water down Eby's neck.

Eby said, "Accident," and waited for more wind. "Go get Whitcomb." He turned around to brace his shoulders on the logs. Burnett brought him the filled dipper. Eby took the water between gusts of wind; he let the dipper drop. "George Millard. We were hunting. I packed him a ways but thought I better let him lie and come get help. I tied a piece of shirt around his leg. He shot himself below the knee."

"I'll take your gray gelding, John," said Burnett. "Where's the saddle?"

"In the shed."

Buck said: "Where's Millard?"

"Two miles up that hill," said Eby. "I'll go back and show you."

Burnett moved on to the shed, found Gay's saddle gear and crossed the yard to the meadow fence. Katherine had gone before him with an empty bucket. She banged the bucket against the fence, bringing the gray mare in from its distant foraging. Burnett saddled the horse and brought it back to the cabin light. The group had talked it out.

"My horse is faster than this one," said McIver to Burnett. "You take it. This is the nearest house. We'll bring Millard here. You bring Doc Whitcomb here. How long you think it'll be? It's forty miles to Oregon City — that's eighty for the trip."

Burnett thought about it. "Night all the way. Ten hours, maybe a little better. Five hours coming back."

"Never mind the horse," said McIver. "Break it down if you got to."

"I'll pick up another horse along the way — maybe a couple of changes. Should be back tomorrow afternoon." He was in the saddle, listening to the talk going back and forth. Buck said: "No trails where Geroge is. Easier to walk than ride."

"We'll catch up a couple blankets."

"Give Harris a horse. He's done up. We'll need a lantern."

"Somebody's got to go tell Mrs. Millard and fetch her here."

"I'll do that," said Lord.

"No," said Katherine, "I'll do that." She came to Burnett and said, "Take care," and touched his hand, and stepped away. He turned the gray over the yard and set it into an easy run across the meadow.

32

HE swung north through Billy Lord's notch and came upon country he hadn't seen since arrival. The sky was clear and full of stars from horizon to horizon. A black sky was always flat but a starred sky fitted down upon the earth with a bowl's curve. There was the thinnest scratch of a moon but neither it nor the stars shed much light; the rolling hills made their silhouettes around him, the meadows sent out a faint glow, the timbered stretches were tunnel-dark. The trail had not been used enough to be potty, but neither could he depend on it being free from deadfalls. Had he been on his own business he would have kept the horse largely at a walk, but in present necessity he pushed it to a run over the meadows — trusting to the beast's sense of danger rather than his own — and dropped to a walk in the trees. From Lord's to the crossing of the nearest creek was a matter of six miles and in this distance he passed three cabins whose lights still shone. The sound of his horse brought people to the doors and he heard them hail after he had gone by, their voices round-shaped in the pressing night. Beyond the creek there was but one light for several miles, this to his left in the lower level of a prairie; it stood alone in the sea of darkness, winking as a star would wink, and for half an hour it stayed with him until the trail left the edge of the prairie and moved into a hilly country all through which the coyotes were crying.

At the first river he spent half an hour in the search of a crossing. Beyond, the trail broke into several little fingers which confused him and he found himself sitting on a stopped horse in the middle of a thicket which apparently had no exit. He beat his way back to the river, cruising its banks and looking for light spots against the forest black. He made several tries before he came into a small valley, and he halted there with nothing to go by but the stars and his sense of where Oregon City ought to be. He crossed the open space and reached the edge of timber and drifted along its edge until he found a break-through where the horse seemed willing to go. He reached the summit of a low ridge and saw nothing before him but the dim bulk of more timber and hills; he back-tracked to the short valley, swung along it more directly westward and followed it, once more reaching timber; but this was a thin stand and when he got through it he found himself in what appeared to be a round meadow. Directly before him was a house, all dark; a dog crouched somewhere and set up a furious barking.

"Hello in there."

Something squealed, something scraped, and a woman's voice murmured. "Take care." The door opened and a man's voice came at Burnett. "Who's that?"

"I'm on my way to Oregon City for a doctor and I need a fresh horse. Think I've lost the trail."

"No, you're on it," said the man. "Do I know you?"

"Rice Burnett."

"Well, I'll be dod-blasted," said the man. "Etty, light the light. Get down, Rice. Etty, make coffee."

"No," said Burnett. "No time."

The woman was up in the room; a light flared and its yellowness sprang through the door, outlining Alpheus Stricklin.

"Who's hurt?"

"Millard shot himself in the leg."

"I'll get my horse," said Alpheus. He went into the cabin a moment, later appearing in shoes, flannel nightgown and a knit cap; he retreated behind the cabin while Burnett removed the gear from McIver's horse. Stricklin's wife came to the doorway, wrapped around by a quilt; her hair hung beside a broad, plain, dark face. "Is it bad? Poor Miz Millard!"

"I don't know. How've you been, Etty?"

"Fine — fine," said the woman. "We don't see nobody. I wish Stricklin had settled closer to folks. Nobody nearer than the Pettys and they're four miles. How's Martha Gay? How's everybody? Anything new happened?"

"She's fine. We're set in for the winter, working hard. Gay's not too well. Lockyear married Roxy Kitchen."

"No!" said Mrs. Stricklin. "Such a thing . . . It ain't to be believed!" She was silent a moment, struggling with her curiosity. Then she said: "You and that Edna girl married yet?"

230

"Wrong man, Etty. She took Moss Rinearson."

"Ah," said Mrs. Stricklin, a long breath falling from her. "Mrs. Irish makin' out?"

"She will."

"And how does it go with Buck and Miz Howard? And, oh yes, that poor little Lavinia and her man?"

"They're eating. That's all you can say for anybody." Stricklin returned with his horse and stood by while Burnett laid on the saddle and buckled the halter.

"I'm so hungry for talk," said Mrs. Stricklin. "I could sit and sit and pump and pump."

"Come down and make a visit," said Burnett.

"Oh, it's so far, so terrible far. Everything's so terrible far. Stricklin says there'll be a good road by here someday with people goin' back and forth plenty but I don't believe it. We're just all sort of lost out here. Don't expect I'll ever see a town again. Everything's so terrible far."

Stricklin said, "Go straight west for maybe an hour. Then you'll be on the edge of prairie. When you cross the river go downstream a mile or so, and you'll come to a big clearing — old Indian campground. Then you strike north and the trail gets plain."

"I'll change horses coming back. Have you got another Whitcomb can use?"

"Sure."

"So long," said Burnett and left them. The trail was moderately straight and he followed it from meadow to grove, over brushy little creeks and past alder thickets and cedar marshes and at last came upon a river which, nearing a junction with the Willamette, was broad but shallowed by gravel bars. He made the crossing, he found the Indian camp spot. The country cleared and cabins began to emerge more frequently from the shadows; in the first paling of dawn he saw the glint of the Willamette to his left and for a short time followed its silver windings. At full daylight he was once more in the timber. When he passed through this he began to hear the undertone of the falls in the still morning, and at last came upon the shock and glitter of the river tearing itself apart on the rocks. Passing along the base of a black bluff, he entered town, asked Whitcomb's whereabouts from the first citizen he saw, and so arrived at a small white house back of Main Street. Whitcomb answered his knock, looked at him, and said: "Who is it?"

"Millard shot himself in the leg."

231

"Come in," said Whitcomb. "There's breakfast on the table. Finish it out while I round up my horse."

"Get another for me."

They were out of town, bound south, in half an hour. "You might as well have stayed back and slept," said Whitcomb.

"Rather return with you."

"I know," said Whitcomb. "Emergency, somebody dying . . . It hits people that way. They'll do anything when somebody's in trouble and needs quick help. Turn themselves inside out, ride, give, nurse — anything necessary." He went on a long distance but still had the thing in his mind; for beyond the falls he had something else to say. "How kind we can be at such times! How brutal we can be, not meaning it, when there's no crisis, only average trouble and disagreement. You know what Christmas really is? It's crowding into one week the things we ought to have done all year long. If we minded the decencies, just the ordinary decencies, there never be any need or reason for Christmas. And we know it, too. How damned well we know it. How bad is Millard's leg?"

"Don't know. The shot was below the knee. Eby said he tied something tight above the hole to stop the bleeding."

Whitcomb shook his head at the information but made no comment on it. The day was clear and warm and beautiful, the sky blue, the not quite evaporated dew on the meadow grasses sparkling in the morning's mild sunshine. They passed through long wet-odored forest aisles in which stillness lay so deep as to seem to be the layered accumulation of ten thousand years. Little creeks charged briskly across their route; they forded a river, caught the first sight of the prairie and moved on at a better pace.

"I'll have somebody in Oregon City take back the horse you borrowed from Stricklin."

"No — let him do it. His woman needs an excuse to get to town."

"Your perceptions," said Whitcomb, "might make you a good doctor. On the other hand, if they're so strong they soak up other people's miseries, you might be a bad doctor."

"Misery's hard to look at, any time," said Burnett.

"Physical misery is," amended Whitcomb. "But the Creator did one good thing when He made us. While it lasts, pain's bad. When it goes we forget it. If the memory of pain accumulated in our minds like a bank account, we'd never stand it — we'd kill ourselves."

They came into Alpheus Stricklin's round meadow and found Stricklin, wife, and two horses waiting. Mrs. Stricklin had coffee and deer meat and bread ready and while the two changed gears, Stricklin counseled Burnett. "I went down to Petty's this morning. He'll have a couple more fresh horses on the trail when you reach there. That's ten miles." They downed the coffee and took bread and meat with them and went away, Mrs. Stricklin's voice coming after. "Stop on the way back, doctor. I have got some complaints."

As they ran up the short valley beyond Stricklin's the doctor finished his meat and bread and grew talkative. "Most of her complaints are imaginary and I shall wipe them away with a few spoonfuls of something sweet or something bitter; the things which are real with her I'll possibly not be able to help at all." Then he added, "It's a wonderful thing how powerful the mind is."

"Living around people, you don't have to face your mind so much," commented Burnett. "Living alone, you do. I've seen a lot of solitary men. They're either damned strong, or damned queer." He changed the subject. "Have a look at Gay while you're there. There's something wrong with him. One arm seems lame — he keeps rubbing it — he handles it like a stick of wood."

Again the doctor took the news thoughtfully and made no comment. They crossed the second river, ran steadily through timber and meadow, and came to the edge of the prairie. Along that part of the trail they found Petty waiting with two fresh horses; they swapped and went on, and in early afternoon they reached Lord's notch and turned south. The Gay yard contained a dozen neighbors when they arrived. Whitcomb dropped from his horse, loosened his saddle bags and went into the cabin.

Burnett crawled from his horse and spoke to McIver. "Your horse is at Stricklin's, twenty miles up."

"Never mind it — I'll take care of that."

He walked to the wash rack outside the cabin, and scrubbed hands and face, and lighted his pipe. Inside, he heard Mrs. Millard crying, and Millard's very low voice answering the doctor. Katherine came out and took his arm and led him to the camp bench. The big fire burned in the yard, coffeepot and stew kettle swung over it. She went into the cabin for dishes and brought Burnett a meal from the fire; she sat across the bench while he ate.

"How's he making out?"

"I don't know," she said. "He's not said much — not complained. The leg looks queer."

The neighbors drifted over. John Gay sat on the bench, watching the cabin's door. Presently Mrs. Gay emerged and walked a few feet into the yard, twisting both arms in and out of her apron; and then she turned back into the cabin. Whitcomb appeared and gave the camp bench a look. "I'll want that bench inside pretty soon." He sat down and got his pipe and filled it and lighted it; he drew heavy on it. "You might put a kettle of water on the fire, Katherine. I want to wash." His face settled, grew bare, grew angular. He seemed to Burnett to turn himself into another man — a hard man, a cold man. Looking about, he estimated the men watching him. He spoke to Harris Eby. "Have you got pretty steady nerves? I'll need you." He nodded at Provost. "And you," and his attention moved past the women, paused at Collingwood and went on, and stopped on McIver. "You," he said, and finally he noticed Lot White. "I want you, too, but I want your blacksmith's muscles, I don't want your prayers."

"What is it?" asked Burnett.

"I have got to take off Millard's leg above the knee and it will require four pretty strong men to hold him down."

"Oh, God," murmured Mrs. Provost. "Oh, God." Burnett's muscles tightened, a short shock hit him in the stomach and left its uneasiness behind. He watched the stubborn expression come to Katherine. Mrs. Irish said: "Is there anything you want from any of us — anything?"

"I want you ladies to take Mrs. Millard home."

"Oh," said Mrs. Buck, "she won't want to go."

"Get her out of this yard," said Whitcomb. "Beyond the meadow. Half a mile away. When the knife hits him his voice will carry that far." He rose and moved to the washbasin and took it to the fire; and he stood there, sucking the last smoke from his pipe, until the water began to steam in the kettle. He filled the basin and went to the washstand to clean his hands. Finished, he knocked out his pipe and walked into the house.

Mrs. Gay appeared in a moment with Mrs. Millard. Mrs. Millard said, "I'd rather stay, Martha." She put aside Martha Gay's arm; she turned to go back. The other women walked over the yard and got around her and Mrs. Provost said, "We'll go on a bit." Mrs. Millard moved with the pressure of the women but she moved slowly and she said in a more rapid voice: "Why — what's he going to do to Millard? I'll stay here — I'd rather — I won't leave him." She was carried onward, her voice trying to rise above the other voices; she made an attempt to swing but arms circled her and the talk continued quick and smooth, riding over her words,

234

riding over her questions; they passed through the gate and started into the meadow.

Whitcomb came to the door and made a sign. The four men he wanted — Eby and Lot White and Provost and McIver — carried the camp bench into the house. The door closed. From the meadow Mrs. Millard saw it and she raised her voice and fought at the other women with her doubled fists, and broke through and came running back. Lattimore got to the door before her and placed himself against it; she struck at him, she hit him in the face, she threw her shoulder against him and tried to go around; her face was long, stubborn, crazy. Lattimore trapped her hands. "You can't do it, Nancy," said Lattimore. "Stop that — stop it." The women came around her again in a smothering circle. She quit fighting Lattimore; she let the women move her away from the door; she turned and put her head against the cabin wall.

Whitcomb's voice went on very quietly inside the cabin, Millard now and then breaking through with equal quietness. Presently the talk ceased. The bench legs scraped the puncheon floor. There was silence for a short time, followed by Whitcomb's voice, much briefer, much lower. After that the silence built up until Burnett found himself braced against it. Everybody in the yard stood with the same stiff expectancy, everybody watched the cabin. Mrs. Provost's chin lifted, her lips parted, and her shoulders rose until they could go no higher and she began to tremble. Katherine turned about and walked rapidly away. Mrs. Millard, against the house wall, lifted and pressed her hands flat against the logs, pressed her listening ear against them.

From Millard came a short surprised, "Ah." He caught himself and spoke to Whitcomb; and Whitcomb's voice went gently on a little while. Then Millard's voice shot upward in a solid cry of pain which carried on and on until the waiting for him to run out of breath strained Burnett. The sound stopped, the man's sucking lungs threw spongy echoes into the yard; the cry came again, higher and higher, breaking into surging, grunting gasps of agony. "Ahhh — Ahhh — Jesus — Ahhh — Ahhh!" Mrs. Millard stretched her hands high over her head and began to claw downward across the rough-barked logs.

Burnett followed Katherine. Sensation went creeping along his legs. He thought of Whitcomb's knife making its cut straight through flesh to leg bone, going round and round until the cut was clear. Sound came steadily from Millard's throat, whooping, hallooing, gurgling, gasping, cursing, unbearably intense. His manhood was departing from him; the

235

cry lost its deep quality; it turned into a scream. Katherine was fifty feet ahead, walking fast; she had her hands tight-locked over her chest, had her head down. She looked around and slowed when she saw Burnett and he came up and caught her arm and they moved on together with the scalding cries following them. "Ahhh — ahhh — a-huhh!" They were hurrying into the meadow but they never got beyond the sound; they came to the trees and stopped. Burnett settled his back against a fir. He listened to Millard's strength die out; the screaming shifted to a feminine tone, it shortened, it bubbled, it fell to an exhausted moaning.

Katherine moved against him, settling her head against his chest. He put his arms around her and felt each sound strike through her; she was a target, quivering at each bullet.

"Hell's here," he said. "It's right here."

The sound from the cabin slowly diminished; there was nothing left to come out of Millard. If he survived this, Burnett thought, he was a good man. Why should he want to survive it? Not for pride — there was none of that left in Millard now. The sound ceased, Katherine grew still, whispering. "I hope he fainted."

"Fainted — or dead."

Far out on the meadow's other edge he saw young Joe Gay crouched like an Indian, both hands clapped over his ears. Nobody moved in the yard; they were statues facing the cabin. Mrs. Millard was still at the cabin's wall, hands high above her. Time went on, everybody still, everybody waiting. It was an hour, or perhaps longer, when the cabin door opened and he saw Lot White come out. He felt the wire-tense strain leave Katherine; her body settled easier against him. He said to Katherine, "All right," and turned her back to the yard.

Lot White moved through the yard and on down the trail, hands hanging full length and scoop-shaped; he stumbled and caught himself and went on. Harris Eby emerged from the cabin with something wrapped in a cloth; sweat streaks, long since dry, netted a face turned ash-gray. There was a bitter pucker around his lips. He went on with the bundle, disappeared in the barn and appeared with a shovel, and crossed the meadow to disappear in the trees. McIver and Provost came out; then Whitcomb stepped through the doorway and spoke to Mrs. Millard. "All right." When she turned from the wall Burnett noticed her bloody fingers and he looked back to the cabin wall and saw the deep, red-splashed claw marks on the bark. She went into the cabin, Martha Gay following. Whitcomb got the basin and went to the water kettle at the fire. He filled the basin; he stooped to wash, but presently he settled to one knee and steadied himself. When he was through he filled his pipe and came over to Burnett and Katherine.

"Did he make it?" asked Burnett.

"So far," said Whitcomb. He was still a bare, hard, cold man.

Mrs. Millard was crying. She kept saying, "Oh Millard — Millard — God help you! God help you, Millard!"

Mrs. Provost said: "Gram and the Old Man will stay with us."

"We'll take Joe," said Mrs. McIver. "I guess John and Martha will want to sleep in their wagon — but where'll you go, Katherine?"

"Collingwood's."

John Gay spoke to Whitcomb. "You'll be stayin' awhile?"

"Long as necessary."

"Then you'll sleep in the wagon, Joe and I'll take the barn, and Martha better go with the McIvers."

Lattimore said: "We'll watch Millard's stock."

Mrs. Gay came from the cabin and stood absent-minded before the group; she put a finger to her lip and looked around her. It was her recollecting, "let-me-see" expression. Mrs. McIver said to her, "If anything's wanted, you'll let somebody know?"

"To be sure," said Martha Gay. "Now we have got to think of sleepin' — "

Her husband told her how it had been arranged. Martha looked at him a moment, the smallest trace of shortness on her face. "I'll not leave," she said. "I'll sleep in the barn. How could I leave?"

Whitcomb emptied his pipe. "Better think of some sleeping, yourself," he said to Burnett. The cruelty of the thing was in his eyes; it was around his mouth, making a stranger of him. Burnett went to the shed and found his gear and came out to the fence and clapped his hands, bringing in his horse from the farther end of the meadow. Katherine followed. When he was ready to go he turned about and watched her a little while; she smiled and impulse caused him to reach for her hand, and her fingers fitted around his palm and held on. "You sleep," she said.

"See you soon."

"All right — soon."

The neighbors were going down the trail afoot; he passed them and settled to a steady run and soon reached home. Watt Irish had cared for the stock while he was gone, for the cows were down the meadow and milk pans were full and the fowls fed. He pulled off boots, pants and shirt and rolled into bed. Directly before he fell asleep, which was almost immediately, he remembered Millard's agony, and suddenly the shadow of the pattern was there, as something seen deep in water — unreachable and shapeless, yet throwing off the emanation of its presence. Nature built men and tested them to the limits of their endurance, and was unsatisfied with even the strongest; and this careless creating hand, failing to find the form and the substance sought for, built and smashed and built again. The very persistence of creation seemed to say that from the dust of the destroyed imperfects would sometime come the one dreamed shape.

33

ON the third day following the operation Millard was partially out of pain and ate a little and seemed to have a chance of recovery. He was thin, he was dull-minded, his vitality was as a column of water fluctuating up and down a gauge; but he had gotten to the point where he saw the possible end of his torture and he was proud of himself, and pride gave him the spirit to hang on. He even managed a show of humor. "I must be a sinner. Only sinners last like this."

Whitcomb had stayed with him without break. There was nothing he could do. The fight was entirely Millard's. Yet the doctor's presence gave these people a sense of security which, though he knew it to be bottomless, he could not disturb. This was the first day he felt able to break free for a little while. He needed the air, he had promised to go see Mercer's youngest son, and in his mind was the hope of a meeting with Lucy Collingwood. When he left the house Gay followed him to the barn.

"Ralph," he said, "say nothing to anybody about this but I want you to have a look at my arm."

"What's wrong with it?" asked Whitcomb, although his eyes had already given him some information.

Gay took his right arm and lifted the left. "It won't work by itself. It's numb. At first it was only in my finger tips. Now it's clear up to the elbow and where it ain't altogether numb it's got a steady ache. I don't sleep any more."

"What else?"

Gay ran a finger across his chest from armpit to armpit. "There," he said, "like I'm bein' pushed together. Cramped — crowded. Don't seem to get full breathing. Kind of a heavy feeling."

At Whitcomb's sign the older man removed coat and shirt and in the half light of the barn, Gay's ears cocked for the sound of his wife's voice, the doctor's fingers tested Gay's arm from fingers to shoulder; and he tapped Gay's chest, made various probing explorations at various joints, and ended by looking into Gay's eyes. When it was done Gay put on his clothes. Whitcomb tried Gay's pulse. "Think it might be a stroke?" Gay asked.

"You don't seem to be headed that way," said Whitcomb and asked a great number of questions. He filled and lighted his pipe. "How long has it been going on?"

"It was in the gorge, first."

"I'll give you something to drink when I come back."

"I'm no woman for medicine and I'd as soon know the truth."

"If I had the truth, you'd get it. I don't know. It may be a strain, or something pinched. It might be the result of a bruise. It might be rheumatism. The simplest thing's always best to think; and it's best to think it'll pass. Most things do. But — it could be anything else. It could be something a long way off from your arm. I don't know."

"Well," said Gay, "it's a serious thing. My feeling is I'm going to die of it. I wish I knew what it was."

"I wish I could tell you. There's not much I know. There's not much I can do, or any doctor can do. Set an arm, cut a leg — simple syrups for simple things — a little of this, a little of that. That's not much. A thousand things go on in your body. Once in a long while I'll reach something and fix it. Not often. It's your body and most of the time the only thing I can do is sit by and watch you get well or die. There's not many times in my practice I can say I helped anything, or saved anybody. We don't know much."

"Don't tell Martha anything," said John Gay.

"I won't," said Whitcomb and rode over the yard into the trail. Martha, he realized, already knew.

After Mercer's he took a roundabout way through the settlement, paying his respects at a dozen cabins; and crossed at the Irish ford and turned home. For three days the closeness of Lucy had haunted him. Listening at night to the tortured threshings of Millard, he had thought of her; since his last meeting with her he had built a thousand warm and colored images of her in his head, each one comforting him, tantalizing him; in his mind the love scene had been played out often, the tentative approaches, the words so carefully chosen, the touch of her hands, the growing of the thing between them until, seeing encouragement on her face, he broke the restraint and took her. The rest was all glory and delight; it was poetry and cannibalism, it was wonder upon wonder, it was the matching of soul and appetite so complete that when he was through envisioning it he could only shake his head at the great hunger which fed these phantasies until they glowed brighter than any light the world held.

When he sighted the Collingwood cabin through the trees the excitement came again and for a moment he was hopeful, he was eager. But he had not slept since reaching the settlement and weariness bore him downward. By the time he was abreast the cabin he had almost talked himself out of the visit; but she had seen him and she was in the doorway and when her smile came to him the grayness left his mind and he thought, *Why have I always got to muddy things up by thinking too much?* He reined in the horse before her. He felt wonderful, he felt self-conscious. Her neatness never failed to surprise him for though she had the common lot of work to do, and had no more wealth or leisure than any other woman in the settlement, she always took pains with her appearance. Much of the time, in his profession, he came upon people in their slack moments but he had never seen her at such a time.

"Coffee's on," she said. "Come down."

He let the horse stand and went inside and for want of better conversation he repeated something he had said before. "Coffee's hard to come by. You should take care to whom you give."

"I do take care," she said. "I'm very particular."

"Where's George?"

She was at the fireplace, handling the water kettle; she had her back to him. "He went over to Rinearson's to see if he could be of any help."

"Nothing he could do there that I can see. They tell me Whit took to the woods — and the marshal's gone back to Oregon City."

"It was just his notion," she said. "He likes to be helpful." In his present mood, perceptions alert, he tried to make something of the remark, but her tone was casual. It was only a remark, nothing intended. She made the coffee and set it against the fire. "Be done in a minute. How've you been?" She gave him a closer attention. "You've not had much sleep."

"Catnaps. I thought I might see you at Gay's sooner or later."

"I couldn't think of a thing I could do to be useful so I stayed away. Katherine's slept here and I've heard how it's been. Is he really better?"

"He'll make it unless something happens in the next day or so."

"I admire him so much. I keep wondering why he had to be the one to go through such a thing." She rose to pour the coffee and set on cream and butter and bread. "It's silly, but there are times I can't help rebelling. Even if it's beyond anybody's power, it's still unjust. . . . No sugar, Ralph."

"Next time I come from Oregon City I'll bring a little in my saddle-bags."

She thought about it and gave him a straight look. "Would that be so wise?"

"I didn't think of that. But would you take it?"

"Yes," she said, "I'd take it."

"Well, then, to hell with wise or not wise."

She laughed and she shook her head at him. "You like to pretend you're one of these hell-for-leather men. But you're not. You're quite serious. You like to think of yourself as a skeptical man. You're not that, either."

"I fool a lot of people."

"We all do, and that's a good thing. Wouldn't it be embarrassing if we didn't — couldn't? Still, I'm not sure we fool as many people as we think. When I look at Gram Gay I feel she knows just about everything about me, and about everybody else for that matter. She's the only old person I don't pity for being old. It's not possible to pity a person that strong. You just hope you can be something like that when your turn comes to be old."

"My turn's come already," he said.

"You've no gray hairs yet, no deep lines." Watching him, her laughter came back. "Is it sympathy you want?"

Her color was good, her eyes clear, her expression firm; she was in better health — or in better mind — than he had seen her before. Vigor held her shoulders up and gave her animation. Her hands were quiet on her lap; her hair was smoothly done and a pair of earrings stirred when she moved her head.

"Now, Dr. Whitcomb, don't look at me with such professional eyes. More coffee?"

He shook his head. It amused him to think how carefully he had, in his moments of daydreaming, fashioned and rehearsed the phrases he had meant to use. They were no good to him now. He had never been so unsure of himself. On the previous visit he had gotten close to her and he

241

had left with the feeling that she had promised something at the next meeting; returning, he had expected to go on where they had left off. But he neither saw nor felt anything of that closeness. She was friendly but she wasn't the Lucy Collingwood he had almost kissed, and he thought to himself: *You don't know a damned thing about women.* Apparently there was no such thing as progressing from point to point with them; if they moved to a certain place one time, they weren't there next time. It was mood that governed them, not logic. He caught himself on that; he knew better. It was mood, but there was always logic behind the mood. Not man's logic, but theirs, and their logic was for all its seeming contradiction more straightforward than man's. Well, she had thought it over and her common sense had stopped her; perhaps she was telling him now, in this proper and pleasant way, that she had better command of her emotions. He put his phrases and his hopes aside. If this was her wish, he would make no more moves; for she was old enough to know what she wished to do, and argument had no part in it. What he wished for was a woman — this woman — coming to him freely. It wasn't seduction he wanted.

He had finished the coffee and laid the cup on the table and he had his eyes on the scrolled brown pattern of the cup while he went through his thinking. She made a small motion with her hand, drawing his glance, and he saw that her lips were rounded by the warmest of smiles. "Oh Ralph — Ralph," she said, and shook her head at him.

He shrugged his shoulders and his own smile, he thought, must have been wry enough to betray him. "Well," he said, and rose and moved to the door. He stood there, watching the soft sunshine sparkle on the deep dull green of the timber. "Strange business. Christmastime, temperature sixty-five or thereabouts, and green grass all over hell and gone. Home now we'd have the snow alleys shoveled from house to barn."

She said nothing. Looking around he noticed she had risen from the table and stood at the fireplace, turned from him. He remained irresolute in the doorway, watching the trail's foreshortening as it ran through the timber toward Gay's. He said, "I hear George intends to run for the legislature."

Her answer was short. "Yes."

"Who's going to do the work around here?"

"I don't know."

"None of my business, but he ought to give that some thinking."

"We all ought to do more thinking than we do. We should all be reasonable, do the right thing, live the right way, never make the wrong move. It's harder for some people than others. It's not so hard for you, is it?"

"I shouldn't have offered my advice," he said. He was embarrassed.

"But you didn't answer the question."

"You should know the answer," he said. He was as short as she had been and he was sorry for it at once, and tried to turn it. "Pretty here with the sun on the meadow."

"Then the sun goes down and it's not so pretty. When I'm here alone I catch every sound. They're like big boots stamping down an empty hall. I'm the empty hall. You don't know much about loneliness, do you? Even my thoughts rattle in the emptiness, and if I cried who'd hear and what would it matter? Year by year I dry up little by little. I'm alive — I have something left. What shall I do with it, what shall I do with myself? Go crazy like poor Roxy? I know her better than anybody else around here. I know what was inside her and I know she heard that terrible rattle in nothingness. Even Lockyear is better than what she had. These women with their husbands, so comfortable, so blind — why should they judge her? What do they know? I listen to my heart beat and feel blood go through me to every part of my body, and it crowds so hard I could burst. But down in the center of me it's dryer and dryer, emptier and emptier, and it's spreading, and one day there'll be nothing but dust in me and I'll be afraid to look in a mirror. So much, so much — but nothing to do with it; and then it's gone and I'm wasted when I wasn't meant to be. Lot White can't tell me we were given life to spoil like that. That's a worse hell than anything he can think up."

He swung over the room and turned her about. Even then there was uncertainty in him; only the shock of her words, with their implied suggestion of his failure, pushed him through the barrier. When he put his arms around her and saw the lifting of her face, doubt died. He kissed her and he was no longer a critical man. He had meant to be gentle — that too was his planned way of telling her how deeply he felt — but the touch of her lips broke his restraint, knocking down his reserve; the taste of her made its demand for a wilder taste; possession bred the intolerable wish for more possession. He used her roughly but he scarcely knew it. She drew off, her face tense and dark, and she looked at him in a strange manner and came back to him with her own rush of feeling. They hung together, swaying side to side, arms clenched about each other, pressing in until strain tired them. She slid her face aside, against his face,

243

whispering: "I was desperate. I thought you meant to go away and not come back."

"I did. I thought you didn't want me."

"Oh, Ralph, I was only trying to make myself presentable to you — attractive."

"You'd look attractive to me in a wet blanket."

"You just think so. You'll never catch me looking like that. I've kept my hair combed and my nice dress on for three days."

He glanced around the room, at the two small chairs, at the rocker, at the bed. He took her hand and crossed the room and sat on the bed. She stood before him, looking down, prying into him with her glance, and he saw a streak of uncertainty go through her; and the delay made him self-conscious. She saw it immediately and dropped beside him. He put his arms around her but the awkwardness hung on. She whispered, "Turn about," and dropped back on the bed. When he swung she drew him to her and then the awkwardness went away. He was the stag and she was the pool; but no matter how much he drank there was one more swallow he needed. He eased himself beside her for comfort and they were motionless for a long run of time, until he grew conscious of the open door and of the soft soil across which anybody might silently come. He rose and went to the door to look around the meadow; he came back and sat beside her.

"Now that begins," she said. He didn't catch her meaning and she nodded toward the door. "Expecting to be discovered, little tricks, wondering when we'll be caught up."

"You're sorry."

"No. Never, never. It's like a lot of things. Maybe it's too bad, maybe it's wrong, maybe it's — everything. But it had to happen. Like poor Millard's leg. What can be done about it? Nothing. I've wanted this to happen so much that there's been nothing else in my mind. I've been absent-minded — crazy, walking back and forth, not knowing what I was doing." She took his hand and laid it over her heart. "That's got to beat for somebody or what's the good of it?"

He shook his head, smiling about it, sad about it. "We're worse off than we were before. We've got something but we want more. There'll always be more we want. It's like an engagement which can't end in marriage."

"You knew it would be that way. You've thought about it a lot. First time was in the wagon, in the gorge, wasn't it?"

"Yes."

"After you left I lay there and thought and thought and thought. Your hand touched me. It burned for a long time. It spread. I didn't sleep much." She watched him. "I think it's worse on you than on me. Please don't worry about it. Maybe it'll help you to know that I think whatever I get from this is good. A little or a lot, all of it's good. I won't complain." Then she surprised him with her directness. "Do you want to talk about George?"

"Hadn't given him much thought."

"Then let's leave it that way."

He said slowly, "You know what I want."

"Yes. That's all right."

"When?"

She said: "I'll leave it to you." But she saw the quickening in him and she added, "Right now would be dangerous."

"Could you get to Oregon City?"

"George talks about making some trips. I'll go along when he takes one there. I know he wants to go to Fort Vancouver for something, but I can stay in Oregon City while he goes."

"That's it," he said. "How soon?"

"Soon," she whispered. "Oh, so soon."

He went to the door again and had a look into the meadow and came back. He was amused at himself. "People do the damn'dest things."

"Are you surprised?"

"No," he said. "It's fine to be people." He saw the signal on her face and he dropped to the bed and it was the same thing over again until his sense of danger began to work at him. He rose and drew his watch. "Somebody in the settlement — Mrs. Provost, maybe — is keeping tab, you can be certain." He gave her a hand and helped her up.

"I suppose I ought to be worried," she said. "Maybe I am — oh, I don't know. Yes I do know. I'm not." She moved a mirror and looked at herself and made quick adjustments of her hair. He stepped behind her, catching her reflection in the mirror; her lips were swollen and the steel-pointed stubble on his face had reddened her chin. She looked back to him from the mirror, her eyes sending their special meaning to him and when she had finished with her hair she came about and laid her hands on his shoulders. She was pleased with him and with herself, she was confident and gay; he couldn't see a single flaw of morbidness anywhere. She gave him a light kiss and drew her hand across his jaw. "Don't you be disturbed. It was good — it will be good. Do you like me?"

"More than that, Lucy. I — "

She stopped him, laughing. "Tell me next time." She gripped his arms and shook him. "Oh, darling — soon, soon. Now you go home, and I hope you'll be as miserable alone as I'll be." She went to the door with him, watched him lift to the saddle and ride away. From the end of the meadow he looked back and caught the kiss she blew to him. Entering the trees he thought of how confident all this had made her, thinking ahead to the consequences which came of his interfering in her life. But none of that appeared to touch her. It was the first things first with women; everything else was blown away before the wind of their primary reasoning. Thinking of her all the way to Gay's, he was very gentle, very thoughtful, very happy.

34

HE identified Lot White's voice, rolling from the cabin in prayer, as soon as he reached the yard and he got off his horse with an irritation quite close to intolerance. But as he stepped to the cabin's doorway he was taken by a mellower mood and it occurred to him that in Lot's eyes he was as much a bigot as he thought Lot to be; and so he kept his peace when he saw Lot, Mrs. Millard and Mrs. Gay kneeling beside Millard on the bed. Millard's eyes were shut but he wasn't asleep, for his hands moved across each other nervously. *Exhausting him, and maybe shaking brimstone coals all over him, he thought.* Raising his head, Lot White noticed Whitcomb and a be-damned-to-you-I'm-goin'-to-do-it-anyhow expression came to his face. He finished his prayer and rose to speak to Millard. "You feel better now, brother? Ready to meet your Maker? Resigned to it — got the glory of it?"

Millard kept his eyes closed; his voice was weak. "Am I supposed to be scared or happy?"

"Feel glory," said Lot White. "God and devil are strugglin' for you — don't you worry who'll make out best."

Millard's hand crawled up to his chest; he tapped it with a finger. "I'm doin' the strugglin', Lot."

"Be humble, man."

"To hell with humble," said Millard. "I made the grade and I'm damned proud of myself."

246

Whitcomb caught the blacksmith's eye and drew him from the cabin. Lot, expecting trouble, met it more than halfway. "Don't tell me," he said. "I won't listen. I know God — you don't. I feel him — you don't. I love him and I believe in him — you don't. I'll not listen."

They went walking over the yard, a long time silent. Whitcomb saw a stem of grass, gray and dead, sticking up from the mud; he reached for it, held it between his fingers. "Look. There's Millard. He's got barely strength to hang on, no more. You ever been sick? Really sick? Flat in bed, ready to die?"

"No."

"Then you don't know how everything pinches down until one small grain of strength makes the difference. Anything can destroy it — a word, a thought, a draft of air, a cough. Then he snaps, like this." His finger came lightly across the gray grass stem and broke it clean.

All the while Lot White had steadily shaken his head and when Whitcomb was through he had his certain answer ready. "You don't believe, so you don't see. Neither you nor I nor him has got any say in whether he lives or dies. You think you made your finger break that stem? No you didn't. God wanted that stem broken and he moved your finger. If God says Millard stays alive, all the wind on earth could blow through that door and not disturb him; if God says he dies, it'll take a wind no bigger than enough to tremble a cat's whisker to do it — for God's in the wind, God's the wind itself."

"So God was the bullet that went through Millard's leg, and God pushed my hand when I took off Millard's leg — and he is solely responsible for the agony Millard went through?"

"That is so."

"Why?"

"It's not for you and me to know, Ralph."

"There has got to be a reason," insisted Whitcomb.

"Buried deep in the book whose pages you and I ain't ever goin' to see. We're sinners, we're all sinners, and we got to suffer."

"Why?"

"Because it's so."

"You say I don't believe in God," Whitcomb pointed out, "but if he guided my hand when I took off Millard's leg, then he must have wanted me to be his instrument. Why did he choose me? Why not a better man?"

"I don't know," said Lot White.

"You think the devil might get in me — might be in me?"

"He certainly could be."

"Well, Lot," said Whitcomb, "do you think maybe he might crawl into you, and send you into the cabin to kill Millard by tiring him too much?"

"I am the Lord's man," said Lot White.

"You're entirely sure of that?"

"I am."

"He sent you a sign — he spoke to you personally — he told you that you were above other men in understanding, mercy, purity of heart — past anger, past meanness, past judgment of others?"

"It would be unseemly to answer that question."

"Well, Lot," said Whitcomb with a show of good nature, "I shouldn't have begun the argument. I serve my way, you serve yours. I shan't trouble your people, but you must not bother my patients."

"Now, then," said Lot White, "I want to talk to you." They were beyond the yard. Lot White halted, faced Whitcomb full on. He rose slightly on his heels. "You're an educated man. You've read books. You can use words like whips and knives and things that stab. You're proud of your learnin'. You have thought about mysterious things I ain't ever heard of. You know a lot. You know so much about so much that there's nothin' fixed and fast in your soul, nothin' shinin' white, nothin' pit-black. You don't think much of sin, you don't think much of glory. What am I against you? Nothin'. I'm an ignorant man. I got no strange ideas, I got poor words — I am a rough and homely fellow. But I know one thing, and it's enough for me, and it's my life, and I believe it so much I'd cut off my arm for it. There's nothin' in the world big enough for you to cut off your arm for. That's the difference. Yet around this settlement you are a respected man and your influence has got power to move folks, but I am only that old fool Lot White. I know what they think."

"Why, Lot," said Whitcomb most gently, "everybody knows your heart's right."

Lot White brushed the remark aside. "There's right — and there's wrong. We're all sinners, we're all losers, we suffer and we pay. It's a hard world, it was meant to be, it's the soul's testin' place, that's what it is. But there's right and there's wrong, and men must support right because it's always tremblin' in the balance. You have got the power, they listen to you. You have got the example to set, they watch you. I can preach for a month, but you come along and by a word or a laugh you can wash my preachin' away."

"Lot," said Whitcomb seriously, "I've argued with you. I've sent you away from my patients when I thought they needed rest, but I've never spoken against you. I'd never knowingly unsettle any other man's faith."

Lot had been looking toward the ground as he listened. Now he raised his disturbing light eyes and drove his glance into Whitcomb. "You are about to do a wrong thing. Don't do it."

It took Whitcomb a moment to realize what Lot White meant. When it came to him he grew quietly and enormously angry. "I'll have no interference in my private life."

"There's no private life when others are concerned."

"Let it alone," said Whitcomb brusquely.

Lot White sighed and his big shoulders settled; visibly strong emotion possessed him though he kept his voice down. "You could be such a good man — but you're such a bad man. You have troubled me with your questions. You have made me falter. It's your words that have got the maggots of doubt in me this minute. I ain't ever going to forgive you for it. Now you're going to trouble other lives. If that's all your education means to you then it'd be better if all the schools were burned and you were dead." He wheeled, walked over the yard to his horse and rode away.

Beyond the Collingwood place, in the timber, he left his horse and knelt against a tree; and he made a long prayer, and at the end of it he said: "He's not your man, God. Not your man at all. Give him light. Strike him, tear the evil from his bones. Let not this thing happen which is about to happen, for if it happens, what am I to think? It'd be better to take him from the earth right now. Give me a sign, O Lord. Let me know what to believe, for I am lost and I don't know where to walk. There's no power in my limbs and my voice has lost the call. Why is this, when blind men thrive around me? What have I done? Give me a sign, oh my God, for I'm failin'."

35

LIGE EBBETT had gone into the hills hunting, leaving Lavinia alone in the farthest southward cabin of the settlement, beyond Rinearson's, beyond Kitchen's. It was middle afternoon, the constant grayness of the timber even then creeping across the short meadow to the cabin. She had eaten a piece of bread with tea, she had industriously cleaned the room, she had patched a shirt. Now, stepping to the doorway, she unexpectedly discovered two Indians crouched against the cabin's wall.

She was a thin, quiet girl of seventeen, possessing little, expecting little, and inclined to efface herself in the presence of other people. The shock of this contact with the Indians sent fright through her and thus temporarily rooted she watched the two come toward her. One of them made a motion at his stomach, opened his mouth and stuck a finger into it. She knew he meant food, but food was the scarcest of their possessions, limited to half a sack of wheat, some tea, a few cooked pieces of venison and a loaf of bread on the shelf. Much as she was afraid of Indians, she was afraid of hunger more, and she shook her head and stood her ground.

The Indian nearest her made his sign again in a more peremptory manner. Both were miserable specimens, ragged hair hanging in oily hanks about their heads, grease-dirty, rank-odored, and with inflamed eyes overcast by pale patches. She shook her head again, whereupon both Indians reached out to shove her aside and to go rummaging around the place, finding the wheat and the cold meat and the bread. Meat and bread they tore into pieces which they divided and began to eat on the spot. Seeing herself despoiled, Lavinia's fear melted before the outrage and she said, "You filthy creatures — scat — scat! My bread, no!" She looked about her, saw the broom, seized it and rushed forward, striking the handle into the ribs of the Indian closest by. He was not injured but he was stung; clamping a chunk of meat between his teeth, he caught the broom, broke it and took one of its pieces and rapped Lavinia over the head. She closed in, she scratched him, she grabbed his shirt — a white man's flannel shirt — and ripped it up the front. Before she could do more damage, the Indian caught her, kicked her in the stomach with his moccasined foot and shoved her through the door. She ran around the house to the shed and seized a pitchfork. Meanwhile the Indians, finding no more food, upset such hand-made furniture as the room contained, banged her iron kettles on the floor and jumped through the doorway. Coming about the cabin's corner she saw one of them packing off her best blanket and she cried, "You drop that," and ran at the Indian with the extended pitchfork. She got the bare end of it into the calves of his retreating legs; she tried to overtake him but lost distance; she seized a rock from the ground and flung it fruitlessly at him; and she came to a stop and watched both savages lightly run to the trees and disappear. Going back to the cabin she looked at the casual damage about the room and sat down to cry. When she was through crying, which was the result of failure to stop the Indians rather than of fear, Lavinia put on a shawl and started for Rinearson's to spread the news.

36

ON New Year's Eve Burnett had had supper with the Hawns and found the visit uncomfortable, Hawn very quiet and Louisa disappearing as soon as the meal was on the table. It seemed to Burnett that even some of Hawn's friendliness had vanished; and later, returning to his own place, Burnett made the guess that Hawn, no longer happy with his wife and watching a good life fall to pieces, blamed the settlers for it.

Returning, Burnett got a good fire going — the wind having brought the snow-chilled air from the mountains — and lighted his pipe to do some thinking about himself. The methodical streak was on him at the moment and a new year was time to take stock.

He heard a horse cross the dark, and Ralph Whitcomb's hail. He swung the big water kettle over the fire before he turned to the door. Whitcomb said: "You've got a boarder for the night. I'll light out for Oregon City in the morning." He stepped down to take the gear from the horse and to dump it in the room. Burnett slapped the horse through the meadow gate and came back to the cabin. Whitcomb had settled himself at the fire. "Had supper — don't want anything. I'm here because I didn't want to eat away any more of the Gay's grub. They've got a hard scratch before summer."

"We'll all scratch, but we'll make it," said Burnett. "I am, at this moment, pretty sick of deer meat and I've eaten enough boiled wheat to crow like a rooster. When I was over at the French settlement I ate half a jug of honey straight. Frenchmen just laughed at me, but they understood."

"Hunger's a powerful disturber."

"How's Millard?"

"He'll make it."

"How will he get around — how will he plow, get on a horse, ford creeks, go hunting, kneel with a crosscut? It's a hell of a country for a one-legged man."

"This afternoon he told me he'd been thinking about a wooden leg in his mind, with a flat bottom for crossing soft fields. He's a Yankee for tools. He'll make himself a leg that looks like a country store."

"Takes it well," said Burnett.

"He's proud of himself. Not many survive that operation." Whitcomb bent forward on the chair soaking in the fire; he was a dark, able-shaped man, large shoulders and arms and hands; he dressed better than the settlers and his hands were soft — otherwise he didn't resemble a professional man. "Even so," he reflected, "the experience will change him. He's a survivor when the rules say he ought to be dead. That makes a difference in what you think."

They talked a little, they sat silent. Burnett made a pot of coffee, and took a tour around the yard and came back. That reminded the doctor of the latest news and he told Burnett of Lavinia Ebbett's fight with the two Indians. Burnett shook his head. "I'm sorry about that. We're brewing up a fight, and it shouldn't be."

"I wouldn't expect you to be sympathetic with Indians," observed the doctor.

"I know Indians. They're people. All people are alike."

Whitcomb said: "The more a man sees, the less he can condemn. Then he's out of step with his neighbors, for they want life to be straight yea or nay."

Burnett freshened his pipe. Whitcomb, he thought, acted like a man with something on his mind which he wanted to share but couldn't. That classified it as a personal problem, which brought Burnett's guess around to Lucy Collingwood.

"It goes farther," Rice said. "If a man sees both sides of everything, he can't be much of a fighter for anything, and then he's out of step with himself." The remark, like so many others, came out in its own casual fashion. He hadn't thought much about it. Now that he had said it, he began to think about it; and other notions, sleeping as this one had slept, stirred without form in his head. It occurred to him then that each man — never knowing it — had a good deal of wisdom soaked into him through the years of his living, an unrealized fund waiting to be drawn upon; maybe the difference between a man like Gay and himself was that Gay knew of the fund and drew upon it and trusted it while others passed it by through ignorance.

Whitcomb nodded. "You're saying the same thing Lot White said a few days ago. He said if education didn't make a man stand on the right

252

side of things, it had better be destroyed. I gathered that he believes virtuous ignorance better than educated doubt."

"I can't follow that all the way," said Burnett. "What's education? One of the smartest men I knew couldn't write his own name. But he could describe a piece of country he passed through so that you saw it and smelled it. Everything he did seemed to be the right thing to do. Any man that knew him respected him."

"You know damned well education isn't a matter of books," said Whitcomb. "It's experience."

"That's not enough," said Burnett. "Everybody gets experience. It's all we get. But some it helps, and some it doesn't."

"If a man looks at the stars and a feeling comes to him and he wrestles with the feeling and tries to make sense of it, he's being educated."

"You make any sense from the stars?" asked Burnett.

"I said *try*," pointed out Whitcomb. He helped himself to more coffee, stirred his finger around it.

"It's the old bone we're chewing on," said Burnett. "Stay ignorant and be happy. Get wise and grow sad. Be ignorant and believe just one thing, and fight for it, and die feeling you've had a hell of a good life. Be wise, and wonder if anything's worth fighting for, and end up asking why you were born at all."

"Truth and beauty, according to the poets, are two names for the same thing, and truth is supposed to set men's spirits free."

"But it doesn't," said Burnett. "I go tell a man the truth. Then we get in a hell of an argument, whether it's true or not. If he doesn't want to believe it, I don't convince him. If I convince him, it makes him miserable. Men don't want to change their superstitions. They're like blankets, dirty and full of fleas; but they're warm and the man's been sleeping in them so long he don't want any new-fangled blankets." He grinned at Whitcomb. "What the hell we talking about?"

Whitcomb looked around the room. "Why aren't you married?"

"And the same to you," said Burnett, cheerfully. "But about this truth business. When I look around I see a form to most things — water and soil, sun and rain, seed and fruit — everything works out neat. It's only when you get to wondering about man that you get off the track."

The doctor made a gesture. "We start from here, knowing nothing. We're going there — away down there to the end of the journey where we'll know everything about everything. We're just a little way along, neither here nor there. We know something, not much. We're afraid to leave home, because it's familiar. We're afraid to walk forward because we don't know what we'll find — we're afraid there's nothing to find when we get there."

"Round and round she goes," said Burnett. "But don't let Lot White hear you say that or you've got an argument."

"We've had several," said Whitcomb. He grew serious and restless. He made a long study of the fire and Burnett sensed the man's wish to share something with somebody. "Whether it's heaven or sleep, what does that matter here? We've got this thing to live as comfortably and as usefully as possible. There's some freedom, some joy possible. But, no, we must not laugh in the face of impending doom. We must be grave, we must bow to angry gods and be fearful. Dead soon enough, we have got to strangle ourselves little by little before we die." He struck a palm sharp across his knee. "What mockery. If there's a God with compassion in him, he must be sad for the barbarisms we commit in the name of morality."

Burnett bent forward to catch another light for his pipe. He didn't look at Whitcomb. "You talking against the rules or against your conscience?"

"Ever settle anything with your conscience?"

This was what Whitcomb had come for, Burnett understood. The doctor, wanting a woman, had got himself mixed up with the right and the wrong of it; he was on the edge of the great jump and couldn't quite spring free. He wanted help. Burnett rose and crossed to the door. He told himself, *He thinks I've been through this enough times to give him some advice.* The wind had blown the mists out of the sky, the stars glittered frost-sharp. Wind smell was keen around him. The doctor's horse stood with its head hooked over the meadow fence. He thought carefully of an answer, and the answer got longer and longer in his mind as he tried to cover something which couldn't be covered; and he grew impatient with himself and said it as briefly as he could.

"I knew an old fellow in St. Louis, one time, about ready to die. He said the only things he regretted in his life were the things he didn't do. I wouldn't be surprised if he was mostly right. There's a consequence to whatever we do, even if we don't do it. We pay for it. So, do we pay for something, or nothing?"

He turned about to find Whitcomb closely watching him; and suddenly the doctor rose smiling. "Yes and no. The same old thing."

"Certainly."

The doctor got his bedroll and opened it on the floor. "No," said Burnett, "you sleep on the bunk. You've had some bad nights."

254

37

DURING the night he heard one of the horses go scudding across the meadow; and he lay awake a moment, listening for further sound. In the morning he cooked breakfast and watched Whitcomb travel down the trail; and he milked the cows and took a short walk into the meadow to find some kind of print on the ground which might explain the horse's momentary fright. He saw nothing and, with pick and shovel and ax, he moved up the creek a short distance to begin work on the mill-race which he had earlier surveyed. Harvest time was six months away. During that time he had to finish the race way, build the mill house, make the wheel and mount it, set in the stones and rig up the bins for wheat and flour. He had to chop a wider strip through the timber to make a wagon road, he had to plow his land and plant. He had to plow for Mrs. Irish, he had to spend time with other neighbors cutting the main road between Lord's notch and Walker's. Each chunk of labor he set in its order; the eighteen-hour days ran solid from now until harvest.

As he worked on the ditch, cutting through gravel and roots to the lower hard soil, he set himself into the slow swing of the six months. He was a runner who, with long miles to cover, would break himself if he ran too fast too soon. He had no fat on him now; he was muscle, bone and calluses — he was so fined down that he was conscious of his energy paying itself out pound by pound as he worked, felt its quick renewal after mealtime, felt it pay out again in late afternoon. Sometimes, overstrained, he lay in bed at night with his body a dull lump through which his drawn nerves traced their streaks of heat; sometimes his energy collected and broke through his discipline and he rose to pace the floor with the male torment upon him.

During the afternoon he became conscious of motion somewhere in the woods around him and he stopped to light his pipe and to dredge the day for its reports. Nothing came to him yet his warned senses refused to settle. Deep in the timber south of the creek a gun sounded, those outrolling thicket-strained echoes thinly arriving; and later he thought he heard the subdued rustle of brush in the same direction but nearer at hand. This was when he laid down his shovel and stepped to his rifle tilted against the nearest tree. Catching it up, he ran his glance along the dark margin of fir, alder and willow across the creek; close beside a tree — half visible and motionless — he saw a man's shape. In those shadows the shape was not to be identified but it didn't appear to be an Indian. Burnett lifted his rifle and took a steady aim. The man came out of the brush and into full view immediately, waving a hand across his body. It was the marshal. He waded over the creek.

"What the God-damn' hell?" he said.

"I was about to mistake you for an Indian," said Burnett. "You're lucky."

"Man," said the marshal, brisk and pointed, "you and me don't track well."

"Walk in plain view around here," said Burnett, "and you're all right. What's your business here?"

"To do what I damn please."

"Fly right at it."

The marshal gave out a short laugh and he shook his head. He raised one hand to make a circle over his head and presently two men broke from the timber upstream and moved forward. They were both strangers to Burnett. One of them said, "He ain't crossed the creek this morning."

"Well," said the marshal, "he's over there somewhere," and pointed to the woods southward. "And he's got to come out somewhere." He lowered his head to think about it, and he sighed. "My God, I could eat the horns off a bull." Having dropped his plain hint, he continued to look at the ground, waiting Burnett's invitation. To any other man Burnett would have issued such an invitation instantly; but the marshal was after a man; good or bad, the man belonged to this settlement and therefore the marshal was no friend of Burnett's. The invitation didn't come and after a spell of vain waiting the marshal shrugged his shoulders and drew the two men a few yards down the creek and murmured to them. He came back to Burnett. "If you see that boy, tell him to give up. He might get out of it easy, on trial, but if he ain't goin' to come in, then I got to shoot him if I see him, for he's sent me warnin' through his dad that he won't be took. That's bad business. Tell him to come in. He can't run east. That's a hundred miles of mountains to nowhere. He can't go south. That's empty for eight hundred miles. He's stuck right around here and it's just a matter of time before I get a bead on him. I told his dad to tell him. He wouldn't listen to his dad. You tell him I don't fool."

Burnett nodded and watched the three men walk over the meadow and disappear into the timber toward Lattimore's. He thought: *He'll creep back here to watch.* It was late, but he worked on the ditch until the shadows began to sift in and the cows moved across the water and stood waiting at the gate. He milked and turned the cows back to the meadow. When he entered the shed to lay the milk on the shelf he heard a chunk of wood strike the shed's wall. He left the shed and stood a moment, thinking about it; and he got the ax from the chopping block and circled the shed and stepped toward the timber, not fifty feet away. Whit's voice arrived from the deeper darkness. "I've got to eat."

"Wait till she's dark then crawl in on your belly."

"He around?"

"Went down the trail, but I believe he cut back. I'll hit a pan when I want you to come." He took a few cuts at a branch with the ax and dragged the branch back to the yard with him and threw it in the shed; that was for the marshal to puzzle about if he happened to be watching. It was fully dark then. Watt Irish came up for the milk.

"Pass anybody, Watt?"

Watt said: "Old Man Rinearson's at Lattimore's. The marshal's around there somewhere watchin'. Old Man Rinearson says to tell you that if Whit shows up here, tell him to go to Gay's and get a horse waiting there — but to stay off the trail. Tell him to go to the French settlement then and see if he can't find some trappin' outfit that's bound for California. Old man says he'll stay at Lattimore's, so the marshal will keep watching that place."

"All right," said Burnett. "I'll tell Whit. He's here."

Watt marched away with two full buckets of milk. Burnett cooked supper and fried an extra skillet of meat; he ate his meal, put the meat on a plate and poured coffee into a bucket and carried these things to the shed. He banged the bucket with his knuckles, presently hearing Whit come around the shed. "Here," said Burnett quietly, and drew him into the shed's full blackness. "Here's your grub. I told you to crawl."

"Tired of it."

"Your dad's at Lattimore's, keeping the marshal interested." He gave Whit the instructions. Then he said, "But you're a fool if you do it. You're better off if you stay here and let me go find the marshal. That man's foxy and he'll find you anyhow. He's got a couple others around here. They've got you pretty well pinned down and they'll give you no time to talk."

"I won't do it," said Whit. "I ain't goin' to hang."

"You might get cleared. There were two of you. Nobody can prove you fired the gun."

"I ain't goin' to do it," said Whit. "I told the old man to tell the marshal to go to hell. I'll shoot him if I see him."

"He'll do the same thing."

"I'll take care of myself. Won't go to California, either. Tell the old man I'll wear that marshal down till he quits and I'll be livin' around here when the whole thing's forgotten."

"Don't do it. Quit trying to be like Lockyear."

"I didn't say a word about him, did I?" Whit ate the meat and drank the coffee. Burnett heard him reach around his pocket for a pipe. "Not now — not here," said Burnett. He lost patience with the boy. "Don't you know you're just short of being dead? That fellow means business. Stop being careless."

"Ah," said Whit, "to hell with him." He made no more attempt to smoke. He got up and moved to the edge of the yard.

"Go around the house and get on your belly and crawl across the meadow. Stay away from the trail."

Whit disappeared, leaving no word behind him; he wasn't crawling for the soft echo of his traveling feet came back. Burnett washed his dishes and filled his woodbox and he was about to go to bed when he heard a shot break over the meadow. He caught up his lantern and lighted it; he seized his gun and set out at a run toward the woods.

Old Daniel Rinearson, standing with his buttocks to the Lattimore fire, heard the shot and flung back his head as though the bullet had struck him; on that sly, netted face the dry flash of agony showed. He clapped both hands together and he groaned and rushed from the house, Lattimore after him. He ran over the meadow and into the timber. Lattimore heard him say: "Son — son," and grow silent. He stumbled in the dark, he collided with trees, he clawed his way forward, and now he called at the top of his lungs. "Whitley — where are you?" A light danced on the trail ahead and little by little the shape of men grew around it.

Lattimore said, "Daniel, let me get ahead of you there," and he overtook Rinearson and tried to catch the older man's arm. Rinearson flung up his hand and struck Lattimore's fist away. He cried again, "Whitley!"

258

He ran faster toward the group standing in the trail. Burnett held the lantern, swinging it back and forth. The marshal and the marshal's two men screened the ground until Old Daniel, reaching them, knocked them aside with his shoulders. He stopped and his head sank toward Whitley on the earth — the latter's body lying loose, face down, one hand tucked beneath his chest, one reaching outward with the fingers dirtied by the soil he had clawed in a last moment of pain. His hat was gone, his yellow hair streaked with mud. There was no bullet hole visible and Daniel, going to his knees, pulled his son half over, saw the drip of blood and the vacant face, and let the boy roll back.

"My God — my God!" The broken wind of his running sawed in and out of him. He cried, he suffered for air, his skin grew scarlet, the cruel lantern light glittered on tears running down his raddled cheeks. "Son — what for, what for, oh, my God, what for? Jesus — my son, my son!" He bowed his head. Kneeling, he laid his hand on the boy's body and stroked it. He clenched his teeth and he shivered from inward cold. His words came out between the gasps of crying, spaced apart, low and stuttering. "What'll I tell your mother — oh, what'll I tell her?"

The marshal's voice was dryly regretful. "Couldn't do nothin' else. He wouldn't be taken, and I didn't propose to be shot. Young men, I don't know, they can't be talked to. They don't take it. We'll move him back to Lattimore's." But Old Daniel didn't hear, and the group was reluctant to break into his tragedy, and stood in waiting silence.

38

IN January winter came, the kind of winter they had left behind them and were lonesome for. Even so, it was a mild thing. The wind blew steadily from the east, bringing sharper temperatures; thin ice formed in water-buckets and glittered as a ragged edge in the slack eddies of the creek. The high mountains grew whiter, the sky was blue, the sun bright and heatless. By early morning the cattle stood stiff-legged at barn lot gates, their breath cloudy in the air. Burnett brought the red hen and the young chicks into the cabin at night. The earth began to harden and frost dropped more leaves until all the yellow color in the timber was gone, leaving only the solid green of the firs. Fern and brambles and weeds settled to their wilted, gray clumps. All through the settlement chimneys sent up their continuous spirals of smoke and in this brittle atmosphere voices carried so far that Mrs. Millard's voice, a quarter-mile away in her cabin, seemed to announce her in Burnett's meadow; and lights winked across the dark with sharper brightness. Toward the end of January the temperature dropped and thick ice formed and one night the snow began and fell vagrantly for three days, edging the fir boughs, drifting blue-cast hummocks against tree trunks, layering the earth with its shallow crust; and the stillness of this still land grew greater.

Burnett finished the ditch before the ground got too hard to work. At upper and lower ends he came within four feet of the creek before quitting — these sections blocking out the creek until he built a headgate; when he got that done he dug away the end sections and let the water through; even at low stage the head of water dropping from upper creek to lower creek, through the race, was enough to turn his wheel. He built supports at either side of the race to hold the wheel; the wheel itself he delayed making until late spring weather, for it was a large affair to be constructed piece at a time on its mountings. Meanwhile he fashioned his other parts at night in the cabin. For the shaft he ripsawed a twenty-foot length from an oak tree and dressed it round with plane, drawknife and rasp, measuring his diameter as he went along; where the shaft sat on the bearings he nailed in a thick collar of leather. From two large maple roots he designed his bevel gears which were to transfer the power of the wheel to the shaft of the millstone. This was the tedious chore, the contrary grain of the roots bonding the wood into a marblelike stubbornness. For the first dressing-down he turned the roots over the fire on a spit, charring the chunks into working shape.

When the snow came he put aside the mill work and set out to widen the trail between his place and Lattimore's, and now he knew road making was harder than he first had imagined, for this timber was old, much of it twelve feet or more in diameter and stretching upward beyond two hundred feet; the labor of cutting it was too much. Wherever he struck such giants he bent around them, hunting clearer patches, hunting thinner firs. He hired Watt to saw the fallen trees into lengths short enough to be rolled aside; he made a tunnel beneath the stumps and started fires, and watched them die, and started them again, and experimented until he had invented a system of cross tunnels to create a draft; but it was a slow thing, for the first heat started the wood's wetness and the whole top of the stump bubbled and sang. At night he watched these inflamed eyes gleam through the timber; and at night, too, when he was unable to endure his own company, he walked to the neighbors to sit, to smoke, to listen to stories he had heard often before; but it wasn't the stories that mattered — it was the closeness, the sound of voices, the thawing out of solitariness, the strength, more real than the strength of meat, which these meetings renewed. It was pretty clear to him then: People were compass needles pointing to each other. People were meant to touch.

He traveled to Lattimore's, to Provost's, to Mercer's; he found himself going oftener and oftener to Gay's. The four miles grew shorter.

Toward the end of the month, Whitcomb came from Oregon City to pronounce Millard ready to move; and Gay hitched the big wagon for the first time since the crossing and took him home. The neighbors made a celebration of it. The roundabout women cleaned the Millard cabin. Daniel Rinearson slaughtered a cow, a meal was cooked, and everybody was in the yard to meet the big wagon when it reached the yard with Nancy Millard and her husband and the Gays. Lot White let go with a huge "Praise the Lord," and made ready to make a sermon; but Billy Lord started a song, and the song took hold while Lot White stood solemnly by and shook his head at this lost opportunity. He looked from face to face and a settled expression came to him and he seemed to see them all as from a distance; he was a stranger looking upon strangers, and he dropped his head and went into his own thoughts. Nancy Millard came down crying from the big wagon. Men stood by to help Millard, but nobody offered a hand and Burnett, observing this unexpected backwardness, found himself stirred by the comprehension and the pity it implied; each man knew what a disaster such a thing was in this country, and each man felt himself in Millard's place and knew what Millard wanted. Millard wanted to be let alone. He had made himself a crutch. He let himself over the wheel; he rested his good foot on the wagon's hub, brought his crutch down, hopped to the ground, and clapped the crutch under his arm. Supported by crutch and wagon wheel, he looked to the cabin twenty feet away and let go his grip on the wagon wheel and made it to the house. He hooked an arm around the doorframe and turned about, the broadest possible smile on his face.

"Why, hell," he said, "I got this thing licked."

A great fire burned in the yard. Around it they ate, the weather sharp and still. Millard sat before it in a chair, the rest of the men standing or crouched nearby. Old Daniel said, "Never mind your plowin' this spring. The boys and me will do it."

"No," said Millard. "That's no way for a one-legged man to start life. I propose to do everything I did before and I propose to do it as well."

"You got a burden to carry," said Lot. "Lord's will. Bear it humbly."

"I don't hold with that," said Millard. "I had two legs for forty-six years. That was fine. Now I got one leg. That will be fine, too. I'll plow, I'll ride, I'll hunt bear. And that's the end of it."

With that, he settled the subject, and the talk went to other things.

The women had drifted to the cabin for its greater warmth, for a greater freedom to discuss the latest gleanings of gossip. Mrs. Mercer spoke to Old Daniel's wife. "I hear Edna's going to have a baby."

"So she says," responded Mrs. Rinearson and looked Mrs. Mercer squarely in the eyes.

There was an interested silence in which every woman did some counting of the months. Mrs. Mercer said: "She don't show yet, naturally."

"You've had babies, Netty," said Mrs. Rinearson. "You ought to know when they start showin'."

"No, she wouldn't show. It'll be, let's see, July, won't it?"

Mrs. Rinearson laughed. "I hope so, Netty." Then she said, "You hope so too, don't you?" And she went into the yard to find Rinearson.

Netty Mercer said to the others: "Of course I hope so. Heavens, what else would I hope?" Afterwards, most casually, she added: "I ain't seen much of her lately." Mrs. Crosby started to speak, looked toward Katherine and kept her silence.

Mrs. Gay said, "Where'd Ralph Whitcomb go? He was to've come here to eat."

"I saw him start back through the notch," said Mrs. Lord.

"Lucy and George didn't come, either," said Mrs. Provost. "That's strange for George. He don't miss meetings."

"Him?" said Mrs. Mercer. "The man wants attention so much he'd take a bath in public if he thought we'd look."

"You think they had words?" asked Mrs. McIver. "George and Lucy?"

The ladies hesitated. They had the thing in their minds and were eager to speak but were restrained by the need to show some properness.

"He's so wrapped up in himself he couldn't see anything about anything," said Mrs. Provost.

That remark took care of the proprieties. "Well," said Mrs. Kern, "if he don't see what's to be seen there he's blinder than any man I know. Nobody could be that blind."

"He could," said Mrs. Provost.

"I think he knows but pretends he doesn't. Because if he let on he knew, he'd have to do something — and what could he do?"

"Same thing any other man'd do," said Mrs. Mercer.

"Oh, no," said Mrs. Provost. "Not him." There was agreement around the group on that; the opinion on Collingwood was almost unanimous.

"Well," said Mrs. Mercer, "what on earth's the matter with him?"

Mrs. Millard threw up her hands and laughed. "Oh, Lord," she said, and clapped her hands on her knees; everybody else was smiling. Even Mrs. Gay showed some humor.

"Poor Ralph," she said.

"Well, poor Lucy, too," put in Mrs. Walker.

"I don't know," said Mrs. Gay in her hesitating, gentle way, "it's not a thing to excuse, but — "

"It's for her to stop," said Mrs. Provost.

That was a challenge to Mrs. Millard's sense of equality. "Oh, I don't know. It's no more a woman's place to stop it than a man's. Who starts those things, anyhow? Men."

Mrs. Lord turned her fat and seamless face toward Mrs. Millard. "What if they didn't?"

"And that's where they've got us at their power," said Mrs. Millard. "They're sly. They start things we can't stop. We do things we oughtn't. Then they act innocent. Oh, the creatures."

"Well," said Mrs. Gay, "as for those two, the right and wrong is clear enough. And still — "

"Let her put up with what she's got, like any woman's got to do," said Mrs. Millard. "And let him marry somebody, which he ought to have done a long time ago."

There was no answer. There was neither agreement nor disagreement; these ladies sat thoughtful, wrestling with a very practical matter and finding sympathy and judgment at odds.

Katherine, usually silent among these older women, spoke with some irritation.

"Is it any of our business?"

Mrs. Millard said at once: "Of course it is. We have to live together."

"No, what's inside a cabin is not our business. I like Lucy very much. I'd not care to see anything hurt her."

263

"In a thing like this," said Mrs. Millard grimly, "she'll hurt herself more than anybody else will. That's where men have got us. They can walk away and sing songs about it. We can't."

Mrs. Lord's baby face was cool to Mrs. Millard. "Don't you touch a hair of my Billy's head — which is gettin' a little scraggly, I'll admit — or I'll come down here and peek through your window all night long, and what'll you think whose business is whose business then? Katherine's right."

"Oh, I suppose she is," said Mrs. Millard. "I always do a lot of talking. I got to put him to bed. He's been up too long."

The ladies rose and went out to find their men and go home. Katherine stopped at the cabin's corner, catching Burnett's attention, drawing him over. "Supper tonight, if you want to come."

"I'll come."

The break in the day had done him good. He was rested, he had been well fed; he was alert, chesty, and he was strongly aware of her. She watched him with her smile.

"You're laughing at me," he said.

"No, I'm not."

He made half a motion to take her arm, remembered the neighbors around, and checked himself. Her smile quickened. She lifted her head, eyes closing a little as she held his attention, challenging him until she saw him lift, until he was half of one thought and half of another, the rashness growing. He had always been proper toward her but he wasn't now, not quite. She stood a short time longer, her manner daring him, and thereafter she said: "Tonight," and left him. She was pleased with herself. Edna could have done it no better.

Millard settled into bed with a windy groan of comfort. "By God, I'm glad to be back. Good as they've been to us I'm glad to be here. When'd I sleep here last?"

"Christmas Eve," said Mrs. Millard, and went about the room to pick it up. There weren't many dishes; the neighbors had brought and taken away their own. "We've got beef for a couple weeks. You want to eat it every meal or you want to go sparing?"

"Every meal," he said. "I got to catch up with myself." He put a hand over his head and lay still.

"It hurt?"

"No," he said. "Just thinkin'."

264

She went about her work and it was a good five minutes before she spoke; and her words were somehow stiff. "Well, I'm glad you're back, too."

"Had a time of it, ain't you?"

"Now, Millard, don't make fun of me, don't make me mad when I don't want to be. I'm trying to be good — it's your first night back here — I'd hate it if we said anything. Please."

"All right." He stirred himself around the bed. He moved his good leg; he tried to move what was left of his other leg. He flexed the muscles of that leg, but nothing happened; he felt the muscles stir a little bit and he worked at it — and then he remembered that those muscles weren't there. He drew in a long breath; he let it out quietly. He drew a hand over his face and shut his eyes and was still. He renewed his effort, thinking of the muscles which remained above the knee. He felt the stump move slightly. Inside his head he spoke to the stump. "You son-of-a-bitch, move." He tried again; he tried several times and felt some response; then he was exhausted and his face was cool-damp. He discovered his teeth were gritted together. He relaxed; he lay still.

"Gay don't look good to me," he said.

"I wanted to ask Martha but she never spoke about it."

"Nobody in the family does. Awful queer. Last few days he's looked feeble, like it was hard to walk or stand up. Hell, he came off the wagon here slower than I did."

She said nothing. He listened to her work at the dishes and he felt— because he knew her so well — the storm piling up within her. He had no notion what caused it but it was there. He waited; behind the hand over his face he smiled as he waited.

"Millard — you asleep?"

"No."

She set a dish on the table with force. She came along the bed until she was at its foot and could face him. "I can't stand it much longer, I can't. Roxy's been in my head all day, all week. Who knows what's happened? She hasn't been back to see her people. She hasn't visited anybody. She might be dead. I waited today for somebody to say something about it. I held myself back. I waited, wondering if anybody cared. Not a word was said, not one word. I can understand why women might not want to speak of it. Women are cowards. But you men sat around. You talked about everything. Not a word about her. If there was a spark of decency in any of you, it'd be on your minds. You're afraid. You don't want to face that man. You keep saying, 'It's his wife — don't interfere — it's his wife.' You're afraid, that's the only reason. You'll let her be beaten and starved, you'll let her be killed because you're afraid. Oh, God, Millard, I can't bear it any longer."

The dam had burst, the flood poured out. This was the pattern. He held his hands over his eyes and listened to her words go on and on in their rhythm of violence; her voice rose higher and the shrill tone made fluttery vibrations against his eardrums; then suddenly she broke off and turned to her work.

"You through?" he said.

"I mean it, Millard," she said. "I think I have got to do something or go crazy."

"She'll be down for a visit pretty soon. Then you'll not worry. It'll work out."

"It'll work out — it'll work out," she mimicked. "Always that. That's men."

"Well," he said, "we're home again."

On that afternoon Lorenzo Buck and his wife walked wordlessly home in the beginning twilight and separated at the cabin, she to go to her work inside and he to milk, to look after the stock, to do the little chores. When they were done he circled the place, using his eyes to see what strange or unusual things might be seen; for on the way home from Millard's he had noted a wolf track in the thin snow, larger than any dog's. It was dark when he went into the cabin. His wife had made coffee and they had their small meal, bread and coffee with butter. The children were with the Ebbetts and would remain there for the night. He shook the fire together and filled his pipe, and stood in the room's center, speculating on the amount of tobacco he had left and how long it would last him. His wife had settled to knitting; now and then, with careful indirection, he watched her. He walked to the door and opened it, appreciating the path of moonlight running across the snow. Through the trees he made out the smallest wink of Monteith's place nearer the creek. He cleared his throat.

"Everything all right?"

Having no answer, he turned about and found her looking toward him, hands lying over the knitting. She said: "You been thinking about something, Lorenzo?"

"Just wondered if everything's all right."

"I'm not worried about food. We'll need a deer or two, and I shall have to be careful about wheat. But we'll make out."

"Oh," he said, "we'll make out. That don't trouble me."

He returned to the fire, pipe thrust straight out, lips drawn back; he rocked idly on his heels, he put his hands behind him. The firelight gave to his mild face a shine of benevolence but his eyes were thoughtful. He waited quite a while before speaking again.

"You're satisfied?"

She smoothed the piece of knitting against her knee, she watched her hand. "We've got as good a cabin as anybody. The land's good — I like to look out and just see Monteith's smoke over the trees, not too far, not too near. It's not a lonely place." She seemed to be thinking of something else to say, but at last resumed her work.

His head dropped lower, he stared steadily into the fire. "You miss some things though, I suppose."

"In a strange country, that's to be expected. I'm not complaining."

"Well," he said, still watching the fire, "I just wondered if everything was all right." He removed his pipe, tapped it against the fireplace stones and held it in his hard hand.

"We'll make out," she said.

He made a short nod. "That's right," he said and added, "Believe I'll turn in. Tomorrow I'm goin' to work on the road." He left the cabin and made one more circle around the place, and came back. After he had gone to bed he settled himself on his side, facing the wall, back to his wife. She abandoned her knitting and sat watching him, the pleasantness of her face fading. He wasn't asleep, she knew, for his hand lay finger-spraddled over his head. He was a considerate, methodical, stubborn little man. He wasn't at all like her other husband.

Now that was queer, that was sorrowful. It was barely four months and it was still hard to think of Harper Howard not alive. Sometimes when people spoke to her and said "Mrs. Buck," she had to stop and remember that she was the one they meant — she was Mrs. Buck, not Mrs. Howard any more. He was a nice man, Lorenzo. When would the strangeness die? When this quiet way came on him and he began to ask her questions in soft persistence, she knew it hurt his feelings to realize she wasn't toward him the way she had been toward Howard. He had a sentimental streak. They all had it. Howard had it, but Howard was different; it was all right to say foolish words and carry on with him, because it had started when they were both young. It wasn't right with Buck; she was an old woman,

267

he was an old man. It embarrassed her. They had need for each other, and that was all right; but it wasn't decent to talk about it or fuss over it. He wanted to say words with it which she couldn't say, couldn't ever say again. There was a time; then the time went, and it didn't come back. She watched the fire a long while.

39

AFTER the meeting with Whitcomb, Lucy was nicer than usual to her husband. The strain of waiting for Whitcomb to gather courage and the endless back-and-forth argument in her own mind was over. The act had been committed, the doubts were no longer important. She had never felt so well, so happy or so important. She had to restrain her cheerfulness, for she could never be certain of George Collingwood's perceptions. Sometimes she was sure that, wrapped around so tightly by his own interests, he saw nothing; at other times she suspected his manner to be a screen through which he watched her most closely. But in her happiness was a pity for him. Knowing loneliness herself so well, she thought there were times when he too must suffer from it; and this made her kind. She talked more to him, though this was difficult. His reticence, so long developed, was hard to break through. Now and then, in this mood, she noticed that he watched her as though he were puzzled. Once — once only during the succeeding days of the month — she was unexpectedly taken aback by the idea that perhaps it was still possible for them to break the barrier and come together again as they had in their earliest days of marriage. That was her bad day. George had gone off on one of his increasingly frequent overnight trips to visit some settler he hadn't met before; she walked around the cabin, she slipped on her shawl and tramped the trail; she lay in bed, thinking about it. But she knew it was no good. The thought that it might be possible — that it might at least be the thing she ought to try to do — gave her a dark and dreadful feeling and then she knew she no longer wanted to go emotionally back to George. She had made the crossover from one man to another; there was no way of returning.

But if her doubt was gone, possessiveness took its place and supplied its own kind of misery. After Whitcomb's departure she stood in the doorway at some moment in each day to make a ceremony of remembering how he had turned at the edge of the timber to wave good-by; and each day she rehearsed the moments preceding the kiss, and the intenseness of her longing as he stood indecisive between his desire and his judgment, and the desperateness which had come into her when she thought he meant to give up and go away; that was when she had spoken of her loneliness. No, she corrected herself, it wasn't desire and judgment which had deadlocked him; it was desire against a lack of confidence in himself. He had passed the youthful egotism which felt itself irresistible and he had an older man's acute fear of making himself appear ridiculous. That had been a hard thing for her to bring him through.

On his second visit, almost a month later, she saw him for only a moment. George had been home and Whitcomb, pausing at the cabin, spoke a pleasant word to both of them and went on. He played his part very well, she thought. Almost too well — for the casualness of his manner sent its splinter of fear through her. Could he have changed his mind? She soon rid herself of the notion but the rest of the day was bad. Sight of him intensified her impatience to be with him, the month behind had dragged interminably, the months ahead grew longer and longer. They had so little, they could expect so little; each lost opportunity was tragic. In this state of mind she once more felt her life slipping by and her body drowned in its stopped-up wants; she had the greatest difficulty making herself cheerful for George on that day.

He had long since begun a list of every settler south of Oregon City, on both sides of the Willamette. He was, in the matter of names, an industrious packrat, returning from each trip with new names which he added to the list in his elegant handwriting. He was very proud of his handwriting; he was most serious about the list. In some manner, he had made a picture of himself in public life, and it seemed to fill some need in him as nothing else had done; and in his quiet, obscure and tenacious fashion he went after what he wanted, putting on his two suits of appearance for the two sides of his life. Among people it was the affable, courteous, straining-to-please suit; at home he sat in the dark shawl of his ambitions, poring over the lists, dreaming his dream, mysterious, intent, listening to the whisper of fame.

After supper that day he brought up the thing she had not dared mention, though she had in a dozen ways tried to lead him to it by indirection.

"I'll do a week's road work, starting tomorrow. Provost has got some neighbors for it and we'll grade Lord's notch. Then next week I'd like to go to Oregon City." He was diffident. "I thought that maybe you'd like to make the trip."

She said, "I don't know — I don't know what I'd do there."

"Well, it's a change. We'll put up at the hotel. I want to go across the river into the Tualatin for a couple days but you'd not be lonely waiting. We've got a few dollars you can spend for things."

She let the silence go on a short time, and said: "I'll go. When?"

"Week from tomorrow. We'll be gone four–five days. Joe Gay will look after the stock."

Afterward she had the feeling — as the lightest breath of air across her face — that behind his mild glance was a knowledge of what was in her mind. Was it real or had her conscience begun to create its illusions?

Two weeks after Millard returned home John Gay finished his night's chores and came in for supper. He struck his foot against the doorsill, stumbled, and flung both arms around the casing to support himself. All members of the family were in the room and saw it but nobody said anything. He didn't look at them. He recovered his balance and let his shoulder touch the casing a little while, for he was unusually weary and his breath ran fast. Katherine came over and put her arm around him.

"Supper will warm you."

"Yes," he said, "that's it. Supper's what I want."

He ate little, drank a good deal of coffee, and sat by the fireplace until the dishes were done. Young Joe slipped away to his night's spooking through the timber; the old couple went to the wagon. Katherine left the cabin long enough for her father to get into bed and then returned. Her mother had drawn a chair beside the bed and sat there with her sewing, saying nothing and pretending to see nothing; in time of trouble it was Martha Gay's inclination to grow confused and silent.

Gay spoke to his daughter. "I was telling your mother that I'm a little run down and I think I'll stay in bed a few days and rest up."

"Lord knows you got it comin' to you," said Mrs. Gay. She thought of something and laid her work aside. "I didn't shut in those geese," she said and left the room.

Katherine settled on the bed's edge. She took her father's hand. "I'll have Rice go to Oregon City for Dr. Whitcomb."

"That will do no good. I saw him when he was here. Don't tell your mother. It's something he can't find. I wanted to hold this off a little longer but it got hard work stayin' on my feet." He was pale, he was old.

270

Though not an austere man he had always kept his emotions under control and it was physical weakness now that brought a glistening dampness to his eyes. "Awful lot of men have got children that cause 'em worry. Like Whit, like Edna, or Roxy, or Provost's oldest boy. Neither you nor Joe ever caused us a minute of trouble. You're going to be all right, both smart and steady."

She bent to kiss the top of his head, to smooth his pillow-ruffled hair. "Oh," she said, "I don't know. There was some trouble. Remember when I fell in love with Harvey Crockett? What was I — twelve, I guess."

A smile appeared in his eyes. "That takes me back."

"Mother was worried. You weren't. I was mad at you because you laughed at me. Harvey and I planned to run away. Did I ever tell you that?"

"Didn't tell me but I knew it at the time."

"We were awfully sly about it. How did you find out?"

"Harvey's father said he'd found a blanket roll wrapped in the barn. Harvey had got it ready. There was a pound of bacon in the blanket roll, an old pistol, some coffee, couple tin plates and cups, and hickory nuts. So I came home and looked around and discovered you'd wrapped some stuff and had it under your bed. Can't recall what all you'd wrapped together. Where'd you and Harvey plan to go?"

"We were going to walk beyond Lee's Bridge, I don't just know where, but Harvey said he knew he could get a farmer to rent him a piece of land and a cabin, and we'd go to housekeeping on that."

"Well, Harvey's father kept an eye on him, didn't say anything. I never mentioned it either and it petered out. Always wondered what happened."

She said: "One day we got to talking and I asked him how old he was, and he told me, and I discovered he was three weeks younger than I. It was such a shock. I just didn't love him any more and the whole thing died. So you knew about it?"

"That's right."

"Maybe you didn't know everything about it," she said.

He looked at her a moment. "You got to remember there was a time when I was twelve, too."

"Is it always the same, at twelve?"

"Just about. Some people, when they get through it and get older, regret what they did. That's a foolish thing. Twelve's twelve. It's wrong to

271

use the knowledge you got at one stage of life to judge what you did earlier. Anyhow, twelve's a fine time, mistakes and all. If I went back I'd be glad to make the same mistakes again."

"I wonder where Harvey is now?"

"Memories," he said. "Sweet as sugar, strong as vinegar. People — people are mostly afraid. They hold back their hands and never touch the apple, and spend the rest of the time wishing they had. What's the use of digging a well if it don't fill with water?" He was silent, turning gently on the bed as pain got at him; he laid a hand over his eyes. "That Edna girl, you think she's still in Rice's system?"

"How'd you know that?"

"Had a few women in my blood at one time or another. You'd not think, I suppose, somebody's mother warned me to stay away from her girl or get buckshotted."

"Weren't you serious about the girl?"

"I did my running around and I was serious each time. That's what I want to tell you. About a man — about Rice. It's possible for him to love a second woman as much as he thought he loved the first. He will have some sentiment about the first one, but that's another thing."

"I know that," said Katherine. "But something's got to happen before the change is any good. He's got to know the first one wasn't what he wanted."

"That will take care of itself," said her father.

"You don't know Rice."

"Rice or any man, that will take care of itself."

She shook her head; she was silent for a short time. Then she said, "Why didn't he take her? I wonder what it was."

"You're not apt to find out, for he don't know. No man's got reasons about a woman; all he knows is what she does to him and how she makes him feel. A man's a peculiar thing. By himself he's got no more shape or purpose than a cloud of dust blown over the desert. He's nothing but a dream of something that might be until he looks at a woman, and then he sees himself and knows what he is and turns real. If it's not one woman to show him, he'll go on till he finds another, for the whole thing's beyond his power to stop."

She turned to look closely at him. He had not talked to her in such a manner before. All her life she had been certain of him; he was the familiar rock of her childhood and girlhood, the one motionless, unchanged landmark in the changing years. Now he was a kind stranger watching

272

her. She wanted to cry; she lowered her head to kiss him and lay with her cheek along his hair.

"It won't be Harris, will it?" he asked.

"I don't know. I don't think so, but I don't know. If it has to be, it will be. You know we can't choose things as we'd best like to."

"Muff . . ." he said. It was a name he had used on her long ago, and had put away. "Muff, don't think about that. Not for a while. Let this work out. Practical's practical, but I want it better for you. I don't say Harris won't do well. Fine man there. But that's another thing. Don't you get impatient. You have got a long way to go and it's best to try for a good start. Talk to your grandmother. She knows more than the lot of us put together."

"It would please you to see me settled," she said.

"It'll work out," he said. "Keep it in your mind—that it will work out. Good and bad are neck-and-neck in the world but I have always believed the thinking of good will produce it more times than not. People draw things to them by their thoughts. Nothing so strong as the pull of a thought. Someday we'll know more about that." Martha Gay's voice said, "Shoo-shoo," in the yard. Gay lowered his voice. "I will not get off this bed again, but don't tell your mother."

She said, "You're mistaken." But her grandmother's strain of dark-earth mystery was in her, and the touch of her father was cold. She lay still, her head against his head.

Hawn came down to Burnett's quite early one morning and squatted by the fire while Burnett cooked his meal. He shook his head at Burnett's invitation to eat. "Had mine," he said and fell into long silence. Burnett made no attempt to break into it; he had finished eating when Hawn made a short one-fingered gesture across the air. "Well, it's through. She left. In the middle of the night. I was sleepin'. Crawled over me—didn't wake me—it's a trick she had, I don't know how. She's straight Indian now and a quarter way back to her own folks."

"How far they live?"

"Hundred miles."

"When you going after her?"

"No good. When she left me, she left a man she don't want any more. If I went after her I'd be lowerin' myself still more in her eyes. I could bring her back but it wouldn't be Louisa. It'd be a squaw crouched in the corner watchin' me like an animal on a chain."

Burnett squatted on the opposite side of the fireplace. Hawn's face was the face of a man looking down the sights of a rifle. "She was like that," he said. "No argument, and nothin' half way. One day she'd stuck a knife in anybody for me. Next day I wasn't worth it. I don't know much about white women, only knew two. But they're not like that. They can be anything, you never know how much or how little. Maybe God made 'em to be more things than an Indian girl. But when he did it he took out of them the strength to be one thing bigger than anything."

"What was wrong?"

"Me," said Bob Hawn. "When you people came I sort of let myself think I was a white man again and I looked at white girls and I got a little bit sad. The minute it got in my head Louisa knew it." He rose. He said, "By God, I'll miss her."

"Go try."

Hawn shook his head. "She won't come back, but I'll wait a month. Then I'm goin' to burn down the cabin and pull out." He moved to the door and watched the meadow. "It'll do me no good now. I was a squaw man and white people didn't want me. I'm no squaw man now but I was once and the smell's on me and they'll still not want me."

"Well, what the hell do you want to be, one thing or the other?"

"That's it," said Hawn quietly. "I'm nothing. I'm halfway between and I'm spoiled for either."

Burnett turned his back to Hawn to put away the dishes; when he swung around Hawn was gone.

Mrs. Millard banked the fire, set teapot and cup and bread and butter on the table for Millard and laid her cloak about her shoulders. "Just going to Lattimore's," she said. "It won't be long unless she gets to talkin' too much." She crossed the meadow in a direct line to Lattimore's but when she got to the edge of the creek she followed it until Burnett's came into sight. Here she slid into the screen of alders and went by his place; farther up she crossed the creek, passed Hawn's and eventually reached Lockyear's meadow. Along the way she noticed a yard-long chunk of a fir limb which fitted into her hand and this she took as a weapon, more and more concerned with Roxy's safety; the most brutal possibilities worked in her fertile mind and gradually she worked herself into half a trot, half a walk, growing angrier as she advanced on the cabin.

Cal Lockyear was at the doorway. She said: "Where's Roxy?"

He looked at her with his sultry disposition showing. "What the hell you doin' up here?"

She started to move by him into the house; his arm struck across the doorway, grazing her face and checking her. "I didn't ask you in," he said. "Go mind your business."

She saw Roxy in the room's corner and in these shadowy quarters Roxy's face was obscure, but Mrs. Millard thought she saw bruises and she took a step backward, raised the club with unexpected quickness and brought the end of it across Lockyear's jaw. His hands came up; he lunged forward to catch the stick and missed it and she had the opportunity to jab its point into his chest, and again into his face before his reaching arm seized the stick, twisted it from her hand and flung it aside. Boots came beating around the cabin and Veen Lockyear's voice called, "What in hell's the matter?" Mrs. Millard, blindly furious, flung herself at Lockyear. She gave him a full raking with her nails, she slapped him, she knocked off his hat, she made a grab for his ear. He got her around the waist, pinning her arms, and he let go with one hand and hit her three times with his full palm on the side of her head. "You God-damned meddlesome witch! You're a woman, why don't you stay a woman? You don't want to be a woman, I'll treat you like a man!" She tried to bite his arm. He hit her again, harder than before, bringing blood to her nose. She hung on but she had a fainting feeling and she was only half aware of Veen Lockyear driving himself between. She fell backward to the ground. "Oh, my dress," she thought and got up and found Veen struggling against his brother.

Veen called at her. "Go on, get out of here."

"Roxy!" cried Mrs. Millard and rushed for the cabin's door. Lockyear broke away from his brother, reached her, and struck her in the chest, sending her to the ground. He said, "Where's the club, you female bastard, I'll give you a taste of it!" He stooped for the club but Veen kicked it aside and closed with his brother again and hung on as the larger man flung him around. Veen yelled, "For Christ's sake, woman, get out of here or get killed! He'll use a gun."

"I don't care. Roxy!"

Cal Lockyear said, "I'll give you just about a minute to move out of my sight, woman, or I'll take you and Roxy and strangle you both in the creek."

Veen said, "He'll do it too. Now you go. Quick."

Mrs. Millard began to cry. She was defeated, she was sad, she was bitter

275

and outraged. Half blinded she turned away, fearing for Roxy more than for herself. In the trees, beyond Lockyear's, she halted and put her head against a fir trunk and let herself go, and was exhausted when she had finished. Then she went on. Before she came into her own meadow she looked at her clothes and she tucked back the shaken pieces of her hair; and she made a show of cheerfulness on entering the cabin.

Millard had his eyes closed and he seemed asleep. She tiptoed by him, thankful for the opportunity; but suddenly he said: "How was your visit?" He was on his back, looking to the ceiling.

"Oh, it was nice, you know Nellie Lattimore, she talks."

"She does," said Millard. "She was here while you was gone, and she talked." He turned his head and gave her a long look. "Where'd you go?"

"Oh, Millard . . ."

His voice rolled against her. "Where'd you go? What's the matter with your clothes? What's your face red for? You go to Lockyear's?"

"I wanted to see Roxy. I wanted to know. I had to know."

"He hit you?"

She looked at him, she said nothing. Millard rolled on the bed, got his good foot and his stump over the edge, and sat straight. "So you did it."

"I couldn't bear wondering about Roxy. Millard, I couldn't bear it any longer."

"You interfered and he hit you."

"He'll remember me," she said. "I left my mark on him."

"Here I am," he said, "a man with one leg, and he hit you, and I can do nothing about it."

"Nothing for you to do anything about anyhow," she said. "Not a thing. He's been beating her, I know. I'll never rest . . ."

He looked up to her with an expression that stopped her talk. He said: "You know I've got to take care of that, don't you?"

"Nothing of the sort. I don't — "

"Soon as I get out of this bed and walking, I'll have to go kill the man."

"Millard! Don't ever think of it! What would you do against a man like that?"

"When will you learn," he said gently — "When will you learn?"

"I'll not have you thinking such a thing."

"Don't ever speak to me again about it," he said. "I have got to do it."

She stared at him and meant to argue, but he watched her with a coldness she had not received from him before and of a sudden she walked by him into the yard and began to cry again.

276

40

LOCKYEAR watched Mrs. Millard disappear in the trees. He became conscious of the stinging tracks of her fingernails on his face and he drew a hand over his cheeks and found blood on it and for a moment he swayed forward with a notion to go after the woman. Then his glance touched Veen close by and his impulse was diverted. With no warning, he raised an arm and punched his knuckles flat into his brother's mouth, driving the smaller man to the earth.

"Don't ever interfere with me again," he said and stepped into the cabin.

Roxy hadn't stirred from her position in the corner. She said nothing, she watched him with a sly and timid attention, her eyes following him. He wheeled about, his words jumped at her. "That time you ran off — that got people thinking about you and me." He moved toward her, witnessing the stiffening of her body, the recoil from him. "Christ," he murmured. "You pull away. A crazy fool, uglier than any damned dog I ever saw. You pull away. Nobody'd look at you, no other man in this country. Nobody wants you but you don't want me touchin' you." His glance was a hot iron prodding her. It gave him pleasure to see fear break her face with its spongelike contractions. "I ought to tie you to a tree somewhere up in the timber and let you rot there. By God I ought to." He laid his hand on her shoulder and felt her shiver beneath its weight. "Don't do that to me," he said sharply. He crossed the room to the doorway and spoke to Veen standing in the yard. "Don't come in here," he said and shut the door.

Veen said nothing. He crouched on the dirt. He heard Roxy make a short sound and he heard his brother's words rap at her. They were struggling. She said "No," and said it again several times in a small and desperate tone. She struck the cabin wall and cried out; then Veen heard her drop on the bunk. He rose and walked to the creek, the sound of the water covering the sounds from the house. He settled on his haunches, throwing rock after rock into the water. It was a quarter hour before Cal emerged with his rifle, went to the shed for his horse and rode beside Veen. The smaller man could always recognize the deviltry his brother had committed by the shifting brightness in the latter's eyes; it was there now.

Cal said: "If she had as much sense as an animal, I could train her. The hell with her. You want her, you can have her. I don't want her any more."

"Send her home then," said Veen, watching the creek.

"No."

Veen continued to watch the creek. Cal said, in a slightly more reasonable tone, "You oughtn't to have monkeyed with me. It's your own fault I had to knock you down. You know better than try to get me not to do something."

Veen said nothing.

"You can go to hell," said Cal. "I don't beg anybody's favors, and not from a cripple like you. You go sulkin' around on me and you can get out of my way." He turned and drove the horse across the meadow and into the trees.

Veen rose and went into the cabin. Roxy lay under a blanket on the bed; her clothes were a heap of torn rags on the floor. She rolled her head to look at Veen. He settled on the edge of the bunk. "Too bad," he said. "Too bad."

"He's my husband," she said. "I can't do nothin'."

"Why don't you run off — go back home?"

"He'd come and get me."

"He's crazy, gettin' crazier. He ain't got any more pity in him than a snake. He's my brother, but God, I hope someday he pays for all the things he's done. I sure hope so."

"I got to stay," she said. "I can't go anywhere. He's my husband. I got to stand it, I guess." One arm came up, slid around his neck and pulled him down. She said, "Don't you go away. You got to stay here, if I got to stay here."

"All right, Roxy. All right."

Lockyear forded the creek and bucked his way through brush and thick timber, thus avoiding Hawn's and Burnett's. He crossed the low ridge behind Millard's, skirting Walker's, Purroy's, and Kitchen's. He was unusually crafty this day and when he came to the break of timber and looked into the small valley occupied by the Rinearsons he had not been observed by anybody. The cabin farthest removed from him, half a mile tant, was Old Daniel's; the one nearest at hand, sitting directly ahead of him, belonged to Ared. Between this place and Old Daniel's, its back crowded against the firs and its front facing the long narrow meadows of the valley, stood Moss Rinearson's cabin. Edna was at the moment busy by a fire in the back yard, stirring something in a big iron kettle. Across the meadow from this cabin, a quarter mile from it, the three Rinearsons were slashing a road between the valley's upper and lower meadows. Hanging well back in the firs, Lockyear advanced until he was behind Moss Rinearson's place, left his horse and crept forward to a tree at the edge of the yard and here settled in the thicket to watch Edna fifty feet away.

Clothes boiled in the kettle. Edna churned them with a stick, arms and shoulders swaying in rhythm, mind obviously far from the chore; her face was stolid with her thoughts and now and then she lifted her head to throw a glance into the meadow and at times the fire's turning smoke rose around her and she stepped back to catch her breath; steam from the kettle dampened and loosened her hair and she made impatient jabs at it with her hand.

He said: "Don't be bothered about lookin' pretty."

She didn't start at the unexpected voice; she made a slow turn and saw him and almost immediately she swung her head to look across the meadow at three Rinearsons. "Always spyin'," she said, and resumed her work. The stick went around and around in the kettle.

"Like to make men miserable, don't you?" he said.

"Not you," she said.

She stared at the boiling clothes; she turned the stick. Her voice was slow and curious. "What'd you marry Roxy for?"

"To have a woman. What'd you marry Moss for?"

"Because."

"He ain't enough," said Lockyear. "He'll never be enough. He's a man you can lead around like you want. That's why you married him. You'll get sick of that."

"You better go."

"Come over here," he said.

"No."

"You're afraid."

"What'd you come this way for?"

"To see you."

She ceased to turn the stick. She stood motionless, she grew solemn. "Why couldn't you be a good man?" she said.

279

"What the hell for?"

"No," she said, "why couldn't you have been?" She looked over the meadow again at the Rinearsons and she turned and walked to the tree. He caught her arm and drew her on, his expression unsteady and violent. "No," she said. "No." She hung back but her resistance was half-hearted. He drew her deeper into the timber. She said: "No, leave me alone." He stopped and put his arms around her and his accumulated impatience made him jerk her forward. Her head bobbed back. She stared at him, her face loose and shaded, an odd numbness on it. She turned her head from side to side. He gave her a rough shaking, slid a hand behind her head and hauled it hard against his face; he wheeled her around as he kissed her, he gripped her hair, he squeezed her head between his hands. He said, half incoherent, "Pale — weak — you're not that! Give it to me, come back to me! God damn it, you want me or you wouldn't have come. I want you! Give it to me, slam into me, let it come out, it's there!" Suddenly he turned and, with his arm around her waist, half walked and half ran deeper into the trees.

"No," she said, and fought at his encircling arm. "No, I'm going back."

"It's got to be," he said. He pushed her through the brush, he halted and looked about him and he gave her a quick shove; as she fell, he fell with her. She lay still, watching him; her mouth was slack, the numb, obscure expression more and more pronounced. She closed her eyes, rolling her head back and forth on the wet earth; she groaned, she opened her eyes and looked at him. "I can't help it," she whispered. Her mouth widened in a grimace resembling pain, she flung her arms about him and brought him flat over her.

Moss's voice rang sharp through the trees. Edna gave Lockyear a push, knocked him aside and sprang to her feet. She looked around, caught Lockyear's arm when he got up and shoved him toward the horse. She made a signal at him to move on, then she thought of her clothes and swung her skirt and found the green-stained muddiness on it and she made another gesture at Lockyear and watched him lead the horse quietly on through the timber. Moss's voice rose again, but she stood still until Lockyear had gotten beyond sight; afterwards she brought her fingers down through her hair to disarrange it and took a bit of dirt from the ground and smeared it over her face. She drew a deep breath, let out a scream and rushed through the brush into the clearing, straight at Moss and into his arms. Old Daniel and Ared, still at the far side of the meadow, ran forward at the sound of her voice.

"It was an Indian," she said to Moss. "He knocked me down. He almost did it, but I screamed and he jumped up and ran away."

Moss ran into the house for his gun. When he came out with it she stopped him. "Don't you do it. He had a gun, too. He'd kill you. I think there's some more in the brush."

"We'll get in the cabin," said Moss and pushed her before him. He stood at the rear doorway, gun lifted on the brush. Old Daniel yelled, "What's up there — what's up?" He ran over the grass and came hard-breathing into the cabin, Ared behind him. "What the hell is it?"

"She was on the edge of the timber and a buck grabbed her and threw her down," said Moss. "She screamed, scared him off."

Both the other men had their guns in the cabin. Old Daniel seized his weapon, swearing. "Well, by God, we'll fix that."

"No," said Edna, "don't you do it. I think there's more than one."

"How you know?" demanded Old Daniel.

"I heard a lot of bushes wiggle," she said. "I heard some grunting."

Moss said: "You sure he didn't do anything to you?"

"I screamed too soon."

Old Daniel said, "We'll go to my place. We'll send out word to everybody and have a meeting. It's time we got this worry off our backs. We'll make up a company and go up where they live and clean 'em out. Come on quick."

They left the cabin and went rapidly over the meadow and had gone a hundred feet or so when Edna said: "My washing," and stopped.

Old Daniel looked at her. "For the love of God, girl," he said and caught her arm and hurried on. Two or three minutes later he turned his head to give her a glance in which a great deal of curiosity lay. They continued forward as fast as they could travel, Moss looking behind every few steps.

41

THE news spread from one cabin to another in the course of two hours and by late afternoon all the men of the settlement were on their way to Old Daniel's place. Lattimore relayed the information to

Burnett. "It's war," said Lattimore, "that's what it is." He was excited. "Maybe they're out in the brush now, ready to sweep through — kill and burn, kill and burn. Maybe we're too late. Jesus, I think we ought to've wiped 'em out long ago." He was apprehensive and as the two rode the timber-bordered trail toward Rinearson's he humped himself on the saddle as though expecting a shot from the brush at any moment.

Everybody had gathered in Rinearson's yard by the time Lattimore and Burnett reached the place. The attack on Edna, and the earlier pilferage in Mrs. Ebbett's house, had at last hardened discontent into anger, Burnett saw, and anger had passed to purpose without a great deal of discussion. With this also was a changing of the quality of their fear; to this point they had not deeply believed they were in danger of a general attack from the Molalas; under the stimulus of excitement they began to believe it and looked toward the near hills with their imaginations creating a vision of shabby warriors erupting from the trees. Gathered in a loose semicircle before Old Daniel's house, the settlers discussed the situation back and forth and gradually talked themselves into a frame of mind. For once in his career George Collingwood caught public temper clearly, made a ringing, resolute speech and received general approval. To Burnett's notion that agreement with a man they regarded poorly showed how far they had gone. He stood silent, closely listening; he observed Edna occasionally appear in the doorway to look on. She met his glance and seemed to wish to talk to him, but he stayed where he was.

Old Daniel said: "We ought to organize a volunteer company."

"Why," said Mercer, "it's scarcely necessary. Let us just pick up our guns and go up there."

"No," said Old Daniel, "this free-for-all skirmishin' don't tend for good results."

He had sentiment with him. They understood organization, civil or military; it satisfied their notion of doing things. Provost said, "We'll need a captain. I nominate Daniel."

Old Daniel said agreeably, "I don't mind, boys, if that's what you want, but don't do it just because I called the meetin'. I'll serve one way or another."

The nomination evoked some favorable response; it ran into silence elsewhere. Old Daniel's son was dead and it was his daughter-in-law who had been attacked. That gave him some support. But Old Daniel was a wealthy man, a close and arguing man who had showed nobody any generosity with his beef when the need was on the settlers; and that was

282

against him. Election time of any sort brought out the independence of these people; their equality was a hard thing. Billy Lord let his glance roll around the crowd. "Hell," he said, "the only man here that knows Indians or ever fought 'em is Rice. I put him up for captain."

Old Daniel's voice was quick to break in, much tarter than it had been. "I didn't ask to be captain and I don't know as I care to run against anybody. I ain't goin' to stand around here and have my teeth examined to see if I can bite an Indian better'n Rice."

Rice said: "Withdraw the thing, Billy. I'm not in favor of a battle."

"What's that?" challenged Old Daniel. "You want us to stand by and let this happen some more? You want women to be ruined, you want people to be killed? Now, then, Rice, what's wrong with you?"

"You've got thirty or forty Molala men up in the brush. They feel bad we're here. In their shoes we would too."

"That's no good for an argument," broke in Lattimore. "We ain't botherin' them. They're comin' down after us. It's no good."

"If a man does something to me," said Rice, "I go after the man. I don't shoot the hell out of the settlement he lives in. Get your company and go after the bucks that did this. Don't attack a whole village."

He had little support. Several men shook their heads at him and McIver said: "Now, Rice, how you goin' to sort out one or two Indians from fifty Indians? They all look alike to me. Anyhow, if two–three would do it they'd all do it. They're all the same."

"It makes no difference to you whether you shoot the right Indians or not, so long as you shoot two–three Indians?"

McIver answered indirectly. "I ain't tender about Indians and I'm surprised you are."

Provost said, in a more persuasive manner, "We got to scare 'em, Rice, or they'll keep pickin' at us. They'll think we're afraid, then they'll get hold and raise hell. You know that about Indians."

"So you go up there and start shooting," said Burnett. "And hit squaws and young ones as well as bucks."

"Oh, I don't know," said Old Daniel. "I'm a good enough shot to hit what I aim at."

"It's been done by men with better eyesight and better aim than you've got, Daniel. I don't like to see a dead Indian woman. None of you'll like it either, and you'll get to wondering whose bullet it was. Look here, you're snowballing this thing too big out of nothing. There's no massacre in sight. There's only some hungry bucks floating around. Make up a small party and go up to their camp and have a powwow. Take a little grub for a present. Smoke a few pipes of tobacco with those people. Talk it out. What we've got is a situation where one side knows nothing about the other, and we're both afraid. Let's go see these people."

"I ain't afraid of any God-damned buck Indian I ever saw," stated Old Daniel. "And I don't propose to lug grub to any of 'em, and I don't propose to squat in a circle with some tricky creature who attacked my daughter-in-law. I don't propose to be friendly with a shiftless, ignorant, dirty bunch of savages I can't trust, don't like and don't want around me. You listen to me, Rice. I do business with my own kind. I stick with my own kind. I don't make allowances for thieves and thugs when they attack my own kind. I am downright disappointed in you. You want 'em to come down here and wrestle with Lavinia and Edna again? It's all right to be fair. It's fine to be big-minded, but there's an end to that. Far's I'm concerned it ends right here. If this crowd of men don't want to march up there I'll take my sons and a few others and go up there myself."

"That's your business," said Rice.

"You bet it is. And it ought to be your business, too. You live here."

"So I do. And when a Molala jumps me I'll settle with *him*. I won't ask the whole country to march up the hill and wipe out the entire village of Molalas."

Provost said in a reasonable way: "You're wrong, Rice. If we don't make a show, they'll get worse. You know Indians."

Rice shook his head. "You boys have made up your minds about it so there's no use arguing. But it's a mistake. When you start shooting there'll be somebody killed that oughtn't be killed. It's unnecessary."

Lige Ebbett broke in: "We goin' to talk all day and do nothing? Let's vote on a captain."

"All in favor of Daniel say so," called out Provost.

They elected Old Daniel. They chose Ryal McIver and Elam Walker for lieutenants; there was a lively contest between Gay, Eby and Moss Rinearson for sergeant. Somebody called for election speeches and each man made one. Somebody said, "One Rinearson's enough for office. This thing turnin' into a family affair?" Moss said immediately, "I'll withdraw." On a show of hands Eby was made sergeant.

Old Daniel assumed his captaincy without delay. "Now men," he said, "if I'm captain, I propose to be captain. I ain't goin' to march half a mile, call for a vote, and march another half-mile. We got to get this thing done

284

—and right away. We'll meet at Mrs. Irish's meadow five o'clock in the morning. Bring whatever guns you've got and grub enough for a couple days. That ought to be long enough. If Rice thinks they're such reasonable beasts we ought to convince 'em without delay. You know a little jargon, Rice—so you can do the powwowin' for us."

"Won't be with you."

"Well, by God," said Old Daniel, "that's a fine thing, not to throw in with your neighbors."

Lot White spoke up. "Rice, what's in your craw?"

Burnett said: "What kind of religion do you believe in, Lot? Have you got a Sunday kind and a Monday kind?"

"Who sheddeth man's blood, by man shall his blood be shed," answered Lot. "There's your answer. There's our command to go chastise the savage."

"There's no blood been shed."

"Why," said Lot, "it's logical to believe it would be shed if we don't go forth and stop it. Now don't you argue with me about Scripture. The Lord fights for us and expects we shall fight for Him. And there's a heathen race, not fair in the Lord's eyes whatever. I'll be marchin' right along with my neighbors. If I ain't squeamish about this thing you got no call to be."

The crowd waited for an answer. The feeling around Burnett was quiet, odd and reserved. He had gone against the will of the majority. He said to Lot, "Don't you ever come to me with your preaching again. I'm like an Indian in one way. A man can't speak two things with one tongue, and when you divide people into two meadows, one to eat the Lord's grass and one to starve on the Lord's stones, I don't want your sermons." He turned to his horse, got on the saddle and rode away from the meeting. He felt the sudden isolation from his neighbors, but more deeply than his isolation he felt his failure to bring them to a moderate temper. He had argued the case poorly, he had become stubborn too soon, he had drawn off too soon. John Gay could have brought them to reasonableness; and as he thought of this he realized how great was the power of an upright man's reputation and the power of a reasonable man's voice. John Gay was a great man, the force of his character working through this settlement in its many ways. Now he thought he saw something. A word was a weapon—like any other weapon, it needed a skillful user—but a word was the greatest of all weapons. A bullet reached only half a mile and struck only one target, and was spent in a second. A word reached

285

through all these hills, across the land, around the whole earth, and struck its ten thousand targets and set off its reactions which lasted a long time, sometimes years; sometimes longer, for the words of some men — spoken ages back — still were striking around him, striking inside him.

Men straggled through the five o'clock darkness to assemble at the ford. Mrs. Irish's cabin lamp flashed against a light-falling rain and voices grumbled around the group. Daniel Rinearson called the names of his volunteers. "Where's Hawley, where's Lathrop? Speak up — speak up, we can't fight no Indian battles down here. Form a double line men, form it. We'll make two platoons. McIver, you command first platoon, Walker, second. Come on, boys, don't stand rump to the wind. We got this to do and no use draggin'. Form line."

Lattimore said: "What the hell's lines for? Let's just start walkin'. We ain't goin' to be in any line when we get to shootin'."

Old Daniel said, "Who the hell's captain here? I ain't runnin' a hay crew, I'm runnin' a company and I want it to look like a company and act like a company."

Not much was said. The settlers milled slow and sluggish into line; they stood lumplike and silent while Old Daniel moved back and forth to count noses. More men came into the clearing. Lot White called out, "Mercer's sick, he won't be here."

"Well, where's Lathrop, where's Hawley?"

"Here," said Hawley.

The line grew longer and as the waiting went on, the settlers grew restive. "Come on, Daniel."

"We ain't got everybody."

"We got thirty. How many Indians we goin' to fight?"

"All right," said Rinearson. "We'll march in a column of twos. I want a pair of scouts hundred yards ahead — Eby and Lattimore, you start ahead. I want a man a hundred yards behind the column. Hawley, you do that. I want flankers out, hundred feet to each side. Kitchen and Moss to the left. Snearley and Cross to the right."

Kitchen said: "That ain't practical. I'll be snarled up in the trees, or crawlin' on the side of a hill for the next ten miles. What we so careful about? No Indians down here."

"God damn it," said Old Daniel, "have we got to vote on every time we spit or turn around?"

286

"Well, he's right on that," said Provost. "Nothing down here to worry about. We won't need no flankers till we're in the hills."

The crowd agreed with Provost and Old Daniel said irritably, "All right, don't do it, then."

"Let's go," said Walker.

Lattimore said: "I'd as soon wait till we're sure we got everybody. The more, the easier."

"Ah," said Hawley, "we talkin' or we goin'?"

"Men," said Old Daniel, "we don't know what's ahead, but we'll do what we got to do. I want no runnin' back, I want no gallopin' around if we get in action. Keep cool and do what I call out. Keep those pans dry." His command came out as a whooping, "Column of twos — for'd, march!"

The column set off in its curious fashion, the head stretching like the pleats of an accordion, the back end lagging. Presently the line was entirely in motion, tail hurrying to catch up with the forward part; it crossed the meadow, entered the trees and filed by Buck's place. Mrs. Buck handed her husband a parcel of food and kissed him. They passed Lattimore's. At Burnett's, Eby dropped out a moment to go into the cabin and speak to Burnett at his breakfast. But Burnett shook his head and Eby went on. It was still dark when they reached Lockyear's, no light showing in the cabin. Beyond this place the creek entered a narrow gorge and the trail, having no other place to go, moved into the timber and up the face of a hill by one looping turn upon another. The steady rain turned the dirt slick; they went slipping and grunting along the stiff grade, plunged into the hard darkness of the forest. Occasionally a word came down the line, "Keep closed up — keep up." Occasionally a faster moving man collided with the man before him and small explosions of temper broke the preoccupied quiet. Voices sank lower and the mood of the column settled. A steady wind made its minor roar far above them in the treetops and at times shook down sheets of water. Somewhere back in the column a man's out-of-breath grumble rose, "Tell him not to walk so fast," but Old Daniel towed his company upward without pause, through the first coffee-colored stain of daylight, across a short clearing into whose sodden grasses their feet deeply sank, and on through the timber again. They reached the creek's canyon and skirted it for a little while, catching the glitter of the broken waters below; they labored along the face of a ridge, the trail curling around one massive fir trunk and another, reached its summit, and arrived at the

287

edge of another mountain meadow. Here they halted to catch a wind they needed. Walker overtook Old Daniel.

"My God, you runnin' to a fire?"

"I am sixty-one years old," said Old Daniel. "What's the matter with you young fellows?" He watched the men at the rear of the column come from the trees one by one; he watched them sag against the fir trunks, settle on their haunches, prop themselves against their guns. Billy Lord arrived last, the sound of his lungs like the swashing of a crosscut saw through a log. Old Daniel shook his head. "It's a soft generation, by God. You can't walk, drink or fight like mine did. Now then, I want flankers out, I want two men ahead, one man behind. We can't be more'n five miles from that Molally camp."

At this elevation rain clouds dragged the earth, the light was gray, steam shimmered on the meadow; the wall of trees beyond the meadow was obscure.

"She still up?" asked Walker.

"Nothin' but up," said Old Daniel.

"Rather have my Indian fightin' on flat ground."

"Indians and women, you got to catch 'em where you catch 'em." Old Daniel walked around the group with his bow-legged springy stride, making a show of his endurance. He cocked his hat over his eyes. He said, "Keep your guns covered. What the hell you got there, Durbin?"

Durbin Young extended a ten-foot pole with a butcher knife lashed to its end; he pointed it directly against Old Daniel's stomach. "Ain't it somethin', Daniel?"

"You goin' to tickle 'em to death? Now, men, we ain't far off from that outfit. Keep close together. Don't nobody straggle. Don't make any more noise than you got to. Don't no man fire till I say so."

"Think we been seen yet?"

"It's a question," said Old Daniel. "Well, for'd."

The settlers re-grouped themselves; the line curled over the marshy meadow in tighter shape than before and entered the trees and tackled a hill rougher than the preceding one. "How the hell they ride horses on this," said Provost, "I don't know." At the next meadow they saw the relics of a camp. It was then time for full daylight but the clouds were still close about them and the rain hung on. Everybody was soaked through and enveloped in the steam of their own private exertions. Now the trail made a long gradual climb through the trees, and the trees grew smaller and farther apart and presently the company reached the

288

edge of a larger meadow than they had previously passed. The creek ran through it, ragged brush grew along its edges, and the tents of the Molalas stood directly before them.

"Spread out," said Old Daniel. "First platoon right. Second — left. Mind me now, boys."

"Wait a minute," said McIver. "This is funny. Ain't an Indian in sight."

"Well, it's rainin'," said Old Daniel.

The settlers trickled through the trees to make a broad front against the Indian village; they crept, they crouched, they kept well within the shelter, their talk fell to a whispering, they looked about with a whetted concern — to the darkness of the timber behind them, to their neighbors on either side, to the Indian shelters shrouded by the pearly fog before them. Nothing alive showed itself — man, woman, child or dog. No horses browsed in the fore part of the meadow; neither were there shadows of horses in the thick mists which obscured the yonder end of the clearing; but above each lodge was a small curl of smoke.

"Inside," said Old Daniel.

"Then there'd be dogs or horses outside," said Provost. "They been here — they heard us or saw us — they got out."

"Look sharp behind," warned McIver. "Everybody look sharp."

Everybody, hit by the same notion at the same time, wheeled. Fred Lattimore slowly circled a tree, gun raised to sweep the timber behind him; its turning muzzle yawned on Lorenzo Buck. Lorenzo dropped flat. "You eternal fool," said Buck, "point that thing somewhere else."

"No, no," said Old Daniel, "they ain't back of us. They're yonder beyond the lodges. Now, men, don't start shootin' at shadows. We'll go right straight forward to the tents. If they're empty, we'll sweep across the meadow to that brush. Come on — come on."

He walked into the clearing with his last warning. "Keep them pans dry." The settlers broke from the trees, the raggedness of the skirmish line most pronounced. Old Daniel, thirty feet ahead of his company, reached the first tent and brushed its door flap aside with the muzzle of his rifle; he put his head through the doorway and drew back. He shook his head. "Nothin' in there but a hell of a bad odor." The company moved by the first tent while Old Daniel pressed forward to inspect the second tent; he walked along the line of tents, searching each one. The village was deserted.

Meanwhile Provost read his own story in the fresh-cut prints on the muddy soil and followed these prints as they led toward the creek and continued southward beyond the creek through tall brush toward the firs farther on. He made a signal with his hand. "This way," he said and led the company to the creek.

Old Daniel trotted back from the end of the village. "Who the hell's captain here?" he shouted.

"You want Indians or you want a long walk for nothin'?" retorted Provost.

Old Daniel hurried to the front of his men and splashed across the creek. Waving his gun overhead, he plunged into the brush and became only a noise crashing through the thicket; the settlers began to take voice as they rushed on, throaty, shrill, lung-deep. Old Daniel's voice, trying to override the confusion, made no impression but somewhere a tremendously excited shout rose above the general racket. "Here — here!" The crashing grew as men wheeled in the direction of the summons. A gun exploded, Old Daniel raised a war-cry. Fighting through this jungle of willow and alder and chance vines, the settlers broke into an open stretch lying between the brush and the trees beyond — and came upon the Molalas. Women and children and animals were at the moment disappearing into the trees, but the men had turned to make a stand with their guns and their bows. Old Daniel yelled, "Charge," and moved forward at a walk, gun flung to his shoulder.

The settlers advanced a short distance, then began to drop one by one to their knees to take aim. Provost shouted toward Daniel, "Come back here you damn fool or you'll get shot from behind!" Flint smashed on steel, no explosion following; for the steady rain got at the powder and wetted it beyond ignition. The Molalas, witnessing that dry volley, ceased their shifting retreat, turned about and came forward in weaving, evasive motion. Suddenly Harris Eby, carrying a revolver whose cap was not as readily affected by the rain, trotted toward Old Daniel, his gun making its lone explosions in the day; on his heels came Durbin Young with his butcher knife lashed to the ten-foot pole. Arrows whacked the ground or went breathing by. At the end of the skirmish line John Mercer, owning the only other cap-and-ball in the company, began to fire.

In rain and fog and confusion there was nothing clear. Up and down the skirmish line men sank to their knees to pour fresh powder into their pans beneath the shelter of their overcoats. Meanwhile, Old Daniel, edging farther and farther from his company, found himself engaged with a Molala who had singled him out. The Molala, his powder as wet as Old

Daniel's, took his dead aim on Old Daniel, pulled the trigger and got no flash; and he dodged as Old Daniel took aim and tried again. Both men, slowly circling each other and slowly drawing together, clicked gun hammers repeatedly on soaked powder until Old Daniel dropped his gun from his eyes to find the Molala not ten feet from him. He stood a moment in shocked surprise at the nearness of the Indian; he stared across the space, he let go with a wild yell, he reversed his useless gun to make a useful club of it and sprang forward. The Molala leaped aside and rushed into the nearby timber.

Half a dozen shots had been fired, all from the two cap-and-ball pistols which alone worked in the wet day; there had been a brief scurry of arrows. Durbin Young stood in the clearing with his butcher-knife lance extended toward the green timber; nobody, red or white, lay on the ground, nobody had been hurt, and the Molalas were gone.

Old Daniel rallied his lieutenants around him while the company tried to pour dry powder into the wetted pans. "Well," he said, "they got away. We'll follow."

Provost said: "Follow where?" He pointed at the wall of timber which faced them; it was a barrier which, viewed from the meadow, seemed a thousand miles deep. "How the hell you travel through that stuff? There's no trail."

"They did it — we can do it."

The company gathered around to join the argument. "I don't know," said McIver. "They might be waiting for us to do just that thing. Looks like a fine place to get lost in, get cut off, get butchered up one by one."

"We come up here to get Indians," said Old Daniel.

A single arrow, flung from afar, passed between Old Daniel and Harris Eby, and to a man the company dropped.

"Men," said Old Daniel, "we'll withdraw to the brush."

The settlers turned, crawled a short distance and rose and trotted to the shelter of the brush, there pausing to watch the trees. Nothing could be seen of the Indians, and after squatting a quarter-hour in the steady rain the settlers grew restless.

"It gravels me to go back and say we did nothing," said Old Daniel.

"Burn the village," suggested McIver. "That'll make 'em move on."

"We'll burn," said Old Daniel. The company threaded the brush, crossed the creek and came upon the village. "Two men go into each tent, pile everything in the middle and set 'em on fire. Rest of the company will stand guard. They might crawl back to make a fight."

But while Old Daniel looked on the company dissolved before him, each settler struck by an idea that hastened him to the lodges. There was a great rummaging around and the settlers came out presently with whatever plunder they had found. "Great God," said Old Daniel, "ain't this a fine fight? Lattimore, I hope that blanket infests you with fleas till your woman drives you out." The fires were started and in a short time the line of tents glowed bright against the dull day, burst into clear flame and burned furiously for a little while.

"They won't come back," said Provost. "And they won't bother us any more, either."

Eby said: "Wonder how they'll live?"

"I ain't goin' to bother my head about that," said Old Daniel. "Well, men, form lines and we'll start home."

The settlers made a loose shift of a line before Old Daniel's dissatisfied eyes. Last men came down the street and guards drifted in from the creek. Harry Mercer, burdened with an Indian basket, a captured Hudson's Bay blanket, and a gun, dropped his prizes to take a better grip on the gun. He swung it parallel to his legs, balancing the piece with one hand; the nose dipped when he stooped to catch up basket and blanket. He tightened his fingers around the gun and in so doing he squeezed the trigger, released the still-cocked hammer and exploded a charge which had failed to catch on half a dozen previous tries. Old Daniel raised a penetrating cry, slapped both hands behind him and fell to his knees. "I'm shot! Boys, I been hit!"

The company rushed around him; Mercer flung away his gun and rushed forward, shouting "I killed a man!" — He knocked his way through the group. "Daniel, you dyin'?"

"Don't think so," said Old Daniel. He was still on his knees, still with both hands pressed behind him. He had a thoughtful expression; he drew his hands away, saw blood, and sent them back for further exploration. Mercer and Eby took him by the arms and lifted him and, as they turned him about, the company saw that Mercer's stray bullet, tearing Old Daniel's trousers, had made a light and grazing trail across his buttocks.

The company waited. Old Daniel showed the men about him a peculiar expression, took a tentative step or two forward, and spoke briefly.

"We'll go home now."

The company passed into the trees and moved down the dark trail, each man burdened by his new possessions. Very little was said, but at the first clearing Harris Eby, trudging thoughtfully along, suddenly broke into a long laugh.

"What's the matter with you?" asked Old Daniel.

"Men," said Eby, still laughing, "we just fought the battle of Huckleberry Mountain against the savages. We're Indian war veterans and maybe someday we'll get a pension. Twenty years from now, the way we'll no doubt tell it, it'll be a hell of a big battle."

Old Daniel gave him the briefest possible glance. "I don't see a damned thing funny about it," he said and went on without further talk. The settlers filed down the trail like a string of gypsies, Molala possessions hanging from them at every angle. Now and then Eby broke into his chuckle, drawing the irritable edge of Old Daniel's glance. The captain's pride festered within him.

42

AT noon Burnett returned from his road work in the timber, made a meal, and stood awhile at the cabin's doorway with his pipe to watch the smoldering stump fires send their sleazy smoke through the trees. The work so far done scarcely made a scratch in that dense stuff; it would require two months' of the hardest labor to cut a passable way for wagons, and this labor was somehow to be squeezed in with other chores equally insistent, all to be done by July harvest time. He knocked out the pipe and started back to work.

Half over the meadow he lifted his face to the fine rain falling and knew he would do no more this day. The smell of the earth was strong, the hills boiled with mist, his restlessness was too much. Returning to the cabin, he got his gun, tucked powder flask and hunting knife beneath his coat and struck into the timber. Work trimmed him too fine, ground him too thin and the feeling was upon him again that he was a harnessed horse plodding the furrows back and forth. The strain of this long haul had begun to have its effect — the incessant push of things to do, the long hours, the monotony of poor food and an empty cabin, the gray color of life, the need for patience and drudgery which never grew less, the knowledge that harvest time with its release was still months away.

He climbed steadily through water-drenched underbrush, the mist growing so thick that his passing body stirred it. He came upon a trail and followed it until he reached a fork — one route, made by the cat animals, sliding beneath the logs and through narrow places, the other route looping around these obstructions and printed with the tracks of deer and bear. It was an hour's work to make the top of the ridge; along this high ground he had previously shot several deer but none of the tracks he saw were fresh and the way at last became so rough that he slid into the adjoining ravine and bucked his way to the crest of the next ridge. Beyond — unseen in the day's clogging mists — the land rose toward high mountains eastward.

He reached a fallen tree whose root system made a ragged disk in the daylight and under this partial shelter he crouched to watch the visible part of the ravine below him and the deer run which came from the lower depths and passed nearby. Water dripped from him while he rested and made a pool around his feet and collected inside his boots. He grew cold and left the shelter, following the deer run downgrade into the denser fog. On all sides of him the crowded timber disappeared into the mists above, and through those far-off tops the wind steadily sighed. The ravine grew more jungle-like as he dropped into it, brush rising head high about him, and windfalls and broken branches and litter made a rough floor from one ravine wall to the other, completely covering the creek which rattled beneath.

Faint motion in the growing grayness of the mist stopped him. He ran his glance along the opposite slope of the ravine and saw a deer poised in the brush.

He dried his pan before shaking in powder; he shielded the pan as he brought up the gun, fired and watched the deer jump high and drop; he laid aside the gun — carefully noting where he placed it — and bucked a path through the brush until he found a log which had fallen in such a way as to make a kind of footbridge across the tangled debris. He thought, *Hell of a place to kill meat,* and tested the log before he began to walk forward.

It lay perhaps ten feet above the unseen creek, supported by logs beneath it and weighted down by other logs over it — all these lying in a matchstick tangle and covered by branches and duff rained down from the high timber. He kept his eyes on the deer, which had ceased to struggle; ten feet forward he surged his weight against the log again to be sure of it and felt no weakness. He came to a cross-log running more nearly in the direction he wanted to go; he moved to it, took three easy steps forward — and heard the sharp crack of its old wood. As it fell, he threw

294

himself forward to hook arms and chest over another log nearby; he missed; he plunged straight down through the heavy layer of branches; he heard more logs give way; he reached the creek and sank into its bubbling mud and violently turned himself as he saw a shadow move past his eyes. He was struck across the thighs and in the small of the back, and he went sliding and tumbling into the strange darkness, making aimless motions to defend himself. A log thundered over him and came to a grinding pause; he was scraped by a falling knot. He felt no particular pain when the shifting of the deadfalls ceased and he couldn't immediately discover what had happened. A rain of old twigs and bark chunks and rotted fir needles descended for a short time; then that quit.

He sat in a strange position, buttocks gently settling into the half-water and half-mud of the creek; but as he sank, his knees and lower legs remained motionless and presently he felt the strain of his crooked position and reached around in the semidarkness to find support, and caught hold of a slender, partially decayed log behind him. The weight of his arm broke it and it fell against him, the disturbance releasing other logs farther away, so that again there was a cracking and rumbling and settling around him and a fresh rain of twigs. This ceasing, he discovered the newly broken log to be at his back, holding him from further descent into the creek.

He hooked his arms over the log behind him for leverage and stiffened his body to pull his legs from the mud. They were lodged and wouldn't slide. He bent forward and felt a log perhaps a foot in diameter, smooth with age, lying across his legs above the knees, so buoyed by the mud that its weight was not painful. He twisted his legs and sought to drive them deeper into the mud, to work them around, to shift them into a different position; but none of his effort broke them from the trap. They seemed to rest on a broad, water-smoothed stone, the back of his knees fitting into the curve of the stone, the lower part of his legs hanging along the farther side; thus, with the log above and the stone below, he was like a man imprisoned in stocks. He was able to work one leg perhaps six inches sidewise and to lift it somewhat less than that distance upward, but the other leg was fast-bound and when he passed his hand over the log lying across his thighs he touched the swell of a boll on its farther side and discovered a limb projecting downward from the boll into the mud. He rocked the foot of his trapped leg and felt the pressure of it come up the limb. It was the limb which pinned his foot — his left foot — against the stone.

He rested a moment, then he swung his upper body farther to the left and raised his right leg to make a straight pull. But the stone beneath him lay at one level and the found of the log over him lay at a slightly lower level and he could not maneuver his leg into any position which would give it clearance; he tried several times and stopped when he felt pain build up behind his knee; he was sawing his leg against the stone's ridge. He lay back, resting again. It couldn't be done that way. He had somehow to free his left foot from the branch and give himself more flexibility.

He sat in a doubled-over position, hips deep in mud and water. The first shock had passed and feeling gradually lessened in the lower parts of his body; sensation came sluggish and delayed when he moved his toes. He unbuttoned his overcoat and drew out his hunting knife, and he bent forward to lay the knife across the limb, and sat idle in this forward cramped position to review the possibilities he had. The limb, cut through, would free his left foot and perhaps permit him to sink his whole body low enough into the creek to slide sidewise until he got himself clear of the rock — if the rock didn't extend too far — and thus draw his legs from beneath the log. Otherwise he could only chip away at the underside of the log to give his legs the clearance they needed. Which was best to do? Would the log settle and crush his legs against the stone if he chopped away the branch? He struck the branch with his free leg and felt it give; it didn't seem to be supporting the log. He struck it again, thinking he might crack it, but he couldn't move his feet fast enough through the mud to lend any force to the kick; and then he decided to cut the branch and so set to work.

He had left the cabin around one o'clock, he had been two hours traveling the hills; it was now about three with a darker and darker stain showing in the heavy fog. Above him was the ragged hole created by his fall and through it came a wan light which was of no value to him. Hands and knife were in darkness and he worked by touch, shaving off the limb's bark and coming upon the cross-grained inner wood. The hunting knife had a six-inch blade with a handle nearly as long, and a notion occurred to him and he reached into his pocket for his bandanna, wrapped it around the point of the knife, and thus was able to make a drawing knife of it, shoving it through the wood with both hands. This presently tired him, since his upper body was strained against his trapped legs, and he rested back and watched the day die through the overhead aperture.

In another hour his cows would come to the yard fence and stand waiting to be milked. Usually when he was away overnight he asked Lattimore or Watt Irish to take care of the stock; this day he had warned nobody. In the morning the cows would start bawling for relief and if the wind didn't spring up that sound might carry as far as Millard's. Otherwise there'd be no likely visitors. Hawn's visits were infrequent. The Lockyears would pay no attention if they passed the cabin. Except for the possible warning of the cows, or for some unexpected visitor, it might be a week before his absence was noted around the settlement. Katherine would miss him by that time.

He returned to the limb, shaving it sliver by sliver. There was some pitch in it and long seasoning had given it a marble hardness; in his cramped position he could put no great force on the blade and when it occasionally jumped from the wood he lost his balance and fell back to the log behind him. It grew dark and the rain strengthened and he heard the increased roar of the wind high in the timber. The water no longer bothered him greatly; numbness made its insulation around him. Some time after dark—two hours, three hours, he had no way of estimating—he gave the limb a kick with his loose foot and heard it snap, and reached forward and pounded his fist against the branch until it fell free.

He put the knife in his pocket, taking great care with his motions; he ground himself deeper into the mud to bring his legs at a greater slant between log and stone and pulled himself back as far as the barrier behind would permit, to discover he couldn't crook himself in any position which would free him from the trap. Next, he bent forward to hug the log and to slide his legs one difficult inch at a time toward the left, hoping to find an end to the stone, or a dip in it; instead he came against a swell in the log and could go no farther; he worked to the right and made at best a foot when stone and log stopped him with their tighter fit.

He returned to the loosest place in the trap and ceased to work; exercise had warmed him enough to make him feel the contrasting cold; his mind quickened. Little miseries began to accumulate—the stillness of his legs, the steady run of water against his body, the chafing of wet clothes against wrists and neck, the cramped position of his crotch. For the first time the sensation of entrapment spread through him. The effect of it was to turn him violently active. He plunged himself deep into the mud, hoisted his legs as high and as stiff as he could manage and hauled roughly back with his body. He ground his flesh into the stone, he struck his knees repeatedly against the log. Then that blind revolt passed and

297

he took control of himself. He was embarrassed by the moment of panic.

With the greatest of care he took the knife from his pocket, spraddled his legs and began to stab away the bark at the bottom of the tree. Only this possibility remained; to carve an alley a foot wide and perhaps a foot deep through the log to give his legs the necessary clearance over the stone. The bark was half an inch thick and soon stripped aside. *Eleven and a half inches to go,* he thought, and gouged the knife point shallowly into the slick, obdurate wood; he drew the knife away and laid his finger on the track he had made and pulled off a sliver of wood the size of a toothpick. He sat uncomfortably humped. *All night,* he thought. *All day, maybe another night.* For a short while doubt moved as loose, greasy ripples along his body, and he remembered he had done this before, in another fashion, in Sonora: he had gone out and out until there was nothing but formless pain in him and nothing but clouds — as real as this mist — about him; he had gone so far out that he felt final bits of energy roll around within him as the sediment water at the bottom of a dirty pail. He thought: *Same thing again — but it's a long way to go before I get that far.*

He bowed his shoulders and moved the knife back and forth across the bottom of the log. This was Friday — Friday, the 12th of March. It seemed at the moment an important thing to remember, though he couldn't understand why.

43

ON that same day Collingwood and Lucy started for Oregon City, staying overnight at Stricklin's and reaching Sydney Moss's hotel in town late on the following afternoon. Lucy lay on the bed to rest while Collingwood walked around the small room with his thoughts. He stopped at the window overlooking the street; he thrust his hands into his pockets and jingled the loose silver there. "I want to go down and see a few people," he said. "I want to find where the Kellys and the Nations went."

"Why?"

"They settled somewhere on the other side of the river. They liked me — they might do me some good. If they're not too far away I want to go see them. They'd take me around their settlement and introduce me to

298

everybody. They might speak a good word for me among the neighbors."

"These people can't vote for you, can they? Don't they live in another district?"

"No, I'm not running in their district. But making friends, getting known, it's a peculiar business. You never know where it begins or ends. You never know where the seed's going to land when you cast it." He came back from the window and stood by the bed. He had on his air of quiet importance; his mind was very active, he was scheming, he was dreaming. In the private world he had built for himself he was a happy man, for in that world he was big and hadn't yet known failure. She realized that even now he was thinking beyond being elected to the legislature; otherwise he would not be going outside his own district to meet people.

"You've got something else in mind," she said.

His glance brushed her and traveled on. His habit of secrecy was too strong to let him be candid with her. Everything he did was by indirection. It was his enormous sensitiveness which made him hide himself, she thought, or perhaps his memory of past failure in other ways caused him to cover himself. Possessed by tremendous ambition, he nevertheless had a knowledge of his weaknesses, and he tried to bury them so deep that neither he nor others would see them. He was shifting and indecisive, he took on the color of his surroundings, and was easily swayed by the temper of other men; he scarcely had a positive character of his own. Yet he was quietly stubborn, he was driven by a wish greater than his fibers could support. The sadness of it was that, having destroyed himself before her by his lack of any dominant quality, he would sooner or later destroy himself before any man who came to know him well. He could neither hide himself nor create the force he lacked.

He said, in his considerate voice: "You won't mind being alone?"

"No."

"I'll come back to the hotel before I leave town." He took time to wash and brush and have a look at himself in the mirror; then, giving her a short glance and a nod, he left the room. She lay on the bed and immediately forgot him as her imagination bred its excitement. Her thoughts ran from one practical thing to another. "How shall I let him know I'm here? How will we meet? There, or here — no, not here, that's impossible. How can I get to his place and not be seen? It's such a small town. Suppose he's out in the country on a visit and won't be back until after I leave? O Lord, don't let that happen." She heard George's voice on the stairway and she sprang from the bed, gave her dress a swift smoothing with her hands, looked at herself in the mirror, and was at the window when George rapped on the door. She said, "Come in," and waited until both men were in the room before turning to them.

"See who I met right downstairs," said George.

Whitcomb made his bow, smiled, looked about the room. "A regular icehouse of a room. The river makes everything damp. Have Moss bring you a warming pan."

She shrugged her shoulders, she was indifferent. "Remember the gorge, Ralph? When will you both stop thinking of me as delicate?"

George said: "Ralph told me where the Kellys live. It's five miles south, on the other side of the river. I'm going to go over there now and visit around. It'll be late tomorrow, I suppose, when I get back." He looked at the doctor. "Would it be too much to ask you to keep Lucy company at supper tonight? This table downstairs is pretty much a man's affair. I'd not like her troubled."

She couldn't be certain — perhaps it was again her conscience-livened suspicion — but she thought she saw the moving of secret knowledge deep back in her husband's eyes. She gave him an embarrassed, brisk retort. "It's no compliment to be foisted off from man to man, George, and no doubt Ralph's got his own affairs."

Whitcomb drew a watch from his pocket. "It's half after four. I've two things to do. I'll see you downstairs at six. It'll be a pleasure. And it's best. Some of Moss's patrons warm up at the saloon before they eat." She noticed the locket — which she had noticed several times, and each time with a growing interest — fixed into the heavy chain and she thought: *I've got to find out about that.*

"Will that be all right, Lucy?" George asked.

"Yes." She made it as cool as she could. "Now, then, both of you go along."

Whitcomb stepped into the hall. George opened his wallet and found two gold pieces and gave them to her. "We can spare this, if you see anything you want." He paused a moment and watched her with his polite, veiled manner. He bent, gave her a light kiss and said, "Tomorrow late," and left the room.

She called after him, "Take care," and closed the door. It was one of those remarks, she thought, which had become as automatic and as meaningless as most polite words between people. It hadn't meant anything for how long? For ten years. She remembered the day and she remembered the scene when George, listening to the rough and suggestive words passed to her by Harker Meloney, had made no move to knock the words back through Harker's teeth. Later he had only said, "He had a couple of drinks — he didn't mean it." At the time she had thought he was a coward; now that she was older, she wasn't altogether sure — for he had a strange tolerance, a queer forgiveness in him, a shrinking away from things which were disagreeable. Never had she known him to break into one clear moment of honest, forceful emotion. It had never been mentioned between them, but sometimes she thought he knew where it had begun.

There was no chance to say anything during supper, for they sat at a common table crowded with men — teamsters, travelers, a settler in from the Tualatin, the ferryman, an attorney, a scattering of bachelors, a pair of lank, bony-faced French-Canadians from the Prairie. Afterwards Ralph walked to the foot of the stairs with her and they had a moment beyond earshot of the others. "I saw you come into town," he said. "I went directly home and told Mrs. Barnes I wouldn't need supper and to take the rest of the day off. She's got people a mile out of town. . . . Would you come?"

"Yes."

"It's a small white house behind this street. When you leave here, go to Abernethy's and turn left at the little lane. I'm at the end of the lane. There's nothing too close to me, and it's dark. I'll go there now. How long will you be?"

"Ten minutes."

He smiled. "Too long — a lot too long."

"That's nice," she said, and watched him go. She returned to her room and spent a short time with her hair. She watched the mirror closely, she looked straight into her eyes and had no wish to avoid them. She felt wonderfully well. She was alert, she was stung by the thousand needles of excitement, she thought of odd little things and she thought of the one big thing. She laid on her hat carefully and bit her lips to brighten their color. The rain and the fog would redden her cheeks and the darkness would make her eyes seem deeper and this was how she would look to him when she stepped through his door. She left the hotel, crossed to Abernethy's and entered the lane, walking as though going nowhere. She saw the house and looked around the darkness and discovered no other travelers in the night; he opened the door before she quite reached it, shut it behind her and took her immediately. She had a fleeting glimpse of his face before she closed her eyes and saw the expression upon it. He was more intemperate with her than he had been at their first meeting in the cabin and she gave him back the same intemperance. Presently he stepped away, shaking his head. "My God, Lucy, I could beat you to pieces."

"That's it, that's just it."

"I ought to have some restraint," he said.

"Don't talk about restraint. I can't bear the thought. It's a way people kill each other. I'm half dead of it now."

He took her coat and hat and laid them on the room's table. "Well, here's my house."

"I want to see it — I want to see where you walk and stand and sleep and eat. I'll have a lot of time to think about you, later. I want something to think about, where I can see you when I think about you."

It was a plain, angular, even a homely house. The front room had a rosebud paper on it and held a table, four chairs, and a tin stove. The kitchen was painted brown, walls and floor. There were two bedrooms, both furnished and both small. "Who sleeps in the extra one?"

"Mrs. Barnes."

She went into the extra room, moved around it and came out; she walked into his bedroom and stood at the dresser, touching the things on its top — brush and comb, scissors, razor and mug, a jar of buttons, a packet with thread and needles — all arranged in a military row. She looked at herself in the mirror behind the dresser and caught his glance following her from the doorway, and as she swung about he came forward and put his arm around her waist. She said nothing; she waited, her head tipped against his shoulder, and after the silence had gone on a little while she raised her glance and saw that he had been closely watching her; she smiled and walked to the front room's stove, holding her hands over it.

"Cold?"

"I think it's damper here than where we live."

"It's the river."

He came beside her but this time he held his hands away from her. He said: "Do you want coffee?"

"No — not unless you do."

He shook his head and looked beyond her to the front window. "I think I ought . . ." He crossed the room and rolled down the shade and

302

came back. Unexpectedly, she was embarrassed and looked steadily at the stove but from the corner of her eyes she observed that his face had settled, both the warmth and the roughness leaving it. Something struck both of them and changed them; they weren't close now, they were strange to each other.

He said: "It's odd how George brought me up to you tonight. Do you suppose he's got anything in his mind?"

"I don't know," she said. "Would it matter to you?"

"Not to me. I'd not like it for you."

"It's past time to think about that, isn't it?"

She was at the moment in a contrary state of mind, puzzled by him and irritated at herself. She tried to keep this from her voice, but the chance remark slid through his guard and hurt him, for he said, "I guess it is," and though he didn't move she had the feeling that he drew away from her.

"What did I say, Ralph? What was it?"

"The truth, mostly. I think too much."

"Well, what are you thinking now?"

"You didn't like me to draw that blind, did you?"

"It gave me a funny feeling."

"I know."

"Just for a moment. It's gone. It did you too. I saw it on your face. You were thinking this was, well, something that happens all the time. Now that I'm here and it's possible, it's not the same, it's not what you thought it might be like."

"No," he said. "I was thinking . . ." He checked himself and he was angry with himself. "Why have we got to do this — paw it around and around until there's no shape to it?"

Now she could look directly at him. She was cool, she was reckless. "You really meant to say, Why are we ashamed of ourselves? But I wasn't when I came into your house." She walked to the table and put on her hat; she let him help her into her coat, but she kept her head turned from him and when his hands touched her shoulders she stirred away and went to the door. She faced the door, more and more angry; she felt beaten and bitter. She thought, *All this — and nothing comes of it.* Her body was so brittle with the piled-up strains within that she felt one sharp blow would shatter her. He came beside her, looking down with the tight expression returned to his face. He was abrupt and distant. "I'll walk back to the hotel with you."

"I came alone," she said. "I can go back the same way." As he opened the door she added, "I had something when I got here. I've got nothing now. We talked it to death."

He pulled her back and kicked the door shut. She whirled and gripped his arms and settled against him. "Ralph — Ralph — what happened — it was bad — it mustn't ever happen again. Don't let me say those things — don't ever look cold at me."

He turned her. She said, "Wait," and threw off her coat and hat and left them on the table and walked into the semidarkness of the bedroom.

She said, "What time's it?"

"Around twelve."

"I'd better go. I'll need a light."

He brought the lamp from the front room and went back to stoke the stove. When he came in again she sat before the bureau mirror, working at her hair. He stood behind her and he dropped his hands over her breasts.

"Now," she said, "I'm not modest."

"Time's past."

"Oh? You think you can come storming at me now, any time, day or night."

"Yes."

"Well, you can." The reflection of her face in the mirror was soft-amber from the lamplight. She was gay, she teased him with her eyes. "What happened to us for a minute? What got into us? I was desperate — oh, Ralph, that must never happen."

"You had it right. It was too much talk."

"We didn't talk much. But it came so suddenly."

"Too much thinking, then. Too much yes or no. Too much black or white. All of that nonsense."

"Well, it's gone."

"Entirely gone."

Her hands lay momentarily still; her lips rolled back as she laughed. "I got to thinking, right in the middle of it, what would you have done if somebody had come to the door and said there was a man with a broken leg to be fixed?"

"He'd've suffered for a while."

"You've got a proud look. You're saying to yourself, 'I did it.'"

"I've got a woman," he said.

304

She finished her hair and laid her hands on the table and became thoughtful. "I never thought it would happen to me. All I saw was years of nothing. I suppose that's what most people see. And put up with it. I expected to put up with it, too. I don't know when I noticed something on your face. Way back on the trail. I was suspicious of you a long time, but I watched you every minute."

"It was pretty easy to see. I was a dead giveaway."

"The night in the gorge you came to the wagon — that was when I decided I would, if you asked. You don't know how hard I hoped you'd ask and all the things I've done to put myself in your road."

"I'm not good at this business."

"You're not sure of yourself. That's strange. You're a doctor and you've known so many women that you ought to understand about them."

"What ought I to understand about them?"

She spoke carefully. "I believe you put too much value on their standards. You're afraid you'll disturb something. With a happy wife, you might. But if she were happy she'd not listen to you and there'd be no harm done. As for the others, like me, what are standards worth when there's nothing for them to love?" She reached an arm backward and drew his head to her head. "Now I've got something and there's my standard. Next time we meet — "

"Next time . . . " he said. "Now that begins. When's next time? We've had just enough to want more, to make waiting worse."

"It'll always be that way," she said. "You've thought about it as much as I have. You know there's nothing for us but a meeting here and there, a lot of hiding and scheming and heartache when things go wrong and we can't meet. I don't dare look glad when I see you. I can't come to you and put my arms around you. I can't eat with you, and talk with you and sleep with you all the nights we've got left. But it's all we have — we've got to stand it. What if we didn't have this much?"

"Will you be back in town again?"

"Not soon. I can't make this trip often without George wondering."

"Then I'll have to come to the settlements."

"Anywhere, anywhere possible," she said. "In the brush, behind trees, in the mud, anywhere."

"If it worked out . . . in your cabin?"

"Yes. I won't like it too much, but yes. Does it sound so bad? I can't help it. Oh, maybe I could, but I don't want to. Whatever I must do with

305

you, I'll do. Don't you know that someday the neighbors will get wind of this, if they haven't already?"

"No question about it."

"Well, don't mind it. I'll stand that, too." She rose and came to him, and he held her and felt the light brushing of her mouth across his cheek. She was gay again and went into the front room for her coat and hat.

"I'll walk to the main street with you." At the door he stopped her and they swung into each other. He thought he was emptied out, but the pressure began immediately and in a little while they were at each other with the same roughness as in the beginning. She drew back her head and laughter bubbled in her throat. A dreamlike looseness came over her; she closed her eyes, she whispered, "It never quits. Are we natural, or are we peculiar?"

"We're caught."

"I don't like that word."

"There won't be a time when we're satisfied. I want more of this. I want more beyond this, beyond the moment, beyond the wall of your flesh. You'll be tired and marked up tomorrow because I've pulled at you so hard with my arms. I've tried to break through, get closer. There's the misery of it. We never get that close."

"You have me, though. There's nothing I want to hold back."

"If our bodies were shadows we could pass into each other and there'd be one shadow. That would be it. That's what we're trying to do. If Lot White would quit trying to bring lightning out of heaven and look around on earth he'd see what God is. This is God — you and I trying to make ourselves into one shadow." He looked down at her with his extreme solemnness. "I love you."

The lightness left her face, her eyes turned brilliant, her mouth was unsteady. "Say it again and I'll stay the rest of the night."

"I'm ready."

Her ease returned. "We must be healthy. Now you know I'm not delicate. Well, it's good to be honest. It's good. Shall I take off my hat and coat?"

"Won't do to have you go back to the hotel at five in the morning."

"You're more cautious than I am."

"That's so."

He accompanied her along the lane, kissed her and watched her go on through the muddy gloom toward the hotel; she walked on quickly, paying no attention to the few lighted shops around her or to the straggling

306

men still abroad and it was that confidence which gave him the worst blow of the day. She knew, as well as he, that they could have nothing more than they were having, that no happy end could come of it. It was a trap which would scar her worse than it would him; still, she stepped smiling into it. In this matter any woman was braver than any man.

44

HE chipped the log, he grew tired, he put the knife cautiously into his pocket, he rested a little while and drew out the knife to work again. Now and then he passed a hand through the forming notch and stripped back the stringy wood slivers with fingers which had scarcely any sense of touch remaining. He was increasingly slow in his handling of the knife, for he worked close to his legs and risked slashing himself if the knife slipped aside from the wood. During the longest hours between midnight and first light he measured what he had done and guessed he had cut two inches into the tree and at that point he drew himself together and brought his legs back for another try; but his knees wouldn't come between the space between log and stone.

The strain got him in the base of his neck and at the small of his back and the stretched muscles along his legs occasionally registered twinges of pain. Except for these sensations he was a man without legs, he was a torso bedded in the mud, a stumplike animal crouched under the deadfalls, swaying forward and grunting as he worked. The rain thickened, the wind rose to a roar in the high trees, and he heard the rifle-shot crack of branches breaking. A considerable distance above him one tree, ready for such a wind, came down in a series of splintering explosions; the effect of its fall trembled through the log jam and shortly afterward a small wave of water splashed against his back.

He put the knife away, the repeated jabbing turning his arm lame, and he settled into something which was stupor rather than sleep. The lesser miseries were blocked out; the greater miseries got through — the coldness striking the spots in him which were still sensitive, the raw aching of his wrists, of his cramped body, the endless sawing of the water against his flanks. But the greatest of the miseries was the thought of the trap itself. Though he knew he could not pull his legs free, the wish to pull them free grew much worse; unable to lift himself from the water, he had sudden surges of wild necessity to lift himself. Even in the haze of his half-conscious state these surges came, to make him struggle as little as possible, for his energy grew thinner and he needed all of it to work the knife.

Somewhere along the night he was entirely still and almost nothing got through, and when later he came out of this coma he saw the hole above him show its raggedness against first light. He was wet outside, dry inside. He scooped water with his palm, tasting the woody mud, he beat his hands together until he began to feel his fingers return to him individually; and he straightened against the log and reached for his knife. It wasn't there.

He thought a moment: *Don't recall using my other hand* — but he tried the other pocket. Neither pocket held the knife. He was still slow-thinking; he pushed the front of the overcoat aside and tried his inner coat pockets. He searched the overcoat pockets a second time. Then he was still and his mind began to work. He ran his hand along the top of the log on the guess that he might have stuck the knife into it for safety. He went through his pockets another time; he made each motion deliberate but the knowledge began to close in. He thrust his hands straight downward into the mud, reaching as far as he could turn his body, exploring the mud to the extreme limit of each arm. He drew them out, washed them in the surface water and returned to his pockets; and after that fruitless gesture he again churned and squeezed and sifted the mud between his fingers. Once he thought he touched the knife handle straight below his left side — which was where it should have been if it had fallen from his pocket — and he turned until his dead knees woke and he tried for one more inch of depth and failed to find anything. He washed his arms around the water; he laid them over his chest.

This creek flowed into another creek which, in turn, came into the settlement's creek below Lattimore's. He would die, he would rot, he would float down that creek piece at a time. *Might even make a taste they'll wonder about.* He would end up a skeleton crouched under this log jam; that empty skull pan would see or feel nothing — but it would know as much, lifeless, about the sky it faced as he knew now, alive.

He wasn't like Hawn's trapper who, dying, knew too late what he should have been and what he should have done. How far out did he have to get before that came to him?

It was better the way the old man had put it: "The things I regret are the things I didn't do."

He straightened to the log and got his arms beneath it, now willing to risk what he hadn't before and collecting his strength into his arms he tried to unseat the log. If it rolled down on his legs and broke them, he would at least be free. There was no give to the log and he lay back and ceased to care. The things a man regretted were the chances offered and not taken. Refusal was a drawing back; to take was to move — and to move was to be alive. Edna . . . he could have taken more of her. What did his refusal amount to, he about to die? One thing not bad. What had he refused? One more shock of life. Against this outward chill of water and wind and against the inner chill of death, the warmth of her body was a strong thing. But his turning mind went away from her and he remembered Katherine crouched by the fire, intent on its mysteries, and then he had the feeling of a man who, walking steadily toward a city at the end of a long day, watched darkness cover the city, and in the dark he took the wrong trail and never saw the city again.

He watched day grow dismally through the hole above him. He rose and once again tried to pull his feet clear and had no luck and settled back. The cold crept deeper into him, the walls went down one by one; but the central place was still intact, for his heart beat steady and he had no idea of letting his mind make an early surrender.

Who said the gate was up there in that cold empty stuff? We live here — our work's here, but we stand frozen and throw foolish questions at the sky. When I get out of here I'll ask no more questions. The gate's down here. Look down, look around. It's all here.

Once again he tried to pull his legs through the hole and felt the smallest possible streak of pain come to him from his knees; and afterwards he began to pluck at the splinters of the log with fingers which had no sensation. *Better that way. I'll dig this thing out with my hands. Won't feel a thing when the flesh strips off.*

Hawn heard the bellow of the cows when he came down the trail around noon that day; he turned in and noticed there had been no fire in the cabin during the morning. Burnett's saddle horse was in the meadow but his gun and powder flask were gone from the wall. Hawn milked the cows and cut a short circle around the yard's edge to see what he might discover in the way of tracks; on the rain-washed earth nothing was to be found. He beat about the timber where Burnett had been cutting road and saw that the stump fires were dead. From there he walked to Lattimore's.

"No," said Lattimore. "Ain't seen him. Come to think, didn't hear his ax in the timber yesterday either."

"He wouldn't walk off from the cows that long," said Hawn, "and them stump fires are too damned hard to start for him to let 'em die. Horse is home, gun's gone."

"If he'd meant to leave he'd told me about the cows," said Lattimore. "If his gun's gone he went on a hunt and got delayed. Couldn't be too far, because he went on foot."

"Sounds like an accident. Which way you think he'd go to hunt?"

"Don't know."

"I'll cross to Millard's," said Hawn. "I'll move out that way and hit the settlers and see if I can find anybody that saw him. You go straight down the trail and ask. Go over to Lord's too. If I don't find anything I'll come back and we'll see if we can't catch his trail back of the cabin."

Mrs. Lattimore, listening to this talk, tossed up her hands, "Oh God, he's dead! Lockyear's killed him — I know. He's dead, all bloody in the brush somewhere — Oh God, poor Rice!" She went crying into the house. Lattimore cast a sidewise glance at Hawn.

"Females," he grumbled, "they get so God-damned wrought up." Rain stung through the thin cotton of his shirt, his ramshackle body shivered. He went into the house, got a coat and came out. "But she could be right about that," he said and moved down the trail.

Hawn crossed the creek to Millard's, found no news of Burnett there, and passed on to Mercer's, Monteith's and Kern's. Howard Kern said: "I'll go down to McIver's and Crabtree's. You go straight on as far as Ebbett's. Come back this way."

Hawn crossed the ridge to Rinearson's and continued to the Kitchen cabin. There was no news there and none at Lige Ebbett's. Ebbett said, "He ain't ever hunted on this side of the ridge." Then he said, "I'll walk back with you," and picked up his gun and went along. Returning to Rinearson's, Hawn found Old Daniel ready with Ared. "I sent Moss down to Shafer's place. They'll go to the ford and come up to Lattimore's and meet us." As he retraced his route, Hawn found men waiting for him and when they discovered he had no news they ducked into their cabins, came out with guns and coats and joined the party. He had fifteen settlers by the time he reached Lattimore's. Mrs. Lattimore said, "Everybody's gone on to Burnett's." At Burnett's all the men of the lower settlement were gathered. Hawn counted twenty-five in the meadow. Katherine Gay was with them.

Lot White came back from a private search of the upper trail. "I don't see any tracks."

"You couldn't read a track anyhow," said Old Daniel. He pointed to Hawn. "That's this man's business. If we all get to trampin' around the brush nobody's goin' to find anything. Let Bob run this. What you want us to do?"

"It looks like he went huntin' afoot," said Hawn, "though why he'd do it on a day like yesterday, I don't know. He didn't go down-trail and didn't go up-trail. I looked both ways. So he must've gone into the brush, this side of the creek — or the other side." He looked across the creek and shook his head. "Not there. You couldn't break a way through that stuff with a cannon."

Billy Lord said: "He hunts them draws over there," and pointed to the hill directly beyond the meadow. "Because he's come out of 'em by my place a lot of times."

"Stay here," said Hawn and crossed the meadow. The settlers waited before Burnett's cabin — their bodies pulled together against the steady rain — and watched Hawn reach the brushy edge of the hill and go along it at a fast walk, bent over, intent on his reading.

"Like a hound dog," said Rinearson. "He knows his business."

Harris Eby looked at his watch. "Two o'clock. We better find something — she'll be dark in three more hours."

"Well, he couldn't go too damned far," said Provost. "He'd not want to pack a deer more'n a couple miles through that country."

"Wish we had some whisky. He might require a shot of it."

"We'll take along some coffee," said McIver, and entered Burnett's cabin to get it.

"You'll play hell lighting a fire up there," said Mercer. That comment brought a notion to Harris Eby and he crossed to the shed and rummaged around for pitchwood. He found a chunk of it and shaved small splinters from it and put the splinters in his shirt pocket and buttoned his coat. Hawn, ducking in and out of the brush, disappeared from their view.

Lattimore said: "Lockyear keeps runnin' through my mind."

Rinearson said: "There's no question but what Rice has had an accident. He wouldn't leave his stock neglected. He's been out in this stuff all night. If he's alive he's in poor shape."

"He knows how to take care of himself," said Monteith. "He's a good man."

"A God-damn' good man," said Rinearson.

Hawn's cry from the brush moved the settlers over the meadow. He had found a trail and had gone part way up the hill's slope. "Come on single file — don't get ahead of me and bust up these tracks."

"New tracks?" asked Rinearson.

"Can't say. Rain's been at 'em."

He worked his way through the wet brush, showering water behind him; limbs slashed at the party and Billy Lord grumbled, "World never was made for a big man." The slope was steep, the ground slick; the party lagged and stumbled and drew deep for wind. Hawn walked the hill in long strides, upper body so tilted that his face skimmed the rising ground, and he made his darting turns as the trail bent, and jumped over logs and went straining on. The party fell behind him; the thicket crashed to their bodies. "Christ's sake," called Lorenzo Buck, "where's he at now?" A little later the column overtook him. He was at a standstill, studying the forks of the trail in a light that grew duller and duller.

"Wait," he said and vanished.

They heard him rustling around the huckleberry and vine maple and dead branches somewhere forward; they heard him quietly curse himself. He came back, eyes pinned to the earth. Rinearson stood in his way; he gave the older man a quick push and went into another blind part of the timber, beating a noisy way downslope; in a short time he returned and led them on. The trail quit and the way forward was extremely rough, over breast-high logs, winding between great fir trunks, dropping into deep pits. Rinearson lost sight of Hawn. "Where you at now?"

"Here," said Hawn from the shadow of a tree ten feet away.

"My God, I'd hate to have you on my trail."

Hawn turned from the crest of the ridge, towing the column into the ravine, and at the foot of the ravine he caught some kind of trace that pleased him and he tackled the side of the next ridge in the same bent-over shape. He waited impatiently for the column to reach him. He looked into the adjoining ravine and lifted his voice and sent a great hail forward. "Ayee-ee-oo-o-oo — Burnett!" Sound whirled around them, fled off through the corridors and broke into separate echoes. He turned his head, listening, receiving nothing back but the rain and the wind and the rasping breath of the men around him. He got on his knees and crawled downslope a few yards. "Light's gettin' bad," he said. He disappeared and long afterwards called to them. "Come on — straight down."

"Now, by God, I'm lost," said Durbin Young.

They worked their way after him, using arms and elbows to fend off the sharp brush. Hawn swung and came upon a trace and he dropped to all fours, head low, rump high, to stare at the mud. He got up and reached the creek, facing the tangle of logs which carpeted the ravine's bottom. It was then so gray that the features of the men around him were indistinct. "He must of crossed over," grumbled Hawn, "but we got to scout back and forth to find where he went through the brush. God damn, I don't know what brought him this far. Wait."

He parted the brush and came to the log jam; he stepped on a small log, slipped and plunged feet foremost into the mud; a minor storm of broken stuff fell around him and he came cursing up and found another log and crawled over it. By now the shadows had blackened enough to swallow him forty feet distant.

He called back: "Dead buck here. Shot. One of you fellows fire a gun."

"I'll do it," said Eby. He drew up his rifle, sheltering it while he poured powder into the pan. The shot, condensed between the ravine walls, roared around them.

"That ought to reach to hell and gone," said Rinearson; then everybody stood stone-still.

There was the ruffle of wind above, the spatting of rain on the brush, the gurgling of the creek beneath the log jam; there were these sounds but no sound from Burnett.

The settlers struggled through the brush and came to the tangle of logs and men crawled out upon the logs and stood indecisive in the growing dark. Hawn moved back and forth, murmuring his unhappiness to himself. "He came here. There's the buck. What'd he leave it for? Damn my soul, I wish it was light." He let go with his chesty call. "Yah-ee-e-o-oo-o — Burnett!" He reached the end of a log, jumped to another, disappeared in the far brush, rattled around it, and returned. Some other settler, drifting over the debris, lost his footing and went down through the logs with an alarmed yell. He scrambled back and came over to firm ground.

Lattimore said: "We ain't goin' to find anything and there's no use standing around here."

Daniel Rinearson's voice went at him. "We'll stay out here, by God, till we get him. You got the pitch, Harris. Light up a fire."

"Wait," said Hawn. He jumped from log to another. He spoke quietly. "Burnett — where you at? Burnett — sing out."

"Here."

The settlers rushed forward, all shouting at once. Hawn yelled at them. "Stand still a minute. Where — where you at, Burnett?" He crouched on a log and slapped it with his hand. "Above me — below me?"

"Little farther. Under the logs."

Hawn worked his way through the tangle and dropped from sight and in a moment his voice called out of the darkness. "All right, boys. He's here."

The settlers moved in. Lot White wrestled a way through the matted dead stuff and crouched by Burnett. Harris Eby crawled forward to smash the litter aside. "Broken leg?"

"I just woke up," said Burnett.

"Slept well, no doubt," said Rinearson.

"Nothing's broke. Legs caught under this thing."

Eby scrambled over the log, big body sinking into the loose mud until his feet located the log and the stone and discovered how the trap was set. Men edged forward, hopping from log to log, beating their way through the tangle, dropping through the interstices. They made a ring around this place and flung their advice briskly back and forth. Lot White called: "We got to get some axes."

"No," said Harris, "there's hands enough to lift it. This is the log. See what's on top of it — and move that stuff away. Then we'll budge this thing."

They crowded forward, blocked each other on the narrow walkway of the logs, made useless motions in their desire to be helpful. "Over here, lend a land."

"We got to have a pry for this one."

"Billy, God damn it, don't roll that thing till I get out of here."

In the pit, Hawn and Lot White got their arms beneath Burnett to cradle him above the water. Burnett murmured, "Don't lift me too high. Legs are caught."

"Say when you feel the strain on 'em," said Hawn.

"Can't feel. Bob, recall the beaver you trapped? I been a beaver in a trap. Know just what they think. Damned nice of you men to come."

"Why," said Lot White, "you think we'd let the devil take one of our own? Lean on me, boy. We got the devil on the run now."

"You're all right, Lot."

Lot grumbled. "Old Lot — he's all right — he hollers and he whoops and folks smile at the old fool — but he means well — he's all right. Lean on me, boy. Don't use your strength, use mine. I got muscle if I ain't got sense."

"Anything hurt you?" asked Hawn.

"No. A little tired, a little cold."

It was around five o'clock then. At nine the column returned to the meadow, dog-weary and wet. Burnett, an arm about Eby and an arm about Lot White, swung his feet and half supported himself as he walked.

Katherine ran from the cabin. "Rice . . ." she said and bent in to catch sight of his face. "Rice — what . . . ?"

"Not a thing," he said.

She stood aside to let Eby and White carry him into the cabin. She called, "Get those wet clothes off him." She remained outside, watching the settlers straggle through the night toward their cabins; she heard their thin talk waver and sink in the distance. Eby came out a little later. "He was in water, dropped under a log, since two–three o'clock yesterday. Lot will stay."

"I'm staying."

"I know that," he said. "But he'll stay in case you need to send for something."

"I've got coffee. Come in."

"No," he said, and looked at her. "That's too damned many people," he added, and went away.

She stepped into the cabin and crossed to the bed. Burnett lay on his back; his face was whisker-black, the bleakness of his experience hadn't thawed from his features.

"Coffee, Rice?"

"Make a tub of it."

She turned to Lot. "You bring in all the wood you can find. I'm going to keep this room hot till hot won't have it, all night." She poured the coffee and came to the bed with it and found he had closed his eyes. She waited a moment, then said, "Rice," gently, and saw that he was asleep. She put the coffee away and stood watching him. Lot White, coming in with a load of wood, noticed the change and settled the wood quietly on the floor. "It must have seemed a long time to him," she said.

"God saved him," said Lot. She turned her head from him, but he was an inquisitive man and he bent to catch sight of her face and saw tears in her eyes. "Sometimes," he said, "it means something, don't it? I don't know why folks are so blind and deaf that they got to be beaten and tortured and crippled before they'll let the Word come in. I don't know why they cry for mercy when they are sick, and forget it when they're well. You're a proud and healthy girl and you give it no thought till this man's hurts make you see. Now, then, girl — you ought to give thanks."

"I do, Lot."

"No — you ought to get right on your knees in the middle of this room and let God see you humble and say so out loud."

"Maybe," she said, "people give thanks in different ways, and maybe people think of God in different ways. I don't see a face and a figure the way you do. I think of mercy and kindness and pity and understanding — and love."

"Words," he said. "Words. Everybody says those words. Everybody believes those words when the believin' is easy. If words made heaven we'd all have heaven. But till man humbles himself openly in the eyes of the Lord those words ain't strong enough. Pride keeps you off your knees, daughter. You don't want to look foolish to me. Pride makes men fight, they don't want to look foolish to others. Pride — that's the devil, too. We believe but we don't believe enough. Till we cast this pride away and believe one thing so much we feel no shame to kneel and confess before all men, till this comes we're sinners bound for hell. You know why we're sinners? Because we ain't got strength to do in the sight of all men what we believe in our hearts."

"Lot," she said, "sometimes you say things which go against other things you say."

"God is a wind which bloweth everywhere, and night is day, and day is night."

"Why did you go up to fight the Indians?"

"I only know what the spirit tells me. And the spirit said, 'Go fight the heathen.' "

"Bring in some more wood."

He tramped silently back and forth with his loads of wood until he had a corner of the cabin filled. She said: "You want me to cook you something?"

"No," he said and drank his coffee, and stood at the fire with his stubborn face bemused. Now and then he looked at her as if to renew the argument; at times he seemed solemn and depressed and he made small motions with his hands to accent the silent words going around his busy head. He drew a great sigh and turned to the door. "I'll be in the shed should you want me."

"Good night, Lot."

"Good night, daughter."

After he had gone she pulled the blankets around Burnett's neck and lightly ran her fingers across his forehead to brush away the drying mud. Color hadn't yet come to his face; it remained sallow. She settled on her knees, laid her arms across him and had thoughts which, in their way, were prayers. When this was done she rose and took Burnett's clothes and hung them before the fire. She spread her coat on the floor and settled on it and, half waking and half asleep, passed the night.

45

HE was cheerful next morning and breakfast lifted him with the quickness of a drink of whisky. He said to Katherine, "You go outside while I put my clothes on." The rain had stopped and now the meadow exhaled this wetness as a thick, crystal-sparkling mist so rank with the odor of earth that it was a taste at the back of her mouth as she walked abroad. This was early March when, according to her memory of the east, the land was still lifeless, but here the yeast was working and ferment was around her and the fog of it came up like smoke to make its dense pall which erased hill and timber; from the distance of a hundred feet she looked back to see the cabin enveloped in this drifting steam. She heard the cows at the fence and she went to the shed for the pail and milked them. Presently Lot called her to the cabin.

Burnett was in bed and in poor humor. "Damned legs like rubber. They bend."

They pained him now, she noticed, for he turned them slowly, he shifted, he showed a cranky expression; his face was flushed and his eyes were heavy. Lot said: "What you think you're made of? You imagine you can sit in the middle of a creek thirty hours and bounce around like a ball?"

"He needs a bath," said Katherine. "Where's your tub, Rice?"

"I use the creek."

Lot said, "I'll fetch Lattimore's." He was back in half an hour with a big half-keg into which Katherine poured a kettle of boiling water. Lot lugged several buckets from the creek to temper it and Katherine went to the shed and stayed there for half an hour. Lot, when he called her in, was dripping wet. "I had to hold him in the tub. His legs are half dead." Burnett lay with his hands over his eyes; the pain had grown worse. Katherine swept the puddled floor and set on a fresh pot of coffee to boil while Lot emptied the tub. He said, "I'll be back this afternoon," and went away with his burden.

She settled on a chair beside the bed. "Can you feel your toes, Rice?"

"On fire."

She put the chair at the foot of the bed and shoved the blankets away from his feet and rubbed them. "Chilblains. What happened up there?"

"A log broke on me when I started across the creek. I went down and the log pinned me."

"Suppose," she said, "the search party hadn't found you?"

"I'd've had to drink the creek dry to get out of it."

She was thoughtful. "We're not very strong. A thousand accidents can kill us. A log, a rock, a little bit of fire, a minute under water, a cut on the wrist — just a small blow on the head. It makes me feel like an ant with the shadow of a big foot over me."

"That's what Lot would say."

"I know. He talked to me last night."

"He talked to me all the time he washed me, asked a lot of questions. What did I feel when I was there, what did I think about, was I humble, was I afraid? Did I hear anything from beyond?"

"Did you have time to think about very much?" she asked and went on with her rubbing.

"Mostly it was, 'How do I get out of here.' When that petered out — "

"You mean you decided you wouldn't?"

"So long as I had a knife to dig away at the log with, I figured I'd make it. When I lost the knife in the mud, I knew it was a close thing."

"Then what did you think about? All the things you shouldn't have done?"

He shaded his eyes with his hand. "All the things I didn't do. And I said that if I had this to do over again I'd not ask a lot of foolish questions that have got no answers."

She smiled, "Oh, Rice," she said, and in a moment they were both laughing. "Don't tell Lot that. It would hurt his feelings."

She laid the covers over his feet and drew the coffee from the fire and brought him a cup.

He sat up to drink it and he relished it thoroughly and lay back. "This business of waiting to get to heaven to lead a happy life spoils too much here. It's like a traveler eating a meal so fast he don't taste it because he's got to catch a train. That coffee's damned good." He shifted on the bed and grew irritable. "The stump fires are out, the road's a long ways from done. So's the mill. It'll be time to plow when the weather changes. And here I am, wasting time."

She looked down at him smiling. "You see, Rice? You think of tomorrow same as Lot thinks of heaven. Tomorrow — but not what's here right now." She walked to the fire and stood before it, her back to him. "Lot White's not the same. He's troubled — he's kinder. I wonder why?"

"Maybe something jarred him out of the notion that everything's so damned simple. I like him better. He's doing these chores for me as though it gave him pleasure."

She came back to sit beside the bed. "It does give him pleasure. Don't you know he's a humble man, even when he seems most positive? He knows people laugh at him sometimes. That would humiliate you or me, so it must humiliate him sometimes. But he goes on doing these things, hoping we'll see something by his example. What do you want to eat?"

"Whatever you can find."

"I'll fix it pretty soon."

"This settlement," he said, "is a peculiar thing. We're all inside a circle. We have got to act alike, think alike. I was an unpopular man for not going along to fight the Molalas. We all bend the same direction; if anybody tries to bend against the rest, he's squeezed into shape. But when the crowd came up to find me, I saw the other side of it. If somebody gets lost outside the circle everybody else fights like hell to get him back in. We do bad things to each other, but we hang together against the thing that tries to kill us. We're killed in the long run — but we don't stand alone."

He was drowsy and closed his eyes. "It would be better, though, if this community didn't use its will like a whip on people that don't think the way it thinks."

"Maybe it knows we'll only hurt ourselves if we try to be as free as we'd like to be. The older people have been through it. They've been in love. They've been strong, they wanted to do as they pleased. When we get to be fifty, will we hate the rules that bother us now?"

"I won't waste much time thinking about that. When I'm an old man I'll act like one. Right now it's a good feeling to be alive, taste water, do some work, kiss a woman."

"You want that now?"

"Yes."

She bent down to kiss him. In a moment he was asleep.

She pulled the blankets about his shoulders and watched pain's uneasiness stir his flushed face. In summer, when he had his place fixed, his mill started and his first crop harvested, he would turn to her; there was that much of the methodical mixed in with his restlessness. It was coming. He wouldn't live alone and he had got closer to her in the past weeks. If she encouraged him more, it might come sooner. He would think, when he asked her, that he loved her; but Edna was the woman most mixed up in his emotions and she was still there. Part of it, Katherine suspected, was a feeling of obligation he owed Edna for what she had given him; the rest of it was Rice's own creation, for he was a powerful dreamer and he had made Edna into the image of his wishes. Most men dreamed things into women; this was the way they got married. The hard thing with Rice was that though he had perhaps begun to know Edna was not all he had thought, he couldn't put her from his mind and move immediately to another woman. He couldn't swing lightly from dream to dream.

She bent forward, watching him with her patience. She thought: *How do I change you?*

He was still asleep when Mrs. Millard came in with a basket covered by a towel. "Mrs. Rinearson sent some biscuits and here's a dab of that plum jelly left. He all right?" She sent her curious glance about the room, she looked at Rice and at Katherine. "You been here all night?"

"Lot's been here with me."

"Oh, I didn't mean that," said Mrs. Millard indifferently. The two stepped into the yard to talk. "Some men are like stumps. They sit and rot away and nothin' ever happens to 'em. But some are lightning rods that draw things. The stumps ain't very interesting to live with, but the lightning rods cause you misery." She shook her head at Katherine. "Poor child — poor child. All that you've got to learn — all that you've got to bear."

"What would you have done with your life if you'd not married Millard?" asked Katherine.

"Married somebody else."

"No — what other thing do you think would have been better?"

"Better — better," said Mrs. Millard, impatiently. "This is no world for better. Katherine, you ought to take a trip to Oregon City, just for the visit. Ain't Eby goin' that way sometime?"

Katherine smiled, whereupon Mrs. Millard pointed into the cabin and shook her head. "Wait on him, then, hand and foot. Be a slave. Waste your time while he plays God and makes up his mind. No, you go away and see how quick he ain't God any more." She crossed the meadow and followed the trail through the trees and hadn't quite got to Lattimore's when she met Lot White, he bound back to Burnett's.

"You don't need to hurry," she said. "They're all right."

"Fine — fine," he said. He was never certain of Mrs. Millard's disposition and never inclined to test it. "How's Millard?" he asked and stirred his body around to indicate he wanted to be on his way.

"Come over and visit. He needs company."

"I will," he said. "I'll come tomorrow and console him."

She surprised him with a smile; she took his arm and turned him about. "No, you come now." He had no ready excuse and so he went along with her and settled into a chair beside Millard's bed and made himself agreeable. During the middle of the afternoon he rose to go, but Mrs. Millard urged him to remain and got him on a line of talk which occupied him until dark. When he rose again she insisted that he stay for supper; it was beyond seven when he left the cabin. Millard swung his guns on her as soon as the guest was well beyond earshot.

"My God, what'd I have to put up with that for?"

"Well, you're lonely."

"Not that lonely. What've you got in your mind now?"

"Better those two were left to themselves awhile."

He gave out a strong laugh. "If that's what you're after, you ought to've had Lot stay here all night." Growing serious, he gave the problem some thought, and disagreed with her. "It won't work. They both got firm minds."

"Firm minds can be changed," she said. "It's comin' anyhow, but it ought to come sooner than it is. He might see some other girl, half as good but twice as bold — like Durbin Young's girl — and that would be too bad. That Katherine, I don't know why she don't help herself. It's clear to me she's waiting for him. And it's so easy. He's a man. He's vain. It wouldn't take anything at all to stir the animal in him."

"My God, Nancy, you think it's always a man fallin' into some damned trap a woman sets?"

"They're all the same. Before marriage they got to be encouraged because they're mortally afraid of being tied down. Afterwards they got to be subdued because they get too overbearing."

"If women really believe that," he said, "I wonder why they bother about gettin' married at all."

She swung on him. "That's just what you'd like, too. A new one every night. No responsibility — just sleep and run. Oh, you'd love it. That's why we play our tricks — because it's a man's world we're trapped in and we got to play tricks or we'd have nothing. Millard, don't say things to make me so angry."

Katherine woke him for his meal and found him cheerful; she cleaned the dishes and stood at the doorway to catch the air, and felt his restlessness accumulate.

"Your father better?"

"No."

"When I was arguing with the boys about going up to fight the Molalas I thought of him. I did a bad job. He could have talked them out of it."

"You know what he wanted to be when he was younger? A musician. But he had no schooling and no way of getting it. One time he said something that made me feel bad, because I knew it came right from himself. He said nobody'd ever know how many people might have changed the world with their good ideas if they'd been able to learn enough to get the good out. That's why he's so strong-minded about schools." She was at the doorway, watching the meadow. She turned back to seize her coat and shawl, saying, "I'm going over to Millard's for a while," and abruptly left him. Down the meadow he heard voices and in a moment Edna came into the cabin.

She moved on to the bed and her close look said, "Remember?" and brought back what had been between them. She removed her coat and settled on the edge of the bed. She said, "Whiskers — whiskers," and rubbed her hand across his jaw and bent to kiss him and rested heavy on him. "What were you doing up in the hills anyway? Just walking to keep walking? I know why. If I'd been here, you'd not gone. I could keep you home."

"You could keep anybody home."

She raised back from him, laughing. "I know it," she said and ceased to laugh. "You mean a lot of things by that. You always thought a lot of things about me." She looked around the room. "She been here all day?"

"All day — all night."

"Damn you," she said and was angry. "What'd she leave for? She don't like me. Is it so easy for you to change? From me to her?"

"Stop that."

"Well," she said, "she's no different than I am."

"Stop it."

"But you think she is. You always thought so. Where'd you get such funny ideas about women?"

"Where's Moss?"

"Cutting a road between our place and the old man's."

"Everything all right?"

She shrugged her shoulders. "I guess so." She brushed the subject aside, impatient with it. "Why have we got to talk about that? You don't care."

"Better not come here any more."

She rose and moved to the doorway and looked upon the meadow a moment. She came back to settle beside him. "You want me?"

"Yes."

She tapped a finger on her chest. "That's what I can do." She waited for him to speak again and presently whispered her encouragement. "All right."

"It won't do. Why don't you let go?"

She darkened and grew sullen. "I'm not holding you. Let go yourself if you want," but she bent down. "I can't help it, Rice. It's not all my fault. It's as much yours as mine."

"I know," he said.

She straightened, her face catching up a keener attention. "Well, there's no use worrying about it. I don't believe much in thinking about things. We can't take a knife and cut it out of us. It's there — let it stay there. It's good, isn't it?" She lowered herself. "I miss you."

He said: "You going to come back here every month to remind me? It won't do."

She lifted herself from the bed. "Won't do — won't do," she said, and went around the room, touching the table, touching the walls. She stopped in the corner of the cabin and kept her sidewise glance on him. "You're afraid."

He turned on the bed. "What do you want? Make up your mind."

"Ah," she said, "it's always that. Everything's got to have a reason, got to be this or got to be that. Things aren't like that. They just are. God, Rice, how can you be cold, how can you not want me? You started it. You want me to change, like it never happened? I won't, and neither will you." She moved back to him. "You marry that Katherine and I'll never leave you alone. You see. You won't be free from me. She'll know it, too.

323

She'll know it when you sleep together. What's she? Ah, Rice — nothing. But she's made you think there's a difference and that's what made it bad between us and made me go marry Moss." She stooped to lay her mouth against him with a groaning sound and she kissed him and whispered, "I shouldn't have married him. I know it now." She rose, got her coat and shawl, flung them carelessly on and moved to the door. She swung to watch him and the keen look came back to her and her shoulders rose in a gesture of confidence at what she saw. She said, "I'll see you again," and smiled to herself as she left the cabin. Reaching the trail she paused to throw a glance in the direction of Lockyear's place. Her expression tightened. In a moment she turned homeward.

She was in the room long after she had gone; she was a heaviness around him. He rolled on his side and pushed his feet to the floor and sat on the bed's edge to put an experimental pressure against his legs; they were stiff and painful and his bruised knees ached. She wouldn't leave him and he couldn't leave her. He stood up and stepped over to his clothes and sat in a chair and dressed himself. He was at the fireplace when Katherine returned.

"Oh, Rice — don't be foolish."

He was out of sorts with himself. "These feet were made to stand on — and I'm going to stand on 'em till they get well or buckle up. There's too much to do around here to waste time in bed."

She said: "There's a piece of steak in the Dutch oven."

"Where you going?"

"Home."

He came over to her with his ragged temper in his eyes and reached about her with his arms and kissed her. She swayed back but he hung on and she let him have his way for a little while and broke clear. "It wasn't as good as the other time," she said and left the cabin, walking thoughtfully home. She knew. *That damned woman,* she thought. Fury built up as she moved through the dark trees, and it kept on past Lattimore's, Provost's and Irish's. By that time it began to settle and her patience came back. *How do I change him?*

46

HAWN made his way through the brush and stumps of Burnett's road work a week later to say so-long. "I'll be gone a week. Take anything I got at the cabin you need."

"Which way you headed?"

Hawn only said, "Just prowlin'," and departed. At the ford he paused a moment to visit with Mrs. Irish, then crossed the creek and soon put Rinearson's and Ebbett's behind him. All he carried was gun, powder flask and possible sack. That day he passed over Waldo's hills and camped beside the Santiam and lay back from his campfire with his pipe, recapturing for a moment the wildness of this land as he had first known it. This far south no settlers had yet penetrated and he thought to himself, "This would be good for a year or two, till they come. Then move another fifty miles and squat till they catch up. Just keep a little ahead, until I'm an old man, and then it won't matter." He crossed the river next morning, found an Indian trail leading southeastward beside the river and toward noon came to the old camp in which he had first seen Louisa. There was nothing here now, only the brush growing where the village had been, and after a short pause for sentimental reflection he moved on, found a fresher trail and pursued it through fern and timber and across fire-scarred meadows, and so eventually caught sight of the village squatted beside a creek.

It was the old man's village, Louisa's old man. It looked smaller than the other village had looked five years before — only a dozen brush-and-skin lodges lined between water and woods. White man did that, Hawn thought. White man with his whisky, with his guns; with nothing more than his smell in the country he did it. He saw a group of squaws crouched at the creek, at the far end of the camp, and he saw the old man walk from the tent with a long-legged young man. They both came forward, the old man squinting between swollen red eyes, the young man's glance unfriendly. The young man had a gun.

The old man said, in jargon: "I will keep the horses. It is not my fault if you don't keep the woman."

It was the swap the old man was thinking about, the horses traded for

Louisa five years ago. "I don't want the horses," said Hawn. "I want the woman."

The young man broke into talk and spoke a long while to the old man and stepped a pace backward and kept his black eyes on Hawn. The old man shook his head, answered the young man with one sentence, and said to Hawn: "Beat her if you want her to go home. I will not beat her if she wants to stay." He pointed to the tent.

Hawn walked the length of the camp, pushed aside the tent's flap and found Louisa crouched at the far side. Her arms were clasped around her body, her face was dirty and her hair ragged; she looked at the ground and wouldn't raise her eyes.

"We will go home now," said Hawn.

She said nothing; she sat stone-still with her downcast eyes. She was beyond the boundary, so far beyond it that he knew he would never reach her. Clothes and face and manner — she wasn't the Louisa he had known. He said: "The cabin is empty."

She had no answer. He settled before her and reached out to catch and lift her chin, compelling her glance. Her eyes were dead for him, her mouth tight against him; no stranger could have given him a look of greater emptiness. He drew his hand away.

"Louisa," he said, and made a gouging motion before his chest, "your fingers went in there. I have no heart. You took it. We will go home."

Had she been a white woman, he might have found words to persuade her; but she was the purest of Indian in her thinking, and he had no way of reaching her. In her eyes he had failed her, he had ceased to want her, he had ceased to be proud of her; and when she believed this to be so, she ceased to value him. Neither recognition nor feeling got through the walled expression and as he rose to lay a hand on her head he had a sudden feeling of sickness; for her hair was gritty with dirt and he realized that she, the neatest of women, had let it become so; in a way it was her act of mourning. He left the tent and walked through camp to the trail. The old man watched him go; the young man had disappeared.

Directly beyond camp the trail entered timber. Passing through the forming shadows he heard a small rustle of brush behind him and he turned to see the young man step from the brush, gun lifted and aimed dead on him. He took a sharp step aside but the gun's muzzle followed and he saw the muzzle jump upward at the same moment he felt the bullet strike and knock him down. He turned on the soft earth, blinded, and he groped for his gun and felt his hand lose its power. In the distance he heard a woman's scream. He ceased to care about the gun. He made one more turn, catching the soft rushing of feet toward him, and directly before he died he felt Louisa's hands on him and he heard Louisa crying.

47

IT seemed like spring, but this was now country of which the settlers had no certain knowledge. In doubtful mind they brought out their plows and made test furrows across their fields and crumbled the damp earth in their hands and watched the sky, and visited back and forth to swap their opinions. The winter wheat was new-green in the fields, but wheat was hardy. The spuds ought to go in, but they had too little potato seed to risk it rotting in a premature planting; as for garden stuff, one good frost could kill. Presently the more venturesome went at it, and soon everywhere in the settlement men were rolling the gloss-black coils back from their moldboards, and harrowing and dragging and casting seed, and many a woman, hungry for the relief from waiting, took up a shovel to break her own garden plot.

Katherine dug the great fat angleworms from her shovel chunks and marveled at them in her hand. It was wonderful soil. They had been warned about deer working at the gardens and when she had the first hardy stuff planted she slashed out alder saplings, trimmed them, dug holes around the garden, set them in and tramped them down; she interlaced the upright stakes with willow branches to make a woven fence. Harris Eby came up to do the roughest of the field plowing, but she and her brother Joe managed the rest of it. Burnett went down to give Watt Irish a hand; and he teamed with Lattimore to break Millard's ground, for Millard's stump was still too sensitive to bear the wooden contraption he had invented for it.

The clearing went on, the brush fires never ceased to burn. Fences began to march along from meadow to meadow. The grass lost its winter dullness, turning tender-green, and the cows picked up in their milk. Mrs. Provost took her basket abroad to the fields and harvested a mess of dandelion greens which, wilted down with a little vinegar and seasoned with a chunk of salt pork, accented her hunger for green things until she wanted to cry. One day Mrs. Gay brought in an onion from the winter planted sets; stripped of its old husk, it was perhaps an inch thick and three inches long, and she watched Gay eat it and relish it so greatly that she walked from the cabin and stayed away half an hour. Geese moved south in V-shaped clouds, the far sound of their voices waking people in the night. Ducks settled on the swales. Travelers began to come through, these being winter-bound emigrants looking for land, and though the hospitality of the settlers was very strong, the strain of extra meals on their meager supplies troubled them. Yet in every cabin the feeling of release grew and the sweat and mud and weariness of spring was good. The long trail across, the long winter — this was done; the crops were going in, the time to harvest lay directly ahead, barring catastrophe.

Buoyancy was everywhere. Men formed crews to do road work; a rough bridge was put across the ford; the grade through Billy Lord's notch was worked down and graveled; and during late April a leggy man with a full beard and a pair of driving gray eyes stopped in at Gay's to say he was a lawyer in a country that needed very little law and therefore he was disposed to teach an eight-week term of school by subscription, ten dollars the pupil. He had heard Gay was a forward-looking man.

His trousers were patched and his coat met him too soon at cuffs and shoulders; but this was the shabby uniform common to all men in Oregon. Gay judged he had a temper, for he was narrow between the eyes — and such a disposition, with wild boys in a classroom, would do better than Christian meekness. As for his teaching qualifications, they were better left unquestioned. It appeared he could speak the English language, write it and perhaps spell it; since he was a lawyer he no doubt could handle common figures. This was enough to start a school on.

"I'll pay ten dollars for my son," said Gay. "Now I'll tell you what to do. Go to Daniel Rinearson's. He's got no sons for school, but tell him I'd appreciate it if he throws in. If he does, it will convince some other neighbors. Then go to Provost. He's got four for school. You had better make him a wholesale rate. Next, try Buck; then Mercer, then McIver. When you get these, the rest will see it is a good thing and they will join. Then go to Burnett, up this creek four miles, and ask if he'll get a few men and put up a school cabin. It'll take a couple days. As for the location, it ought to go at the ford. That's central and it's where there'll be a little town one day. The school will sort of begin it. Tell Mrs. Irish I said she ought to give the land for the school. You can batch in the cabin when it's up. Meanwhile, make yourself at home here. Come back and tell me how you make out."

The lawyer — his name was, he said, Henry McGregor — slapped his knees, rose and went away. In one day of hard walking he secured ten subscribers and twenty-three pupils. Within four days Burnett and a crew had a log house forty feet long and fifteen wide erected; it was larger than necessary for a school but it would do for a meetinghouse also and for a church. Lattimore had no children for school and he had made no contribution, but his objection was violent. "It don't make no difference if it's free now. I see what's comin'. You'll get the damned thing up and next year you'll want to slap a tax on everybody to run it. It's just Gay's way of slidin' through the back door with this education business."

A week after the lawyer's first appearance in the community he faced his first day's class. They were of all ages from seven to Durbin Young's twenty-year-old son; four of the boys were somewhat taller and heavier than the lawyer; on these he kept his eyes as he talked.

"Your people have paid ten dollars a head to give you schooling. I shall see you get it." There was no furniture in the room save three long benches made of half logs planed flat enough to write on. The lawyer placed his pupils before these, and nailed two charts to the wall, one with the alphabet inked on it and the other containing the numerals and an example of each of the arithmetical processes. "Now, then," he said, "we'll learn the letters. Then we will learn words. When I point to a letter you will say it with me."

"I know the letters," said George McIver, "and I can spell."

"Do you?" said the lawyer, and let his eyes fall on Ryal McIver's big son. "It will be a treat to you, then, to sing out louder than the rest, so they can hear how it ought to be. Repeat after me, *A as in cat. Also as in mate. Also as in ball.*"

The class repeated but George McIver remained silent.

"I didn't hear you, young man," said the lawyer.

"I didn't talk," said George.

"Well," said the lawyer, "you are a strong-minded man, and so am I, and the room's not big enough for both of us. Do you back up or do I?"

"It's a foolish thing," said George. "I know all those letters."

"My boy," said the lawyer, "we are all free and equal in the courtroom and in the graveyard. But in this classroom I will say, and you will do. Do you think you can whip me?"

"Think I can," said George McIver.

"I wish," said the lawyer, "all knowledge could be imparted this rapidly. Come outside."

Lined against the cabin wall, the class had its first lesson. George was rough and willing, the lawyer was as cool as a man breaking a horse. He backed away while the young man did his wild swinging; when George grew eager and rushed in the lawyer struck him three times and knocked him down and seized him by leg and arm and threw him in the creek. George rose and started home.

"No," said the lawyer, "I have got ten dollars to teach you and I'll do it. Go back in the room."

He had been an unfriendly man in the beginning. With the class again lined before him, he was kinder. "There is but one way to learn anything and that is learn it. I don't hold with easy things. I hold with hard things. Cold water's better than hot. Meat feeds you but sugar won't, and misery's the greatest teacher. We are going to repeat these letters . . ." and he smashed his tough palms repeatedly together . . . "they wear holes in your head. Fifty years from now you'll remember 'em. I am going to teach you to know what you know. Repeat after me. *A as in cat. Also as in mate. Also as in ball.*"

They stood on their feet three hours, singsonging the phrases he threw at them. They twisted and grew tired and careless, and suffered from the need of going out; but he held them there. When he was through with his lessons he said: "Now I will give you a little taste of the world all this leads to," and he thrust his hands into his pockets and threw back his head and began on Shakespeare. His voice rolled and rose; he closed his eyes, his tongue formed each bump of each bumpy word. He clenched his hands and roared at them; he opened his eyes and grew sad and his voice ended on a whisper. His glance searched them a moment; he said in a dry voice, "Be here at nine tomorrow morning."

When Ryal McIver saw his son he said: "What happened?" George told him. Ryal said, "Well, by God, I think we got a good teacher," and laughed.

Burnett had thought of it and had mentioned it around; and one morning he came to the Gays' with his crew of ten neighbors and fell to trimming right-sized logs in the timber. Gay hadn't got out of bed since he had lain down to rest and it was the general belief now that he never would walk again; but the one room of the cabin was too small for day's work and an invalid too, so Burnett's idea was a dogtrot house, which was a second cabin built in line with the first, the two connected by a common roof. The covered-over space between — about twelve feet wide — could be used as summer kitchen. With a fireplace and furniture, the second cabin became a second room, this for Gay. By noon they had the logs raised, the pole rafters up and the fireplace framed in. Eby and Provost mudded the fireplace while the rest split shakes and laid on the roof.

During the afternoon, everybody being at work in the yard, Katherine stepped into the old cabin, moving quietly around her father whom she thought asleep. He had only been musing, with his eyes closed. "Where's your mother?"

"She and Gram went up to see Mrs. Collingwood."

He had aged so much that it was hard for her to bring back the image of what he had been. He had no energy and his face showed the shrinkage and the clawing of a pain which he could no longer hide. "Nice of those boys to put up that room but you know I'm not going to use it very long."

She laid her hand on his hand and said nothing.

He said, "I'm not certain your mother knows. She ought to see it, but she's a great woman for not seeing the things she don't want to see. Joe don't know — boys don't catch up with these things."

"They've said nothing."

"People don't talk about death much when it's close by. I'd like to see the first crop of wheat cut, but I don't believe I'll make it. This thing took hold slow but she's going faster now. I feel it breaking through. I'd like to see Joe a couple years older, I'd like to see you married. Naturally I have got regrets. But I want you to know I'm not afraid of it, and I don't seem to feel it oughtn't happen. If I was stronger I guess I'd fight more, but things seem to be getting a little farther away all the time. Three months ago I felt like I owned this place. More like a fellow on a visit now." She recognized a semblance of humor once so strong in him. "I've thought lately we're all just visitors."

"That's what Lot would say."

"I have never criticized Lot publicly. He means to do good and people have got to treat good ideas with respect. But I wish he wouldn't spread so damned much sulphur around the premises. I'm not much for this thunder and lightnin' business. Don't see this the vale of sin and sorrow he makes out either. Believe things work out pretty well here and will work out better as time goes on and we learn more."

"I've wanted to ask you," she said. "Would you like to have been something else?"

"I had some wild notions as a young man. That's a hard age. But there's only a few people who can ride the big white horse at the head of the parade. Not necessarily the best people or the smartest or the most honest, but people that saw the chance and had enough gall to take it. In the long run I don't think they're any happier than the rest of us. Little flies bite us. Big flies bite them."

He hadn't answered her question and she knew he wouldn't. He was silent, going as quietly through a spasm of misery as he could. She brought him a cup of water and held him up to drink it; she felt the unpadded bones through his skin. He lay back. "I want this claim kept for Joe. When you get married you'll move to your husband's place. I expect your mother and the old folks will stay here with Joe. But you'll help out. It will be all right. I'm not worried. Your mind's not made up yet?"

"No."

"Don't marry till you're clearly certain. I ought not say this, but for you to marry just for comfort or just to get rid of bein' single — that would be as bad as a downright bad marriage. I do wish one thing. Wish I'd stopped work more often to've played with you and Joe. We put these things off, and then it's late."

"I remember a lot of fun we had. Nobody could have had a nicer childhood than I had."

"Well," he said gently, "it was fun."

Martha came back with Gram to make supper and the crew finished the cabin and came in to visit with Gay for a short time and went away. Burnett stayed on to eat.

A little short of twilight Ralph Whitcomb, riding in from Oregon City, came upon Collingwood's and checked his horse to watch the yellow light of the open doorway. He hailed the house and when he stepped from the saddle Lucy was in the yard waiting, immediately saying, "George has gone — till tomorrow." She made a small motion toward him but he shook his head at her and stepped inside. He was embarrassed by his carefulness but when he put his arms around her the feeling went away and his kiss had a young man's force. The same accumulated desire was in her; they clung in this straining wish to break through each other until she tilted her head to laugh at him, to show him the brightness of her eyes. "It gets worse, doesn't it?"

"Toothache that won't stop."

"Tooth, toes, heart, all over, everywhere."

"I'll go on to Gay's and eat. Then I'll say I've got to make the rounds and I'll come back. Will that be all right?"

"Come as soon as you can. Don't get to talking and forget me."

"When I come back I'll leave my horse in the trees. It'll be about an hour."

"That's so long," she said.

"There's no reason to this thing."

"You want reason?"

"No. I want you. I've been thinking of a thousand things to say to you. I've been tortured. My bed's a damned cold thing. I go around with my head full of wool. I feel your hands on my back and I think, 'My God, how much time we're wasting.'"

His words moved through her with their incitement and her face took on a dreamy sensuousness, lips parted, eyes heavy. She whispered, "I'll take down my hair," and followed him to the doorway and watched him ride on.

He saw change in Gay and knew there was no hope. After supper he sent the women out of the cabin and made his examination. Burnett stood by the fireplace with his pipe, saying nothing.

The Old Man crept close to the bed, looking on with his distant curiosity. "What's the matter, John? You feelin' poor?"

"A little rheumatism," said Gay.

"Don't run in the family," said the Old Man. "You're bilious. I used to bet bilious. Give him something to purge his liver, Whitcomb. There was a root my old man used in Kentucky. Wish I knew what it was. Give him somethin' to clean him out. It's spring. Eat some new grass. Horses know that much." He stepped into the yard and went wandering on toward some chore half formed in his mind.

Gay said to Whitcomb: "Wasting your time. I don't feel much outside, but I sure feel a hell of a lot all the time inside. How long, you think?"

"I don't know. I told you that before."

"Leave some kind of medicine," said Gay. "It will make Martha feel better. And don't say anything about it to the family. You're staying here tonight?"

"I'll sleep in the shed. But I've got to go around the neighborhood first."

"Fix me a pipe, Rice. I don't taste it much, but I can smell it." He took it and dragged smoke deep into his lungs and relished the flavor. "Bad habit's always fine. Got your seed all in?"

"Except the late stuff," said Rice.

"She'll look good about July. Stuff will roll off the vines, we'll be hog-fat with plenty, we'll forget how hard the first year's been. In time we'll get tired of poor things and make better ones. Joe's going to see a better country than I saw, and his son will see it better than Joe. That's it — that's the whole story."

Whitcomb smiled and shook his head. "If we'd be content with that we could make ourselves a fine life, nobody poor and nobody rich. But we won't be content. The itch won't let us alone."

"If we didn't have the itch we'd be like the Molallies. It's a necessary thing. Your trouble is you look at people and see what they could be, and it makes you sad to see they're not wise enough to follow a straight road in the direction of the blessed life. We start for the top of the hill, then we get pulled off on some wild goose chase and we're back down at the foot of the hill. But I think we're farther up the hill now than we were couple hundred years ago. We do make some progress. It's slow, but we make some. We'll make more."

"Some mornings I believe that," said Whitcomb. "Some mornings I don't."

"You're an educated man," said Gay. "I'd gladly gone through life with one arm to know what you know, for learning puts a light on the world an ignorant man never sees."

"Don't make that mistake," said Whitcomb. "Learning starts with the man, not with the book."

"I only say one thing," reflected Gay. "Thinking just to be thinking can be a dangerous business. It can pull you back and forth till nothing's clear, and it can take the wallop out of your fists. We're made of rough stuff, for we've got rough work to do and if thinking makes us too tender to do it, then we're of no account." He handed the pipe back to Burnett with a look of distaste. "When tobacco don't taste good there's not much left."

"I'll see you later," said Whitcomb and left the room.

Katherine came in to stand by Burnett and Gay's eyes went to his daughter and admired her. He nodded to Burnett. "Like her grandmother. She's got a firm disposition, good sense and good health, and a lot of devilment."

"That's the way you used to sell horses in Missouri," said Katherine.

"I always told the truth."

"So far as you went," she said.

"You see the devilment?" Gay asked Burnett. Then he added, "Good thing to have," and seemed to lose interest as weariness overtook him, and presently Burnett left the room with Katherine and crossed to his horse.

"I'll walk to Collingwood's with you," she said. "I want to see Lucy."

He took her hand and, leading the horse, went on through the bland night; a warming soil threw its sweet odors around them and moonlight was mellow stain in the shadows. She was thoughtful. "He's never talked like that — like he wanted us to know him." Then, as she went on, he knew how much she had thought of her father's coming death and how directly she had met the fact. "We'll stay on the place. There's enough of us to do it. We'll not leave, we'll not give up what Dad started. Joe's old enough to work as a man, and there's hands enough to help him. In four years it will be his."

"You'll have all the help you ask for."

"The neighbors have their own troubles. But we'll stay. I hate change. I hate to be scattered around, a piece here, a piece there. I didn't want to leave the old home, but now we're here and I'll never move again. I want to belong somewhere, I want to keep around me all the things I live with, keep close to the people I know. I don't even like to see people move away, it takes something from me. I wish everybody who came here'd live the rest of their lives here, in this one settlement. I'm going to. Every day of my life I want to look out and see the same thing, same trees, same meadows and creek, same trail. People that move and change and throw away things — they get smaller and smaller. When I get old and my children grow up and go away, that'll be the cruelest thing that can happen to me. Maybe I ought to have been born a tree. They never move. When I step into a house I expect to stay there — and I'll want a big attic to put things in, because what means something to me one time, always means something to me."

He said nothing and in a moment she looked at him. "Are you listening?"

"Was thinking of all the places I've scattered myself around."

"Men have to roam awhile."

"I saw a lot of places and met a lot of people. An old Crow grandfather squatted on a hill watching the sky thinks the same things we think. A Crow mother blows on her baby's neck to make it laugh, same as you will. Was a time when I traveled with pretty hard men — the easy kind don't stand up well in the mountains — and I thought then you could boil everything down to a man's belly. Give him good food and give him a woman and he'd want nothing else. When I knew those fellows better I

335

found out they were all packing around appetites that buffalo meat or a woman's body wouldn't cut."

They came to the Collingwood meadow and walked over it. The door of the Collingwood cabin was closed but pencil streaks of light came through the log cracks. He said: "Poor job of mudding in." He thought he heard voices, softly pitched, in the place.

"Appetites . . ." she said. "Go on."

"When these fellows came into camp they were sour for being alone up some creek a long time. Soon as they got together, it was like a drink of whisky. I never knew but one man that ever pulled out from his partner when trouble came. Nobody had any use for that fellow afterward. I never knew a good man that wasn't respected. Made no difference how rough a crowd it was, those fellows knew quality when they saw it."

"But you left that life."

"Well," he said, "it ran out. It . . ." He shrugged his shoulders. "I don't know."

They were almost into the timber beyond Collingwood's when she stopped. "You don't know yourself."

He turned to her, still holding to the reins of the horse, and when he saw the tense and faintly stubborn set of her face, he knew she wanted to be kissed; she had made up her mind, she had dropped her guard. Last time she hadn't liked it, but Edna had been around that afternoon to disturb the air. Maybe she had even tasted Edna on him, for women had a keenness about things like that.

He let go the reins, drawn on by a signal from her as clear as anything Edna could have shown him. In his past affairs such a signal meant going straight through without limit, and as he watched Katherine he saw no difference. He wanted to see a difference, for she wasn't Edna, she was none of the other women he had known; she was many things in his mind, made up of her talk and her gestures and of his growing fancies concerning her. But there was no difference and then he became aware of how much all women were at the mercy of these old signals and words which were so brutally inexpressive. Thoroughly bad women and thoroughly good women used the same signs. There were no other signs — only these few which covered everything from the necessity of two illiterates clamped together and rolling in the dust of a dark country lane to the loveliest poetry love could stir. He couldn't know what wonderful images were in her as she waited for him. For that matter she had no way of seeing the truth in him; they had to stand here unexplained, frozen

336

into the tenseness of doe and buck suddenly come upon each other; it was as though nature, wanting only one thing out of humans, had made them mute to keep this act unchanged.

The whicker of a horse in the nearby timber checked him, and he swung with his instant suspicion and seized Katherine's arm and led her to the deeper shadows. He called, "Who's that?" The horse whickered again, directly before him; reaching out, he felt its reins tied to a fir, and he ran a hand over saddle and saddlebags.

"Don't pay your visit now."

"Who is it?"

"Ralph's in the cabin."

"Oh. Poor Lucy."

"I'll walk home with you."

"No, it's nothing I mind. I hope nobody comes by. Poor Lucy. Nothing for a husband and only half of Ralph."

"Half's half."

"You didn't mean that, did you?"

"Best they can do."

"Best a lot of people can do, but it's still poor shrift. It's twice the misery she had before. And no end to it. You want that to go on?"

"It'll go on till it runs out."

"I don't want it to go on," she said. "It will break her right down the middle of her body. She'll be nothing — not George's wife, not Ralph's, not anything. She'll get to hating herself and she'll get to hating Ralph."

"George, too."

"He's not worth hating. I've thought a lot about it. I've . . ." She turned back to him. "People have got to make do. They have got to decide. If I must take a man I don't love, I expect I'd take him, for a single woman's nothing, she's dead. She has got to send Ralph away, or she has got to go away with him."

"Looks to me Collingwood's not in love with her now."

"Oh," she said, "he's not to be respected." She hesitated a moment, and then he heard the decisive side come up, the lean and dark side. "If I were Lucy I'd leave Collingwood. I could endure not loving a husband, that's common, but I couldn't stand not being wanted. I have got to be wanted to be any good. . . ." Her manner lightened. "We talk about so many things!"

He thought, *I passed it by and she's laughing at me.* He was irritated by his slowness. When he drew her forward she swayed aside with a light gesture of protest, but he checked her. "No," he said, "I'm not Colling-wood."

She was laughing. "Hurt your pride?"

"Katherine."

"Like that name?"

"Fine name."

"Like the way you say it."

"Katherine."

She put her hands on his shoulders, and the smile settled and she dropped her head to rest it against his chest. He never knew where she was, never in the way he knew where Edna was.

"Katherine, lift up."

She pressed her back against his holding arms. He tightened them. "No," he said. She was motionless, waiting for him to be through, or listening to herself; then restlessness stirred her and came through her arms. She raised her head. "It's not fair," she murmured. She drew a breath, her face shadowed and moving reluctantly inward. "It's never fair." The weight of her hands increased on his shoulders and when she reached his mouth he felt a second reaction against him and a half-hearted impulse to turn away. He held on. She seemed heavy to him, wanting him and not wanting him, undecided, liking it but not liking it, afraid. But her lips stayed with him and the flimsy little strings that held him back began to break and the rest of it came on, the blind thing, the unkind thing, the thing that had no conscience; the growling, bitter, un-bearable thing that stiffened his legs and closed his arms around her and made him scheme to carry her beyond herself. She ceased to be heavy; she was a willow bending gracefully to him; she was a willow no more, she was angry with the same anger he had, she was motion in his arms, mouth feeding at him with strong appetite. She cried in her throat and flung her head aside. "Let me stop." She came back in violent aggressive-ness, fingers biting through his coat. She struck her head on his chin. "Make me stop."

He let go and watched her struggle with herself. She stared at him, she came nearer and ran her fingers across his forehead. "You're sweating."

"I'm crazy."

"I'm crazy." She took his hand and laid it against her chest. "Feel it beat. I'm shaking."

"I'll walk back with you."

"Oh, no — it wouldn't do — it would be — no." She lifted her hands

338

and pressed them against the sides of her face and drew a long sigh to control her breathing. She said, "You stopped. Put your arms behind you." She came in and gave him a kiss and moved quickly away. "You stopped."

"Sure you don't want me to walk back?"

"No. Go home now. I'll wait a minute. Get on your horse."

He climbed to the saddle and said, "Good night," and turned away. As he entered the trees he heard her call his name and he swung around. "No," she said, "keep going. Good night." He was well into the trees when she called again.

"Rice."

"Want something?"

"No. Good night."

"Good night," he said, and rode on. His sweat-damp body felt the chill of the colder air lying in the firs, but he felt fine; he sat straight on the saddle and caught every odor of this dark place and his spirit made spinning turns through him and waves of tenderness unsteadied him. Nothing was like this — not Edna, not any woman he remembered, was like this. Nothing was like this. The shock held on, memory bringing back smaller shocks, and the goodness of it went into the marrow of his bones. Nothing was like this.

When they were through, Lucy made coffee for Whitcomb and they sat at the table, very quiet, the hunger of love and the intemperate words of love exhausted. Her face was drowsy; memory quickened it and now and then humor lightened it and when she looked at him he saw the shared thing there. They were comfortable with each other; the strain was gone.

"I've got to make the rounds before I go back to Gay's," he said. "But I don't want to."

She smiled. "I did that to you."

He finished his coffee and rose to tie his stock and get into his coat. He stepped to the fireplace. "When will next time be?"

"I don't know."

"That's the bad part of this."

"Don't start regretting. It'll spoil this."

"Not regret. The more we have, the more we'll want."

"We went through that last time. There's nothing to be done about it." She tapped a spoon against her cup, keeping time to a tune in her head. The spoon stopped and her manner changed. Her voice was flat. "He'll be home tomorrow. He'll be polite to me, he'll ask me how I've been, he'll get out his list and add names and dream over them, he'll stand behind his queer screen and watch me from the corner of his eyes. But he'll want me and I'll have to do it. I can't bear the thought. I'm not his any more, I'm yours and it's a terrible thing to touch him."

He said, "In this territory it's the legislature that grants divorces."

"He's ambitious. He wouldn't let me have a divorce. It would lose votes for him. And what could I say? Do you think I could say we're no longer in love and I don't want to go on with it? Your legislature would tell me to go home and put up with something that a lot of other married people put up with."

"You've thought about it," he said.

"I've thought about everything I could think about. Nothing will work. We both knew that when we started."

He locked his fingers behind him and watched the fire. She was the direct one. Most women were; even in the height of ecstasy they could look forward to the consequences. But he had to admit that he too had looked forward. All day he had pondered Lot White's warning — that was the day he had operated on Millard — and he knew that if Lot saw something here so would other neighbors. He ought to tell her but he couldn't bring himself to it.

Her voice turned him about. "When you're solemn I know you're fighting something in your head. Don't."

"I knew how it would be," he said, "but not how strong it would get."

"We're very placid now. We're reasonable — and that's when it looks dark." She reached over and took his hand, whispering, "Wait another half-hour. We'll not be reasonable then. That's best."

"I have got to have you."

"You do, you know you do."

"Nothing certain, ducking around, waiting for somebody to get out of the road, making plans that fall through."

"Don't go over it again."

He turned behind her chair and laid his arms around her. She caught his hands, lowering her head to them. "You're harder to manage than I am. You're older — you ought to be wiser — you ought to be practical."

"I love you, that's the trouble. This thing will work on me till I'm apt to tell George he can move out and go to hell."

"Stop it, Ralph."

"All right," he said, and bent to kiss the top of her head. She drew his face down and whispered to him. "Let's start again."

"I've got to make the rounds."

She left the chair and went to the fireplace to set the coffeepot aside. His mood infected her and her temper was no more stable than his; she grew impatient with him. "It's so long between times that I'd think you'd think of some excuse to forget the neighbors."

"All right, I'll forget them."

"No, I guess it wouldn't do."

"Well, that's it. When will next time be? Can you get to Oregon City?"

"I don't know. Not soon."

"I'll come here in three weeks."

"Maybe he'll be away again — maybe he won't."

He was irritated by her sudden distance from him. She was unreasonable without warning. He moved to his greatcoat and got into it and stood hat in hand waiting for her to turn about from the fireplace; she kept him waiting, she was deliberately punishing him. He wanted to go over and kiss her but even that closeness had gone. He thought: *There'll never be anything settled between us.* He said: "I'll stop a moment on my way by in the morning."

"Sometimes I don't understand," she said. "One minute you can't wait, you've got to tell George and get him out of the way. The next minute you're careful about the neighbors, you're cold."

"We're both that way."

"We ought to know enough to be sensible. We're not young people."

"It's not a sensible thing," he said. He hadn't meant it to sound as it did; it came out wrong and hurt her.

"Maybe we'd better stop then," she said. She turned about. "I suppose that was in the back of our minds from the beginning, that it was really impossible. We were just pulled over our heads."

"Well," he said, "good night," and moved to the door.

"Aren't you going to answer me?"

"I can't argue you into something you don't want."

"You never argued me into it in the first place. I made up my own mind."

"Changed it now?"

"Well, haven't you changed yours?"

"No," he said.

She stared at him and obviously meant to hold herself against him, but

341

a swinging impulse weakened her and she crossed the room quickly and hooked her hands around his neck. "Ralph — how can it get this way — it mustn't — I know it's hard — but it mustn't! Stop being reasonable — stop it."

"The hell with the neighbors," he said. "Let's start again."

"All right. Now."

The fire was small, the room cold. "There's still time," she said, "to visit some of the people."

"It's all right. I don't care."

"No, we've got to be a little watchful. A little. I was thinking, suppose George came home early?"

"Might be a good way to settle it."

She rose. "You get out of here now." When he was ready to go she drew him to her. "Next time — next time — soon . . . I wish this had happened months ago, years ago. Oh, how much time we've wasted. Wish I could lock you in a closet and draw you out whenever I wanted you. Haven't some of your women patients ever tried to — "

"One did," he said, and kissed her and left the cabin.

Going back through the night to Gay's — he had decided against visiting any of the settlers — he realized neither of them had been very level-headed. It wouldn't get better; it would get worse. Hope would swing them up, but doubt would shake them to pieces. How many millions had gone through this misery of denied possession since the first man had described it in the Bible — he himself no doubt having suffered from it?

48

COLLINGWOOD returned from his trip the following day, saying very little to Lucy; he caught up with his chores around the place and that night plunged himself into his list of names. He appeared tired and he was brusquer than usual. She wondered if he had discovered anything about her through the neighbors and she pried at him with her indirect questioning.

"Where did you put up last night?"

"At Deans' — over by the Mission."

"Did you hear about Gay's new cabin?"

342

"No. What happened?"

Then, she thought, he hadn't stopped in at any of the neighbors and hadn't heard anything. "Oh," she said, "Rice Burnett got some men and put up another cabin so Gay would have a place by himself."

"I wish I'd been here to help," he said. "He feeling any better?"

"I don't think so. Whitcomb was here yesterday. He dropped in to see us a moment but he didn't say anything."

"Oh," he said and went on with his work at the lists. It didn't appear to stir anything in him but she wasn't entirely satisfied.

"How was your trip?"

"All right. There's a man over on the bottom who's announced himself for the legislature. I don't think he's known, and he's a sort of a damned fool to boot, but it will make me work harder."

That was it, she thought. "When is the election?"

"Two weeks."

"There's a good deal of work on this place you ought to do."

"After election I'll get some time. If I make it there'll be maybe a month at Oregon City, of course."

"That will leave me here alone."

"Come to Oregon City with me if you want." It was so casual an invitation that she knew he had thought about it and didn't really want her to be with him. He added, "I've got to make another trip up there and I thought to start tomorrow. You want to go?"

"No."

She picked up her sewing, thinking more and more of his frequent trips away. Politics accounted for them, yet she knew that he was quick to see a good-looking woman and that he was warm enough, when he chose to be, to attract some of them. He had tried Edna, he had tried others and had been successful more than once. He might have another woman now. She said: "Do you think you'll win?"

"Yes," he said.

"You're not ordinarily that confident."

"The men who could easily beat me," he said, "don't want the job. They think it a waste of time. They think men in politics are all crooked or fools and won't sully themselves with it." He leaned back from his work to display an interest in this subject; in his voice was the slight tone of cynicism. "If they get crooks or fools it is entirely their own fault."

"Don't you feel a little strange over what they might think of you for running?"

343

"I'm not so blind I can't see," he said. Then definitely she heard a note of bitterness. "But I'm not too proud to take the crumbs these gentlemen scorn. I know what they think of me." He looked at her with an uncharacteristic directness. "You had thought I didn't. They play a little game with me to my face. I play a little game with them. In the long run maybe my game's the better. We'll see."

"I didn't know you hated them," she said. "Is all this neighborliness you show just a play?"

"I like to be useful," he said, not quite answering her. "I like to be well thought of."

"You're after something else, not just this job."

He looked back to the pages of names before him and she saw him struggle with his secretive impulse. Presently he said, "Yes." She didn't press him. She returned to her work. He sat idle and afterwards he grew curious. "I expect you think this is all foolish, as the rest do."

"It's your judgment," she said. "But I'd like to see us make something out of this place, the way others are doing with theirs."

"Oh, I'll get to it."

"I don't know when."

The remark irritated him. "I'll do it. I'll do it as well as some of these damned fools going around laughing at me. Someday they'll know." He checked himself and turned to his names and said nothing more until they were in bed. "I don't know now why I came to this damned country. It's not my country, and it's not yours. I guess I wanted a new start, same as everybody else, but I'm not going to spend my life digging spuds out of the ground or following a pair of dumb cattle back and forth across the plowland. There's opportunity here, everything's just starting. When I get a foothold, when I get known all around the territory, we'll probably move to Oregon City. A little political influence opens a lot of business doors and I shall find where the money's to be had, and go into some sort of business while I'm playing politics." Once again the small boy's resentment would not stay down; it slipped through his careful cover. "I'll demonstrate something to these people, by God, I will."

She lay still, waiting for him to want her, bracing herself against it and dreading it; but he made no move to her and then she knew he had some other woman. She thought of it a long while, relieved and feeling freer yet lightly stung by the knowledge he didn't want her.

"We haven't got much of a life, have we?"

"No," he said. "Haven't had for a long time."

344

"What's to be done about that?"

His moment of directness was over. He hid himself with an evasive, "I'm pretty tired. Let's let it go till another time."

He was a failure to himself as well as to her, she thought, and when he stepped from his secrecy and had to make decisions which would oppose other men, his world would fall apart; he was like a man who, having rehearsed a dive from a high place a thousand times in his mind, walked to the actual cliff and could not force himself to jump. Now she believed she knew why he was so quiet; he knew it about himself.

He rose long before daylight, cooked his own breakfast and slipped away without disturbing her and at three o'clock that afternoon he entered Oregon City, put up the horse and set forth to begin his methodical business of entering the shops of this town. Some of the people he already knew and he took time only to say a few words by way of keeping himself in their minds. At other places he began by looking at things he indicated he might need; shortly he introduced himself, spoke of the settlement from which he had come and in turn asked a good many questions of the shopkeeper concerning business conditions, the future of the territory and politics generally. He had long before learned the art of making a man important to himself by gravely listening to the man's opinions, and toward the end of each visit he dropped an opinion or two of his own which subscribed to the man's opinions; and so he canvassed the town. He took pains to look up the territory's leading citizens. He talked to Abernethy and he was introduced to Peter Burnett when the latter came into the store; both men, being highly political, were interested in his description of conditions down his way — for they too knew the art of listening. This he understood, and played a sober and not too talkative part; and he left with the feeling that they would remember him and regard him as a valuable man to know from his community.

Short of suppertime he stepped into a little white building which served both as a dwelling and a store with a few shelves of bolt goods, ribbons, buttons and women's stuff. The bell tinkled when he went through the door and in a moment a woman came from the rear of the place; she was about thirty-five, slightly florid but still attractive, owning hazel eyes which looked upon him a moment and opened with a delayed warmth.

"You're in town again."

"Yes," he said. "Have you got some ribbon, just a small piece, about so wide?"

"What color?"

"Some kind of green."

She found two or three spools and laid them on the counter, watching him while he studied the ribbon. "Your wife would do better picking it."

"She's not here."

"You must do a lot of traveling."

"I suppose I get around the country as much as anybody. I'll take just a yard of that."

She cut it and rolled it and took his money; she stood back, in no apparent hurry to end the meeting. "Have you got a lot of business around so many places?"

"Yes," he said and looked down at his clothes. "Expect I ought to get back to the hotel and rub some of this mud from me. The trails are knee-deep."

"So's that street," she said, nodding beyond the door.

"You ought to get a man to fix your walk."

"Men are busy and I've none I can order around."

He loosened his manner toward her and set his eyes on her. She looked back with what he took to be a considerable interest, and for a time they were weighing each other, making their guesses. He judged she had experience enough not to be fooled if she didn't want to be and experience enough to bring him on if she chose. He thought he saw the signal. He turned his attention to a bolt of goods on the shelf and he reached forward to touch it and brushed her shoulder. "That's a nice thing."

Her smile remained steady. "It'd be too old for your wife."

"How could you tell?"

"You're a young man," she said.

"I'll feel old tonight," he said, "in a dismal room at Moss's place."

"I expect so," she said. She was listening to him, she was waiting; there was a wariness about her eyes.

He grew restless, color came to his face and he took a forward step and half raised his hand toward her; then the gust of daring blew itself out and he pulled his hand aside to touch the bolt again. Without warning she tipped her head and laughed at him and stepped back. "Is that all you want?" she asked, nodding to the ribbon in his hand. She was no longer waiting as she met his eyes and he thought he saw dislike in

346

them; she had been ready to play the game but now, for no reason he could understand, she was through with him.

"Yes," he said, and walked out, stung by her amusement, humiliated by the failure. He returned to his room, looked long at himself in the mirror. "God damn her," he thought, "what'd she see? What'd I do wrong?" It was the same as it had been with Edna; both women had searched him out and hadn't liked what they saw. He washed and went down for supper and at the common table he listened to the conversation until he had some notion of the men around him, and presently he caught the drift of their thoughts and joined the talk. For a short time he enjoyed himself, for he talked well before strangers and thought he sensed approval in them. The proprietor, Sydney Moss, he didn't like. Moss was a man with an agreeable manner which took men off guard, and a sharp tongue which upset them; and Moss had a set of eyes which seemed to regard nothing highly. When they touched him, Collingwood felt uncomfortable.

He left the hotel and walked to the street's end, and took a stand by the shore to watch the flooding river cast its waters over the ragged rock reef. The rumble of that thunder was a pulse in the night and a tremor under his feet; and a mist rose from the whirling basin at the foot of the falls, milk-sallow in the moonlight, and whirlpools rushed round and round and gave out the sound of a giant mouth sucking. The power of it impressed him; turning to look along the street, he drew himself square and he thought: "You people — you ignorant, greedy, heartless people — I'll make you know me. You'll eat it, you sons-of-bitches. Every one of you that's done it, I'll remember, and you'll eat it."

He walked back as far as the saloon where, at this hour, the men of the town had gathered. He was tired and he hated to rub shoulders with the crowd again, but he took hold of himself and stepped into the place. Halfway down the bar he discovered Ralph Whitcomb. Whitcomb motioned to the barkeep for an additional glass and poured him a drink. "What brings you here?"

"A little business. I'm glad to see you."

"Everything all right in the settlement?"

"Gay's a little worse."

"Nothing's to be done about that," said Whitcomb. He put both elbows on the bar and considered his glass. He had a sad face, Collingwood decided, a sad face at times marked by irony. But it was a square face with a vigor to it and Collingwood, who admired decisiveness above all other qualities in a man, envied the doctor. It was hard for him to find a common ground with Whitcomb; he never quite caught on with the man.

"Lucy's looking well," he said.

Whitcomb nodded and said, "That's fine," and continued to watch his glass. A question occurred to him. "How you making out on this campaign?"

"It'll be all right. The neighbors are with me. . . . I meant to ask a favor. When you go around the country you might mention my name — put in a word. I'd appreciate the effect."

"I'll do so if you want it, but I don't know why you want a time-wasting thing like that. What's it good for?"

"I think," said Collingwood quietly, "I might be useful. Coming down our way soon?"

"Week or two."

"Be sure to drop in and say hello. Lucy likes you."

Whitcomb pursed his lips; he raised a hand to pass it across his face and he turned to give Collingwood his attention. "Have another drink."

"No," said Collingwood, "I'm going to bed. I'll give Lucy your regards."

The doctor flushed. "All right," he said.

Collingwood returned to his room and stretched on the bed, physically weary, and he remembered the woman in the shop and he thought: "What in God's name was the matter?" He thought of his wife, of Whitcomb, of Moss's strange-regarding eyes, of all the careless laughter he had overheard men use on him, and he was weary of his riding and weary of himself; he said aloud, "What's it worth — what's the use of it?" He rose, looked long at himself in the mirror, undressed and went to bed.

He was in the saddle by daylight, bound back; he passed the mill at the end of town, following the road squeezed between bluff and water to its summit. He was then above the falls and he thought he heard a voice penetrate the roar of the tumbling waters; turning the horse about he rode to the rim and noticed a group of men huddled at the shore line with their interest riveted to something in the river. Out there, when he looked, he discovered a raft lodged at the brink of the falls, precariously lodged between two boulders and supporting a figure spread-eagled on it, arms gripping its either side, toes hooked over its end. Collingwood sent the horse down the road, swung beside the river and galloped toward the watchers.

The wish to help the helpless figure on the raft pushed them so close to the river that the lapping water touched their feet; they were a dozen men and a boy of fourteen whose shaken voice sailed repeatedly and vainly against the roar: "Gil—hang on! Hang on! Hang on!" The boy broke from the group, raced along the shore to a small log and shoved it into the stream. One of the men called after him.

"What you doin' that for, son?"

The boy came back. "I don't know." He gritted his teeth together. He was crying. "*Do* somethin'."

The man said: "We got to wait for the rope, boy." He looked to Colling-wood and dropped his voice. "His brother out there. They were playin' on that damned raft and it slid into the fast water."

"*Do* somethin'," cried the boy. "It's goin' to slide off those rocks!"

It was about a hundred feet from shore to the nearest rocks of the horseshoe reef stretching across the river. Water flowed smoothly forward to the reef, cramped itself between ragged boulders and broke into white froth as it reached the lip of the reef and flung itself into the basin forty feet below. Mist rose from the basin and settled as fine rain on the watching men. Through the mist Collingwood watched the raft lift and fall to the rough waters. It was at present lodged between the rocks, at the mercy of some extra push of the current which would work it free and send it and its passenger down the ladderlike falls to the whirlpools of the basin. Each surge of the raft shifted the boy on the loose logs; he righted himself; his cry now and then came through the thunder of the water as the thin piping of a sea gull.

"Men," said Collingwood, "we have got to do something."

They took their eyes from the river to look solemnly at him, and returned their attention to the river.

"By God, we have got to think of something," he said. "We just can't stand here and watch him drown." He scanned the shore and saw nothing but a sharp point which obscured the beach beyond. He had no idea in his head; it was only a wish to look well before these men which made him break into a trot and run around the point, there to discover a boat drawn on the gravel. Still with no idea, he dragged the boat to the water and towed it back. He anchored its bow on the gravel and looked steadily toward the boy on the raft. The crowd shifted toward him. A man said:

"What you thinkin' — to take that thing out there? It won't do. You can't row against the current."

A file of men appeared from the town and ran forward. The boy broke from the crowd about the boat and raced toward them and came back with a coil of rope. Men seized the rope and paid it out along the beach; the new arrivals straggled in with other sections of rope.

"Ain't long enough."

"Tie three–four coils together."

"That's no use — you can't throw a hundred feet of rope."

"What the hell we get it for then?"

"Somebody said to."

Men tied the rope sections together and one man slowly rolled the joined pieces into a loose coil. Collingwood, standing by the boat, watched another man take one end of the rope and fasten it to a chunk of driftwood; then the man handling the coil slowly swung the driftwood around his head until it gained momentum, cast it out upon the water and let the current uncoil the rope in his hand. The driftwood bobbed along the current toward the falls.

"What for?" asked Collingwood.

"Maybe the current will set it over to the boy, and he can grab the rope and we'll pull him in."

"It won't set over," said Collingwood, pointing. The driftwood was far short of raft and boy, sliding toward a side eddy of the falls; the man operating the rope hauled it in and the group made a semicircle by the river and stared in silence across the water.

Collingwood reached for the rope's end and tied it to the bow of the boat. "This current can be rowed against till you're close to the rocks. We can set the boat right on the mark, drift it down to the raft. Boy makes a jump for the boat — and you fellows on shore haul in."

Collingwood's glance went around the group and found each set of eyes falling from him. "It'll work," he said. He had no answer from them. He looked over the river, watching the violent play of the raft against the rocks. Now the avoiding eyes returned to him, for he felt the surreptitious interest play against him; but as soon as he brought his attention back to the group the eyes fell again. He said: "Haul in when I grab the boy." He gave the boat a shove from the gravel, jumped in and fitted the oars into their rowlocks. The current grabbed the boat and swung it downstream, but he pulled the nose about and rowed upstream and outward until he was in line with the raft; then he let the boat drift toward the raft.

The rope, stretching from boat to shore, began to catch the hard push of the current, dragging the boat's nose downstream. Collingwood rowed against it with full strength and signaled ashore and saw men tying other sections of rope on to give him the slack he needed; but each added yard of rope thrown into the water gave the current more surface to push on, and as Collingwood approached the broken waters at the reef he could no longer handle the boat. The raft was twenty yards ahead of him, vague in the mist-clouds rolling densely over the falls; the sound of the falls shook him, the suddenly accelerated current seized the boat and flung it forward. He dropped the oars and knelt in the boat, watching the turning white face of the boy on the raft. He cried, "Jump," but he knew it was a hopeless thing, for the boat slid off and the gap grew greater and then he looked to the men ashore and waved both hands in signal to haul back. There was no answering pull. The boat leaped upward as the broken waters tossed it toward the rocks. Crying again — scarcely hearing himself above the roar — he saw the crowd rush along the edge of the water. They had lost the rope, he realized, and he fell face forward on the boat's bottom and gripped the cleats with his hands. The boat struck a rock and tipped, and water filled it, and he was carried upward and he went falling, strangling, dying, downward across the rocky ledges of the falls into the whirlpool.

From the shore, men saw him tossed clear of the boat as it sailed outward beyond the reef and disappeared and they saw the raft, struck one time too many by the current, rise vertical and hurl its clinging passenger free. Collingwood and boy and boat and raft vanished in the crying mists below the reef.

The boy ashore turned and ran away from the river, crying, "Mother — mother — mother!" Somebody said: "Who was the man?"

There was a pause until another man recollected him. "Collingwood, I heard him say in Abernethy's last night. From somewhere in the valley."

"Damned brave man."

49

WINTER was for Lockyear a cage against whose bars he flung himself with increased resentment. There was no patience in him to endure himself at idle times, no ability to stand the tedious hours. He was a man with no cushion between thought and action; as soon as his mind conceived, his muscles stiffened to execute; and so he was constantly jarred by the convulsive motions of his temper, flung back and forth between short spells of brooding and violent activity. It was as though he had been born with unformed cells where the reflective part of his mind should have been and could not receive the gentling lessons of experience; he was a stallion, knowing only his own existence, dumb to half the pain he suffered in his search to eject himself into the receiving mare.

At intervals he ranged the trails for no other purpose than to release the energies he could no longer contain, but otherwise the dripping wall of woods held him to the cabin. He had no friends, he was increasingly unwelcome to the settlers, there were no diversions during the short gray days and the long nights; once during February he scouted the land along the Willamette for a hundred miles; and in March he visited Oregon City. He had nothing to keep his hands busy, for he had no ambitions, no farm to make, no buildings to set up. On several occasions he returned to Rinearson's valley and hung back in the trees, watching for Edna, but he got no sight of her; and these times he returned home in a more explosive mood. He ate, he stood at the door, he lay on the bunk to watch the ceiling, his temper creating its threat. Veen and Roxy never ceased to watch him, to be cautious around him; he was an unpredictable animal they were forced to live with. When he was within the cabin there were fewer than a dozen words said during a day's time; when he was gone Veen and Roxy relaxed, but even then they were careful, for he had the stealth of a cat in his walking, and often appeared with no warning.

Toward the end of April, returning from one more futile prowl around Rinearson's, he stopped at the top of a ridge to catch a long view of the settlement along the creek — the cabins lying in their cleared places, the groves of timber between, the fences squaring plowed fields turned green with new crops, the spiraled smoke rising from chimneys, the occasional moving figure in one yard or another, the traveler creeping along the trail. He watched the scene for perhaps half an hour, missing none of its detail, hands folded across the saddle horn, shoulders stooped; when he was done with his gazing, and had been further incited by his thoughts — for he realized he looked upon a scene in which he could never have a part — he moved on.

He reached the cabin at suppertime, ate, and made up a hook and a line to whip the creek in the twilight, catching nothing. He squatted against the cabin's wall with his pipe, watching Roxy go to the creek for water but not thinking about her and ignoring her when she passed him. He had Edna in his head. The outsideness of his place among these people, the hours of nothing around the cabin, the walking for no reason, the appetite which stung like ginger through his body — these drove him at her. She was all he saw; there was nothing else to see. The thought formed and locked him into his decision; and then he was a man who had to act. He got his gun from the cabin, oiled it and re-charged it; he polished the butt with his palm and set the gun away. He went to the creek, flattened to drink and rose and stood beside it, listening to some far-off sound. Behind him, Veen dropped an armload of wood beside the fireplace, that crash roving through evening's stillness. He circled the yard at a long, loose walk, traveling faster with each circle; now he was driven by the idea and he went into the cabin and sat on his bunk, shoulders bent, hands over his knees, and stared at the fire. Roxy was in her corner, in the shadows; he knew she watched him though she seemed to see nothing. Veen, on the floor with his back propped against the wall, watched him with the same indirection. He couldn't catch the glance of either when suddenly he looked at them. It pleased him. They were always afraid of him; they were more afraid tonight.

"You foolin' with each other when I'm away?"

Veen said: "Stay around and find out."

"I don't care. Go ahead. You doin' it?"

"If you don't care — don't ask."

Lockyear stared at the girl. "Ugliest woman I ever saw, but she'll do for a cripple like you. She ain't had much. She's hot. Do it at night when you don't have to look at her face."

They said nothing. He rose and stood nearer the fire; he turned and went slowly toward her and then her eyes lifted and she drew herself back to the wall, shoulders flat against it. Veen said, "Leave her alone." Lockyear moved in. He raised his arm and let it settle on her shoulder and felt the shrinking of her body. He closed his fingers into her skin, not hard. "Let her alone," repeated Veen.

"You been doin' it?" asked Lockyear.

Her face was solemn, afraid, homelier than before. Having met his glance she wouldn't take her eyes away; he tried to stare her down but couldn't. "What's the matter?" he said. "I'm a snake that's got you hypnotized? Tell me what I asked. You doin' it?" He slid his arm downward, fixed his hand around one breast. Her breathing quickened and he caught the rapid strokes of her heart; she was afraid of him but afraid to move when he touched her. Suddenly he dug into her breast with his fingers and twisted. She screamed.

Veen cried, "You son-of-a-bitch," and he seized a chunk of firewood and flung it into Lockyear's back. He was on his feet with another stick when Cal swung and rushed him. He drove the chunk into Cal's chest, wrenched it back to strike again, and had it knocked from his hands. The older Lockyear hit his brother flat on the mouth, caught him and closed his two hands around Veen's throat — tips of his fingers behind Veen's neck, thumbs hooked across Veen's windpipe; he pressed Veen against the wall and squeezed until he shut off the smaller one's wind.

"God-damned good time to kill you," he said.

Veen punched his doubled knee into his brother's belly and drove the bigger man away; he leaped forward — a broken noise in his throat, a crazy cast to his face — and jabbed his extended thumbs forward, missing Cal's eyes but ripping the skin beneath; he ducked Cal's arms, rammed his head into Cal's chest and got his arms locked about his brother and pushed him against the bunk. Cal tripped and fell on it, and used his hands to fend away Veen's blind swings; then suddenly he gave out a yell of rage, caught Veen around the body and flung him to the floor; and as Veen started to rise Cal kicked him back and whirled to catch up a chunk of wood. "I'm goin' to batter your brains — this time I'll do it." He turned with the stick and flung it, missing. Veen wrenched himself upright, snatched Cal's gun from its rack by the fire and pointed it at his brother.

"Put that down," said Lockyear.

"Stay there," said Veen between broken gusts of wind.

"No — put it down," said Cal, and stepped forward.

"I've made up my mind," said Veen. "Don't do it."

Lockyear shouted at him. "Don't tell me what to do!"

"Come on," said Veen. "Come right on into it. I'll put the lead low — right through your gut, right through your liver. You'll scream for an hour. Come right on."

Lockyear stood still.

Veen nodded to Roxy. "Pick up your things and walk home. You ain't goin' to stay here any more. We've had enough."

Roxy came out of her corner, ducked under the gun and went to the door. She turned back, speaking to Veen. "You better kill him — you better, or he'll do it to you. Go ahead, kill him. Go ahead. Do it now."

"Go home," said Veen. "Go on quick."

354

She disappeared, her feet striking soft in the yard. The sound died and Veen's coarse breath ceased to rasp the room. He shook his head, splashing blood on the floor. "I ought to do it," he said.

"About the girl . . ." said Cal. "That's all right. I'm sick of her. She can go."

"Don't go after her."

"I would if I wanted, but I don't want to. Put the gun down. Better with us when there's no bitch around here. You been usin' her."

"Shut up," said Veen.

"She was a good thing for you. You ain't had much of that stuff. Only woman you'd ever get to look at you. Women don't want cripples."

"Shut up."

"Put the gun down. The hell with it."

Veen laid the gun against the wall and stood by it while he watched his brother. Cal shrugged his shoulders and sat on the bunk. He reached for his pipe and ignored his brother. "We'll quit this fighting."

"All right," said Veen and turned to the back door. From the side of his eyes, Cal watched him drop his guard; then sprang unexpectedly over the small space, seized Veen, swung him, hurled him to the floor. He fell on his brother, sinking his knee into Veen's stomach. He caught Veen's shoulders and lifted and lowered them and pounded the little man's head against the floor until the latter's body went loose. Afterwards he rose and took his gun and settled on the bunk to wait. Presently Veen groaned and rolled his head back and forth and reached out aimlessly with his arms.

"You hear me?" asked Cal.

Veen sat up.

"That's to teach you something," said Cal. "Don't ever lay a hand on me again. Next time I'll kill you. I don't care about the girl. Don't want her around any more. You think I don't know you been foolin' me? Hell, ten times a day. You been draggin' yourself around half-dead. She's sucked the sap right out of you. By God, she wants you to kill me. She's got you where you'd do it, too. I don't want her here any more."

Veen sat stooped. Blood ran steadily from his nose and he swayed side to side to soothe the pain in his stomach. He said, "I'll leave."

"Try it," said Cal, "and I'll tie you down and smash the bones in your other foot. Then you won't walk at all."

50

ALL through April Burnett worked on the road; each morning, stoked with food, he crossed the meadow, followed the road he had chopped out and came before the barrier of trees yet to be cut; at noon, hollow with hunger, he ate again and returned to the barrier; at twilight, weariness greater than hunger, he turned home. In the morning he had so much energy to spend; at night he had spent it. He hacked and twisted and cleared and burned his way through the forest five feet, ten feet, a day. He left two months of his life in that timber; during the first week of May he dropped the last tree at the margin of Lattimore's clearing and he looked back to see the two months of his life as an aisle between the firs. From Lattimore's meadow he could see his own cabin half a mile away. He touched the stumps along the way when he returned home; this was half a day of his life, this cut stump; this was half a day, this corduroy stretch over the swampy spot. Later, from his own yard he watched Lattimore's lamplight dance through the corridor.

The road was two months of his life; the cabin, fences, shed, millrace, lumber pile — those were four months of his life. Six months of his life lay around him; he saw it and touched it; he had frozen it in this one place so that it would not slide down the tunnel of the past. It was a good thing to look on his life; when he was an old man he could say this was what he had been and this was what he had done. Beyond his time, after he was dead, it would burn or rot or the creeping brush would erase his work and erase the memory of him; but that was beyond his time. It occurred to him that Katherine had this in mind when she had said she never wanted to move, never wanted to throw away anything she had liked or which had been part of her life; she wanted all the pieces accumulated around her in one place.

It had been his habit, after work and supper, to saddle the horse and go down to Gay's; this night in the odored spring darkness he traveled the trail again, past the Lattimores', Irishs' — dropping a bucket of milk there — past the dark shell of the schoolhouse, past Provost's, Collingwood's. The familiar shadows and sounds and shapes closed about him as the warm blankets of a bed into which he had beaten out comfortable indentations for his particular bones; and in such a mood he had great regret for his traveling years. They were gone; the man back there was a shadowy man.

Gay and Katherine and Mrs. Gay were in the new cabin. Martha said: "You see Joe anywhere on the trail? Always running with the Provost boys, or the Dunmores. You'd think a long day's work would make him tired. This country's making him wild."

Gay said: "If he ain't wild now he'll be flatter than old beer later."

"I don't doubt that Sophy Cartwell's running with them, too."

"Joe had any fights with the boys lately?"

"He'd not tell me. Why?"

"I recall the first Sophy Cartwell I knew," said Gay.

"What's that got to do with fighting?"

There was no power left on Gay's face for smiling; his amusement was back in his eyes, made vague by clouds of pain rising from his flesh. Observing it, Martha said: "I know what's in the boy, well as you."

"Then let it be."

"I won't have Sophy Cartwell trapping her way into this family. Joe's too young for it and if I'm going to have a grandchild I'd like to be sure whose it is."

Gay said, "Mill finished?"

"Another month," said Burnett. "The road's just slashed."

"If I had it to do over," said Gay, "I'd not've worked so hard. Back home, every time I picked a peach from the orchard I thought, 'It ought to be a juicy peach, there's a gallon of my sweat in it.' I got awful serious awful fast. All the people I liked did the same. I make out now it wasn't intended so."

Burnett thought: *He's Hawn's dying trapper, seeing too late what it ought to have been. He's the old man in St. Louis regretting the things he didn't do. Right road, left road — which was the best road now there's no more roads?*

"Go hunting," said Gay. "Go fight somebody."

"That reminds me," said Burnett. "I had no luck arguing the crowd out of fighting the Molalas. You could have stopped them."

"I'd not've tried," said Gay. "There's time when men are not to be argued with. You didn't go with the bunch. I'd've gone and tried to catch 'em when they were in a more reasonable mind. You got to put up with a lot to gain a little — and it's better to gain a little than gain nothing. The only gains we make are little ones."

His words came shallow from the top of his mouth.

357

"That's enough talk," said Martha and sent Katherine and Burnett from the house.

The last of washday's fire glowed red in the yard. Gram drifted gray and half seen in the shadows beyond it; from the big wagon rose the Old Man's steady snoring. Katherine said: "You see the change in him? It won't be long."

They walked toward the trail from it across the meadow by the creek. Day's warmth rose from the plowed ground, and odor rose with it — musky, stale-rotted, effervescent-fresh, yeast muck stinking, pale green tendrils breathing. The creek broke white across its stones, this whiteness penciling the shadows, and moonlight shaped the alders crooked against the water. The creek flowed; and coolness was a stream flowing above the creek, the edges of coolness lapping them as the creek lapped the shore.

"He was talking to me — telling me something," said Burnett.

"The old always try to tell us something. But it's hard to know what they're saying. It's all mixed up in them. They know — they don't know. They're trying to leave something behind that's wise, but they're not sure, no more than we are. . . . He wanted to be a musician."

"Suppose he had been. What would he be saying now?"

"The same thing. It makes no difference." She settled at the creek, her hand bringing him down. She tipped her shoulder against him for support.

"Good man — good man."

"He's been lying in bed all these weeks, trying to think what his life's been. We'll do it, too." A cloud moved beneath the moon to darken the night; in the deep hills the coyotes were crying. "That's lonesome," she said. "Good lonesome. Like bones picked clean, like rock or fire. It's not mixed up with anything else. Do your feet still hurt?"

"When the weather's cold."

"They'll trouble you a long time."

He waited for her head to turn, he bent inward. Her mouth was quiet, almost giving, not quite giving, and as soon as he pressed forward she drew back and her laughing whisper brushed the darkness. "Oh, no." She rose and drew him with her. "Cold here." They crossed the field and came to the trail, and turned into it, and back again toward Collingwood's. The moving cloud gave motion to the earth around them — the meadow creeping beneath their feet, the fence lines crawling forward, the hills bending. Pale wool fluffs of light lay banked against the dripping soot of the fir shadows, the coyotes were calling, the small wind thickened with the scent of fir resin. They passed into the vault-black timber and the motion of the earth ceased.

"That a bear I hear?"

"Tree groaning in the wind," he said. "Big tree, deep groan." He took her hand; her fingers closed solid around his palm. He was restless, neither pleased with the kiss he had given her nor happy with her answer; they weren't as close now as they had been before. She had moved away from him and he didn't understand her and wasn't easy in her presence. Collingwood's cabin light wavered through the trees and in a moment they came to the meadow and halted there.

He said: "Whitcomb been back here since George was drowned?"

"Yes."

"They're free."

"We'll see."

"I don't make that out. It's what they've been after."

"Funny things," she said. "Funny things." She turned around. "Can't work all day, walk all night. I have got to send you home."

He took her hand but now it was light in his palm, no pressure there; it waited to drop away. She walked beside him, slightly ahead, and he quickened his pace to keep up with her, but she was still ahead of him and he got the notion she was smiling to herself.

"What funny things?"

"Don't you know? When's the mill to be done?"

"In time for the wheat — barely. Late July."

"Then the waiting's over. Then we're settled. It will never be the same again."

"Nothing's over," he said.

"What's not over?"

"Nothing's over."

Gay's clearing was a streak through the trees and the cabin lights made yellow patches against the dark. "Yes it is," she said. "Things don't wait."

"What's not waiting?" She was only a step before him but the illusion of a greater and greater distance between them got strong and he pulled her to a stop. "What's not waiting?" She was stiff, waiting to be released; she was on guard and her mouth was cool. He tried to break through the coolness, and felt a small agitation within her, a willingness and a coming back to him, but suddenly she whirled and seized his arm and moved rapidly on, out of the trees and across the Gay meadow to the fire.

She touched the coals with her foot, rousing a shower of white sparks. "It's late." She looked at him keenly and he saw the roundness of her eyes and the almost blackness of them. Laughter was on her mouth and he felt helpless before her confidence. He said, "Good night," and rode away.

She crouched at the fire, took a stick, and poked at the coals. Her mother called from the cabin, "Now don't spook there all night, we've got a lot to do tomorrow," and she answered, "All right," and watched the coals. She heard Gram's light feet whispering over the yard and felt the old woman's eyes peering at her. Sensation ran through her body, and collected and made its heavy places; she jammed the stick into the coals, broke it, flung it away and looked over to Gram. The old woman looked at her and nodded and seemed pleased.

"No," said Katherine.

Gram moved her shoulders indifferently.

"It's Edna," said the girl.

Old Gram shook her head. "Then why's he come here?"

"Because he can't go to her."

"No," said Gram. "I've seen it too long not to see what I see. He'll be back."

"It's hard," said Katherine. "It's like being squeezed in a vise."

Gram settled to the ground, nodded and drew a palm idly over the ground, gathering dirt; she turned her hand to rub the dirt around her palm. She said, "That's good stuff. We're made of it." She rose and walked toward the wagon. From the house Martha called, "Katherine — come to bed," in an aggrieved voice. Katherine hovered over the fire, watching purple color flutter through the sullen coals. She laid her hands on the dirt, pressed them down, drew them up, laced them over her knees. She watched the fire.

51

EACH finished chore bred other chores. The road was done but at some slack time it needed widening, grading, and graveling in the wet spots. These he added to the list of work for fall and winter work and as the list lengthened he saw that the second year would be no easier than the first. Throughout the settlement other men would be discovering the same thing; there was no free land, no painless plenty. The first people in a new country were the ones who best knew the cost of every usable thing. Having so much to do and only his hours and his energy to do it with, Burnett found himself calculating each piece of labor with a kind of miserliness he had not possessed before; he had to balance one necessity against another and to ignore that which was less important. Even a lost bucket became a serious thing, for it took all of a day's work to make a new bucket. More and more he became the conservative, weighing his wish to do things against his ability to do them, and in this way he came to understand the skepticism of the older ones when faced with something new, and their preference for the things which existed as against the things which might be; they remembered the hardness of creating what they had and were repelled by the thought of carelessly throwing it aside.

He turned to the mill wheel, lining the shaft from the creek to the site of the millhouse, and building on paddles and sideboards and braces; he opened the head gate and watched the wheel turn to the water, and discovered that it revolved at uneven speed, and he spent three days changing paddles and adding counterbalance strips. He laid the bed for his lower millstone, framed-in the millhouse, built bearings for the shaft which held the stones. With the help of Billy Lord and Lattimore and the schoolmaster he set the stones one over the other. He built a loading platform and a chute to feed the wheat between the stones, and troughs to catch the flour as it trickled from the furrows of the nether stone. These things done, he opened the head gate and put his mill in motion and made a trial run with half a sack of wheat. Now he found that his stones did not evenly grind and he used up the better part of four days re-aligning the shaft.

He worked against time as June came on; he worked from the beginning of light until light faded, and did his chores by lantern light, and cooked a quick meal, and fell asleep as soon as he struck the bed. He grew stale, his cooking no longer pleased him. He shot a stringy deer and found no flavor in the meat; it supplied him with strength but dissatisfied his taste, and he had spells of thinking of jams and relishes and sweet and sour flavors until sensation tortured him. One day Billy Lord came by to say he was bound for Oregon City and did Rice want anything done there? Burnett got two dollars from his money belt. "Bring me a gallon of the rawest, meanest whisky you can find." He was as sour as he had ever been, he was work-bound, his temper was short. It was the same with the rest of the settlement. Twelve months had passed from the time they had left the Missouri, and harvest was nearing; the long wait was almost over but not quite, and the last of the waiting squeezed them hard. Though it was coming on summer, the slash fires never ceased to burn as the land clearing went on and roads were extended from claim to claim. Somewhere, at any hour of the lengthening days, the ringing sound of an ax could be heard, or the "swash, swash" of a cross-cut saw, or a man's voice cursing his oxen forward. Winter long there had been no release for these people and with them, as with Burnett, was the growing knowledge that what had been begun would not be finished for years. They were accustomed to monotony but they were also accustomed to some kind of explosion which would temporarily break the monotony and as June moved on the tension increased. Everybody felt it. When he dropped down to Gay's at night — and during the building of the mill he went only twice — he found the same tightening of manner; he sat a little while with Gay; he stood in the yard with Katherine, the talk between them of no consequence and hard to make; he came home in a more ragged humor than before, and sat in his doorway to wrestle with a puzzle that grew worse; and went to bed.

Millard, sitting in the sun, watched his wife come out of the hillside brush. She carried a bunch of small yellow flowers already wilting from the heat of her hand; her face was scratched, her hair snagged by branches, and there was a familiar sign around her mouth. It meant trouble.

He said: "Where the hell you go on these mountain expeditions? It's the third time this week."

"Flowers," she said.

"I can pick the same things at the creek, twenty feet from here. You been gone two hours."

"There's a berry the Indians eat. I was looking for them."

"Little bit early."

"Well, it's good to get out of the cabin and stretch my legs."

He said nothing and she threw a sidewise glance at him and went into the house. Presently she came to the doorway. "I meant nothing by that, Millard. It just came out careless."

"No use being mealy-mouthed about a leg I've not got," he said. "I ain't got it. That's the situation."

She said: "I'll be out in a minute. I'll milk."

"I'll milk," he said.

"I'm not trying to beseem you," she said. "I don't mind doing it."

"Done it so long's we've been married," he said, "and I'll continue to do it."

"Millard," she said, unable to quite restrain her militancy, "now you know what it's like to have other people do what you'd rather do yourself in your own way. Every woman born's in that position. Men doing this — men doing that. Always men. Woman does something. Man tears it down and does it over his way. How do you think we feel — made helpless when we don't want to be? At least you've got one leg. For all a woman's permitted to do she might as well have no legs. It ought to make you more considerate."

"Ain't I been?"

"Oh, you're better than most. But you're a man still."

"Intend to continue to be," he said. "When you want a castrated animal, let me know and I'll see can I find one."

"Not like you talk that way," she retorted; but she held her tongue and returned to the cabin. He did the chores and came in with a weariness he tried to conceal, saying nothing through the meal, and soon going to bed. She was restless, making two steps of one; she gave out small exasperated sounds, she walked to the yard and came back and still could not settle in peace.

"What's bothering you now?" he asked.

"Can't I walk around without being bothered?"

"Not that way."

"What way?"

"Like every time you set your foot down you were grinding a man under it."

"Since you been sick," she said irritably, "you say things you never used to say — make it harder for me to bear, make me put up with it. You know I can't fight you like I did and feel nice about it. You oughtn't do it."

"All right," he said. But her restlessness continued and he knew something brewed in her mind.

Burnett hadn't known Edna was in the clearing until her voice reached for him on the roof of the millhouse. "Come down," she said. She stood by the cabin corner, the close smile waiting for him. He dropped to the ground, noting that her shoes were muddy.

"I came through the trees," she said. "I didn't want everybody to see me." She moved into the cabin and waited for him and observed that he gave her body a moment's attention.

"Yes," she said.

"When?"

"Oh, September I guess." Her smile thickened. "No, not Oregon City. That was too long ago."

"Here?"

She laughed and let him stand with his thoughts, until he said, "Well, is it mine?"

"You wish it was?"

"No."

"I do," she said. She had expected him to come directly to her, but he stood away and her smile wavered and then he knew she was troubled, for her manner was unsure and she walked to him and got her arms around him and laid her head on his shoulders. "You smell like cedar," she said. She raised herself and kissed him with a flare-up of her old willingness, and tipped her head to watch the effect on him. "You still like that? Or do you get it better somewhere else?"

"I like it," he said.

"You don't say it right," she said. "Remember the first time?"

"I remember."

"You don't say it right. You make it sound like it's a long time ago. Ever wish things — this thing, that thing — were different?"

"Sure. A lot of things."

"So do I. It hurts to know they can't be. Ever wish we'd not met?"

He was silent, not for the sake of pleasing her or for fear of hurting her, but because he had to think about it. "It was a good thing," he said.

"It was better than good," she said, breathing it in his ear. "It was the best. But I wish we'd not met. I think of you too much. Don't you think of me?"

"You know damned well what the answer is."

"Ah," she said, and was pleased. "Always think of me."

"Too much," he said.

"Never too much. Just lie in bed and think of me."

"I have got to get rid of that," he said, "when I get married."

She shrugged her shoulders. "There's always room for thoughts like that. What difference does it make, being married?" Then she was silent, and he caught the displeasure within her. "When?"

"I don't know," he said, "I was just saying it."

"Oh, I know, Katherine. She had her way — she beat me. Right from the beginning she made herself look like something she wasn't. You looked for it in me. But it wasn't anything at all. She beat me. That's when it started."

"What started, Edna?"

She rested against him. "I wish it'd been different. Wish I hadn't met you. Wish you'd had me more when I wanted you to. Then you'd known me better and there'd not been all this. I wish I hadn't married Moss, I wish I'd waited. I wish I'd known more — I could have beaten her. Then nothing would have happened that oughtn't to. We were all right. It was a lot more than you thought. Lot more than I thought. Because if it hadn't been you, you wouldn't think of me now and I wouldn't mind about you. God, why can't people know more, when they ought to know it — not when everything's too late?"

She was unhappy in a way he had not felt in her; not sullen, not offended at a little thing, but bone-deep unhappy. Her voice thick with it, her body heavy with it. He put his arms around her and at that motion she lifted her head and laid her broad mouth on him, arms pulling, body pushing, hard with him, indiscriminate and unreserved. The warmth soaked through him but he held still. She drew away, again giving him her close look of curiosity, and stepped over to the door. "Why has it always got to be too late to know things? One thing I didn't know. If I had, it'd been different."

"What?"

She kept her back to him several moments. "Don't forget, you started this." When she turned she had recovered herself, the assurance and the teasing expression returned. "Ah, why talk about it? You look thin. I wish I could have come when you got back from the accident. She was here but she didn't do what I'd have done. Did she?"

He was embarrassed and she noticed it, her laughter growing. "That's what I wish — that I'd known more about you." She pursed her lips at him for a kiss and left the cabin. But afterwards, back on the roof, it was the heaviness inside her he remembered. He straddled the ridgepole and forgot to work while he thought about it.

He was at the same work — laying shakes on the mill roof — when Mrs. Millard hailed him next morning. "I have brought you a pan of biscuits. Come down from there and thank me for them."

This was her way, friendliness laced with vinegar; a pan of biscuits and a challenge. She liked him, he thought, but she'd never give him the advantage of being certain of her liking; and when she was roused to the general injustice of men toward women she could despise him as readily as she liked him. She was in good spirits at the present moment. He followed her into the cabin.

"It don't look like the usual rat's nest a bachelor keeps for himself," she said. "You must have had a good mother to teach you what was clean and what was nice. That's where it starts." She gave the room a thorough going-over with her eyes. She looked at the dishes on the shelf; she ran her fingers across them. She shrugged her shoulders at his manner of making a bed, snatched off the blankets and rearranged them. "But you're not near as good a housekeeper as you like to think."

"Didn't think so anyway," he said.

"Man always thinks he can do anything better than a woman. This is a nice floor. I don't know another cabin with one as good. Why don't you scrub it more, before it gets so grimed in it'll never look clean?"

"Short of time."

"Certainly you're short of time. This isn't what you ought to be doing. You've got work enough outside to keep two men busy. You know that, don't you?"

He lighted his pipe and smiled at her obvious hunt for things to disapprove of. She was a good woman, she was a salt-of-the-earth woman; she was, for a man to live with, an unbearable woman. She said: "You know it's silly."

"What's silly?"

"Innocent — don't look at me innocent. Woman can hide things, but I never knew a man clever at it. You know what I mean. It's silly. You trying to be wife and husband. It's silly. I'd think you'd be a little ashamed."

He went to the shelf and got a bowl and filled it with the gray-brown flour milled by his own stones. "First batch," he said. "See if it makes bread. No, I'm not ashamed. Tell you what I am. I'm sick of my own company and my own cooking — and the bed's cold."

"There you are," she said, and said it in a reflective way, speaking to herself as well as to him. "Comfort, cooking, scrubbing your floor, washing your clothes. That's what it means to a man."

"Ever think it might mean more than that to a man?"

"When he's courting her he thinks it does. What a cloud of things he gets lost in! Makes them up and floats around like a fool. In a year that's

366

gone. Well, don't you make up those clouds about any woman. Then you'll not fool yourself or fool her silly brain either."

"Never heard you run a woman down."

"I don't know that I've got any more patience for a woman than for a man," she said.

"It doesn't leave you much, does it?"

She looked back at him from the doorway, half amused, half ready to argue. She was a sharp woman, nobody's fool. "You don't like me much," she said.

"Was I in a fight," he said, "I'd feel better having you on my side than on the other."

"I know. That's what they think about me. I can't help it."

"Wonder how it got that way with you," he said.

She turned her back to him, watching the meadow and the hill beyond. "Same way some people have got weak eyes, long legs. Born so."

"Born half so," he amended.

She turned again and was curt with him. "Don't you go prying. It's none of your business." She resumed her scanning of the meadow. "Pretty here, though I think I'd rather have the cabin turned about to see the creek. Wouldn't be so lonesome for a woman. Creek moves and makes noise. You ought to be married. You really ought."

"Now whose business have we got into?"

"That's different," she said. "What are those berries the Indians like?"

"Huckleberries."

"I've been walking the hills looking for them. You know there's a trail on the ridge across the creek? It comes from Lockyear's way and goes down to Rinearson's."

"Had no time to look yonder."

"He passed me by yesterday but he didn't see me in the brush." Now her voice was angry in a new way; this was controlled and single-minded. Her voice was quiet. "He was walking in a hurry, his face was all animal, all stirred up." She let go with a rough breath. "That terrible man — that beast. I hope someday to hear him being killed. I hope it happens." She was still for a considerable interval. "There's nothing his hand touches don't get hurt. Nothing. It's the third time I saw him. Last time I was clean over on the edge of Rinearson's valley. You know where he's going, Rice?"

"No," he said. He knocked his pipe ashes into the fireplace and filled it again.

"It's been going on a long time — all spring, I know," she said. Then she said, "I know it because I've seen it."

"Those biscuits look nice," he said.

"Don't be a fool. Never mind if her mouth is hot enough to burn a hole in your face. She'll burn holes in other faces, too."

"I thank you for the advice," he said.

"No you don't. You hate me for it, but I'll give you some more. Then tell me to go home. Some men get sorry for what they've done to a girl. Girls know it — they use it. Well now, if the girl did it, she wanted to, didn't she? What's there to be sorry for?"

"All right, Nancy. Go home now."

She turned and considered him and she shook her head; she crossed the room to lay a hand on his shoulder. "They're devils, Rice. They're all devils, and you better be a devil to handle 'em." An expression of compassion came upon her. She bent forward, kissed him and almost ran from the cabin.

He walked to the yard and caught himself a drink from the bucket and watched her hurry over the meadow. He took up his hatchet, laid a bundle of shakes over one shoulder and climbed the ladder to the roof; he anchored the shakes into the roof sheeting and sat back to stare at the ridge across the creek. *Lockyear. Lockyear and Edna. For Christ's sake, why? Any man, any other man, but what did she want with him?*

That was why she had come here yesterday, straight off the ridge from a meeting with him, clothes soiled, shoes muddy, with unhappiness thick enough within her to be cut by a knife. He laid a shake and nailed it in; and rested again. He thought, "Nancy Millard never saw that, she's guessing," but he couldn't make it stick, for he knew Edna, he knew the necessity of those big hips. Moss couldn't drain her; she would exhaust him, dry him to powder and blow him away. And she had come here stained and unhappy. He brought Lockyear before him, face and voice and brutal energy, and he caught the edge, the faint edge, of the truth. The power was there. Lockyear was a match for her. She was unhappy, for no man had penetrated her self-sufficiency. She had never been thrown beyond herself, never had lost command. His own experience told him so; from Oregon City onward she was lodged in him, and after marriage she had returned to keep herself there. But Lockyear shook her and made her dependent; for she was unhappy. She might hate the man, but he had her and she'd go back.

He had believed that somewhere within Edna was an untouched part

368

and this was the mystery which had held him on. Now he couldn't believe it, not after Lockyear. It was no mystery, it was big hips churning because they had to churn. She knew that about herself, and laughed at him because he didn't know it.

He laid down a shake and drove the nail home. There was no mystery. Then he recalled her phrase, "I'm sorry I met you, because that's when it started," and he realized she had come back to tell him it was he who had set her hips into motion. Maybe she wasn't honest about that, but the words stuck in him. His hammer came down, drove a nail deep into the shake and split the shake.

52

BEYOND noon, bound out from Oregon City on his rounds, Whitcomb paused at the Lords' and found both people lazing in the back yard. Lord had built an outdoor bed between two fir trees, a stout contraption of poles, laced rawhide and thick comforters, and sheltered by a canvas canopy which was rigged in such a manner that when he hauled on a rope hanging near his pillow the whole thing shifted to meet the weather. Man and wife lay side by side on the bed, mountainous in shape, faces smooth and childlike. Lord made great work of rising. "God-damn' weather takes it right out of me. . . . Stay to eat?"

He wanted, Whitcomb explained, only a drink of water and then he had to cover the settlement and start back by early morning. A pair of red hens picked around the yard. Dirty dishes still stood on an outdoor table, and through the cabin's doorway he caught brief sight of an untidy room. Winter rain and spring sun had weathered the newness from the cabin logs; a hard scrabble garden slanted along the sunny slope of the hill and a makeshift lean-to, scarcely tight enough to afford animals shelter, stood at the edge of the trees — four convenient firs making its corner posts. He saw no fences about the place. For this easygoing couple, the little they had was enough; there was no acquisitiveness, no push, no worry in them. Judged by the settlement's standards, they were lazy and improvident people and when they got old the community would have them to worry about; yet to Whitcomb this knoll standing above the settlement was a peaceful island. He stepped down to the spring house and had his drink and for a moment admired the view below him. Mrs. Irish's

369

green meadow, the straight garden rows back of her cabin, the glint of the creek running its curved course, the islands of timber along the narrow valley, the clearings lying between. The wheat was high and turning amber in every field; cattle browsed the pastures, the small shapes of people moved with a distance-exaggerated slowness. Everywhere he saw the scars of slashing, the yellow streaks of road grading and the blue curl of brush fires. It was a fine settlement, sheltered in this pocket far from the rumors of trouble.

He found Mrs. Irish and the schoolmaster and young Watt at table, and he could not refuse a dinner ready before him, and ate and paid for the meal by such idle gossip as he had at hand. He had not met the schoolmaster before and found the man a little hard to know, somehow awkward and ill at ease, a suggestion of the domineering mixed with a suggestion of the diffident. The gray eyes were cold and set close, the mouth was fleshy, the face generally intelligent. At the first opportunity Whitcomb left them, turning toward Gay's, and as soon as he passed into the trees he began to look forward for first sight of Lucy's cabin. He was eager to see her again; eager but strongly apprehensive.

"There's a good man," said Mrs. Irish. "An awfully good man."

"Don't expect he makes much of a living," said the schoolmaster. "People have to be pretty sick to call a doctor, and can't pay when they do."

"I'd not guess he cares much."

"Be remarkable if he don't. We're all out here to root-hog or die. Were I in his shoes I'd certainly see to it I got paid in some form — money, wheat, shoes, calico or something."

"He's an awfully good man," said Mrs. Irish again.

"People always like a man that's kind, comes at beck and call, and asks nothing. But they don't love him so much when he presents the bill." He looked at her, he looked at Watt sitting silent over the table. "I imagine I take the hard side of things. I got larruped when I was young and I got no favors when I was grown. Principles get beat in pretty deep that way." He studied Watt a moment and he tried a lighter manner. "That's the way I teach, as Watt knows well."

From time to time Mrs. Irish had cast quick side surveys at her incommunicative son; and now she said, "I wish you'd go up the meadow and fix that fence the ox broke through."

"All right," said Watt and rose and left the room.

"He's always quiet in front of people he don't know well," said Mrs. Irish.

The schoolmaster shook his head. "The boy's jealous."

"Jealous?" Mrs. Irish gave out an uncertain laugh, looked at him and let her glance remain with its smiling. "I never heard of such a thing. A boy of fourteen."

"Man of fourteen," said the schoolmaster. "A hard-worked man who's been head of the family and don't take kindly to another man. And I don't look anything like his father looked."

"But, *jealous*," said Mrs. Irish. "What on earth could he be jealous of?"

The schoolmaster rose, his shrunken coat sleeves crawling back from lank wrists. He shrugged his shoulders and pulled the sleeves toward his wrists and stepped to the door. "I have got half a day's road work to do for Rinearson. He a reliable man — pays his bills?"

"Well able to," said Mrs. Irish.

"I'd not want to waste half a day's work otherwise," said he. "There's too much waste behind me as is."

"I'd never judge you to be a waster."

"It's not that," said the schoolmaster, and took a stand at the doorway, looking into the meadow. He put his hands behind him, laced his fingers together. "I'm one of those men that seldom catch a tide on the full swing. Usually when I jump in to swim, the current's changing and I have to work harder than should be. It took me six years to study law — a twelve-hour job on the side, and my father's debts to pay. I set out to practice in hard times, was forced to turn to farm labor. I come here and the country's full of lawyers with no clients. I don't cry over the matter. It's the way my life works, and I recognize it and expect it to be the same way all through. I only say I was cut out to do two day's work for one day's reward and therefore I have got to rise earlier than most and go to bed later than most." With scarcely a change of tone or a pause, he added, "Had you thought of me as a man you might marry?"

She said, "Why, I hadn't thought of it, I mean I'd maybe wondered — " She stopped herself. She said, "Turn around, Mr. McGregor."

He turned to meet a grave woman. "Yes, I'd thought of it," she said.

He said, "Don't smoke, don't drink. I'm on the tight side. I'm never idle if I can help it. The young ones in school are afraid of me but that's as it should be. I don't make friends easily and people don't make me out for quite a spell. I guess that's because I've had no time to waste, and spending time to talk comes hard. I appear to be a positive man. I guess I am. I appear cold." He let that much stand and after a short interval he put in a short defense of himself. "There is, however, another side to me, and if we got on I'd expect to show it to you."

"Well," she said, "I don't know. I'd not know what to say about myself."

"I don't expect it. You've had hard times. I admire the way you go about it."

She said, "You know I'd have to talk to Watt."

He nodded.

"It's not that I don't know my own mind, but — "

"He's your son, he's fourteen, and he don't like me. Naturally you've got to talk to him."

"Oh, he just don't know you yet. But he's not had much of a life. We've been poor, he's worked harder than he ought, and he ain't had the fun any boy ought. It's too late now. He's not going to get it, because he's too old. Sometimes when he's not around to hear I cry about that. I don't want him to be so grave and I don't want him going through life with his head down, thinking of the next chore to do, not looking up, not smiling, not friendly. If it were only me, I'd give you a quick word on it, for I'm mighty tired of being alone. But it's not only me. I can't do anything to make it worse for him than it's been. I can't do it."

"Go talk to him," he said.

"I'll try to make him see."

He looked long at her and nodded. "I know," he said. "I know it all."

She moved to the door, watching him cross the bridge and move along the road at his ground-chopping stride; and after she cleared the table and stacked the dishes she stepped into the yard and circled the cabin to observe Watt at the far end of the meadow. She made a false start toward him, halted herself and presently, with an air of uncertainty, she crossed the meadow. He had seen her coming but he worked at the dislodged fence rails and paid no attention; his manner was strange, as though he knew what was in her head and she thought: *Maybe he does, he's old enough.* She said: "The beast gets its head through and shoves up. That rail will have to be tied to the post."

Watt said: "Then he'll try another section. I have got to nail a top on these posts."

"That's work."

"Be the end of chasing the critter every day."

He was on his knees and reared back to look toward the road; his eyes sought and settled on the dwindling shape of the schoolmaster. "Where's he going?"

"Rinearson's — road work."

He returned to his job and she stood idle behind him, only half inclined to speak. *Why ought I be afraid of my own son? It's me — it's not him. It's me.* She grew still. She braced herself to speak. He looked back at her with his dry face, with the strained old gravity which hurt her so much to see.

"How long's he going to eat with us?"

"Till school's out, Watt. He's paying. It helps us."

He turned again to his work and his back was hostile. "It don't help much."

"Everything helps."

"It don't help much."

"You don't like him. Why don't you like him?"

Then she saw that he only pretended to work; his hands moved around the fence rail but did nothing. His voice was sullen. Below the sullenness was an uncertainty she hadn't heard from him for a long while; he was a little boy at the moment and he was afraid. "You going to let him marry you?"

She summoned up her courage, she thought of what she wanted to say, she watched his small back stiffen as it waited. "No," she said. "No, there's nothing to that" — and turned back over the field.

Lucy was in the garden hoeing, and she smiled at Whitcomb and turned again to her work. He stepped from the saddle, and spent a moment untying the knotted reins to let them hang on the ground; it was a way of wasting time to cover an awkward moment. Then she straightened and set the hoe aside and came forward, moving a hand around her hair. She said, "The weeds get ahead of me." He tried to catch and hold her glance but it touched him and moved on to the horse. "Is that a new saddle?"

"Yes."

"Have you eaten?"

"Mrs. Irish had it on the table when I got there."

"You'll be seeing Gay?"

"I'll see him, and make the rounds."

She brushed her skirt, she kept her hands busy. "It's warm." Her eyes lifted to him, dropped to her hands. "Well, come in for a moment and rest." He followed her through the door, still awkward and a small amount of anger still rankling him. *I've to break this quick,* he thought, *or it'll get so hard it can't be broken.* He caught her arm and turned her to him and kissed her. She brought up her hands to his shoulders lightly and her mouth was still; he felt indecision in her, as though she debated being generous with him; then it seemed to pass and she waited for him to be through. He knew what it was and he knew nothing could remove it but a passionate outburst on his part. He had to wash it away with words and impetuousness, thereby convincing her that he thought as much of her now as before. As a married woman she had not regretted her generosity to him. But this was different; she was free, she wanted him to look at her as the woman he loved and wished to have, not as a mistress; and she regretted their meetings, fearing that he put less value on her because of them. Since Collingwood's death he had known this would come. The naturalness between them was gone and he could only bring it back by losing his head all over again. Much as he loved her he found it a hard part to play. Outside the conventions they had been themselves; now the conventions required them to ignore what had been so real and to go through the proper moves of a game as though their previous closeness had not existed. He knew what he had to do, but couldn't bring himself to it, and she sensed the delay in him as he had sensed it in her. She turned away from him and moved around the room, making talk.

"He's not the man you saw two weeks ago. I think the family would rather see him die soon than go on suffering."

"Dying has got its own ritual. Nothing to be done about it." How silly this was, they so far apart when they had been so close. It was their minds which made strangers out of them. Reason — reason — it killed. He grew more embarrassed; he had become a small boy, all hands and feet and self-conscious misery. He said, "I'll go on. Tonight . . . Would tonight be all right?" He heard the soft, cautious words and despised himself for them. The gentility of the gentleman. That's not what she waited for. She wanted him to come storming in, half out of his head, and smash her with his insistence. Not these modulated words. *Straight-out . . . Why can't I be straight-out with it?*

She moved her hands, she shrugged her shoulders. "Would it be right?"

"That's what I asked you."

"You're older than I am. You ought to know what's best."

"Since when did we get so concerned about what's best, what's right?"

Her glance raised quickly. Now it was intent. She was waiting, she was hopeful. "I suppose people have to think of those things. Don't they?"

"Why? We didn't before."

"Well, Ralph —" She dismissed it with a gesture. "Oh, come if you wish."

"It will probably be after supper, probably dark." He saw the shadow instantly cross her face and he said quickly, "Or would you rather have it be before dark?"

Her whole body emitted its impatience. "Come when you want."

He nodded, left the cabin and rode on toward Gay's, growing angry at her inconsistency, and his own poor showing. *In a thing like that they all want a club. Why do I make so many mistakes with her?* The first forthright impulse of the day came to him and almost turned him back to knock the nonsense aside, but the self-critical part of him viewed the showing he would play in such a stormy role and the impulse shriveled. *We're in love. There ought not be any excuses or regrets.* But he shook his head at his own ignorance. *You don't know a damned thing about a woman. She wants it proper now. She wants it all tidied up.*

Gay's voice was a whisper in his chest. Whitcomb had to bend toward the bed to hear it. Gay's face was yellow tissue, ill-fitted to its bony frame — cracked, hollowed and overlapped. His eyes had the dulled light of water seen at the bottom of a well. He had been a clean-shaven man; now he was bearded a rusty gray and white; and with beard and withered body and eyes whose vision was set on something beyond Whitcomb, he was not only one man dying, he was to Whitcomb the picture of every man dying. The doctor listened to the slow heart strike and marveled at its endurance. It was a pity that men like Gay, constructed for use and durability, could not make an easy surrender to the inevitable as weaker men did. People paid for being strong. They paid as much as weak people paid for being weak.

Lot White was with the family. Whitcomb sat by the bed a decent while to give out such news as he had and in return received the local gossip, with Gay watching the group around him but not seeming to hear. When Whitcomb left the cabin he was followed by Lot White and Katherine.

Katherine said: "How long?"

"I don't know. When he makes up his mind to quit it will come quite soon."

Lot White jerked one hand knifewise toward the sky. "He has got his cross. He is acarryin' it like a Christian."

Katherine looked into the meadow. She had, Whitcomb thought, the composure of her grandmother — its outward bareness and its inner resiliency. She was not quite Lot White's kind of Christian, hoarding up this life's misery as a bank account for future glory, but she made no comment. Little pleasantries and little solaces didn't impress her.

"You'll stay here tonight?" she said to Whitcomb.

"I'll make the rounds and be back. Anybody in particular I ought to see?"

"Durbin Young's wife."

"I will ride that direction with you," said Lot and crossed the yard for his horse. Katherine laid a hand on Whitcomb as he turned. "Wait." Her glance possessed more than ordinary directness. "You'll see Lucy?"

"I've seen her."

She studied him and tried to make something of the remark and decided it meant nothing. "You'll see her again?"

"Yes."

"She's lonely," said Katherine. It was a bare thing to say, but Whitcomb realized she meant more and he had the notion that he saw the whole community looking at him through her eyes. He flushed. Katherine knew the whole story, everybody knew it — there was no secrecy possible. They had watched the affair. All those eyes — curious, sympathetic, profane, hungry, amused, wise — all those eyes had viewed it. It gave him the feeling that Lucy and he had played out their affair in the center of a meadow with an audience rimmed around it. He was offended and yet could not be, for the curious sensation of a silent good-wishing came from them to him — as though, disapproving, they withheld comment out of their common knowledge of human nature. His thoughts and his hunger and his rebellion — and Lucy's — they knew about those things because they knew themselves; their silence was a kindness flowing around him to tell him they knew about those things. But now they would have their way; through Katherine's eyes they judged him, they spoke to him. They would have their way.

"Be back at suppertime," he said and got on his horse and crossed the creek with Lot and took the trail toward Rinearson's valley.

53

DAYLONG sunlight played upon an earth still softened by spring rain, and warmth and moisture unlocked the peculiar fragrance of fertility, one odor upon another, and quickened the tempo of growth. Rose sunset, violet evenfall and gray dusk took the day by soft degrees into night; and the breath of the earth, dry-sweet and spice-strong, came around Burnett with its vagrant turbulence. The earth was a woman who, long loved and stroked, grew tense toward the moment of explosion.

Burnett stood in the yard a moment; then afterthought took him back to the cabin and he came out with his jug of whisky and rode toward the ford. The Lattimores had already gone down, the Provost cabin was dark; across the creek he heard the Millards talking with one another as they moved to the trail. Farther away, toward Durbin Young's, a deep-chested call rang through the hill notches. There was motion and the sense of motion all around him; everybody in the settlement seemed to be drifting toward the Irish ford. The meadows sent their mild heat against him; the groves, when he passed through, were like pools of cold water; but the sun had worked loose the resin fragrance of the trees and it lay here so strong that it was pitch in his mouth. From a distance he saw the bright triangle of a fire in the schoolhouse yard, and voices began to reach out, sharp notes and deep notes running together in such a way as to remind him of the babble of geese passing high overhead.

At the ford he found half the settlement already gathered. He tied his horse to Mrs. Irish's fence and tucked his jug in the meadow's high grass and went on to the fire.

"Rice," said Old Daniel.

"Daniel. How's your wheat?"

"Fine as frog's hair — twice as pretty." Old Daniel gripped the air before him with his fists. "We got it made, we'll eat." Fire's flame turned his bargainer's face crimson and slick; his eyes roved the circle, saw the women in their own group beyond the men, and settled there with the old stag's interest revived. Ared stood beside him, a plain dull copy of his father, and Moss was beside him.

"Moss — Ared," said Burnett.

Moss nodded; his glance touched Burnett and went away; he had not been a friendly man since the day of his marriage. Harris Eby pushed through the circle, his presence reducing the size of every other man.

"Harris."

"Damned beautiful night."

"It's what they said Oregon was when we were listening to the stories back East. Remember?"

"Remember well. They said nothing about the rain."

"Maybe they said it but we thought it couldn't be more than ordinary rain."

"That was a year ago. Long time ago."

"This time last year we were on the Platte."

"Recall the first Indians we saw? My God, how scared we were."

"Long time ago."

"It was the gorge that like to broke me. Never want to do that again. Never want to be that cold or tired."

Whitcomb came into the circle. "Gentlemen."

"Ralph."

Lights burned in the schoolhouse. In there a fiddle made preliminary scratches.

"Billy get his fiddle back?"

"Borrowed it."

"On the Platte I could have killed him for that damned scrapin'. Later I got to listenin' for it."

"Long time ago."

Rice caught Eby's attention and he gave Whitcomb the same signal. He drifted from the circle, stepped through the darkness to the fence line, and got his jug from the grass and watched the two figures waver across the beam of firelight as they moved forward. "A little cheer," he said and passed Eby the jug.

"Where'd you get this stuff?"

"Lightning struck the cabin, ran down the log, filled the jug."

Harris took his drink, lowered the jug. His breathing stopped. He struck a foot hard against the ground, let out a spongy gust of air and passed the jug to Whitcomb.

"That is correct," he said. Whitcomb drank. Rice drank, and laid the jug in the grass. He counted the fence posts. "Two feet to the left of the eleventh post. Remember that."

"Just say it's behind the post you've got your horse tied to," said Whitcomb.

"Horse might shy and take the post with him."

"Then," said Whitcomb, "you'll want a celestial reckoning. Take that star over that tall fir. Line it up. She's dead on the jug."

"Suppose the star falls," said Eby.

"In that case," said Burnett, "we'll get right down and roll for the jug." He brought it back from the grass, passed it around for a second drink, and hid it again.

"I feel like a good fight," said Eby.

"Who you want to fight?"

"That's the hell of it. I'm too big to fight anybody. Never been able to fight anybody. You boys don't know what that means. I have got to be good-natured. I got to be careful who I step on, like a Percheron."

"I'd think it'd save you a lot of trouble," said Whitcomb, "never have to wonder whether or not you can whip anybody."

"I do, though. I look at some little bastard and I say to myself, 'Wonder if I could lick him? Wonder if he's got more brass than I've got?' But I can't fight him and find out. I'm too big. It's a hell of a thing. And the little bastard looks at me and jabs me with the edge of his eyes and hates me because I'm big, sort of darin' me to fight — when he knows damn well I can't risk breakin' him apart. It's a hell of a thing."

Children whirled through the shadows with their mysterious games, crying, skulking, rushing down the road, vanishing. More settlers came in. The crowd grew larger around the fire and Lot White's voice boomed across the meadow, across the creek, and broke into fragments of echo against the hill trees. "Hallelujah!"

"Everybody packs something like that around," said Whitcomb. "Everybody's got some sort of private business to wrestle with." He laid an arm on the big man's shoulder and laughed. "To be or not to be — that is the question with all of us. Run, sheep, run. Or, don't run, sheep, don't run. Or, why don't I run, sheep — I want to run but if I do, maybe I shouldn't, but if I don't I'll regret not running, so why don't I run, sheep?"

Eby said to Burnett, "He's had his drink." The three strolled back to the fire.

Old Daniel called from the schoolhouse, "Who's for dancin' — here's the music, here's the women — you come here for politics or for fun?" The younger men began to stir, to drift away from the fire, and the younger women moved upon the schoolhouse, their laughter like splin-

379

ters of silver shining in the dark. Edna's voice lifted and Moss drew himself together with an uneasy motion and looked toward her. She was in the shadows, George Provost and Laughlin Mercer standing by her; she was a magnet swinging them from their straight course to the schoolhouse. Burnett watched her shape sway, he listened to her easy voice trade talk with the two men; the tone was idle and amused, but there was something else in it, as there always had been when she spoke to men. He watched Moss grow solemn and fretful and presently move over to catch Edna's arm and go on to the schoolhouse with her. He thought: *You're not big enough for that, little boy.* He felt sorry for Moss. A small streak of jealousy stirred, a sentimental regret of things past, a wonder for what might have been. It was a twinge, it was the last flare of a nerve dying. As much as he knew about her, she still had the power to hurt him.

Millard swung forward on his homemade crutches. "Ed."

"Old three-legs."

"Rice."

The fiddle briskly began a jigging tune. Old Daniel's voice lifted. "Choose your partners!" Rice crossed the yard and stepped inside and searched for Katherine and found her on the floor with Harris Eby. He saw Lucy Collingwood looking on from a corner. Whitcomb came in. "Over there," said Burnett.

"You, too," murmured the doctor.

"God damn it, man, don't tell me I wasted whisky on you."

Whitcomb crossed the hall and made his bow before Lucy. There were women beside Burnett, gathered along the wall, and they had been talking; they ceased to talk and he saw their eyes hard on Whitcomb and Lucy — he saw the closeness of the thought on their faces, he saw the sensations produced by the thought. Lucy shook her head. Whitcomb spoke again and took her arm and the two came over. Lucy smiled at Rice, she smiled sweetly, and stepped into the yard with Whitcomb. Mrs. Mercer, beside Burnett, said, "Ah," and bent toward Mrs. Provost with her murmur.

Three sets moved in and out and around and forward and back to Old Daniel's calling, to the board-flat crash of his hands. He stamped his feet as he called, he swayed, he laughed.

"Ladies to the right, gents to the left!"

Billy Lord sat on a bench, the double folds of his chin settled on the fiddle, moon-round face dreaming, little eyes watching the crowd. Katherine, smiling, faced Eby and flirted with him; they circled, side to side, back to back, and faced each other again, and she watched the big man with her lips parted and her head cocked aside; she flirted with him. Burnett stepped into the yard and lighted his pipe. The older men were comfortable in the darkness, talking.

"Dig down, cut the roots, and let the stump rot. No use burning — it won't burn unless it's old."

"Dig a pit under and keep a steady fire. She'll burn."

"Not fresh fir stumps. They won't burn."

"They'll burn. Dig a pit."

"I don't know. Corn don't look good. We got to have cracklin' hot weather. This ain't corn country. If it ain't corn country it ain't hog country, either."

"It's hog country. There's mast aplenty."

"If it wasn't hog country I wouldn't stay. I have got to have my bacon and salt pork."

Burnett moved on. Moonlight glowed cream-yellow through a thin heat mist and paled the shadows lying banked along the edge of the fir grove. Lord's hill was a dark bump against a darker sky. Music, sound and light rose from this clearing and was sucked into the roundabout silence, the endless, bottomless silence. Warmth still rose from the earth with grass scent and dust scent; the schoolhouse logs exhaled a raw wood odor. He walked on with his pipe. Shapes were around him, two and two, drifting beyond the light, beyond earshot. He came to the timber and drew back from a sudden-rising pair on the earth; turning, he heard the girl's short laugh. Deep in the timber was the threshing of children, their hooting, their long crying. More men stood by the fire and other settlers moved in, and a horseman's shape was vague beyond the fire — the horse stopped, the rider looking on. In the schoolhouse the music quit; he turned back and found Katherine still with Eby.

The room had grown warm and Eby dashed the sudden sweat from his cheeks. "I'd handle a plow all day long and not do this. Which post was it, Rice?"

"Eleven."

Eby went laughing away. Around the walls older people made thick witness-rows, and lantern light darkened their faces and flashed against their eyes until it reminded Burnett of a councilhouse in Mandan country — smoky and dim and crowded — the tribe listening, the tribe looking on, the tribe judging.

Katherine said, "Sober — sober," and laughed at him. She was new to him; there was knowledge in her — the devil was in there. Where was Lot? The devil was all over the place tonight. "Next set?"

"Next set. Where'd you get the jug?"

"Sent to Oregon City for it."

"A man and a jug."

Old Daniel came whooping into the hall, a bucket in each hand, a dipper in each bucket. "Now then," he cried, "now then: Whisky or water? Can't dance without one or the other. Whisky or water?"

"Come over here," shouted Billy Lord. "I have got to baptize this fiddle."

Mrs. Mercer's baby woke from a sound sleep and set up a toylike crying. Mrs. Mercer opened her dress and put it to feeding. Old Daniel circled the room with his buckets and dippers. "Whisky or water?"

Burnett said, "That reminds me — wonder how my jug is." He took Katherine's arm. "We'll go see." He started from the schoolhouse and was halted by the angry bark of a voice and the sudden collision of flesh. Couples moved back from the center of the floor — they were pushed back by the swift, roundabout rushing of young Hardy Provost and Abe Mercer.

"You been breedin' that scab on your nose," said Hardy Provost.

"Knock it off — knock it off," said Abe Mercer. They plunged on, fists spatting; they drew back, wary. Old Daniel moved in with his laughter and knocked down their arms. "You ain't got room enough to fight here. Go outside." He caught them and shoved them over the floor, herded them from the place, and turned back to his chore. "Whisky or water — come on — come on. Warm up that fiddle, Billy. My God, it's been a long time."

Burnett held Katherine's hand and towed her through the doorway. He used his shoulders to press men aside and he got Ared Rinearson's touchy glance; he laughed at Ared as he went by. The two fighters were shadowy in the suffused moonlight, ringed around by a crowd; their feet stamped the earth, they grunted as they struck, their blows were meaty in the night's softness; they were intent and eager. Burnett drew Katherine on.

"Ah — Sophy," she said.

"Which one she like best?"

"One that won't let her alone."

"They're both after her."

"But one will put his will on her harder and make her believe."

382

The meadow was pale, the creek glittered, the hills lay silent; he walked the road's soft dust with her and got down on his knees to find the jug.

"I'll take a taste," she said and sipped at the jug and shivered. "That's enough, that's too much, how can it taste so bad and feel so good?"

He restored the jug to its hiding place and turned with her toward the Irish yard, and turned again to make a slow climb along the trail which led to the summit of Lord's hill, the schoolhouse noise softening as they rose along the slope and the fiddle music making better melody. In the timber to their near left Lot White's voice rose in half prayer and half a shout.

"Now, then, Lord, they have been hard pressed, they have worked till this valley's sprinkled with the salt of their sweatin'. Let them rejoice tonight, Lord, let them freshen on folly, for they have got to pour out the staleness somehow. There will be fightin', and there will be foolin' goin' on in this brush — it's around me, Lord, and I hear it and I could tell you names, but I won't — and there will be things done and things said, and bad bellies tomorrow. But we have got to do it. Angels won't do here, Lord, not in this dust, not to break these fields and chop these trees. Devil, devil, he's here tonight. Keep your eye on him and let me keep my eye on him, but let these people sweeten themselves tonight and drop the hoops that bind 'em, and let the rich old curdled stuff drip, for tomorrow's work again, and there's a lot of tomorrows before we go."

"Listen," she said.

"Good man."

Near the top of the hill they grew tired of climbing and settled side by side to watch the schoolhouse lights five hundred feet below. Lean cloud fluffs drifted past the moon and the strengthened silver light became a motion in the hills, and shadows shifted as slow waves of water against the fir groves, and a crystal haze shimmered on the meadows. He dropped back full length, facing the sky; and distance sucked his spirit outward and upward into that emptiness — into that unbearable, beautiful, star-crusted pit of nothingness. One day he would go out there, falling and turning and spinning through a blind forever which had no top, no bottom, no sides, no nothing. Forty years from now, maybe; it sounded like a long time, but time wasn't anything. Forty years was only the drawing of a breath — and suddenly he felt it, the day he went spinning out into that void; his mind almost reached the actualness of the moment and of the act itself; almost touched it and recoiled, and he lay still and small and insecure and felt loneliness. There was nothing out there; everything was here. He lifted a hand and flattened it against Katherine's back — she sitting close beside him, silent, watching the valley below — and warmth came through her dress and comforted him. She turned her head and looked down at him.

"You warm?" he asked.

"Yes."

"I like that dress, like the way you're in the dress. Katherine, Katherine, Katherine. Swing your head a little — that's pretty against the sky — you've got a fine chin, stubborn sometimes — lower your head, not stubborn now. I see sparks of light in your eyes. Always admired those hands, big strong ones, pick a chicken, hang on to plow handles, pat a loaf of bread, smooth on some man's back, too. Katherine. Very peculiar thing — when I look at your eyes I look toward your hair, but when I look at your mouth the next thing I'm looking at your breasts. Good ones."

"They're for babies."

"Something else, before babies. Something else after babies, too."

"I never caught you looking at my breasts."

"I'm sly. All men are sly about it. But you damned well know I've looked."

"I always know when you're looking at me." She swung and dropped to an elbow and at this closer range she watched his face. "Know more than you think I know."

"How many babies?"

"Five, I think. Two have got to be girls. Girls stay close, boys go away — and I've got to have a family around me. I want Gram to stay alive to see all five." She drew a breath. "Time's short."

Earth's warmth rose from the soil and eddied around them and a soft air drifted with the slope of the hill. He turned and laid his hand on her hip, on its round solidness, on its motionlessness; then he thought of Edna and drew his hand away, remembering the power below the motionlessness, in Katherine, in Edna, in all of them; and he closed his fingers against the edges of her hair and watched a dreaming expression settle upon her face and weight her eyelids; and he thought about Harris, wondering how that was with her, but he put Harris out of his head, for Harris was nothing to him now; he was almost ready. Tenderness had no words; it lay choked in him, it had drawn his hand from her hip. Though that was what he wanted, it held him quiet against his strong desire to pull her upon him and light the blaze.

She dropped nearer and whispered, "Rice," and blew breath on him and watched him; and her smile broke and she rose and gave him a hand and pulled him upright. "We'll go dance — it's been a long time — we'll just dance till the fiddlestrings break. You want to go get another drink? No, not now — wait awhile. Smell summer? Listen, I hear crickets — it's too early for crickets, isn't it? Oh, it's a beautiful land. Think of it, year after year." She seized his arm, she surged against him in sudden delight, and she laughed and swayed and drew him down the hill. He said, "Wait," but she was in haste and shook her head. "No — I want to dance — not talk, now — the music's starting." The fiddle sawed up and down and the flat slap of hands and the steady stamp of feet made a current through the doorway. She led him into the hall and turned to laugh at him, and her lips moved near to whisper, "Devil, devil, nice devil."

Old Daniel's voice bawled above the fiddle's crying. "We ain't barely started. Hell for shoe leather. Get your partners, we're here till daylight cracks! All out — *Partners, salute.*" Crossing the floor, Rice saw Edna in the corner with Moss solemnly beside her, and her eyes called to him and were sullen.

Whitcomb and Lucy went down the road until they came upon the timber adjoining the Provost cabin; and they turned to the creek and made seats for themselves on the stones. They had said little. The strain was still between them and he found himself unable to break it.

"You're tired?" he asked.

"No."

"Hard to be alone in the cabin?"

She hesitated over her answer. "I suppose I ought to say I'm grieving. You know I'm not. The neighbors know I'm not." Afterwards she revealed her puzzled mind. "I'll never know what made him get in that boat and go out there. He wasn't that kind of man. If he was, then I never knew him. I wonder if he did it to tell me something — to tell us all something. He wouldn't kill himself to do it, I know. But he might have nerved himself to the risk, hoping he'd come out of it well thought of. To be well thought of meant everything to him. I wish I knew."

"So you've got some regrets, wondering if you understood him, if you treated him right."

"It wouldn't have made any difference. It was too late. He could have turned out to be a great man and still it was too late. When that thing goes, Ralph, it just goes."

He said: "Is there anything else you feel sorry for?"

She gave him a glance and a brief answer. "No." She seemed offended. She rose from her place. "What made you think of that?"

"I only wondered what was in your head."

"No use mixing things around and around."

His habit of analyzing things was a sore point with him and her remark hurt him. He stood up and went with her along the trail, pride building his silence. Halfway to the Irish cabin she stopped and turned to face him. "Ralph, would you rather give it up, not see me any more? I know men feel some sort of obligation about these things, when they've said things to a woman, when they've had certain things from her. You don't need to feel that."

"Do you want to?"

"No, it's your decision."

Unexpectedly he was disgusted with himself for his involved thinking, for his indecision. All she asked of him was to be straight-out. Meet it and step into it and settle it. She made a small motion of denial when he brought her forward. "Oh, to hell with that, Lucy. My God — what has a man got to do? What change do you think . . ." He stopped himself. It was words again. He kissed her, he drove it in like a spike. She winced for the hurt he gave her but drew away. "You're a rough beast when you forget about yourself," she murmured. "I was sick — I was afraid — you didn't seem quite yourself."

"You know I've not changed."

"I know, I know now."

"What about the neighbors? They know. You don't mind that?"

"Ah," she said, and dismissed it. It didn't matter. He had no doubts in his head about her — that was what she had wanted to know, to make this thing neat for all the time they would have together. The rest, the opinion of the neighbors, was nothing.

He said, "Let's have a dance."

"All right."

"Then let's go back to your place. I've been lonely as hell."

She said, "I'll make you coffee," and looked at him, and saw the expression on his face. She tightened her hand on his arm. "Now," she murmured, half laughing at him, "you're very impatient."

"We'll get Lot White tomorrow. I can't stand any more of it."

"All right," she whispered. "But Lot White first."

"I know," he said.

Old Daniel cried, "*Partners out and back!*" His big hands slapped the time, all the watchers joining in until the beat was stronger than Billy Lord's fiddle. Burnett sashayed out to meet Katherine in the center of the set. Her body swung, her hands made lively little motions before her, almost touching him, and drawing away. Old Daniel called, "*Other partners — forward and back!*" She drew away, laughing. Her lips were active, her face flushed; she clapped her hands while the other pair moved in, but her glance held him, flirted with him. She was a willow bending in the wind. She was the tip of a fire, leaping bright against the shadows.

Harris Eby's voice flung a lonely wolf howl through the room. Mrs. Mercer's wakened baby screamed. The place grew warm, it trembled to the stamping feet, to the beating feet. "*Out and around — and around we go!*" He came forward to meet her. He murmured, "What you afraid of?" He circled and saw the brisker flash of her eyes as she withdrew. The opposite partners came together and retreated. He moved in again. "What you afraid of?" she said, and curtsied and laughed as she fell away.

Rinearson cried, "*All hands round!*"

Turning in the circle, Burnett saw Roxy in the corner, body strained forward, her dream-anxious face not quite real, not quite solid through the curling pipe smoke. Sweat burned on his cheeks. He saw Gram's face staring on with its concentration. Old Daniel cried again, the fiddle quickened, the fiddle died and the shouting rose. Rice drew his palms across both cheeks to squeeze them dry. He fell beside Katherine, walking.

"Of nothing," he said.

She cast a sidewise glance at him. Now she was graver. In and out. Close and far away. "Solemn — solemn," she said.

"I'm thirsty. Let's go back to the jug."

Her laughter rose, "Oh, no."

"That's careful. Lock your door. Don't walk through the woods alone."

Her glance sharpened. "Say that about yourself."

They passed Edna and Moss in a corner, Moss glum. Edna's eyes searched him with somber reproach; she stood aloof. Old Daniel sat on a bench beside Billy Lord, both men florid. "By God," said Old Daniel. "By God, she's a night." Sweat hung like crystal beads from both Billy Lord's chins and dripped into the relaxed belly; he knew the loosening his fiddle had caused around the crowd, for he looked upon the young ones and the old ones with his surreptitious contentment, with his scheming, and he laughed to himself.

"The whisky run out?"

"There's a little."

"Fiddler needs a drink. I am goin' to draw the festerin' of their souls right up to a head, and I am agoin' to bust it."

Women's voices were busy knitting needles crossing each other.

"My mother had got married at fifteen and didn't want me to do it so early. So I had to run off to do it. She never liked my children. They made her feel too old."

"I made Baldwin put in ten rows of onions. I ain't ever again going to be without onions. They keep sickness off."

"If he gets drunk he'll be goaty in bed."

"Look at him watch her."

Hard-shouted laughter rose from a circle of men around the door; the circle expanded, and drew small again and men's heads crept close as somebody else told a story. Ray Lampert came up, spoke to Katherine and took her away to a new set forming. Burnett swung, but she didn't meet his attention; she stood opposite Lampert laughing, waiting for the music.

Billy Lord reversed his fiddle on his knees and tapped it with his knuckles; he shut his eyes and made a shuffling rhythm. Old Daniel began to beat his hands together: "*Tom-Tom — Eyahhh Injun — Injun file.*"

Burnett humped his back, drew his shoulders together and made a small circle, pumping his hands up and down before him, hopping from one foot to the other as he turned.

"*Eyahhh!*" shouted Old Daniel and slammed his boots on the floor to keep time with his hands.

Harris Eby moved in, grinning, while he watched Burnett go round and round with his Indian shuffling. He clapped his hands across his mouth and howled; he bent and fell behind Burnett, pumping his hands, stooping lower. Provost followed Eby, and Old Daniel jumped from the bench to take his place in line.

Burnett moved down the room with his hop and shuffle. He remembered the Mandan lodge, the smoke, the reek of bodies, the dark faces staring out from the walls, the file of Indians in the center stamping their circle around the fire. The line grew behind him, snake-crooked. He buckled his knees as he stamped, he flung his hands overhead. "*Yah — yah — yah!*" The line howled with him. Out from the walls moved the

388

pounding of feet. He bent the circle of men around Katherine; he looked at her and slapped his chest. He shuffled on.

"*Eyahhh!*"

The log house shook to all those boots driving down. Mrs. Mercer's baby steadily cried. Billy Lord, eyes closed, had his head against the fiddle as he tapped it and his voice rang against the walls:

> Men are born and die too soon,
> Lily's in the corn, highaway noon.
> Plums don't grow for angel's fare,
> Hoe your corn while Lily's there.

"*Eyahhh. Eyahhh — uh — uh — eyahhh.*"

Faces looked in from the yard, high and low in the doorway. Gram Gay, seated on a bench, tapped her shoes and clapped her hands. Edna looked on with her unhappy manner. He drew the circle into a tight knot in the middle of the room; he started his arms low and lifted them slow and shivering upward and drew a prolonged howl from the crowd and he turned sweating to the doorway, Eby following, Eby's big hand weighting down his shoulder, Eby's exhausted laughter hard on his eardrums. "God almighty — I'm dry — I'm faintin' dry." They moved into the night's fragrant coolness and past the Irish cabin toward the cached jug. The schoolmaster's high-raked body was outlined in the cabin's doorway. They heard Mrs. Irish crying.

"We can't have strangers doin' that," said Eby. "Maybe he's a man I can fight."

"Not your woman crying," said Burnett. "Let her alone." He searched out the jug and waited for Eby. Eby drank and surrendered the jug, whispering:

"I've not got a woman to cry. God damn you."

Burnett tipped the jug, took his whisky and blew a foggy sound from the jug's neck. "I've not got your woman, and God damn you."

"Well, if you've not got her, who's got her — God damn you?"

Burnett returned the jug to Eby. "I don't know," he said, and took the jug back. "I don't know."

"It was just as certain as honey in the hive," said Eby, whispering again. "Just as certain, till you showed up. Now who's got her?"

"I don't know. Stop whispering. I can hear all right."

"Well, let's go find out. Let's ask her."

"It won't do."

"Why won't it do?"

"I don't know, but it won't do."

"I wish I could get damned good and mean when I drink. All I get is friendly. By God, I wish I could get sore enough to pull down a house, shake hell out of a few trees and get in a good fight. That's what they want. I'm an ox — dumb brute with no harm in me. They don't want that."

"Who's they?"

"Women. They want steady men, but, hell, they don't like 'em. God damn you."

A rider drifted down from Lord's notch toward the schoolhouse, unknown in the darkness; he stopped in the yard, dismounted and crossed quickly to the house and went in. Suddenly a silence came to the place.

"What's that?" said Burnett.

"Johnny-come-lately. Not a steady man. Women like men like that. Out all night — sleep all day — "

Burnett carefully laid the jug in the grass and moved forward. "Let's see," he said, and began to run; for a woman's scream broke and ran on like fine hammers drumming on a tight-strung wire. Eby heaved himself into motion, following Burnett.

Lockyear had crossed the yard in long strides, rifle thrown before him; he knocked aside a pair of men blocking the door, stepped into the room and faced the crowd. For a moment he was unnoticed; it was Old Daniel ready to call a new set, who discovered him and pointed a hand at him and challenged him. "What the hell you want?" Then the last voices pinched out and the settlers watched him as they would have watched a loose bear. He had his rifle thrown forward and as he swung, seeking out somebody, the muzzle of the gun made its arc. He braced his feet and bent his shoulders, long face turning and strange eyes hunting; he discovered Edna and there his glance stopped.

John Millard, on a bench across the room, reached for his crutches and lunged to his feet, knocking aside his wife's interposed arm. He said, "You're the man I want to see."

"Stay back there," said Lockyear.

"You're the man I want to see," repeated Millard, and moved on. "Had I a gun I'd kill you on the spot."

"Stay back," said Lockyear, and flung up his rifle on Moss Rinearson.

Millard planted his crutches far forward and swung ahead on them, driving himself into Lockyear. Lockyear swerved, brought the barrel of his rifle sidewise against Millard's head and knocked the man down. Roxy, small and shivering against the wall, let go with her scream of terror as the rifle swung again to Moss Rinearson, made its gentle, centering motion against Moss's chest and jumped back from its bullet.

Waves of sound choked the room, to oppress and shake the surrounding people. Moss wheeled and made a short, painful hop; his face rose to show its moment of fright, he took one step and began to die as he fell, his hand seizing Edna's dress and ripping it straight down; she tried to hold him, was caught by the weight of his body, and went to the floor with him.

Old Daniel shouted, "Moss," and rushed toward his son. Lockyear made a full circle on his heels, shortening his grip on the rifle to make a club of it. He rushed upon the men blocking the doorway and drove them aside with the gun's threat — grazing Provost's face with its butt, striking down Lattimore's arm — and ran into the yard; he reached his horse before the shock of the scene wore off; he was in the saddle, cursing his horse into motion before the first man — it was Provost — came full-throated after him; he had straightened away from the place when he saw Eby and Burnett close upon him. He turned his horse aside to avoid Eby's body, changed his mind and reined the horse into Eby, driving him to the ground, rolling him, riding over him. The horse faltered and reared and shook Lockyear on the saddle, and in such awkward position he swept his club-clutched rifle toward Burnett, missed his aim and spurred the horse over the yard.

Roxy's scream went on and on. Old Daniel cried, "Moss — Moss, boy — Moss — my son!" The doorway was clogged with men bucking silent, single-minded, through it. Mercer came out of the jam with his rifle held over his head as though he were fording a stream and Burnett, catching sight of the weapon, jumped forward to seize it. At this instant Lockyear had passed the Irish cabin and was at a full run down the trail toward Lattimore's, his body a diminishing shadow, the horse a diminishing shadow. On the broader bulk of the horse Burnett took aim, held it until he was certain of his shot, and fired.

He flung aside the gun and raced on. Lockyear's horse traveled fifty feet before it slowed, dropped its head and tripped itself, and for a short time Burnett lost sight of Lockyear against the darkness of the earth, man and horse mixed in their violent turnings. Eby, pounding forward, shouted: "Get him!" Then Burnett saw Lockyear rise and go along the road a short distance with the evident notion of reaching the timber between this meadow and Lattimore's place; he had not traveled ten paces when a gun barked in the yard — some other settler swinging into action behind Burnett — and the shot, though wasted, changed Lockyear's mind and drove him over the meadow to the creek. He reached the willows and disappeared.

Burnett passed the Irish cabin, reached his horse and got gun and powder horn from the saddle. Eby overtook him. "Wait for me!" Settlers' boots knocked on the hard school yard, scuffing, running; their voices rose in excited halloos. "Wait for me," said Eby. "I got to get a gun!" Burnett vaulted the meadow fence, now catching sight of Lockyear in the pale moonlight, half across the creek.

54

LOCKYEAR was in the trees beyond the creek when Burnett took to the water and sank armpit-deep in his fording; on the far bank he paused a moment to catch the reckless beat of the man ahead and, using that racket as his compass point, he set out to follow. Lockyear's gun, having been fired, was useless and so long as he remained in motion he could not reload; therefore Burnett moved steadily through the trees, bearing from one side to the other as he heard the other change direction and plunge on with no attempt to conceal himself. It was this carelessness which puzzled Burnett, for he knew Lockyear's ability to slip through any kind of thicket with no sound whatever if he wished to do so. The fall must have injured him.

Beyond the creek's marginal brush and alders a narrow meadow lay at the foot of a ridge separating this part of the settlement from Rinearson's valley. Here Burnett stopped. The sound died and he thought that Lockyear had turned possum in the shelter beyond; but in a moment he saw motion and identified Lockyear's shadow sliding along the foot of the ridge, close upon the trees but using the meadow's softer ground to dampen his retreat. Burnett changed his course and moved rapidly down his side of the meadow, less than a hundred yards to the rear of Lockyear and paralleling the man's course. He quickened his stride to close the distance; he crouched to keep himself small.

The shadowy shape limped and went on with a kind of swinging bear-like clumsiness, apparently intending to cross the trail which ran between Irish's ford and Rinearson's, and put himself on the prairie side of the settlement rather than to go into the west hills as he was expected to do. He was canny enough to know the settlers would try to throw a ring around him; perhaps he had made up his mind to hole up in the open rolling hills south of this country, where escape was easier managed.

His mind was soon changed, for voices and the sound of rapid running horses came up the trail from the direction of the ford as an announce-ment of the settlers' pursuit. Lockyear's reaction was to turn immediately into the trees and smash his way — abandoning his temporary caution — upward, along the ridge. Burnett broke into a trot, crossed the open ground and gained some distance on the man by the time the latter entered the timber; once he heard Lockyear let go with a strong swearing at an injury the brush had caused him.

The ridge was part of a larger chunk of rough land to the east and it lay like the thumb of a hand, coming down from the greater mass and terminating suddenly where the trail cut through to Rinearson's. It was perhaps two hundred feet high and when Burnett reached its crest he saw Rinearson's valley lying pale in the moonlight below and the wink of cabin lights at Old Daniel's; and from that direction he made out the distance-thinned calling of voices. This elevation gave him his first no-tion of what the settlers were meanwhile doing, for he also caught the small, broken bits of voices along the upper creek where a group appar-ently had swung into the hills at Millard's place to lay a barrier before Lockyear if he tried to fall back to the higher mountains.

Lockyear had started to descend the ridge, evidently heading for Rinearson's valley; but he had not gone far when he switched his direc-tion and beat his way along the slope of the ridge toward its junction with the parent hill on the east. By this maneuver he lost ground, Burnett now being above him and able to swing his direction in such a manner that he would come ahead of the man. Listening a moment, Burnett started forward at a long slant, slipping through the timber, crawling quietly over logs, meeting the brush with his forward hands, traveling sidewise, letting the brush softly swing behind. So engrossed was he in his own progress that he ignored Lockyear for a short time and pulled himself sharp-still when he realized the man had quit moving.

He settled and he turned his head slowly, not to see — for the black-ness of this lower timber was a solid blackness — but to catch any sound on the flat of his eardrum. He believed Lockyear to be no more than fifty feet away by this time, and at such a distance he ought to make out the man's strong breathing, but he got no suggestion of it above the labor of his own wind and the repeated vibration of a man's voice shouting somewhere beyond Rinearson's.

Then he thought he detected the light and short rustle of brush from a new angle of the timber, and he rose and moved downgrade in easy stages, waking no echoes, and reached the edge of the Rinearson meadows. There was nothing to be seen along the mooncast meadows, but when he looked to the south, toward the rolling hills, he again discovered a shadow wavering close beside the timber. Lockyear was repeating his former trick — to reach open ground and travel beside the thicket; by this shift he had gained ground and possibly thought he had thrown off pursuit.

Burnett followed, using the same shadows to conceal himself. He stretched his pace and as he walked he debated taking the first decent chance at a fair shot; he lengthened his stride again and watched the shadow thicken. A light unexpectedly lifted from the meadow's other side, from Moss Rinearson's cabin five hundred yards away, and with the light came the small voices of men who seemed to be in motion. He watched the light a short time, or until he heard Lockyear's feet break into a run.

Burnett followed suit, coming down on the balls of his feet, rising and falling to the ground's hummocks. The shadow bobbed high and low before him but gradually began to lose the little distinctness it had as the heavier hill eastward threw forward its denser color. Presently Lockyear reached the foot of the hill and left his loud wake behind him as he pressed into the undergrowth and began to climb. As soon as he in turn reached the brush, Burnett fell back to his quieter pursuit. It became evident to him now that Lockyear's fall from the horse had hurt him in more than passing fashion, for his audible course grew crooked and he fought the brush with his arms for a quarter mile or more up the hill, and at that point he seemed to understand — if he had not already known it — that he was being followed and being overtaken; and abruptly his threshing ceased.

Halted, Burnett heard only the diminishing heave of the man's breath; when that stopped there was an occasional flurry of motion from Lockyear as he shifted his position; then that too quit. Burnett rose and moved by in small steps to a place twenty feet from his original stopping place and by equally cautious motion he eased forward until he was close enough to Lockyear to hear whatever motion the latter might make. He had no knowledge of Lockyear's exact location — and Lockyear, cornered, would be dangerous; and so he settled again and waited for daylight to come on. In the distance, at the extreme edge of hearing, a long call went over Rinearson's valley; and back in the hills to the east a gun sent its rolling report outward.

Daylight was at first a trembling of the blackness, a silent cracking of the frozen night. Overhead the sky lost its dark color and grew gray, and trees began to stand as charcoal streaks against the lesser black. Cramped and cold and tired, he rose against a fir's trunk to orient himself, to sweep the trembling, shifting twilight around him. He moved to another tree, knowing the man nearby was awake and somewhere prowling as he prowled, angered by pursuit and sure enough of himself to stand and play this game out. He stepped on, exploring the ragged half definite shape of fallen limbs, of huckleberry bushes and breast-high deadfalls against which the shadows lay with their stony solidity. He dropped to his knees and crawled against such a deadfall and followed the deadfall's length far enough to find himself at the break of a small ravine in whose thirty-foot depth the darkness was beginning to flow as water flows. His stretching hand came down on the slick-cold surface of a snail and his reaction carried him so swiftly backward that his feet struck the deadfall with the small sound of a finger tapping on a broken drumhead. Somewhere he heard the rustle of brush. It seemed to come from below him and, running his eyes along the ravine's bottom — prying through those sedimentary shadows — he caught a wavering reflection of light on the surface of water, on the puddled beginnings of a creek which seeped from the higher hills. A stump stood close by in the water, broad-topped and gray. He watched it a moment and moved his glance onward. Then he thought: "Stump hell — can't be a stump here," and brought his eyes back to it. He saw a pale glow at one end of the stump, like the sallow scar of an ax stroke; then the light seemed to shift, for the glow disappeared. He looked at the pool and saw that its surface was still shining; the light hadn't shifted, but the stump had. Rearing to his haunches he settled the rifle against his cheek, laid the sights on the stump, and searched for the target. The glow appeared again, the scar moved gently into view. It was Lockyear's head swinging on his crouched body. Burnett took up the trigger's slack.

The report was a great explosion in the morning silence. Lockyear's cry followed, ringing desperately through the timber; he rose from the pool, wavered and rushed into the deeper tangle of the ravine, disappearing from sight, threshing along the hillside — not away from Burnett, but toward him in a roundabout charge. *Cripple shot,* Burnett thought, and reared back to load and prime his rifle before Lockyear reached him. Lockyear's grunt came up the ravine; his body smashed at the fern and devil-stock and huckleberry; he got to the rim and plunged into the trees and somewhere stopped. Burnett poured in powder, rammed home shot and wad; he primed, snapped down the pan cover, seated his rod and rose and ran in weaving haste from tree to tree. On the heights of the hill above him he heard another gun sound in signal; up from the valley rose a hard long call. He sidestepped from one tree to another and took temporary shelter beside a deadfall, waiting for sound; now he heard Lockyear breathing — to the right and not far away — and he straightened and advanced against another tree and surveyed the matted vines ahead of him, the stiff tree columns, the crooked arms of a capsized fir root ragged in the creeping light. He watched the fir root, pointing the gun on it, and he caught Lockyear's sudden expulsion of breath. To the left — to the left and close by. He backed away from the tree and stepped around it, gun's muzzle forward, hip high. Lockyear was on the ground, seated and facing him and waiting; he was hatless, his shirt was ripped down the front and in this bad light his eyes were a pair of holes burned against pale skin. Burnett swung his rifle at the hip and fired. The bullet hit Lockyear, turned him and knocked him over. Curled on the ground, he made a violent reach for his fallen gun — such strength as he had going into that effort. Burnett ran in to kick the rifle aside. "Cal," he said, and got no answer; bending, he watched the man die.

From the heights of the ridge broke another gunshot, signaling and asking for a signal; from Rinearson's valley lifted the nearer cry of a party apparently put in motion by the two explosions from Burnett's rifle. He took up Lockyear's piece and fired through the treetops, and loaded both guns and set them against a tree; and he moved down the ravine for a drink and returned to squat beside Lockyear.

He could think of no good this man had done; act by act Lockyear had been consistently bad, as though by birth he had been put into the world to disturb it. With that mind set right and those great energies harnessed, he would have been a powerful man. How was it that these

396

gifts could be thus carelessly flung into a bad instrument? Where was the pattern in such a thing? John Gay called up the best in men, the influence of his life forwarding a purpose which men liked to believe governed them; but a Lockyear canceled a Gay. Where was the pattern there? He reached for a gun and fired another signal and sat back, hearing the shout of men in the timbered heights and the clearer call of those in the valley below. Lockyear lay on a shoulder, his head settled crooked against the ground, his open eyes filmed and dusty. His face had the usual claylike cast to it, the mouth was unsettled, the sullen look was there. With the power gone he was a shabby thing and the threat which bullied the settlement was now unreal. Either death was careless or death was subtle.

He rose and fixed his position for the nearing searchers by a long shout, and heard them rattling through the brush on both sides of him. He made out Eby's voice, and Provost's. He shouted again.

Eby shouted through the trees and sighted him and came forward, leading a party from the valley; the second group shortly afterwards threshed its way up the ravine. They stood circled around Lockyear, watching him with their common silence and their separate reactions. Provost touched the dead man with the toe of a boot. "Now we got a job packin' him out of here."

"Leave him here," said Durbin Young.

"Nothin' to dig a grave with."

Durbin Young said, "Well, let the wolves — " but he checked himself and shrugged his shoulders. "No, I suppose not. Well, we can lug him to the meadow and load him on a horse."

"Where'll we take him?"

"This settlement needs a graveyard."

"Let's get at this."

Eby stepped around Lockyear and caught him at the armpits; he nodded to the others. "Catch a leg apiece." Provost took one leg, Lige Ebbett took the other. They moved downgrade in a roundabout way to avoid deadfalls and root pits and brush clumps, Lockyear's buttocks now and then dragging the earth as the supporting men hunted for their own footing. It was an hour's work carrying him from the timber to the waiting horses in the meadow. Eby got Lockyear into his arms and threw him belly-down over a saddle and, with a man walking at either side of the horse to hold the body on, the party moved toward Rinearson's. Eby fell back with Burnett.

"Don't believe I'd'a' cared to monkey around with him in the dark,

Rice. It was his meat — he was a damned savage. Think you'll have trouble with Veen?"

"I'll go talk to him."

"You sorry about this?"

"No."

The party passed the upper Rinearson cabins, filed through a grove and moved on toward Old Daniel's place, drawing the attention of a few people standing about the yard. Lot White and Old Daniel came from the house and women began to appear as the file of horses and men drew near. Old Daniel stepped forward to stare at the horseshoe shape of Lockyear across Eby's saddle; he turned and put his arms around Mrs. Rinearson, pointing to the body. Mrs. Rinearson shook her head and went into the house, Daniel following her. Presently he came out with Edna. He said: "There's the son-of-a-bitch. There he is." He was crying as he moved on to the horse. He circled the horse and squatted and cocked his head upward to stare into Lockyear's hanging face. "I lost two sons to this son-of-a-bitch. Who shot him?"

Eby inclined his head at Burnett. Old Daniel came over, caught Burnett's fist and shook it, long lines creased his face, his mouth trembled. "God bless you." He walked around the yard with an aimless agitation and began to wave his arms. "Get him out of here — I don't want him within a mile of the place. Get him out."

"Daniel," said Lot White, "he's dead."

"Don't want him around. Whit's out there in the grove. Moss'll be there tomorrow. Get him out of here — don't want him around."

Provost said, "Well, where we goin' to put him?"

They stood about, thinking, undecided. Edna laid her back to the log wall and watched Lockyear; she lifted her head and drew down her lids until the close, nearsighted expression was on her face again; and a shadow moved over the heavy-turned features and she lowered her glance and stared at the ground.

"We got to put him somewhere," said Provost.

"We had better start a graveyard," said Lot. "It will be needed."

"Well, where? You'll be doin' most of the prayin' over the graves. Where?"

"Not here — not anywhere near here," said Old Daniel, and went on crying. Ared stepped in and put a hand over his father's shoulder.

Edna raised her eyes and fixed her glance on Burnett and he saw that she was sad in the close-held way of a woman who had always kept her own counsel, who had always been somewhat scornful of the crying of other people. He had thought this air of steadiness to be the sign of her strength, now it seemed to him it was a lack of deep feeling. Maybe this was all the sadness she would ever be able to show for any misery; maybe no misery could register deeper. Back in her eyes he thought he saw the old call, its suggestion and its promise, which had once so excited him. From that glance and out of that body he had built a wonderful image of mystery. Those big hips remembered him and waited to churn with him again. If he were dead, they would churn as readily for another; one man or another, that was their necessity. There was no mystery. Looking upon her, he remembered her closeness, and the heat of it stirred him and was good, but there was no mystery.

She had been watching him; in her seriousness there was the suggestion of a knowledge of what he was and what he thought, and presently she made a gesture with her shoulders and her face closed out whatever it had held for him and, casting a short glance at Lockyear, she turned into the house.

"Take him to the ford," said Lot White. "We will start the graveyard on the hill below Lord's. It is a good place." Burnett followed the caravan down the trail.

The three men — Ared, his father and Lot White — watched the file of horses and men move away. "Two of my sons," said Old Daniel and bent his head as the tears fell again. "Two of my sons, on account of him. I hope he burns in hell ten thousand years."

"Daniel," said Lot, "that's the Lord's judgment, it ain't yours, and I want you to cleanse your heart. Come with me. We will go into the hills and pray."

"Judgment, hell. What've I got to pray for? What'd I do wrong, what'd Moss do wrong? Maybe Whit did wrong, but what'd Moss do wrong? Give me no prayers."

"You going to rot your soul by carryin' that around the rest of your life? It won't do."

"I will do what I have got to do," said Old Daniel. "I will save mercy for them that deserve it, I'll spend none on them that don't. If I have got to be judged for hating a man that deserves to be hated, why then let me be judged, for I won't change. I won't be meek and mild. Wasn't made that way and can't be that way. I'm dirt while I'm here and by God, dirt's good enough for me." He stared at his son, grief giving his practical face a wizened cast. "All I've got is this boy. What good's my valley to me

399

now, empty cabins standin' where Whit ought to be, where Moss ought to be?"

"Pride of man," murmured Lot and shook his head. "You atryin' to hang on to a piece of earth, you atryin' to populate it and fix it like it was yours. You atryin' to be a king in Israel. You atryin' to be a Pharaoh and build a tomb that will last forever. This ain't your home, Daniel. Your home's up there."

"Don't tell it to me," said Daniel. "I'll wrestle with this earth and fix it the way I want it, if I can. Heaven, I don't know about. This, I do. Let it be pride, what else has a man got to hold him together in one piece? No sir, sleep's comin', but I'm awake now and I will wrestle." He gave his head a violent shake to knock away the tears and he watched Edna come from the house and go slowly along the trail. His head rose and he looked upon her body with his admiration. "Ared," he said, "I want that baby she's got. I want it in this family. I want no other man to get it. You got to have a wife. You'll never get a better one. Now you go talk to her."

Ared said, "I'd not mind, but she's got Moss in her head this minute."

Daniel studied his son, wisdom of a sort trapped in the seams of his face. He shook his head. "You never chased enough women to know 'em, Ared. She can't sleep with a dead man, but she has got to sleep with a man. In a year's time she won't remember the look on Moss's face, no more than a plowed field remembers who did the plowin' last season. Now you go talk to her."

Ared turned after her. She had stopped down the trail, her glance fixed on the column of men and horses now about to pass around the foot of the ridge toward Irish's ford and when he came up she ignored him for a moment, her expression dulled and heavy. Occupied by his own thoughts, he didn't notice her manner. He was a copy of his father without his father's deviltry, and he had no subtlety of any sort.

"I'd like you to consider marrying me," he said.

She brought her glance around, paying him no compliment of surprise or smile or interest. The heaviness hung on while she considered him; she looked down the trail again until the last horse vanished from view and as it did so she shrugged her shoulders and turned to Ared. Now the smile came. She gave out a short laugh and put a hand on his arm. "All right, Ared," she said. "It might as well be."

Burnett left the column when it started up the hill beyond the ford to

400

locate a graveyard; he stopped at his cabin a moment and rode on to Lockyear's place, finding Veen settled against the cabin wall, half asleep in the warm sunlight.

"Where's your brother?"

Veen shook his head. "In hell for all I know or give a damn."

It revealed to Burnett what he wanted to know about the crippled man's attitude toward his brother. "He might be there," he said, and told the story.

Veen turned once on the ground while Burnett talked; for a little while he stared steadily at Burnett but toward the end he dropped his glance to the ground and when Burnett had finished he made a short gesture.

"Well," he said, "there was a time when I'd wanted to kill you for that. There was a time when Cal was a good man. He never had much regard for anybody's rights, but he let people alone. I don't know when the hate started to get the best of him. Once it started, it moved fast and he was bound to kill somebody." He reached into the dust and filled his palm and let it spill. "That Edna woman was what he wanted most. He saw her a few times. I know that, because he'd come back tame for a couple hours. But he was no man to take half of anything. When he wanted something it was a terrible thing—he'd get it or he'd kill it. But if he'd got her, he'd busted her up. Nothin' pleased him long."

"Go down to Irish's. He's there."

"Don't want to see him. It would just stir up the hate in me." He rose slowly. "Now I got to bear the reputation of being his brother. God damn him, even dead he can hurt people. You think I could go see Roxy? You think the Kitchens would care?"

"Go see," said Burnett and rode back to the cabin.

He made a meal, did the chores; he stretched out to sleep and woke at sundown with a restlessness working powerfully through him. He felt fine, he felt cheerful; he did evening chores and cooked supper and sat in the doorway with his pipe to watch twilight sift through timber and settle across the meadows.

The air was rich and warm, and though no wind stirred there was nevertheless the sense of motion all around him—in the rising heat, in the smell of growth, in the shifting colors; and so still was this night that he had the illusion he felt the giant whirling of the earth itself. He could not long remain motionless, and rose to stroll about the meadow, to walk along the fence, testing the rails with his hand, to stand in the millhouse and speculate on the storage space, to return and face the hills with one thought and another running through his head, no thought complete. He walked to the creek, listening to its melody while watching the yonder ridge blacken against the sky; over there, twelve hours before, he had killed Lockyear — and the recollection moved through him as a physically disagreeable sensation. It lasted a moment and was gone. Deliberately he tried to bring it back; deliberately he sought for some blackness in his head as a result of it, but could produce nothing; and then he knew that for him there could be no remorse. An act produced its consequences, but act and consequences were swept on and thinned out by the tide of time, covered over by other acts, and at last forgotten in the accumulating episodes of life.

He circled the meadow again and returned to his cabin; he lighted a lantern, he looked about the room and felt its emptiness to a degree he had not before, and he walked to the yard with well-being stiff and strong in him and discontent plucking at him; he lighted his pipe again, started another circle around the meadow and checked himself. Turning to the shed, he saddled the horse and rode toward Gay's.

Two lights came over the clearing, one from each Gay cabin; when he reached the yard he heard Katherine's voice speak. "Over here, Rice." He found her at the outdoor table, seated idly before it, arms spread on it. He came around the table, seeing the ivory disc of her face rise in the shadows.

"How's your father?"

She shook her head.

"I'll go say hello."

"He won't know you."

"Where's everybody?"

"Mother's with him. The others are in bed."

"Beautiful night," he said. He stood behind her, he let his hands fall to her shoulders. "Beautiful night." He moved on to the table's end, vitality making motion necessary; he slapped the table with the butt of his hand. "I smell something good."

"It's a white flower blooming through the brush."

"Like honey, like a woman's hair. I want to see your dad."

"It's no good. Just remember him."

But he shook his head and stepped around the table; she watched him a little while and afterwards rose. "Why?"

"I don't know," he said. They crossed the yard toward the house. "Some

402

people—when they're gone you think about them and a bad feeling comes when you remember they're not here any more. I want to see him."

She stopped and let him go into the cabin by himself. Martha Gay was in a rocker at the bed's side and she checked its steady swaying and watched him for a moment with her thoughts a long way off. It took her a little while to bring herself back. She rose over the bed, lifting and replacing the blankets around Gay's shoulders. "He won't hear you, Rice. He won't know you." She bent to listen to his breath.

His face even now had the disintegrated expression of death, flesh careless over hard bones, cavern shadows in the sockets, temples fallen, placid mystery registered around the hardening mouth. The fire had retreated to its central place and burned lower and lower as the cold crept in; his vitality was like the emanation rising from the blackened bed of a fire in which one buried coal still held heat. There was no recognition in his eyes. Pain was about through with him, and he lay with that thoughtful patience upon his features which was neither thought nor patience; with that far gazing which saw everything—or nothing. Burnett dropped a hand to the blanket-covered shape, drew it away and stepped from the cabin. Night's air struck him sweet and strong in the face and sank deep into his chest. Katherine took his arm and walked on with him, over the yard, past the shed and toward the trail; her shoulder touched him, fell away, touched again as they went on.

"About all I ever learned that's been worth learning," he said, "has come from people that never tried to teach me, and never knew they did. The things in a good man come out of him—they go through other people. Even the meanest man born feels it. There's no power like it. Your father was that kind of a man."

He swung with her and crossed the meadow and stopped at the wheat-field's edge. She turned, face shining in the moonlight, alert, listening. He thought she had been silently crying and he bent in to identify the glitter of tears, but she moved back and gave her head a sharp, short shake, and the glitter ceased. He swept his hand across the wheat tops, trapping kernels and crushing them between his fingers. "Be ready to cut in three weeks or a month. Been a fine thing if your father could have seen the first harvest."

She had no answer. She was restless, her hands moved and her shoulders stirred; she watched him and the silence was roughened by the turbulence of a discontent making up within her. She stepped ahead and settled beside the creek and seized a stone, flinging it outward. Moonlight caught and froze the upstrike of spray into an instant's streak of silver; the riffles flashed, the tree-crazed pattern of shadows wavered on the water. Strange things rotted in the mud at their feet, and fern and grass and brush sucked in this stuff, and breathed out the damp fragrance of growth. The creek's motion was a sensation which lifted and lowered him; he felt the earth's turning in the pit of his stomach — the giant rolling of it, the great vibrations of it. The wheatfield's shining was a cold shining, the darkness of the fir grove beyond the meadow was a heavy darkness; the mountains were beyond sight but their weight pressed in.

He dropped beside her. She withdrew from his touch, hands clasped over her knees, bent forward, stone-still. She was hard, she was distant. He touched her and pulled her around, but there was reluctance to her motion and the strengthening turbulence seemed to stiffen her body until it seemed to him the strain was ready to break her. Her face moved forward, her mouth was a streak of shadow, her eyes a streak of shadow. He bent in and kissed her. Nothing came back to him. She remained still, critically tasting a flavor; she was wary, locked-up. He put his hand at the base of her head and he swung forward and pressed her to the ground. She turned as though to slide away from him. "No," he said, and checked her turning.

"There's a rock under me," she whispered, and lifted herself while he brushed it away.

She adjusted herself, she rested her hands on her arms. Propped above her, he saw the motionless mouth below and the still surface of her face; and the tension between them was like the coming of a hard wind whose sound was faint in the distance. He lowered himself.

"Yes?"

She said nothing. Her hands had no weight on him. She was waiting, she was listening — listening to him or to herself.

"Yes?"

"Yes."

He brought her head around. Her mouth moved forward and her hands closed upon his sleeves and he felt the hard wall break, the beginning outflow, the gathering insistence. Across the meadow unexpectedly came Mrs. Gay's voice with its splinter-keen note of tragedy. "Katherine — Katherine!" Her body trembled, she crept nearer, fitting herself to him, knees and hips, and her arms closed about him with increased strength. Mrs. Gay's voice came crying again. "Katherine — your father . . . !" Her trembling ceased and he felt wetness break along his cheek. Her hands prompted him and he turned her head against the soft earth and caught a whisper from her as he came upon her, and the illusion of the spinning earth was so strong that he flattened himself to keep her and himself from being whirled outward into the black.